Henr

MW01674685

History of The American War

Vol. 2

SALZWASSER VERLAG

Henry Charles Fletcher

History of The American War

Vol. 2

Reprint of the original, first published in 1865.

1st Edition 2022 | ISBN: 978-3-75258-860-6

Verlag (Publisher): Salzwasser Verlag GmbH, Zeilweg 44, 60439 Frankfurt, Deutschland
Vertretungsberechtigt (Authorized to represent): E. Roepke, Zeilweg 44, 60439 Frankfurt, Deutschland
Druck (Print): Books on Demand GmbH, In de Tarpen 42, 22848 Norderstedt, Deutschland

HISTORY

OF

THE AMERICAN WAR

BY

LIEUT.-COLONEL FLETCHER

SCOTS FUSILIER GUARDS

VOL. II.

SECOND YEAR OF THE WAR

(1862-63)

LONDON

1865

CONTENTS

OF

THE SECOND VOLUME.

CHAPTER I.

CHAPTER II.

CHAPTER III.

CHAPTER IV.

CHAPTER V.

CHAPTER VI.

CHAPTER VII.

CHAPTER VIII.

CHAPTER IX.

CHAPTER X.

CHAPTER XI.

CHAPTER XII.

CHAPTER XIII.

CHAPTER XIV.

CHAPTER XV.

CHAPTER XVI.

LIST OF ILLUSTRATIONS.

HISTORY

OF

THE AMERICAN WAR.

THE SECOND YEAR.

CHAPTER I.

CAMPAIGN IN THE SHENANDOAH VALLEY.

IT was in gloom and sorrow that the usually pleasant springtime opened on the Southern States in the year 1862. Far different were their prospects from those which apparently awaited them in the corresponding season of the preceding year. Then expectation and hope, the excitement of novelty, the anticipation of freedom from a union they detested, and the first bursts of military enthusiasm had roused the people of the South, and concealed from the eyes of the majority the trials, the sufferings, and the desolation which a war such as they were about to engage in would bring upon themselves and upon their country. This enthusiasm and these hopes had been increased by the events of the first campaign.

From various circumstances, more especially from the more warlike character of the nation, the results of the earlier battles had been in favour of the South, and had tended to rouse her people to unbounded confidence, and to an overweening assurance of their own superiority over the soldiers of the North. This feeling had been carried to so high a pitch, that, instead of acting as an element of strength, it had tended to weaken her power, by leading her to disregard, or rather to undervalue, her preparations for defence. Consequently, the North, roused and piqued to increased exertions, rather than disheartened by first failures, put forth her strength, and gradually, but with sure steps, carried the war far from the frontiers, even into the heart of the Confederacy. Scarcely a State but what was called on to feel on her own soil the horrors of war. The Border States at first bore the brunt of the battle; gradually Kentucky, Missouri, and Western Virginia were occupied by the troops of the North; whilst the coast of the Confederacy, assailed by the fleets of the seaboard States, yielded a footing to their armies. New Orleans at length fell, the greatest blow that had been dealt against the Southern cause; great not only from the effect it exercised on the *morale* of the belligerents, but also from the important influence it had on the policy of Europe, either as regarded recognition or intervention. From that time the South awoke more clearly to the perception that on herself, and on herself alone, would the task of gaining her independence and position among the nations fall; if her first enthusiasm was damped, a deeper and more lasting feeling of determination was aroused, which was destined ere long to clear away, if it did not at once break, the clouds which had gathered round her prospects.

New Orleans had indeed fallen, but Richmond still remained; and it was felt that in front of that city must the battle be fought. Yet her position was one of great danger. Within a few miles of the capital was encamped the largest and best-equipped army of the

North; within less than an hour's steam of her quays were anchored the ironclad gunboats of the Federal navy, whilst converging on her from the west and north marched the three distinct armies of Fremont, Banks, and M'Dowell. Weak were her preparations for defence. The unfinished fort at Drury's Bluff had indeed repulsed the first efforts of the ironclads, and the hastily-constructed earthworks joined to the swamps of the Chicahominy had hitherto hindered the advance of the army of M'Clellan; but her situation was so critical and her danger so imminent, that many even of those who were most confident of final success showed symptoms of alarm for her security. Numbers left the city; preparations were made for the removal of the archives of the Confederacy; and a feeling of intense anxiety pervaded her population.

It was at this most momentous crisis, when few could restrain a feeling of doubt and perplexity, that a success, which seemed to turn the tide of victory, crowned the arms of the Southern troops in the Shenandoah Valley. The causes which led to this event must be looked for in the conduct of the Federal Government. From various motives, principally political, such as the necessity of giving commands to generals who represented or could exercise influence over the great political parties, a system of detached operations had been sanctioned by the President and his advisers. Thus in Virginia alone, irrespective of the great army of the Potomac, three several generals exercised independent commands. To General Fremont had been allotted the mountain department of Western Virginia; to General Banks, the Shenandoah Valley; and to General M'Dowell, the department of the Rappahannock. The forces of the two last-mentioned generals occupying positions principally with reference to the defence of the national capital. Each general was at the head of a force sufficient to encourage him to attempt offensive movements, but was without power to carry them through with success.

In order to comprehend the campaign of the Shenandoah Valley, it is necessary to follow closely the movements of these several armies. Towards the middle of April, the three generals occupied respectively the following positions:—General Fremont was at Franklin, a small town in the mountains of Western Virginia near the source of the south branch of the Potomac, with a force of at least three divisions, including that of General Blenker, which had been withdrawn from the army of the Potomac, and had since acquired an unenviable notoriety for plundering.* General Banks having advanced along the north fork of the Shenandoah River, had placed his head-quarters at Newmarket, beyond the terminus of the rail which intersects the Shenandoah Valley, whilst General M'Dowell, with the first *corps d'armée* of about 30,000 men, occupied Fredericksburg on the Rappahannock—the town having been evacuated by the Confederate troops on the 17th, and having surrendered to General Auger on the 19th, under the expectation of an attack by a combined naval and military force.

Such was the position of the Federals. On the other hand, the Confederate troops detached to hold in check Generals Fremont and Banks were under General Jackson, who commanded his own division and that of General Ewell, together with the cavalry force of Colonel Ashby. Possessing true military genius, combined with

* The term Blenkering became common in America to express rioting and plundering.

an accurate knowledge of the country, General Jackson, although inferior in force to his opponents, was more than a match for them in the field; and by availing himself of the opportunities offered by their mistakes, so contrived his movements as to take advantage of their isolated positions, and to inflict defeat on them in detail.

It was on General Banks that the first severe blow fell; in place of merely occupying a defensive position to cover Washington, that officer had advanced for a considerable distance up the Shenandoah Valley, driving, as he supposed, General Jackson before him. Deluded by the retreat of his opponent, and misinformed by the country people of his movements, General Banks transmitted tidings to Washington of his supposed success, which were only too eagerly received. Jackson was reported to be hurriedly retreating through Harrisonburg, towards Stanardsville and Orange Courthouse; and it was expected that Banks and Fremont would effect a junction in the upper Shenandoah Valley, and threaten Richmond from the west. The fact that Milroy, commanding the advanced guard of Fremont's army, had reached Buffalo Gap, in the chain of mountains bounding the Shenandoah Valley on the West, and had driven back a small force of Confederates near the railway which intersected Augusta county, gave some colour to the report.

General Jackson's position was between the two armies of Fremont and Banks, which threatened to overwhelm and crush him. Such might possibly have been the fate of a less able general; but he, on the contrary, saw and seized the opportunity of defeating his antagonists in detail. Having evaded General Banks, he marched rapidly to the relief of Colonel Johnson, who was endeavouring with inferior forces to hinder the advance of Fremont's leading divisions under Milroy and Schenck, and after an unimportant engagement on the 15th of May, drove these officers back to Franklin, forcing them to destroy in their retreat a considerable amount of stores and provisions. Thus Fremont's advance was checked. Then General Jackson without delay, and without communicating his plans to any one, brought his army over the mountains, by paths difficult for troops, to the attack of General Banks—thereby effecting the brilliant movement which not only for the time cleared the Shenandoah of the Federals, but threw a doubt on the power and success of the North, and collaterally was of material service in delaying the attack on Richmond by M'Clellan.

General Banks's head-quarters were at Strasburg, with an advanced guard beyond Newmarket. The *corps d'armée* properly comprised the two divisions of Williams and Shields; but in consequence of the urgent remonstrances of General M'Clellan, who was desirous of the co-operation of M'Dowell in his advance on Richmond, Shields's division had been transferred from the department of General Banks to that of M'Dowell at Fredericksburg. Banks was thus deprived of about half his force; notwithstanding which he retained his advanced position, his left or exposed flank covered by a line of mountains, through which gaps or passes afforded entrances from Eastern Virginia into the Shenandoah Valley. Through one of these passes, in the neighbourhood of the village of Front Royal, the Manasses Gap Railway ran, connecting Manasses Junction with Strasburg, and there Colonel Kenley, in command of a force of about 1,200 men, was stationed. No attack of any importance was expected from that quar-

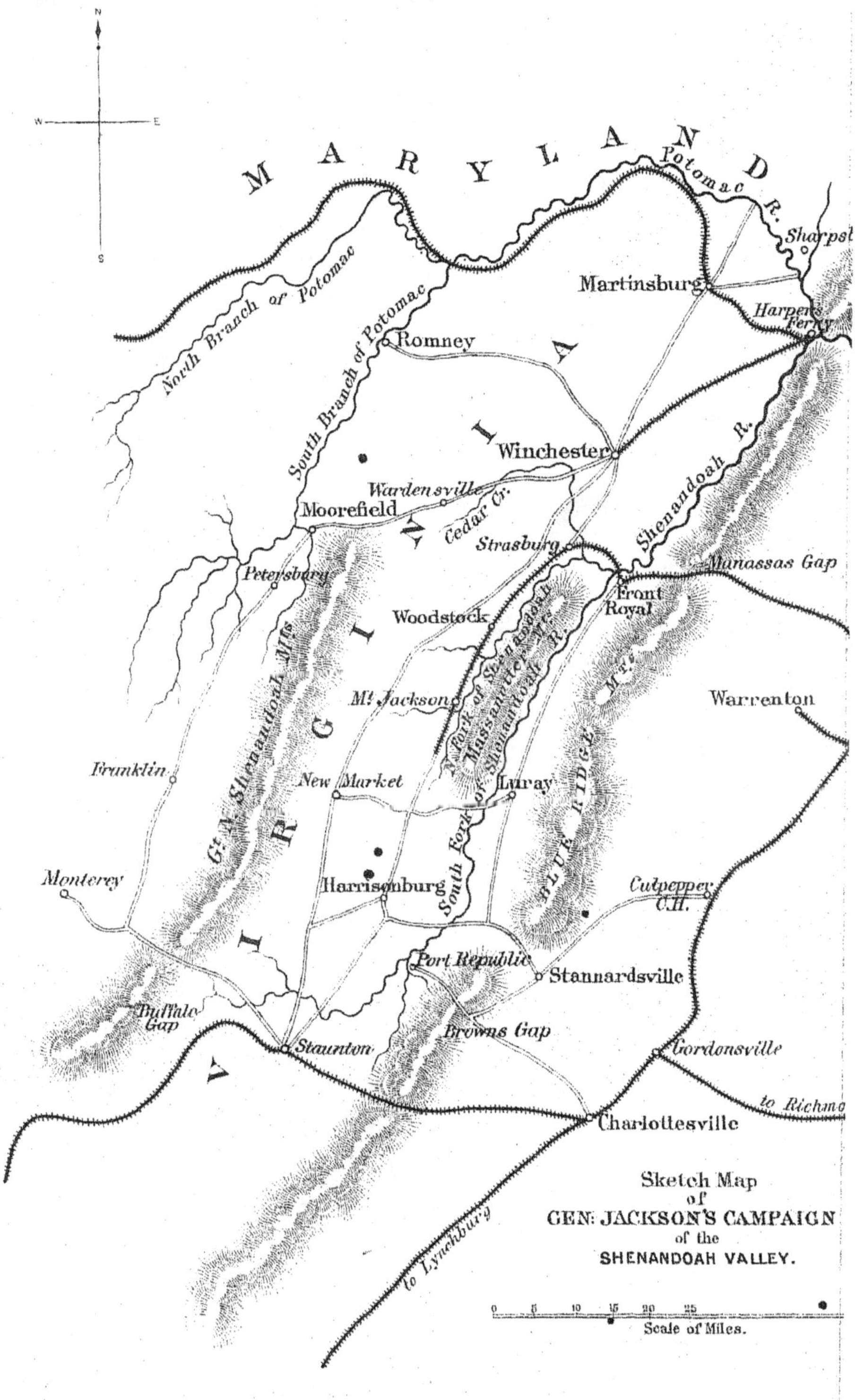

Sketch Map of GEN: JACKSON'S CAMPAIGN of the SHENANDOAH VALLEY.

ter, and the troops were posted more with the object of protecting the place from guerillas than in anticipation of resistance to a regular force. Between Colonel Kenley's force and Strasburg was a line of hills known as the Massanutten Mountain, dividing the two forks of the Shenandoah River. Taking advantage of the weakening of General Banks's force, and of the features of the ground, which effectually concealed the movements of the troops, General Jackson on the 22nd of May advanced down the south fork of the Shenandoah River to the attack of the Federals at Front Royal. By this movement he placed a strong force between Colonel Kenley's detachment and the main body. Perceiving his danger, that officer endeavoured to effect a retreat; but being overpowered by numbers, his force was surrounded, and nearly the whole were either killed, wounded, or captured—he himself being among the killed.

A rumour of this movement of General Jackson reached Banks on the evening of the 23rd, and in consequence reinforcements were at once ordered to proceed to Front Royal. When, however, towards night, despatches arrived from Winchester detailing the full extent of the misfortune, and the probable strength of the enemy, General Banks perceived that his own position was one of considerable danger, and that his line of retreat was liable to be cut off. The reinforcements were immediately recalled, and steps taken for a rapid retreat on Winchester. One other line was perhaps open to him—viz. that over the mountains to Western Virginia—but it would have entailed the abandonment of his waggons, much of his artillery, and the whole of the stores collected in Winchester; therefore it was resolved to march at once on that town, and to endeavour, if possible, by a rapid movement to reach it before General Jackson could forestall him. Even then General Banks did not fully realise his position; he believed the main body of the enemy to be still at Strasburg, and ordering his baggage train to Winchester, covered his rear with the greater portion of his troops.

At 3 A.M., on the 24th of May, the march commenced; but the baggage train and their escort had hardly crossed Cedar Run, about three miles from Strasburg, when they encountered the enemy's pickets, occupying the direct line of their retreat. A few shells fired into the train created great confusion; the teamsters cut the traces of their horses and mules, and, accompanied by other fugitives, hurried back on the main body, and made General Banks aware of the imminent danger in which he was placed. Immediately a change was made in the formation of the line of march, the troops were ordered from what had now become the rear to the head of the column, and the baggage train was countermarched to its proper position; then the Federals, after some skirmishing, resulting in the loss of many of the cavalry and a detachment of engineers, continued their movement, forcing a way through the enemy's troops, which consisted only of detachments from the main body, and arrived at Winchester on the evening of the 24th.

It was there that General Banks received a confirmation of the news of the total defeat of the Front Royal detachment, and also information of the numbers of the enemy. Believing himself to be too weak to hold the position, he resolved on continuing the retreat; but wished first to offer battle, in order fully to test the enemy's strength, and to afford time for his detachments to reach the main body. However, the movements of the Confederates were too quick to allow of the necessary disposition of the troops, which were scattered without order through the town.*

The retreat, which threatened to degenerate into a rout, commenced early in the morning of the 25th; outside the town some order was restored, and the troops took up a position to offer battle; the Confederates advanced, and after three hours' fighting drove the Federals back to Martingsburg, from whence, without much molestation, they continued their retreat to the Potomac. During the night of the 25th and morning of the 26th the army crossed the river, the boats of the pontoon train which had been saved proving of the greatest assistance: on the 26th the Federals considered themselves to be in safety, and, to quote the words of General Banks's despatch, 'There never were more grateful hearts in the same number of men than when, at mid-day on the 26th, we stood on the opposite shore.' The troops reached the Maryland shore of the Potomac in miserable plight; some regiments were almost destitute of knapsacks and accoutrements, which had been either taken off preparatory to going into action, or abandoned in the retreat; whilst a vast amount of stores

* The following is an extract from a national account published in the Rebellion Records, page 63, Documents, vol. v.:—'Presently the enemy's cannon boomed in the rear, and a small cloud of smoke in the sky suddenly appearing and then dissolving, showed where the ball had exploded. Some shell fell among our men, and the panic was quite general for a short time. One round-shot, a six-pounder, passing near me, went directly over the shoulder of my companion, and brushing the blanket of the one next to me, fell to the ground. Guns, knapsacks, cartridge-boxes, bayonets, and bayonet cases lay scattered upon the ground in great confusion, thrown away by the panic-stricken soldiers.'

had been either burnt or left to be captured by the enemy.

General Banks, in his official report, estimated the number of his killed as 38, wounded 157, and missing 711; this, however, cannot include the losses of the detachment at Front Royal. The artillery and the greater portion of the baggage train were saved; and it must be confessed that General Banks, having been completely out-generalled by General Jackson, yet extricated his army with some skill from a perilous position.

Great was the consternation at Washington when the news arrived of this defeat. The President and many members of the Government were not free from the general alarm; telegrams were despatched to the Governors of the Northern States for troops to defend the capitol, and the most exaggerated rumours of the numbers and intents of General Jackson were circulated through the country. The President had but just returned from M'Dowell's head-quarters, where he had arranged a plan of advance on Richmond, when the news of the defeat in the Shenandoah Valley was brought to him, and for the time completely changed his preconcerted arrangements. At the very moment when, on all sides, success appeared to crown the Federal armies, a most mortifying defeat, followed by a still more mortifying panic among even the rulers of the nation, had occurred, and threw doubt on the overwhelming power of the North. At Baltimore, among a large portion of her inhabitants, the news was received with the greatest joy; some even anticipated that the hour of their deliverance had arrived, and that the Confederates would advance into Maryland. Indeed, the most absurd reports gained credence; and it was only after a few days, when a true estimate was formed of Jackson's real numbers, and when there appeared to be no intention on his part of crossing the Potomac, that men's minds regained their equilibrium.

Reinforcements were immediately sent to General Banks, and a scheme planned by which the Confederate force in the Shenandoah should be cut off by the combined movements of M'Dowell and Fremont. The real object of Jackson's advance was, however, more clearly discerned by General M'Clellan, who saw that it was intended to draw off troops from the army of the Potomac, and thus to relieve Richmond. In this it proved completely successful. M'Dowell's corps was no longer permitted to co-operate with the army of the Potomac, but received orders to march for the Shenandoah Valley, so in a great measure disconcerting M'Clellan's plans.

Before, however, returning to the army of the Potomac, it will be well to glance at certain events which occurred about this time in the North, which afford evidence of its interior condition. On 16th of April, the bill providing for the emancipation of slaves in the district of Columbia received the sanction of the President. Already, in a message sent to Congress on the 6th March, Mr. Lincoln had proposed a scheme for aiding by pecuniary assistance any State which might adopt a gradual abolition of slavery, alluding indirectly to the Border States, and averring that the proposition was made as a political measure, in order to separate the interests of the more northern slave States, either under the power of or occupied by the troops of the Federal Government, from those of the South. A resolution to this effect passed the Senate on the 22nd April.

Other evidences of the feeling of the North in

favour of abolition were shown by the successful resistance offered to the police at Washington, armed with legal powers for the arrest of fugitive slaves, by the soldiers of the 76th New York Regiment. As the regiment was marching through the city, the police made an attempt to seize some negroes who accompanied the troops; but the soldiers interfered, and the law officers were driven away with threats of violence unless they desisted from their attempt. Notwithstanding these signs of the increased power in the North of the abolition party, the Proclamation issued by General Hunter on the 9th May, in his capacity of general in command of the so-called department of the South, declaring the abolition of slavery in the States of Georgia, Florida, and South Carolina, met with the disapproval and disavowal of President Lincoln. General Hunter alleged in his Proclamation that martial law was a necessity in those States, and that as slavery and martial law were not compatible, that the former was abolished. As yet neither public opinion nor the Government were prepared for these extreme measures, and they met with the disapproval of a large proportion of the senior officers of the army, who belonged to the democratic party.

Mr. Lincoln at this time was popular in the North, and used his popularity to cover his friends, who had outraged even the elastic consciences of the Members of the House of Representatives. On the 30th April, a resolution passed that House in reference to the alleged frauds on the Government, couched in these terms,—'Resolved, that Simon Cameron, late Secretary of War, by intrusting Alexander Cummings with the control of large sums of the public money, and authority to purchase military supplies without restriction, without requiring from him any guarantee for the faithful performance of his duties, when the services of competent public officers were available, and by involving the Government in a vast number of contracts with persons not legitimately engaged in the business pertaining to the subject-matter of such contracts, especially in the purchase of arms for future delivery, had adopted a policy highly injurious to the public service, and deserves the censure of the House.' This resolution produced a message from the President, in which he took the whole responsibility of the acts of Mr. Cameron on his own shoulders, justifying his conduct by the emergency of the times, and asserting that he was unaware that a dollar of the public funds thus confided without authority of law to inefficient persons had been either lost or wasted. This was a bold statement. The lavish and wasteful expenditure of public money and the frauds of contractors were sufficiently notorious throughout the Northern States, and were facts which even the most violent partizans did not attempt to deny.

The attention of men was, however, so completely engrossed by the struggle in which they were engaged, that much of what would have created alarm and anger in more peaceful times was passed over amid the excitement of the news from the seat of war. The liberties and privileges of American citizens were outraged with impunity, and almost without remark or remonstrance. Mr. Gilchrist, who had been arrested and confined on suspicion of treason at Fort Warren, was discharged unconditionally without trial, after months of imprisonment; and this illegal act on the part of the Government passed almost unnoticed. Verily the Federals, in their anxiety to bring back what they termed the rebellious States under the authority of a

Constitutional Government, were fast permitting that Government to disregard all the checks and restraints which withheld it from the possession of absolute power. The whole attention of the country was concentrated on the progress of the war, and especially on the movements of the army of the Potomac; and leaving for the time the scene of General Jackson's exploits in the Shenandoah Valley, we must return to General M'Clellan's camp on the Chicahominy.

CHAPTER II.

OPERATIONS BEFORE RICHMOND.

THE army of the Potomac had reached the Chicahominy, and measures were taken for effecting its passage. This stream, destined to become famous in history, is of itself insignificant in appearance.* Narrow and sluggish, it flows during a part of its course in a south-easterly direction, almost parallel with the Pamunkey, and finally enters the James River. In dry weather it is fordable in several places; but the adjoining country, for a short distance on either bank, is usually of so swampy a character as to render the fords valueless for the passage of any considerable body of troops. Along either side of the stream a thick jungle of trees, calculated to afford cover for sharpshooters, and also materials for restoring and constructing bridges, hides its current from view. Previous to the destruction of the bridges by the retreating Confederates, the Chicahominy had been crossed by several, in its upper course at Meadow Bridge (about six miles from Richmond), by the Richmond and Fredericksburg Railway; lower down, by the Mechanicsville Road, only four miles from the city; still further down, by the Cold Harbour Road at Newbridge; further still, by the West Point Railway, near Despatch Station;

* About the breadth of the Medway above Maidstone.

and below that bridge, by the two branches of the New Kent Court-house road at Bottom's Bridge and Long Bridge, the latter in close vicinity to the White Oak Swamp. On either side of the stream comprised between Meadow Bridge and Bottom's Bridge, the land sloped up from the meadows or woods directly adjoining its course; and although partially cultivated, and at the time of the first appearance of the Federal army green with fresh growing crops, it was yet thickly clothed with forests, owing to the fact that each proprietor, dependent for firewood or building material on the individual resources of his farm, preserved a portion of the remains of the original forests; whilst the country being but thinly inhabited, was still covered in its less productive localities by the uncleared woods and jungle. Thus, although the land above, and in the vicinity of Newbridge, was comparatively well-cultivated, that part adjoining the White Oak Swamp retained its forest character. On the sides of the low hills which slant downwards towards the stream stood the comfortable houses of the several landed proprietors, surrounded with smiling gardens and orchards, and resembling in appearance the residences of English yeomen. Clustering round them were the cottages of the slaves, and the large outbuildings necessary for barns and farming stock. All bespoke peace and long-continued plenty; and the large fields, stretching downwards from the owners' houses to the low ground near the river, already gave promise of rich crops. Adjoining the Mechanicsville Bridge, about five and a half miles from Richmond, was the small but neat village of the same name; otherwise, no buildings except scattered farm-houses stood between the Pamunkey River and Richmond. Such was the appearance of the country when the advanced divisions of General M'Clellan's army appeared on the hills overlooking the left bank of the stream.

Aware that the struggle for the possession of Richmond must take place on the banks of the Chickahominy, and anxious that every soldier who could be brought up should be present at the apparently imminent battle, General M'Clellan urged on Mr. Lincoln the necessity of the co-operation of M'Dowell's corps; and after some difficulty he so far convinced him of the soundness of his plans as to prevail on him to sanction the advance of that general by land from Fredericksburg. The proposal that the *corps d'armée* should move by water, and so effect a junction with General M'Clellan's left wing on the banks of the James River, was not approved of, as one of the stipulations laid down by the President expressly urged the necessity of keeping General M'Dowell's corps in such a position as to cover Washington. It was expected that these reinforcements, with the addition of General Shields's division from General Banks's department, would amount to 35,000 or 40,000 men; and General M'Clellan received directions to prepare a depôt for their supply at West Point. This plan was, however, frustrated by the result of the operations in the Shenandoah Valley, which was announced to General M'Clellan in the following graphic despatch from the President:—

'Washington, May 25, 1862.

'MAJOR-GENERAL M'CLELLAN,—The enemy is moving north in sufficient force to drive General Banks before him; precisely in what force we cannot tell. He is also threatening Leesburg and Gearey, on the Manassas Gap Railroad, from both north and south; in precisely what force we cannot tell. I think the movement is a general and concerted one, such as could not be if he was acting upon the purpose of a very desperate defence of Richmond. I think the time is near when you must either attack Richmond *or give up the job*,* and come back to the defence of Washington. Let me hear from you instantly.

'A. LINCOLN, President.'

Not being inclined *to give up the job*, but feeling that his right wing was in some danger of attack from the force which had been engaged in watching General M'Dowell at Fredericksburg, but which was now falling back in the direction of Richmond; being desirous also of cutting the lines of railway which connected Richmond with Fredericksburg and Gordonsville, and which might at any time be used for the purpose of bringing reinforcements and supplies into the town, General M'Clellan ordered a reconnaissance in force to be pushed forward in the direction of Hanover Court-house. For this purpose General Porter, commanding the 5th Corps, marched from his camp on the right of General M'Clellan's position at daybreak on the 27th of May, his force consisting of about 8,000 men, including two cavalry regiments. Their objective point was Hanover Court-house, about fourteen miles from the main army, where the enemy were observed drawn up across the road. An attack was immediately ordered, and, after about one hour's firing, the Confederates retired, followed by the cavalry and by two out of the three brigades of General Morell's division. Of the remainder of the corps a portion was detached to burn the bridges over the Pamunkey; whilst one brigade, under General Martingdale, was directed to move at once on Ashland

* The italics are our own.

Station in order to destroy the railway. In so doing, it was attacked by a superior Confederate force under General Branch, and with difficulty held its ground until General Porter, hearing the firing in his rear, moved to its assistance. The Confederates were then repulsed, with the loss of about 200 killed and 700 prisoners. Of the latter, many were brought in by detached bodies of cavalry, who scoured the country in the vicinity of the scene of action. The men captured were principally from North Carolina, and had neither the appearance of disciplined troops, nor the enthusiasm which might have counterbalanced other defects.

In consequence of General Porter's successful operations, the road was open for the advance of General M'Dowell's corps, as had previously been arranged between the President and General M'Clellan; but those who undertook the charge of military matters in Washington destined that general for other purposes, and the greater portion of the troops under his command played no part in the attack on Richmond by the army of the Potomac. General Porter's corps withdrew to its former camp, and General M'Clellan's right rested on Mechanicsville, his left extending across the Chickahominy to Fair Oaks Station, on the Richmond and West Point Railway, within about seven miles of Richmond.

At the end of May, the following was the position occupied by the several corps comprising the army of the Potomac:—The right, under General Franklin, was encamped in rear of Mechanicsville, which was held by a detachment, with advanced pickets posted near the bridge over the Chickahominy, and as far up the stream as Meadow Bridge; on the left of General Franklin, occupying the heights overlooking New Bridge, was General Porter; on his left, but at some little distance, lay General Sumner's corps; whilst across the Chickahominy, on and to the left of the West Point Railway, were the two corps of Generals Heintzelman and Keyes—the latter in advance, the former in support, the extreme left holding the roads debouching from the White Oaks Swamp. The army thus occupied the arc of a circle, stretching from Mechanicsville to Fair Oaks Station; whilst its cord was in the hands of the Confederates. From the camp of General Porter to that of General Keyes, in a direct line, was but a short distance—about three miles; but the intervening space on the right bank of the Chickahominy was occupied by the Confederates, and the only means of communication between the right and centre of the army and its left wing was by an ill-constructed bridge opposite General Sumner's camp, or by Bottom's Bridge, a distance of nearly nine miles. General Johnston had, therefore, the advantage of acting on interior lines, and the opportunity offered itself of falling on and crushing the two corps which had been pushed across the river before assistance could be furnished them by the remainder of the army. An unusually rainy week at the end of May, and the consequent rise of the waters of the Chickahominy, favoured his projects, and induced him to make preparations for a formidable attack on the Federal left wing.

The force at the disposal of General Johnston consisted of four divisions, commanded by Generals Longstreet, Smith, D. H. Hill, and Huger—all officers who had formerly served in the United States army. On the 30th May dispositions were made for an attack on the left wing of the Federals, to take place on the following morning; and orders were sent to General Hill, and communicated verbally to General Longstreet,

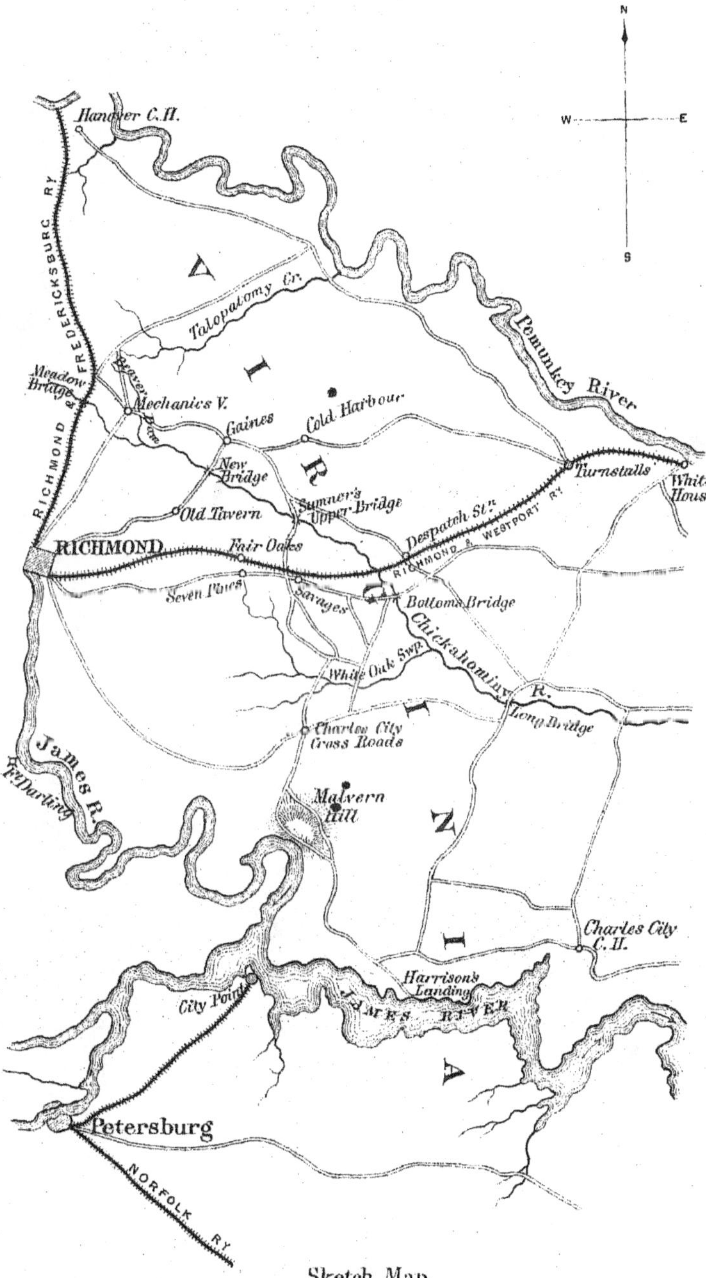

Sketch Map
of
M^c CLELLAN'S OPERATIONS
BEFORE RICHMOND.

to concentrate their divisions on the Williamsburg Road. The attack was to be made by Hill's division, supported by Longstreet; whilst Huger was directed to effect a diversion on the right by advancing by the Charles City Road, and taking the enemy in flank; and G. Smith's division was at the same time to occupy a position at the junction of the New Bridge and Nine-miles Road with the object of attacking the right flank of the Federal column engaged with Hill's division, and keeping a watch lest any attempt should be made by M'Clellan's right wing to cross the Chickahominy. Such were the dispositions made by General Johnston; but the rain, which it was hoped would materially assist the Confederates by causing a rise in the river, and thus separating General M'Clellan's army, so far interfered with the plan as to impede and render partially nugatory General Johnston's dispositions. A terrible storm raged during the night of the 30th, the roads became almost impassable; and although by great exertions three divisions of the army reached the positions assigned to them in proper time, yet General Huger's division was delayed by the mud and swollen streams, and failed in fulfilling the part allotted to it. Hour after hour did General Longstreet wait. At length, despairing of Huger's arrival, at 2 P.M. he ordered Hill to advance to the attack.

What, meanwhile, was the position of the Federals? The same remarkable storm on the night of Friday the 30th had passed over their camps; it was a night not to be forgotten by those who witnessed the continuous flashes of lightning and heard the incessant roll of the thunder, precursors to the tumult of the battle on the following day. The advance corps, under General Keyes, bivouacked in the woods and cleared spaces in the vicinity of the Nine-miles Road, General Casey's division about three-fourths of a mile in advance of the Seven Pines, and that of General Couch on the Nine-miles Road in the vicinity of Fair Oaks Station. A line of woods in front of Casey's division concealed the country beyond, and afforded shelter for the pickets, which were close in advance of the main body of the division. Slight breastworks of earth and felled trees had been hastily thrown up to cover the troops, and the artillery was posted in such positions as to support the infantry. About 10 A.M. on the 31st an A.D.C. of General Johnston, by name Washington,* was captured, and it was supposed that his presence argued the near vicinity of the Commander-in-Chief, and therefore the probability of an attack; but the morning passed quietly, and General Keyes was at Fair Oaks Station, where he had ridden to inspect his lines of defence, when he heard firing, which seemed to denote the presence of the enemy in the direction of the Seven Pines.

Such, indeed, was the case. About 2 P.M. General Hill had advanced to the attack, and, supported by Longstreet, had rapidly driven back Casey's pickets. Some of the regiments did not behave well, and retired hastily to the rear, abandoning their artillery and the camp of Casey's division, which was captured, including the hospitals and baggage waggons. A stand was, however, made at the second line of defence, and an aid-de-camp sent to hasten the supports under General Heintzelman, and also to request General Sumner, encamped on the left bank of the Chickahominy, to cross the river with the two divisions under his command

* A connection by descent of the great General Washington.

General Heintzelman advanced by the Williamsburg Road and the railroad, and arrived in time to assist such part of Casey's division as still held their ground, and that of General Couch, who had been attacked by General G. Smith on the side of the Nine-miles Road near Fair Oaks Station. It was in that portion of the field that General Johnston had placed himself, and had been joined by General Lee, and by the President in person. Some delay had occurred in the advance of General Smith's division, as, owing either to the configuration of the ground or the state of the atmosphere, the firing from General Hill's division had not been heard, and it was at first supposed that he had not moved forward. Thus the Federal supports under General Heintzelman had arrived in time to reinforce that part of the line. Still the Confederates pressed forward, but with severe loss. General Johnston himself was dangerously wounded, struck on the shoulder by the splinter of a shell, he fell from his horse, breaking two of his ribs, and the command devolved on General G. Smith.

In the meantime, after great exertions, General Sumner succeeded in effecting the passage of the Chickahominy by means of two hastily constructed bridges, and brought up his divisions. They advanced along the railway and joined the Federal right, which had been thrown back. It was now evening, but the roll of musketry still continued, interspersed with artillery, although but little of that arm was employed by the Confederates, owing to the difficulty of bringing up the guns through the swampy country. Darkness closed in, but the woods were illumined by the flashes of the rifles from the advancing Confederates. Then was wanted Huger's division, but delayed by the badness of the roads and by the swollen streams, it played no part in the battle, and night at length terminated the contest. The Confederates had driven back their opponent two miles, and had captured nine guns and a vast amount of camp equipage and stores, including those of the medical department, of which they were much in want. The success was, however, attended with severe loss; the Federal smooth-bored 12-pounder Napoleon guns had produced much havoc, and were considered to have been more deadly in the wooded country than the rifled Parrot guns.

During the whole day the Federal right wing, comprising the two corps of Generals Franklin and Porter, remained idle; no attempt was made to force the passage of the Chickahominy either at Mechanicsville or at Newbridge, and so either to effect a diversion by marching on Richmond, or to move to the support of the left wing by the shorter route across the stream. General M'Clellan spent the greater portion of the afternoon on the slopes of the hill in front of General Porter's corps, overlooking the Chickahominy, from which place the sound of the firing could be heard, and even the explosion of the shells seen as they burst high above the forest. He did not seem to be aware of the serious nature of the engagement in which his left wing was involved, and it was not until late in the evening, shortly before dark, that he resolved on ascertaining in person the true state of affairs. During the greater portion of that night the general was on horseback. His first point was the old quarters of General Sumner on the left bank of the stream, but although the camps were still standing, every available man had been marched to the front; the stragglers and the officers' servants having been ordered to proceed to the bridge and repair or reconstruct such portions as had been injured by the swollen stream.

Leaving Sumner's head-quarters, General M'Clellan reached Despatch Station about 9 P.M., and there first heard the true account of the battle. Railway trains filled with wounded encumbered the line, and accumulations of stores blocked up the station. Amidst this confusion, General M'Clellan endeavoured to extract the truth from the various statements made by two voluble informants, and after making himself master as far as possible of the true position of affairs, he and his staff returned to General Sumner's head-quarters. The night was pitch dark, and the gloom of the forest was only illumined by millions of fire-flies. With some difficulty the general reached his destination, and, after receiving and transmitting numerous telegrams, lay down to the rest which he much needed, worn out as he was by fatigue and sickness.*

Both armies bivouacked on the ground that they occupied at the termination of the action, and both were aware that the struggle would be renewed on the following morning. During the night, General Huger brought up his division to reinforce those of Generals Hill, Longstreet, and Smith, whilst the several Federal divisions and brigades which had crossed the Chickahominy late in the evening of the 31st were closed up to reinforce and take the place of the troops which had suffered so severely.

It was indeed an anxious night for both armies, and even more so for the inhabitants of Richmond. Within sound of the guns, almost within sight of the combatants, their safety depending on the events of the

* General M'Clellan was suffering from chronic dysentery.

battle, were the wives, daughters, and nearest relatives of those who were engaged. The President himself was on the field, and it seemed that the battle of the Seven Pines must be that which had been so long looked for to decide the fate of the campaign. The long line of Federal prisoners captured from General Casey's division, as they were marched to the rear, had afforded some evidence of the success of the Confederates; but the numerous ambulances and carts filled with wounded bore testimony to the cost at which the battle had been gained. During the night of the 31st, and the succeeding days, the city of Richmond was one vast hospital; and the ladies of Virginia, leaving for a time the task of furnishing clothing for the troops, devoted their energies to relieving the wants and alleviating the sufferings of the wounded. Short repose was allowed to the dwellers in Richmond on the night of the 31st. At daybreak the sound of artillery awoke those whom anxiety had suffered to sleep, and on either side the advanced troops seized their arms. On the right of the Federal line were two divisions of General Sumner's corps, under Generals Sedgwick and Richardson. On the left of Sedgwick, between the railway and the Williamsburg Road, was General Kearney, of General Heintzelman's corps; and on his left the division of General Couch, of General Keyes' corps. Advancing up the railway was General Hooker's division. The engagement commenced near the Williamsburg Railway about 5 A.M., and lasted until 10 A.M. The Confederates did not evince the vigour they had shown on the previous day; they were opposed to fresh troops, who, undismayed by the repulse of their comrades, advanced boldly to the attack; and the Federals after some resistance regained the ground they had lost on the 31st, and recaptured one of the guns which had been taken from General Casey's division.

Towards the close of the action, General M'Clellan arrived on the ground. He had been delayed by the difficulty of crossing the Chickahominy, which had risen during the night, and had rendered General Sumner's bridge almost impassable. As he approached the battle-field the evidences of the serious nature of the struggle met his eye: the woods were filled with the wounded, who were conveyed with as little delay as possible to the few farm-houses, which had been converted into temporary hospitals, where the surgeons were earnestly engaged in administering to their wants; whilst interspersed with these sorrowful signs of battle were the news-boys almost as busily occupied in selling the last copies of the New York papers, which had just arrived by the train from West Point. General M'Clellan rode forward to where Sumner and the several generals under his command were directing the movements of the troops. The open field was covered with the Confederate dead, and the volleys of musketry in the neighbouring woods marked the position occupied by the combatants. Both sides were, however, exhausted, and about 10 A.M. the firing, as if by mutual consent, died away. The army laid down in the positions they occupied, and slept; the artillerymen stretched like the dead under the very wheels of their guns. Riding along the lines from right to left, General M'Clellan visited the several divisions, and was even received with cheers from those troops who had suffered most severely on the previous day.

During this time his right wing had remained idle.

The Chickahominy was indeed more difficult to cross than on the previous day, but still did not present an insurmountable obstacle. Generals Franklin and Porter's divisions were each possessed of a formidable artillery, sufficient to protect and cover the passage of the infantry; and it is idle to suppose that there was not sufficient engineering skill among the troops to enable them to construct bridges for the infantry. Possibly the artillery could not have been conveyed across the stream, but the presence of the infantry divisions would have been invaluable. However, from whatever cause it arose, whether from a want of decision, or from over-caution on the part of the general commanding, or from his knowledge that neither the subordinate generals nor the troops could be depended on, unless accompanied and covered by a powerful artillery, the right wing did not move; and as on the 31st the Confederates, by the absence of General Huger's division, missed the opportunity of effecting the destruction of the Federal left wing, so on the 1st of June did General M'Clellan fail to avail himself of the advantage of attacking with his whole force troops which had been held in check on the previous day by a part of his army. On the evening of the 31st he might have been unaware of the serious nature of the attack on his left wing, and therefore cautious before he committed the division on his right; but on the succeeding day, or during the night, there was ample time to make arrangements for an advance of his whole force. There were doubtless many difficulties to be contended with, such as the almost impossibility of obtaining a clear idea of the progress of affairs, owing to the nature of the country, which hindered if it did not prevent personal inspection, as also the want of military knowledge in the generals and staff of the army, which often led officers to exaggerate the importance of events passing under their own eyes, and so to submit reports tending to mislead the general commanding in chief. From whatever cause it arose, an opportunity was lost. If Generals Franklin and Porter had shown the same energy as General Sumner on the evening and night of the 31st, the whole army might have crossed the Chickahominy, and the battle of the 1st would on the part of the Confederates have been not for victory, but for existence. As it was, both armies occupied nearly the same ground after the battle as they had done before, with the exception that three Federal corps in place of two were on the right bank of the Chickahominy. General M'Clellan's right and left wings were still separated by a large extent of ground, as their opponents continued to hold the woods opposite Generals Franklin and Porter, and prevented direct communication between those corps and the three corps which had crossed the stream.

On the old battle ground of the 31st the troops encamped. Among the half-buried dead, and the swamps teeming with corruption, arising from the numerous bodies of men and horses, did the soldiers erect their huts and pitch their tents. The water they drank was drained from the graves, and the whole air reeked with stench; the hot sun drew up the vapours from the saturated ground, and the swamps of the Chickahominy became as fatal as the bullets of the enemy. In his first despatches General M'Clellan under-estimated his loss; but he was fearful lest even the numbers he owned to should tend to dishearten his army, therefore he requested the

President to receive his communications as confidential. Ultimately he acknowledged to the total loss of 7,000 men. According to General Johnston's report, the Confederate loss amounted to less than 4,500, of which the whole fell on the divisions of Generals Longstreet, Hill, and Smith. General Huger's division was not engaged. On the 31st it did not arrive in sufficient time to be of service, and on the 1st June it appears that the Confederates were unwilling to renew the action, and fought entirely on the defensive. They had missed their opportunity on the previous day, and were anxious to return to their former defensive tactics.

In General Johnston they lost an able officer, and one who hitherto had conducted operations with much skill. In consequence of his wound, he was disabled for a considerable time, and although on the field he was succeeded by General G. Smith,* yet the chief command was given to General Lee; and thus the apparent misfortune sustained by the temporary loss of the services of General Johnston was more than compensated for by the opportunity it gave of bringing to the front one of the most able men, if not the most able man, that the war has produced. Few men in the old United States army had been more beloved and respected than General Lee: his character was said to resemble that of Washington. Of an old Virginian family, possessed of wealth and position, he had embraced the profession of arms and had served with distinction in Mexico. When the secession of Virginia took place he unwillingly resigned his commission in the army; but convinced

* General G. Smith had been a personal friend of General M'Clellan, and was present at his marriage.

that his primary duty lay with his State, he without hesitation threw himself heart and soul into her cause. His property and family residence lying close to Washington, became the spoil of his enemies, and both were rendered valueless. From a rich man he was reduced to comparative poverty, but, 'not excelling in this 'respect many of his fellow-countrymen,' he willingly resigned all, seeking for no compensation, for the sake of the cause he fought for. Both in mind and person he seemed especially qualified to become the leader and to win the affections of the Southern army. Free from all selfishness, he attached to himself by sentiments of personal affection the generals under his command; of simple habits, and singularly unostentatious in manner, he set an example to the army and to the senior officers of self-denial, of patience under hardships, and of a disregard of all state. He also gave a tone to the army in other and higher qualities. A deeply religious man, he checked the licentiousness too common in camps, whilst in respect of his conduct towards his enemies he lessened, as far as possible, the horrors of war, and in the subsequent campaigns waged in the enemy's country afforded an example of forbearance which many of the Federal generals would have done well to have imitated. His willingness to share privations with his men,* and the cool courage he displayed in action, endeared him to the private soldiers; and if such men as Generals Jackson, Longstreet and Stuart may be said to have been the arms of the army, General Lee may truly be accounted as its head. Such was the

* It is said that during all the campaigns in which General Lee has been engaged he has always occupied a tent, and refused to sleep under a roof, even during the most severe weather.

man now in command of the army for the defence of Richmond.

After the battle of Fair Oaks or Seven Pines, both armies entrenched themselves. General M'Clellan erected field-works, and threw up a line of breast-works, flanked with small redoubts, extending from the White Oak Swamp in a semicircle to the Chicahominy, and enclosing within the lines the railway and the several roads and bridges constructed to afford communication with his right wing, which continued to hold the country in the neighbourhood of Mechanicsville and Cold Harbour. He applied frequently for reinforcements in order to replace the losses incurred by battle and sickness, and asked permission to draw regiments from Fortress Monroe. To these applications President Lincoln replied by promises, and assurances of help from the Shenandoah Valley as soon as General Jackson should have been disposed of.

Not only was the campaign in the Shenandoah Valley supposed (and rightly so) to influence materially the strategy of the General in command of the army defending Richmond, but there was constant apprehension, as was evinced by General M'Clellan's despatches, of a junction between the army of the West, under General Beauregard, and that of General Lee. Therefore, during the pause that occurred in the active operations before Richmond, it will be well to follow up the events in the West, which resulted both from the capture of New Orleans and from the operations in Tennessee.

The battle of the Seven Pines, although indecisive, was yet a proof that the capture of Richmond was a task which would tax all the energies of the North, and the practical experience of the difficulties of campaigning in Virginia showed that the rapid marches and brilliant operations anticipated by the Northern people were either impossible from the nature of the country, or inapplicable to the half-disciplined troops and unpractised officers of the Federal armies.*

* The terms 'half-disciplined and unpractised' are not intended offensively, or even disparagingly. There had not as yet been sufficient time either to form properly disciplined soldiers or to train experienced officers. Doubtless there are instances where talent may, in the case of a general, lead to the performance of even greater tasks than experience, and where enthusiasm and determination may, in the case of the troops, effect the accomplishment of greater enterprises than discipline; but up to the time alluded to in this chapter no Northern general and no Northern troops had given signs of either great talent, or of the intense enthusiasm requisite to counterbalance faults in discipline and organisation.

CHAPTER III.

CAMPAIGN IN THE WEST.

THE fall of New Orleans materially affected the position of the Confederate army of the West, as not only did it deprive General Beauregard of the resources of a great city and of the means of recruiting his forces from its population, but it also opened the waters of the Mississippi to the Federal fleet, and so enabled their gunboats to hinder communication with the western bank, and to render difficult the transmission of cattle and other stores from Texas. Thus, General Beauregard's advanced position at Corinth became difficult to hold, and it was a question whether a more southern line of defence should be adopted where he would be nearer his depôts, and also in a position of greater security. At present he was threatened by the Federal army of the West encamped at Pittsburg Landing, by the combined naval and military force on the Upper Mississippi River, and by the possibility of an attempt on his left rear by detachments of the Federal force from New Orleans.

That the spring campaign would be followed up by the Federals, there was abundant evidence. The capture of Island No. 10 at once allowed of the advance of the fleet under Commodore Foote, which was only stopped by the guns of Fort Pillow. This fort, hastily constructed soon after the commencement of hostilities, was situated about 60 miles above Memphis, on the left bank of the river. High ground had been selected on which to erect the works, and for a short time it offered an obstacle to the further progress of the Federal fleet. The efforts of the naval force were directed to its reduction, whilst General Halleck concentrated all the disposable troops on the Tennessee River.

As has been previously stated, General Beauregard, since the battle of Shiloh, had been joined by the troops of Generals Vandorn and Price from Arkansas, but even with these reinforcements he did not consider himself sufficiently strong to retain his position. However, no rumour of any intention to abandon the lines at Corinth reached the Federal camp; the Confederate force was supposed to be large, and after the lesson taught them at Shiloh, the Northern generals were cautious of committing themselves to an engagement under disadvantageous circumstances. Changes were made in the organisation of the army; and, apparently with the intention of marking disapprobation for the defeat of the first day at Shiloh, General Grant was susperseded in the command of the army of Tennessee by General Thomas. To the troops originally included in that army was added the division of General Pope, who had marched from the neighbourhood of Fort Pillow to the encampment of the main body of the forces near Pittsburg Landing.

With great caution did the army advance; each successive camp was fortified, and careful lines of defence, quickly constructed with the spade and axe, covered the front, and prevented a repetition of a surprise of the pickets, as on the first day's battle of Shiloh.* Attempts were made to turn the enemy's position, and to cut the lines of rail both west of Corinth, between that place and Memphis, and to the east, in the neighbourhood of Decatur. These movements were not wholly unopposed. On the 9th May, General Pope's pickets were driven in, and his division forced to retreat, whilst attempting the capture of Farmington and the destruction of the railroad; but, on the other hand, a detachment from General Mitchell's force at Pulaski occupied Rodgersville, on the frontier of Alabama. The main advance was, however, directed against Corinth, and on the 16th of May the Federal army encamped about five miles from the place, and commenced, as usual, to fortify themselves. There were frequent skirmishes between the pickets. The forest concealed the numbers of the enemy, and afforded cover for his sharpshooters, who, as was asserted, frequently placed themselves in the trees, in order more effectually to pick off the enemy's skirmishers. There was no attempt to storm the Con-

* General Sherman, in an address to his division of the 31st May, dated Corinth, congratulates it on its industry in strongly entrenching seven distinct camps since the march from the camp at Shiloh. The distance between Shiloh and Corinth is about twenty-five miles. A correspondent, writing from General Pope's army, notices the same peculiar features of the march. He writes:—'One curious feature of the advance now is, that of throwing works of defence up along the whole line. The fortifications completed to-day cannot be less than twelve miles in length, extending from the extreme right to the extreme left wing. They are strongly made with logs and earth, lined by rifle pits, and distant from Corinth six miles. Every movement is characterised by extreme caution. To-morrow the lines advance four miles, when another parallel will be constructed. In case any reverse should happen, these defences would be invaluable.'

federate position; and, as was the case at Yorktown, great preparations were made, to end in a somewhat similar result. So close were the Federal lines to Corinth, that the sound of the trains could be heard as they entered and departed from the village; and on the 27th and 28th May, it was remarked and reported to General Halleck that there was especial activity on the railroad, apparently denoting some movement of the enemy. The light and sound of explosions, as of scattered ammunition, was also noticed; and General Halleck at length entertained suspicions that operations of which he was unacquainted were in progress in the enemy's camp; he therefore ordered a strong reconnaissance to be pushed forward, which was accordingly done, and on the morning of the 29th May the Federal troops entered Corinth without any resistance. General Halleck had been completely out-manœuvred; he had concentrated a large army, had preserved the greatest caution, had at length completed his preparations for attack, when his opponent, having also matured his plans, and sent all his stores, wounded, and sick to the rear, drew in his pickets and disappeared. A few stragglers were captured, and possibly a small quantity of stores; but there can be no doubt that General Halleck's campaign was a failure.

General Pope was sent forward to pursue the retreating columns, and grossly exaggerated, if not untrue, reports of his successes were forwarded to Washington; but these despatches scarcely served their turn to delude the people of the North, and in the ridicule they cast upon their authors, were productive of more harm than good to the Federal cause. On June 4th, General Halleck sent the following despatch to Mr. Stanton, Secretary of War:—

'General Halleck's Head-quarters, June 4.

'General Pope, with forty thousand men, is thirty miles south of Florence, pushing the enemy hard. He already reports ten thousand prisoners and deserters from the enemy, and fifteen thousand stand of arms, captured. Thousands of the enemy are throwing away their arms. A farmer says, that when Beauregard learned that Colonel Elliott had cut the railroad on his line of retreat, he became frantic, and told his men to save themselves the best way they could. We captured nine locomotives and a number of cars. One of the former is already repaired, and is running to-day; several more will be in running order in a few days. The result is all that I could possibly desire.

'H. W. HALLECK,

'Major-General Commanding.'

What could be more absurd than such a despatch! The actual facts as relating to General Pope's exploits were subsequently ascertained to have scarcely any foundation, whilst the report regarding General Beauregard was puerile in the extreme. That General conducted his retreat with great order, and received little or no annoyance from General Pope. After evacuating Corinth he took up a defensive position about twenty-five miles to the south, which he held until the 8th, when, owing to the want of good water, he retreated without molestation farther into the State of Mississippi, making Tupelo, about fifty miles south of Corinth, his head-quarters. In a letter published by General Beauregard with reference to General Halleck's despatch, he denied categorically the statements it contained, at the same time owning to certain losses, which evidently gave some colour to the otherwise perfectly false statements of his adversary. As General M'Clellan had been foiled before York Town, so had General Halleck been out-manœuvred at Corinth—that is, out-manœuvred in so far that he had failed to bring the campaign to the issue of a battle. The Confederate army of the West was intact, although its retreat surrendered to the enemy an important line of railway, and also necessitated, or rather led to, the fall of Fort Pillow, and consequently of the city of Memphis.

The war policy of the Confederate States about this time underwent a change. It was found that they were not sufficiently powerful, either as regarded men or means, to conduct operations at a distance from the main supplies, and with the object of defending long lines of frontier. It became apparent that the resources of war must be economised, that concentration had become necessary, and that, consequently, many large districts of country must be abandoned to the invader.

The retreat of General Beauregard's army necessitated the abandonment of Fort Pillow.* The original garrison had been greatly weakened in order to repair the losses of the battles of Shiloh, and, although recruited by volunteers from the city of Memphis, was yet insufficient to sustain a protracted siege. For some weeks the Federal gunboats had poured shot and shell into the work, and preparations had been made for an assault, when, on the evening of the 4th, the garrison, after removing and destroying the greater portion of the stores and guns, abandoned the fort, and embarking on board the steamers, hastened

* This Fort Pillow must not be confounded with the fort of the same name in the immediate vicinity of Memphis.

down the Mississippi. The place was immediately occupied by a Federal garrison, whilst the gunboats without delay descended the river, and shortly afterwards (on June 5th) anchored off Island No. 45, in close vicinity to the city of Memphis.

One last struggle did the Confederates make to save this important place; the small river fleet resolved to interpose between the invaders and their prize, and, although far inferior to their opponents in all the requirements of naval warfare, yet determined to make a final effort and to risk all for so important an object. On the morning of the 6th June, the Confederate fleet of eight steamers was discovered lying off the levee* near the city of Memphis, equipped, as far as was possible, but necessarily very imperfectly, as vessels of war. Seven carried two guns each, one four guns; they were all of wood, but defended by bales of cotton. The fleet was under the command of Commodore Montgomery. The Federal fleet was divided into what may be termed two squadrons—the first consisting of the rams, which moved in advance; the second of the gunboats. The first line was under the command of Colonel Ellet, the whole under Commodore Davis.

The sun rose brightly on the morning of the 6th of June, as each side prepared for action. The banks of the levee were lined with the citizens of Memphis, eagerly awaiting—although with but little hope—the result of the combat. Few indeed could venture to expect anything but annihilation to the small Confederate fleet, consisting, as it did, of fewer vessels, far less powerfully armed, and of construction ill-adapted to the

* The word levee denotes the embankment erected to confine in their proper channel the waters of the Mississippi, and is used as the place where ships load and unload their cargoes.

requirements of war. There seemed no prospect except that of a glorious death. Indeed, it is difficult to account for Commodore Montgomery's resolution to offer battle, except on the supposition that he anticipated the arrival in his rear of Commodore Farragut's squadron from New Orleans, and preferred the chance of battle to capture. Immediately preceding the action, he transferred his flag from the Van Dorn to the Little Rebel, as the former was laden with gunpowder and other Government property. At 6.15 A.M. the action was commenced by the Confederate gunboats, which fired at the advanced line of the enemy's fleet. The fire was immediately replied to, and, under cover of the artillery of the second line, the rams Queen of the West and Monarch steamed boldly against the Confederate fleet. Each selected her antagonist. They were followed by the Switzerland and Lancaster No. 3—both rams. The Queen of the West attempted to sink the Beauregard, but only glancing against her, passed through the enemy's line, turned round, and again engaged her coming up stream. The Beauregard attempted to strike the ram, but missing her mark, fell foul of one of her own fleet. During this time the heavy guns from the Federal gunboats poured shot and shell into the comparatively defenceless vessels, whilst the riflemen from the rams picked off their gunners. The Beauregard was sunk; the Little Rebel endeavoured to reach the Arkansas shore, was run aground, and abandoned by her crew; Commodore Montgomery and some of the men escaped by swimming.* Five of the

* The Cincinnati commercial newspaper thus describes the incident:—'The Little Rebel reaches the shore, when Commodore Montgomery and all his crew break for the timber, and, by the tallest kind of swimming, escape.'

Confederate fleet were sunk, two captured, and one—the Van Dorn—escaped. The whole was effected in one hour and twenty minutes, with very little loss on the Federal side; three men only were reported as wounded. The Confederate accounts owned to the loss of about 50 men killed and wounded, and 100 prisoners, and much as the courage of Commodore Montgomery, in offering battle, may be admired, it cannot but be lamented that so many brave men perished uselessly.

The result of the action was a demand for the surrender of the city of Memphis, which was agreed to, as there were no defenders, and the place was at the mercy of the guns of the fleet. A detachment was landed, the stars and stripes replaced the stars and bars, and the Northern newspapers searched for, and of course reported much Union sentiment. How different was the appearance of Memphis in the spring of 1862 to that of former years! One of the principal points of export for cotton, its levee was usually covered with bales, its wharves thronged with shipping, and its population—both rich and poor—busily engaged in trade. Now scarcely a bale of cotton was to be seen, only a few smoking remnants proclaimed where it had been destroyed; not a vessel excepting the Federal gunboats and storeships lay off the city; the merchants' stores were closed, and the long rows of villas and wealthy houses deserted in a great measure by their male population, who were serving with the Confederate army. The events which followed the capture and occupation of Memphis afforded an additional proof, if any were wanted, of the unanimity of the South. The great trading city had been captured, but no power could restore its traffic, or induce a resumption of its former business. The cotton on the plantations was burned, and but few bales found their way to the North.

After the fall of Fort Pillow and the destruction of the Confederate flotilla, there appeared no hindrance to the passage of the Federal fleet down the Mississippi to New Orleans. The lower part of the river was held by Commodore Farragut's gunboats, the upper part by those of Commodore Foote; and it seemed probable that the two fleets would unite, and proceed to the reduction of the several places on the tributaries of the great river. Such, however, was not now to be the case; a task more difficult than any that had as yet been attempted awaited the Federal fleet, and the defence of Vicksburg was to wipe away the disgrace, if disgrace there had been, of the easy surrender of Forts Henry, Donelson, Island No. 10, and Pillow.

On the 24th of June, both the upper and the lower fleet reached Vicksburg, and communications were established between Commodores Davis and Farragut. It was a formidable force that was thus brought to bear against the hastily constructed Confederate works. Commodore Davis's fleet consisted of four gunboats and six mortar boats; whilst that of Commodore Farragut comprised nine gunboats* and the mortar flotilla under Commodore Porter. In addition to the naval force, four regiments of infantry and two batteries of artillery, under General Williams, had been brought up from Bâton Rouge, and took part in the operations. The progress of the lower fleet had been slow, as it had been necessary to protect the transports from artillery and riflemen, for which the thickly-wooded banks afforded cover and concealment. The troops had often

* During the siege other additional gunboats probably joined the fleet.

been obliged to land to clear the woods of the enemy, and had been marched across the bluffs and peninsulas, so frequent in the winding stream of the Mississippi. Destruction marked the progress of the Federal flotilla: the town of Grand Gulf was burned, and there were slight skirmishes with detached bodies; but no serious opposition was made to the advance until the arrival of the combined force below Vicksburg, on the 25th of June. There the Confederates had determined to make a stand, and to prevent if possible the accomplishment of the project aimed at by the Federal Government, of opening the river to the trade of the Western States.

The position was well chosen for the purposes of defence. Opposite the town the river makes a sharp bend, leaving a narrow peninsula of land immediately in face of the high bluff on which the place stands. Thus the reaches of the river, looking up the stream and looking down, could be seen from batteries mounted on or near the bluff. The town itself is small, and is built on the slopes of the hill; the highest point crowned by a church. A railroad connects it with Jackson, the capital of the State. At the distance of a few miles above the town the Yazoo River, a large navigable stream, enters the Mississippi, after a course of many miles through the State of the same name. Numerous ravines and bayous, running into the Yazoo and the Mississippi, afforded positions which could easily be defended on the land side; whilst the swamps and vast forests rendered the surrounding country difficult for the passage of troops. As early as the end of May the town had received a summons to surrender from an advanced squadron of gunboats sent up the river by Commodore Farragut; but it was not until

June 25th that the siege, or rather bombardment, can be said to have commenced.

During a whole month was the bombardment continued. There were many days of intermission in the fire; but these were followed by more vigorous efforts. Shells both from the mortar boats below and those above the town were hurled on its defenders, the church appearing to afford to the gunners a conspicuous mark. Little damage was, however, inflicted: there were many open spaces in the town, where the shells fell and buried themselves; and the inhabitants who remained took refuge during the height of the bombardment in caves, which they excavated in the sides of the hill. The defenders of the batteries sustained but little injury, and generally reserved their fire until the near approach of the gunboats seemed to threaten a more serious attack. The enemy's mortar vessels below the town were out of reach of their guns, as they were anchored close to the eastern bank, concealed by the forest, and protected from any attack on the land side by a strong detachment of infantry.

During this time, and under cover of the fire, a large body of negroes, about 1,200, were employed in cutting a canal through the peninsula, opposite the town, in order to turn the waters of the Mississippi, and so to create a fresh channel secure from the enemy's guns, by which ships could pass up and down the river. The scheme was attended with great difficulties, and was thought impossible by those who knew the river. Not only had a deep canal through a thick clay soil to be cut, but the forest and tangled jungle had to be grubbed up; and when the work should be finished there was great doubt whether the water could be induced to take the new channel. Whilst this scheme was in progress, five of the gunboats of Commodore Farragut's fleet succeeded in passing the batteries and effecting a junction with the upper fleet. They accomplished the enterprise with little injury to themselves, owing to the bad firing of the Confederates, whose guns were levelled too high, cutting the rigging without damaging the hulls of the vessels.

Notwithstanding this success, the capture of the place appeared no nearer its accomplishment; and on the 15th of July an event occurred which showed that even on the water the Confederates were not entirely powerless. A few days previous, two deserters had brought word to Commodore Farragut that a steamer, built somewhat on the same plan as the redoubtable Merrimac, was lying either in the Yazoo River or in one of its tributaries. To test the accuracy of this information, a reconnaissance of three gunboats was ordered up the river; and after proceeding a short distance they found a barrier of timber, behind which was supposed to be concealed the Confederate steamer. During the night of the 14th the timber was removed, and the steamer issued forth on her bold enterprise. It was, indeed, one of the most daring feats of the war that Captain Brown, commanding the small steamer Arkansas, undertook to perform. With a river steamer, adapted for the purposes of war, and coated with such iron as could be procured, but still of rough workmanship—manned with volunteers from the army, many of whom had never been on board ship, and were unaccustomed to the use of big guns—Captain, or, as he then was, Lieutenant, Brown formed and carried out with partial success the bold scheme of forcing a passage through and destroying the Federal fleet.

The Arkansas had been built somewhat on the model

of the Merrimac; but her roof, instead of sloping to a point, was flat at the top. She carried three guns at each side—one at the bows, and another at the stern; her funnel protruding from the roof. About 5 A.M. on the 15th she left her moorings, and moved swiftly down the Yazoo River. The Federal gunboats saw her approaching, and immediately perceived that she was the long-talked-of ironclad. The Tyler and the Queen of the West, after firing a few shots, which seemed to strike harmlessly against her sides, turned and fled; the Carondilet, ironclad, attempted to bar the passage, but could not stand against her guns—her steam-pipe burst, and she was driven ashore. The firing had been heard by the Federal fleet, who supposed it was from the gunboat Tyler shelling the woods. It had also been heard in the town; and the inhabitants, and the soldiers who were not on duty at the batteries, better informed of its meaning, thronged the hill, and eagerly watched the mouth of the Yazoo River. Nor long did they watch in vain. About 6 A.M. the gunboats Queen of the West and Tyler were descried flying before the Arkansas; and the Federal fleet, totally unprepared for such an enemy, were seen to be in some confusion. On board the Federal ships the feeling was more of surprise than alarm; for it was not supposed that so small a vessel would venture to attack a fleet of fifteen gunboats and rams, carrying upwards of 200 guns. Still the Arkansas advanced, and before preparations had been made to receive her she had come within gunshot of the Federal fleet. Great was the anxiety of the defenders of Vicksburg as they watched the small steamer boldly enter the throng of vessels. Fifteen vessels of war and seven rams lay in her path; but she continued fearlessly on her course. The Hartford and Richmond, with their numerous and heavy guns, fired into her; the ram Lancaster made at her to butt her and run her down; the other gunboats, both ironclad and wooden, poured their shot into her; still she held on her course. She disabled the Lancaster; she poured forth her broadsides to the right and to the left; and, although much injured, preserved her steady track through the whole Federal fleet.

Was there ever a more gallant feat of arms done? Astonished, dismayed, and in confusion, their shots missing their small antagonist and striking each other, the Federal fleet opened out on either side, and left a clear passage for the gallant Arkansas. She rounded the point of land, and amid the cheers of the defenders of Vicksburg anchored under the guns of the batteries. In the meantime the panic had spread to the fleet below the town; one of the mortar vessels which had grounded was set on fire, and the remainder got up steam, and made preparations for flight down the river. But the alarm was groundless, as the Arkansas had been injured in the previous engagements, and her crew* were tired out with their exertions; therefore she remained quietly under the guns of the batteries.

Apparently ashamed of the easy manner in which so small an antagonist had baffled them, the combined fleets made an attack on the batteries late on the same evening, with the object of either capturing or sinking the Arkansas. Nothing resulted from the engagement; and on the following morning the ironclad gunboat Essex made a second attempt for the same purpose. Under cover of the fire from the upper fleet, and with

* Five were killed and nine wounded on board the Arkansas. The Federal loss in the action was, according to their own account, twenty-two killed and sixty wounded.

the expectation of co-operation from the vessels below the town, the commander of the Essex (Commodore Porter) ran the gauntlet of the upper batteries, and approaching the Arkansas, delivered his fire at the distance of about five feet, at the same time attempting to sink her by running her down. The Essex missed her blow, and ran aground directly under the Confederate batteries, and exposed to the fire of riflemen from the shore. Finding a further attack hopeless, and perceiving that the lower fleet made no demonstrations of coming to his assistance, Commodore Porter having got his vessel afloat, put her head down stream, and passing the lower batteries, anchored below the town.

This incident was the last of any moment which happened during the first siege of Vicksburg. The scheme of cutting the canal through the isthmus had failed, and on the 24th of July the fleet of Commodore Farragut having embarked the military force under General Williams, steamed down the Mississippi to Bâton Rouge, whilst the upper fleet took up a position opposite the mouth of the Yazoo River. Thus the siege may be said to have terminated, and the hitherto almost continuous success of the gunboats received a check, which was the more galling, as a larger force had been brought into action during the attack on Vicksburg than in any previous operations on the Western waters.

In order to furnish a connected narrative of the siege, we have been induced to forestall the chronological order of the events of the war. The campaign of the Peninsula had closed in a manner unexpected to the Federals; and as the results of that campaign tended materially to influence the conduct of the war in the West, in so far as the resources of both parties were drawn to Virginia, it will be advisable for the present to leave the Mississippi River and return to the armies on the Chickahominy. Irrespective, however, of military and naval matters, and indeed engaging men's attention even more than the movements of armies, was the conduct of the Federal authorities at New Orleans, which excited to the utmost the indignation of the South, and even awoke an almost corresponding feeling in the nations of Europe.

It will be remembered that the military force which occupied the city of New Orleans was commanded by General Butler, who after the surrender exercised the functions of the governor of the place. How he conducted that government, and how by his acts he roused a spirit of unconquerable hatred in the breasts of a proud race, it must be our province to inquire. On the 1st of May the troops landed at New Orleans, and General Butler immediately issued a proclamation, placing the city under martial law. He directed that the inhabitants should surrender their arms; that no assemblages of people should congregate in the streets; that no flags or other emblems except that of the United States and the foreign consulates should be exhibited; and that the newspapers should not publish articles tending to inflame their readers against the Government or troops of the United States, or, without authority, issue any news of the war or of the movements of troops. The functions of the courts of justice in respect of serious offences were also suspended, and their duties taken by courtsmartial. Such a course of action was no doubt necessary to secure the safety of the troops and the peace of the city. The character of the population of New Orleans was turbulent even in quiet times; much more was it expected that it would break forth into aggressive acts when the presence of an invader had aroused the passions of the inhabitants, and when the taunts of the other states and cities of the South for the easy surrender of the city might possibly provoke her populace to insurrection. If, therefore, General Butler had confined himself to the severity doubtless necessary in dealing with a conquered but still refractory people, few except those biassed by party feeling could have blamed him; but when he overstepped the limits of what may be called the rights of the conqueror, and especially when he gave his consent to the execution of an individual for an act performed prior to the occupation of the town by the Federal army, his conduct ceased to be justifiable on the plea of military necessity, and earned the designation of tyranny, whilst the act alluded to may almost be stigmatised as one of murder.

On the 27th of April, the day following the reply of the Mayor to Commodore Farragut's demand for the surrender of the city, a party of Marines had been landed and the American flag hoisted on the Mint. The same was also attempted at the Custom-house; but owing to the excitement of the crowd it was thought better to desist. The Marines then re-embarked on board the ship of war, and the city was left in charge of the civil authorities. A short time subsequent, a crowd collected round the Mint, and the United States flag was torn down and dragged through the streets. The act was performed by a citizen of the name of Mumford. On the 1st of May, as has before been stated, the troops landed and formally took possession of the city; their general, Butler, at the same time issuing a proclamation of martial law. This law, therefore, came in force on the 1st of May, and could not in justice take cognisance of acts performed prior to its declaration; but the United States flag was torn down prior to the 29th of April, and therefore Mumford ought not to have been tried for any infraction of martial law. For what, then, was he tried? The Confederates had long since been recognised as belligerents, and therefore entitled to be treated as such, and not as rebels. Mumford had given his allegiance to the Confederate Government, and owed none to the Federal authorities; therefore he could not be tried on the charge of treason to the United States Government. The flag was flying in a city which owned the supremacy of the Confederate Government; and although the enemy had by force raised the United States flag over one of her principal buildings, yet he had left no guard to protect it, had not taken possession of the city, nor had substituted any law in place of those already in force. When, therefore, Mumford was arrested by order of General Butler, was tried by courtmartial and sentenced to execution, and when that sentence was sanctioned and enforced, General Butler was regarded by the people of the Confederate States as guilty of deliberate murder.

The execution did not take place until the 7th of June. Mumford met his death with firmness and courage. He was hanged in front of the Mint at New Orleans, protesting, immediately before his death, that he did not consider that he was about to suffer justly. Such was one of the acts which excited an universal feeling of hatred to General Butler throughout the Confederacy. But even this did not render his name so odious as his conduct relative to the ladies of New Orleans. On May 15, the following order was issued:—

'Head-quarters, Department of the Gulf.
'New Orleans, May 15.

'As officers and soldiers of the United States have been subject to repeated insults from women calling themselves ladies of New Orleans, in return for the most scrupulous non-interference and courtesy on our part, it is ordered hereafter, when any female shall by mere gesture or movement insult or show contempt for any officers or soldiers of the United States, she shall be regarded and held liable to be treated as a woman about town plying her avocation.

'By command of Major-General BUTLER,
'GEORGE S. STRONG, A.A.G.'

What could be more atrocious than such an order? It is a well-known fact that one of the great difficulties which a general has to encounter is to restrain the licentiousness of the troops under his command, and their disregard of the civil rights of the population with whom they may be brought in contact; and yet here was the Commander-in-Chief of the Federal forces of the Gulf actually encouraging, and even commanding, violence towards ladies, and leaving it to the discretion of every blackguard bearing the uniform of the United States to insult and ill-treat defenceless women, of whatever rank or position, he might encounter in the streets. When the intelligence of the order reached New York, derived as it was from Southern sources, it was regarded as a fabrication of the enemy in order to inflame the anger of the people against the captors of New Orleans. For this purpose it was doubtless used. General Beauregard immediately issued copies of the order, and directed that, for the information of his army, it should be read on parade. He appended to it the following address to his men:—

'Men of the South,—Shall our mothers, wives, daughters, and sisters be thus outraged by the ruffianly soldiers of the North, to whom is given the right to treat at their pleasure the ladies of the South as common harlots? Arouse, friends, and drive back from the soil these infamous invaders of our homes and disturbers of our family ties.

'S. T. BEAUREGARD,

'General Commanding.'

Through the length and breadth of the South the name of Butler was held in detestation, and the *soubriquet* of the *Beast* applied to him. His treatment of the citizens of New Orleans did much toward enhancing the determination of other cities to endure every evil of war rather than to surrender and lie at the mercy of such men as the Federal Government saw fit to appoint and to support. On the other hand, the very indignation against his conduct in England, and the terms applied to his order in the British Parliament, in some measure warped the judgment of his fellow-countrymen; and in their anxiety to act in opposition to England, and to show themselves uninfluenced by any expression of opinion from that quarter, they considered it their duty as American citizens first to palliate, and then to justify, and even admire, the actions of their general. The press, ever ready to pander to the popular taste, supported the general, and reminded him that he was a free American citizen, and not a subject of Queen Victoria. That these were the opinions of the better classes, it would be almost impossible to believe; but when those classes, either from a fault in the institutions of the country, or from idleness and distaste to enter the arena of politics, allow themselves to be overridden by the uneducated and vulgar majority, they must be content to share with them the blame attached to their conduct.*

There were other acts of General Butler at New Orleans which proved the character of the man equally with those above-mentioned. No doubt he was a shrewd, and what may be termed a strong man, and through terror, and perhaps legitimate severity, he preserved the peace of the city, and even in some respects rendered it more orderly than during the days of its prosperity; but nothing can justify his tyranny to the conquered, and the unjust means which he used to attain his ends.

With such an example before them, Mobile and Charleston resolved to hold out to the last extremity; and the latter had an opportunity of proving the sincerity

* Subsequently, General Butler, in a letter to the Mayor, gave an explanation of his order. The explanation is, however, little less insulting than was the order itself. The following is General Butler's letter to the Mayor of New Orleans:—

'Head-quarters, Department of the Gulf,
'New Orleans, May 16.

'SIR,—There can be, there has been, no room for misunderstanding general order No. 28. No lady will take any notice of a strange gentleman, and *à fortiori* of a stranger, simply in such form as to attract attention. Common women do. Therefore, whatever woman, lady, or mistress, gentle or simple, who by gesture, look, or word insults, shows contempt for, thus attracting to herself the notice of, my officers and soldiers, will be deemed to act as becomes her vocation as a common woman, and will be liable to be treated accordingly. This was most fully explained to you at my office. I shall not—as I have not—abate a single word of that order; it was well considered; if obeyed, will protect the true and modest woman from all possible insult. The others will take care of themselves. You can publish your letter if you publish this note and your apology. Respectfully, 'BENJ. F. BUTLER,
'Major-General Commanding.

'JOHN T. MONROE, Mayor of New Orleans.'

of her professions, as operations were about this time directed against her, and she had a narrow escape of suffering the evils attending the presence of the enemy at her gates. Since the commencement of the war a naval force had been stationed off the harbour of Charleston; and it was about the end of May or the beginning of June that a strong body of troops detached from General Hunter's army in the vicinity of Beaufort, was organised for the purpose of making an attack on the city from the land side. On the 2nd of June the army landed on Seabrook Island, and prepared to cross the Stono River and attack the Confederate forts on James Island.

From various causes, chiefly from the necessity of contracting the lines of defence, General Pemberton, in command of the Confederate troops in and around Charleston, had given up the idea of holding Coles's Island and the mouth of Stono River, and contented himself with erecting works on James Island. Thus, the Federal gunboats were enabled to enter Stono River, and to cover by their fire the disembarkation of the troops on the south-eastern end of James Island. The Confederate lines of defence stretched across a narrow neck of land between the Stono River and the creeks or streams which empty themselves into Charleston Harbour. Their right was covered by a strong work which commanded the Stono River, and so closed that inlet to the Ashley River and the rear of the city; their left rested on marshy land, in the neighbourhood of Secessionville.

Such was the position of affairs in the second week of June. The Federal force consisted of two divisions, commanded by Generals Wright and Stevens, the whole under the orders of General Benham;

whilst the Confederate defences on James Island were in charge of General Evans, acting under General Pemberton. The force at his disposal was far inferior in numbers to that of General Benham, but had the advantage of a strong position. On the 15th June orders were issued by General Benham for the troops to be under arms at 3 A.M., prepared to assault the works in the neighbourhood of Secessionville. General Stevens's division, forming the first line, was to furnish the storming party, which was to advance without firing, trusting to the bayonet; General Wright was to move in support, and guard against any attempt at an attack on the left flank of the assaulting column. According to orders, the troops paraded, and advancing rapidly and without noise, completely surprised the Confederate pickets, and almost succeeded in reaching the parapet of the work. Some of the picket, however, escaped and warned the garrison; the gunners were at their guns, and, under the direction of Colonel Lamar, an eight inch columbiad and 24-pounder rifled gun were levelled against the centre of the attacking column. The effects of the discharge checked the storming party, which was now within seven hundred yards of the battery; and the time gained by this delay on the part of the Federals enabled the two battalions, which properly formed the garrison of the work, to line the parapet. The storming party and the battalions in support, in place of re-forming and advancing against the enemy, defiled to the right and left, and sought shelter in the ditches and behind bushes, or laid themselves down in the cotton furrows, from whence they directed a heavy fire against the gunners and the men lining the parapet. The defenders suffered severely, but continued to work their guns, and replied to the musketry fire. A brigade was now brought up from General Wright's division, in order to support a second attack. Again did the Federals advance, and this time reached a ditch about four hundred yards from the parapet; but there they commenced firing, and did not make a rush for the final assault. In the meantime an attempt was made to turn the right of the position, but with no more satisfactory result. Reinforcements had reached the defenders, and inspirited by their first success in checking the enemy's advance, they held their ground until about 10 A.M., when General Benham sent orders to the generals commanding the divisions to withdraw from the attack.

Thus terminated an action which, had the result been different, might have proved most detrimental to the fortunes of the city of Charleston. Had the Federals forced the defences at Secessionville, they would have been able to establish batteries on James Island, which would have commanded the city, and which would have rendered almost useless the retention of the forts in the harbour; they would also have in all probability reduced the fort which commanded the Stono River, and so have opened a passage for the gunboats into the Ashley River, and, in fact, up to the city itself. That the plan of attack nearly succeeded, is apparent from the reports of the Confederate commanders; that it had every right to succeed, even after the surprise had failed, may be fairly argued from a comparison of the numbers in the field. Even after the reinforcements had arrived, the defenders do not appear to have numbered more than two thousand,* whilst the Federal General could not have had less than six thousand in the field. Of this number the

* General Evans's report.

whole were probably not engaged; and the formation of the ground and natural strength of the position gave an advantage to a small body acting on the defensive. But the same faults seem to have been made at Secessionville as in many of the earlier engagements of the war. The troops were not pushed forward with sufficient energy to the attack; they were allowed to waste their time in firing, in place of advancing rapidly to the assault; and in view of the importance of the end proposed, it is difficult to understand why the columns were withdrawn so early in the day as 10 A.M., when two brigades of the supporting division had scarcely been under fire. The loss in the action on the Federal side was, at the very least, six hundred men, of which far the greater portion fell in General Stevens's division.* That of the Confederates was a little over two hundred.†

The smallness of the garrison of so important a place is a proof how hardly the Confederate Government was at that time pressed for men, and how necessary it had become to provide other means of recruiting the army than by voluntary enlistment. The successes of the North had given a fresh impetus to the warlike feelings of her population, and their far larger numbers, joined to the assistance derived from immigration, enabled her to recruit her armies without undergoing the pressure of a Conscription Act. The South, on the contrary, had exhausted what may be termed the available warlike portion of her population in the first levies which fought the battles of the earlier campaigns;

* General Stevens acknowledged to the loss of 32 officers and 497 men in his division. Colonel Lamar, 'Confederate,' reports to have buried 341, and that 107 were captured.

† General Pemberton's official report.

and in order to supply the gaps in the armies, and to carry on the war with sufficient vigour, she was obliged to have recourse to a Conscription Act. This was willingly agreed to by her people, as they perceived that no partial efforts would suffice for the end in view, but that the whole strength of the country should be put forth, and that this could only be done by enrolling under arms the larger portion of the population, which enrolment would be attained in the fairest and most satisfactory manner by conscription.

Shortly after this failure at Secessionville, the Federal forces retired from James Island to Hilton Head, and no further attempt was made on Charleston until a much later period of the war.

CHAPTER IV.

CAMPAIGN OF VIRGINIA.

IT has already been shown how intimately connected were the campaigns of the York Town Peninsula and of the Shenandoah Valley. The withdrawal of General Shields' division from General Banks, for the purpose of reinforcing General M'Dowell's corps preparatory to a march on the Chickahominy, had invited the attack of General Jackson, which resulted in the complete defeat of Banks; whilst the defeat of Banks, and the panic resulting therefrom, led to the countermarch of Shields' division, under M'Dowell* in person, from Fredericksburg to its former position in the Shenandoah Valley, thereby preventing the proposed

* General M'Dowell addressed to the Government a strong letter of remonstrance on the policy of transferring so large a portion of his force from Fredericksburg to the Shenandoah. His out-pickets had already effected a junction with those of General M'Clellan; and he fully appreciated the importance of co-operation with that general, and of a conjoined movement on Richmond. He also represented that he could better cut off General Jackson's retreat by an advance on the rail between Gordonsville and Richmond than by a march to the Shenandoah. The only answer he received to this remonstrance was a repeated order to march to the Shenandoah. Subsequent events have proved the correctness of General M'Dowell's views. General M'Dowell took little part in the campaign which followed in the Shenandoah, in consequence of injuries he received from a fall from his horse.

co-operation with General M'Clellan, and in a great measure crippling his movements.

After the Government at Washington had recovered from its panic, and had ascertained how small a force General Jackson really had under his command, it resolved to endeavour to intercept his retreat from the lower Shenandoah Valley, and to compel him either to fight far superior numbers or to surrender. To effect this object, General Shields' division, numbering 10,000, was ordered at once, having retraced its steps, to hasten as quickly as possible to Strasburg; whilst at the same time General Fremont, with from 15,000 to 20,000 men, was directed to march on the same point; and the two united were thus to place themselves directly on General Jackson's line of retreat. Thus it was supposed that the Confederate general would be opposed not only by his old adversary, General Banks, strengthened with reinforcements, but also by a force greatly superior to his own in his rear.

No doubt, to an ordinary man, General Jackson's position would have been one of great danger; but previous to his pursuit of General Banks, whilst apparently neglecting the ordinary rules of war, he had calculated the costs; and trusting to his own powers as a general, and to the good qualities, both as regarded marching and fighting, of his men, he had abandoned, or rather greatly endangered, his own line of communications in seeking to defeat his adversary in detail. Having thus with 15,000 men succeeded not only in checking the attack of the Federals in the Shenandoah Valley, but also in greatly hindering, and, as subsequent events proved, in frustrating altogether General M'Clellan's attack on Richmond, General Jackson devoted all his energies to escaping from the net which appeared to be rapidly closing round him. On the 30th of May he made a feint against Harper's Ferry; and on the 31st retreated up the valley, followed as far as Martingsburg by General Banks. In the meantime General Fremont, abandoning his former project of advancing into the upper valley, hastened by mountain roads to intercept General Jackson's retreat at Strasburg. On the 25th of May he left Franklin with troops scarcely recovered from the fatigues of the march consequent on their attempt to relieve Generals Milroy and Schenck, and on the 26th he arrived at Petersburg, thirty miles distant from Franklin. Here the baggage, tents, and even knapsacks were left, so that nothing might incumber the troops on the rapid march which was in prospect. Five days' rations were issued; and thus leaving Petersburg, and passing through Moorfield and Wardensville, General Fremont halted on the night of the 31st of May at the intersection of the Strasburg and Winchester Roads, east of the Grand Chain, but west of the lower spurs of the mountains which shut in the Shenandoah Valley. On the 1st of June the march was renewed; and as the advanced guard was crossing the last of the lower hills it encountered the rear guard of General Jackson. This caused a slight delay, and also proved that General Fremont had arrived one day too late, and that his adversary had escaped. Still Shields might possibly fall upon his left flank, and hold him in check until Fremont should come up. The latter pressed on, and on the 1st of June entered Strasburg, a few hours before the main body of General Shields' division. But again had General Jackson escaped his pursuers, he had passed through the town unmolested, and, in a night of rain, thunder, and lightning, continued his retreat, his rear well protected by Colonel Ashby's cavalry, who checked any attempt of the Federal advanced guard to harass the infantry. With a long train, conveying the plunder and spoils of Banks's army and about 2000 prisoners, Jackson marched rapidly onward, burning the bridges over the streams which crossed the road.

On the 2nd of June, after some skirmishes with the rear guard, Fremont reached Woodstock, and on the 3rd crossed Stony Creek; the cavalry and artillery fording the stream, the infantry effecting its passage over a trestle bridge, and carrying over the artillery ammunition. At Mount Jackson, General Jackson made a stand to cover the passage of his infantry and train over the long wooden bridge which, at this point, crosses the north fork of the Shenandoah River. The artillery posted on the right bank defended the bridge; whilst the cavalry prevented the too near approach of the enemy's advanced guard. When the army had crossed, the bridge was burned; and Fremont's troopers arrived at the bank of the river only in time to see the timbers of the bridge fall into the stream. This caused delay to the advancing column, as it was necessary to repair the bridge, the river being unfordable; and it was not, therefore, until the 6th that Fremont reached Harrisonburg. On that evening there was a skirmish, which almost attained the rank of an engagement, between the advanced cavalry, comprising about 800 men, supported by infantry, and the Confederate rear guard. The former, namely, the cavalry, had pushed on with tired horses somewhat too rashly, and thinking to charge a body of the enemy's cavalry drawn up across the road in their front, fell into an ambuscade and suffered severely; their colonel, 'Windham,' of the 1st New Jersey regiment, falling a prisoner into the hands of the enemy. The infantry, consisting of a regiment termed 'Buck Tails,' coming up in support, were also severely handled by Brigadier-General George Stewart, who commanded the infantry and artillery of General Jackson's rear-guard. This check impeded the Federal advance for one day; and it was not until the 8th that Fremont marched out of Harrisonburg.

The engagement, although resulting favourably to the Confederates, was yet the cause of a great misfortune. Colonel, or rather Brigadier-General Turner Ashby, whilst leading on his men, fell, killed by a bullet from one of the Federal riflemen. He was a man greatly to be lamented. Although not educated as a soldier, yet he possessed all the requirements for a general of cavalry; especially of such a force as he commanded. Of an old Virginian family, his grandfather distinguished in the wars of the Revolution, and noted as a bold rider, his uncles, soldiers of the war of 1812, he inherited the taste for a military life. During the disturbed times, resulting in John Brown's raid at Harper's Ferry, he had raised a troop of cavalry, and was distinguished not only as its leader, but also as the best horseman among the men. When Mr. Lincoln was elected President, he determined to join with and, if need be, fight for his State, whichever side it might embrace; and, on the secession of Virginia, engaged heart and soul in the Confederate cause. His first enthusiasm received a deeper and sadder tinge from the death of his brother, killed in one of the earlier skirmishes of the war; and from this time he relinquished all other pursuits excepting that of repelling the invaders of his country. He shared every hardship with his men, refusing to avail himself of any of the privileges of his rank, and not only led them as an officer, but took delight in individual feats of enterprise and swordsmanship. Conspicuous on a white horse, he exposed himself to fire freely and, it may be termed, unnecessarily; unless it be taken into consideration that he was engaged in animating and leading raw and inexperienced troops. During all the operations in the Shenandoah Valley he had rendered conspicuous service; and had earned not only the rank of brigadier-general from his own Government, but also the admiration of his enemies.* In these terms did General Fremont speak of his death: 'General Ashby, who covered the retreat with his whole cavalry force and three regiments of infantry, and who exhibited admirable skill and audacity, was among the killed.'

Whilst Fremont had been engaged in pursuing General Jackson up the valley of the north fork of the Shenandoah River, General Shields had marched in an almost parallel line up its southern branch, and was preparing to cut him off from retreat through the passes of the Blue Ridge Mountains. Jackson's position was most critical, and it was only by the display of no ordinary generalship that he finally extricated himself from his difficulties and succeeded in turning the tables on his pursuers.

About ten miles south-west of Harrisonburg, the south branch of the Shenandoah separates into two streams near the small village of Port Republic. Both these streams are unfordable, and are passable only by bridges; it was, therefore, of great moment to secure their possession. On the 8th of June, General Jackson, anticipating the advance of General

* The greater portion of this account of the life of General Ashby is taken from Pollard's *History of the War*.

Shields, led about half his force across the bridge at Port Republic over the North River, leaving General Ewell in a strong position about eight miles from Harrisonburg to hold the enemy in check, whilst the long baggage train was crossing the bridge. About 8 A.M. on the same day the advanced guard of General Fremont encountered the enemy, but finding him strongly posted, awaited the arrival of the main body of the troops, and the action did not really commence until 11 A.M. General Ewell had chosen his position well. The ground, covered with dwarf oaks interspersed with pines, concealed his real strength, whilst the rolling hills afforded situations where he could employ his inferior force to advantage. The greater portion of Fremont's army were engaged. On the right was General Schenck's brigade, in the centre that of General Milroy, and on the left General Strahl's; whilst General Cluseret, who had commanded the advanced guard, was in front of the right centre with about three regiments; and the greater portion of General Blenker's division was held in reserve. About 11 A.M. the line advanced. The right, under Milroy, pressed forward, but the left was held in check by a strong artillery fire, and was finally forced to retreat. The retirement of the brigade on the left of the line exposed the flank of General Milroy, who received orders also to withdraw. This he effected without molestation from the Confederates, who were content to hold their position; and the battle terminated at about 4 P.M. It received the name of Cross Keys from a small hamlet in the vicinity of the ground on which it was fought. The loss of the Federals, as estimated by their own accounts, was 664 men; but they also lost, what was of greater importance to the future conduct of the campaign, the opportunity of overwhelming General Ewell, who was fighting with his back to a river, and with inferior numbers, and thus of precluding the possibility of General Jackson's effecting the project he had in view, of falling with his whole force on General Shields. However, events proved that General Jackson, in employing such bold tactics, had not over-estimated the powers of his men.

During the night of the 8th he brought the greater portion of Ewell's division across the North River by the bridge at Port Republic, leaving only a small force on the left bank to deceive Fremont and to burn the bridge. Nothing interfered to frustrate the plan, and Fremont arrived at the bank of the river only in time to see the bridge in flames, and to hear the guns which were playing on his colleague. During the action of the 8th the portion of the army which had crossed the North River under General Jackson had been engaged in an artillery skirmish with the advanced brigade of General Shields' division, which, under Colonel Carroll, had been sent forward to *protect* the bridge at Port Republic, little thinking that its destruction would have been far more advantageous. On the morning of the 9th General Jackson carried the greater portion of his army across South River—the smaller of the two branches—by a bridge formed of planks laid on waggons placed in the stream, and then proceeded at once to attack the troops under General Tyler, who, on the evening of the 8th had come up to support Colonel Carroll. The main body of Shields' force was still in the rear; and thus, although inferior in numbers to the whole force, Jackson was able at the decisive moment to bring a larger number into the field than his adversary. As each regiment crossed the bridge it was brought into action. The Federal force was drawn up across the main road in an open plain covered with wheat. Their left rested on wooded hills, and on a small knoll near the woods was posted the greater portion of their artillery. General Jackson at once noticed the dangerous position occupied by the guns, and whilst he attracted the attention of General Tyler by demonstrations in the plain he sent a detachment, consisting of the Louisiana brigade, to move through the woods, and thus operate on the left flank of the line and threaten the artillery. This was effected, and by a sudden charge the greater portion of the artillery was captured. The line was broken, some regiments retreated in fairly good order, others were completely routed, and in detached bodies took to the hills and sought refuge among the woods. The Confederate cavalry pursued, and the defeat was complete.

Whilst the battle was in progress a portion of the Confederate artillery, supported by infantry, watched the opposite bank of the iver, and prevented any attempts of Fremont to repair the bridge. That officer, becoming aware of the defeat of Shields, sent a detachment of cavalry to open communications with him, but did not make any further attempt at the pursuit of his antagonist. On the contrary, hearing that General Jackson had received reinforcements, and dreading lest a portion of General Beauregard's force should join him, having before his eyes also his own isolated position and the former fate of General Banks, Fremont retreated down the valley. General Jackson withdrew leisurely to Brown's Gap, in the Blue Ridge Mountains, where he covered the Gordonsville and Staunton Railway, and from whence he had easy access to the former place, and so to the direct line of rail to Richmond.

His campaign in the Shenandoah Valley was one of the most brilliant of the war. With a small force of at most 15,000 men he had defeated in detail Generals Banks, Fremont, and Shields, and had so completely paralysed the action of General M'Dowell that he had prevented any reinforcements from reaching the army of the Potomac. The results of the campaign were even more important than could have been anticipated; and in returning to the armies before Richmond we shall see how greatly subsequent events were influenced by the operations in the Shenandoah Valley. The reputation gained by General Jackson in this campaign was not confined to America, but elicited the admiration of European nations. Not only had he shown the greatest talents as a strategist, but he had also evinced the possession of that important qualification for a general,—the power of inspiring his men with his own enthusiasm, and enlisting their support by imparting to each individual officer and soldier (what may be almost termed) a fanaticism for the cause in which they were engaged. Added to these qualities, General Jackson had acquired during the earlier operations of the war a thorough knowledge of the country in and around the Shenandoah Valley, and also the support of the inhabitants, who were as eager to afford information to the Confederates as to withhold it from the Federals.

Not long after the battle of Port Republic, on the 27th of June, the three several armies of Major-Generals Fremont, Banks, and M'Dowell* were consolidated

* *i.e.* So much of General M'Dowell's army as remained after the reinforcements had been sent to General M'Clellan.

into one, and called the Army of Virginia, and the command given to Major-General Pope, who had been recalled for that purpose from the army of the West. This arrangement led to the resignation of General Fremont, who was succeeded by General Sigel.

Whilst these events were taking place in the Shenandoah Valley, the army of the Potomac remained quietly in its lines on the Chickahominy. General M'Clellan applied frequently for reinforcements to replace the losses of battle and sickness, and at length received a promise that General M'Call's division, from M'Dowell's army, should proceed at once by water to the White House. Almost on the very day that these reinforcements arrived the monotony of camp-life was disturbed by an event which tended to arouse the army from its fancied security. The capture of Richmond was looked on as so certain, and the situation of the army regarded so completely as one of offence, that any attempt at attack on the part of the enemy, excepting directly from the front, was totally unexpected. So much was this the case, that the line of railway running from the main camp of the army to the White House, about eighteen miles, was almost unguarded, and its passengers thought as little of danger as when travelling on the line between Baltimore and Philadelphia. Even the important depôts at the White House were unprotected, except by a very small force, and steamers and other vessels lay as securely on the Pamunkey as in their own more northern rivers. Nothing gave warning of the raid for which orders were already given to the officer commanding the Confederate cavalry. On the 12th of June, General M'Clellan himself reconnoitred the ground in the neighbourhood of Mechanicsville and Meadow Bridge, and then moved his head-quarters to the right bank of the Chicahominy, about one mile in rear of the battle-ground of Fair Oaks. On the very next day General J. E. Stuart, with twelve hundred cavalry and two guns—the former under the command of a nephew and son of General Lee, Colonel Fitz Lee and Colonel W. Fitzhugh Lee—and Lieut.-Colonel Martin departed from Richmond, and moved along the Richmond and Fredericksburg Railway as far as Kilby's Station; then turning eastward, they bivouacked in the vicinity of Hanover Court-house, twenty-two miles from Richmond. The object of the expedition was a profound secret, known only to General Stuart, and every precaution was requisite to keep information from the enemy. The troops were ordered to bivouack as quietly as possible, and no trumpets were to sound, as the presence of the Federal pickets rendered concealment extremely difficult. However, the forest afforded a sufficient cover. During the night General Stuart communicated a portion of the orders he had received to the three colonels; and at daybreak the troops were under arms, and marched at once on Hanover Court-house. Here they encountered and quickly drove in a small body of cavalry, and soon afterwards encountered a large detachment of the 5th United States regular cavalry—Colonel Lee's former regiment. This detachment fared no better than the former; they were quickly routed—indeed, sooner than was pleasing to Colonel Lee, who was anxious to cross swords with his old regiment. Several horses were captured, and their camp burned, and it then became a question what course General Stuart should adopt. Should he return to Hanover Court-house satisfied with what had been already done, or should he pursue the bolder plan of marching round the rear of the whole Federal army? The latter, as the more adventurous, and perhaps also the more safe, from being unexpected, was determined on. Taking precautions to mislead the enemy by making especial inquiries relative to the road to Hanover Court-house, General Stuart turned his horse's head towards Turnstall's Station and kept steadily on. When near Garlick's Landing on the Pamunkey, he detached a squadron of cavalry to burn the stores and whatever vessels might be lying there, whilst a few men with his two aid-de-camps were pushed forward rapidly to Turnstall's Station on the White House and Chicahominy rail, to cut the telegraph wires and surprise the small guard at the station. Both plans succeeded. Two vessels and many stores were burned, and the guard surprised and captured. As the party at the station were engaged in obstructing the line of rail, the train from the army was seen approaching. It quickly cleared away the few obstructions already placed on the rails, and the engineer, when called on to stop, suspecting something wrong, put on a full head of steam and hurried on to the White House. The Confederates poured in a volley of musketry, killing several men, but the train escaped, and alarmed Colonel Ingalls, in command at the White House. He took all the measures in his power to defend the stores, whilst the shipping which crowded the river cast off from their moorings, and prepared to make all speed to York Town.

In the meantime the main body of the cavalry had captured a large train of some forty waggons and several prisoners, and after burning a railway bridge, halted for about three hours and a half near the New Kent Court-house. Here they refreshed themselves at the suttlers' stores, who, anticipating no enemy in that neighbourhood, willingly afforded provisions to the men, and were greatly surprised when they were informed whom they were entertaining. Leaving New Kent Court-house about midnight, the cavalry marched at once towards the Chickahominy, which they endeavoured to ford in the vicinity of a broken bridge. The water was, however, too deep, and a bridge with some difficulty, and at considerable risk, owing to the anticipated attack of the Federal cavalry, was built from such material as came to hand. Partly by swimming, partly by the bridge, the cavalry and their prisoners crossed the stream, and on Saturday, two days after they had left Richmond, re-entered the city with 165 prisoners and upwards of 200 horses and mules, besides having destroyed a large amount of stores, and acquired a knowledge of the country and of the position of the enemy's forces. This was accomplished in about forty-eight hours, and with the loss of only one man—Captain Latane, of the 9th Va. Cavalry.

It can easily be imagined with what rejoicings the return of General Stuart was hailed in Richmond. Well might his countrymen be proud of him, for unquestionably he had performed one of the most dashing acts of the war, to be measured not so much by the material results as by the *prestige* which it gave to the Confederate cavalry. The Federal officers, even whilst annoyed and piqued at the disgrace which had been inflicted on their cavalry and pickets, could not withhold the admiration which they felt for so gallant an enterprise, whilst the regular officers were proud to think that their former friends and comrades in arms were not unworthy of the old army, in which they had served together. Often did these feelings of friendship show themselves, even amidst the bitter enmity engendered by war; and although good soldiers, and true to the cause they had adopted, there were many regretful retrospects cast back on the former happy days of companionship, when those now opposed to them in deadly strife were their comrades and friends in a degree not often to be found in the civilian's life.

Very soon after General Stuart's raid the division of General M'Call was brought up to the front and attached to Porter's corps. Affairs resumed their former tranquillity, only broken by occasional skirmishes at the out-pickets; the weather grew very hot, and the effluvia arising from the numerous dead who had fallen in the battle of Fair Oaks, and were but partially buried, became pestilential, and was a cause of sickness and mortality to the troops encamped on the battle-ground.

About the end of June a rumour reached General M'Clellan that Jackson was concentrating a force at Gordonsville, where he was receiving reinforcements from Richmond; and this rumour received confirmation on the 24th from a deserter, who stated positively that Jackson was near Gordonsville, and was making preparations to attack M'Clellan's rear on the 28th. This information was considered so important, that a telegram giving its substance was sent at once by M'Clellan to the Secretary of War. A reply was received, stating that neither the commanders in the Shenandoah Valley nor General M'Dowell could give any information respecting Jackson's strength or movements. Every description of rumour was in circulation, and each commander reported the enemy's pickets in front of him. Mr. Stanton was inclined to believe that Jackson would probably join Lee's army at Richmond; but the War Office at Washington could furnish their generals with no certain information.

By the 25th the several bridges over the Chickahominy were completed, and the lines of entrenchment finished, giving the army a secure base from which to operate, and to which in case of reverse they could retire. All being in readiness, M'Clellan directed an advance by Heintzelman's corps along the Williamsburg Road, in the vicinity of the Seven Pines,—and in compliance with this order, at an early hour on the 25th, two brigades of General Hooker's division were pushed forward to drive the Confederates out of the woods immediately in his front, whilst it had been intended that General Sumner on Hooker's right, should also advance and obtain possession of the Old Tavern and the heights which commanded the New Bridge. Through some mistake, Hooker alone was engaged; and his brigades were subsequently ordered to retire. Later in the morning the attack was renewed, in the presence of General M'Clellan, who rode round the lines of entrenchment, and was received with cheers by the men. He had gained their affections in no common degree; his presence roused them to exertion, and his slightest remarks were quoted, and passed from one to the other along the line. All day the engagement lasted in the woods in front of the Seven Pines. Two brigades of Kearney's division were brought up in support, and, with a brigade of Sumner's corps, continued the action. In the evening half a mile of woods was gained, with the loss of about 500 men; and on the following day General M'Clellan determined to make the grand attack on the enemy's lines. During the whole of the 25th he had remained with his staff in a small redoubt directly in rear of the woods in which the action was going on, and returned to the head-quarters camp, in the main satisfied with the results. When, however, he arrived there news reached him which changed the complexion of affairs. He received a confirmation of the former rumours respecting General Jackson's movements; and in his despatch to the Secretary of War, dated that evening, he almost prognosticated the misfortunes that were about to happen. In these terms he wrote:—

'Head-quarters, Army of the Potomac,
'Camp Lincoln, July 25th, 1862, 6.15 p.m.

'I have just returned from the field, and found your despatch in regard to Jackson. Several contrabands just in give information confirming supposition that Jackson's advance is at or near Hanover Court house, and that Beauregard arrived with strong reinforcements in Richmond yesterday. I incline to think that Jackson will attack my right and rear. The rebel force is stated at (200,000), two hundred thousand, including Jackson and Beauregard. I shall have to contend against vastly superior odds if these reports be true. But this army will do all in the power of men to hold their position and repulse any attack. I regret my great inferiority in numbers, but feel that I am in no way responsible for it, as I have not failed to represent repeatedly the necessity of reinforcements, that this was the decisive point, and that all the available means of the Government should be concentrated here. I will do all that a general can do with the splendid army I have the honour to command; and if it is destroyed by overwhelming numbers, can at least die with it and share its fate. But if the result of the action, which will probably occur to-morrow, or within a short time, is a disaster, the responsibility cannot be thrown on my shoulders; it must rest where it belongs. Since I commenced this, I have received additional intelligence confirming the supposition in regard to Jackson's movements and Beauregard's arrival. I shall probably be attacked to-morrow, and now go to the other side of the Chickahominy to arrange for the defence on that side. I feel that there is no use in my again asking for reinforcements.

'G. B. M'CLELLAN,
'Major-General.

On the following day, the 26th June, General M'Clellan went over to the head-quarters of General Porter, who commanded the *corps d'armée* which alone occupied the left banks of the Chickahominy, as Franklin's corps had been brought over to the right bank some time previously. Porter had, however, received reinforcements by the arrival of M'Call's division, consisting of three brigades, numbering in all about 8,500 men, and denominated the Pennsylvanian Reserves, which had been detached from M'Dowell's corps. This division occupied the extreme right of the line, with pickets extending as far as Meadows Bridge and Tolopatomy Creek, whilst Stoneman with a force of cavalry patrolled the country between Tolopatomy Creek and Hanover Court-house. On the same day, M'Clellan directed his Quartermaster-General (General Van Vleit) to telegraph the following message to Colonel Ingalls, commanding at the White House:—'Run the cars to the last moment, and load them with provisions and ammunition. Load every waggon you have with subsistence, and send them to Savage's Station by way of Bottom's Bridge. If you are obliged to abandon White House, burn everything that you cannot get off. You must throw all our supplies up the James River as soon as possible, and accompany them yourself with all your forces. It will be of vast importance to establish our depôts on James River without delay if we abandon White House. I will keep you advised of every movement as long as the wire works. After that, you must exercise your own judgment.'

By this despatch it will be seen that M'Clellan had determined on the 26th to abandon his base of operations on the Pamunkey for another base on the James River. This scheme had been long thought of, and had even been debated at head-quarters; but apparently M'Clellan had been loth to give up his present lines, which were within five miles of Richmond, for others at a greater distance, although possibly possessing superior advantages for the purposes of attack. When, however, he saw that his army, notwithstanding the accession of M'Call's division, was daily diminishing, and that its total strength did not amount to more than ninety-five thousand men; when he also perceived that the Confederate force was, on the other hand, increasing, and that Jackson's victorious divisions would soon be on his right flank, he determined to carry out the project which had up to this time been only considered. But there was a great difference between making this change of base voluntarily, and at his own time and convenience, and doing it in presence of a vigilant and aggressive enemy.* Still his right wing might possibly

* The Prince de Joinville, in his able pamphlet on the Campaign of the Army of the Potomac, thus speaks of the proposed change of base:—'Ainsi que nous l'avons dit, le général M'Clellan y songeait depuis longtemps, comme à une des nécessités de sa situation,

hold the enemy in check until all had been accomplished, and a victory on the left bank of the Chickahominy might even change the aspect of affairs on the right bank, and render the movement unnecessary.

The position occupied by M'Call's division was very strong; it extended from the upper road leading from Mechanicsville to Cold Harbour and the Chickahominy, following the left bank of a small stream running through wooded and steep banks, called Beaver Dam Creek. The thick woods afforded ready means for constructing *abattis*, and the line of low hills or banks presented convenient positions for artillery and for the disposition of infantry. The weak point of the line was on the right, which was, as it may be termed, *en l'air*, but was protected by the difficult nature of the country and by the cavalry force under General Stoneman. This line was occupied by two brigades of M'Call's division—General Reynolds' brigade holding the right, General Seymour's brigade the left of the line; a portion of General Meade's brigade was on picket, the remainder in reserve. Such was the position of affairs on Thursday the 26th June. On the same day Jackson, who had concentrated his division at Ashland Station, on the Richmond and Fredericksburg Railway, marched from thence through the country lying between the Chickahominy and Pamunkey Rivers; whilst General Branch, belonging to General Lee's army, crossed the Chickahominy at Brook's Turnpike, and likewise

et il avait même pris quelques dispositions éventuelles qui allaient se trouver singulièrement justifiées; mais autre chose était de faire cette retraite à son heure, par un mouvement libre et spontané, autre chose de la faire précipitamment sous la menace de deux armées ennemies.'

marching down the stream, drove in the Federal advanced pickets, and allowed General A. P. Hill to cross the river lower down at Meadow Bridge. Thus the Confederate force was in echellon. The right advanced. General Hill at once attacked the village of Mechanicsville, which he occupied without much difficulty, and so obtained possession of the direct road to Richmond, although the bridge was in ruins. He then, in conjunction with General Branch, with a force of about fourteen thousand men, proceeded to attack the Federal lines at Beaver Dam Creek. The troops defending them had been reinforced by two brigades of General Morell's division of Porter's corps, which acted as supports to the right of the line. About 6 P.M. the engagement became general along the whole extent of the position, although the principal efforts of the Confederates were directed against the Federal left and the lower Mechanicsville Road near Ellerson's Mills. With determination and courage did Pender's and Ripley's brigades of A. P. Hill's division advance. They were acting under the eyes of the Commander-in-Chief (General Lee), and with all the prestige of attack on the foe which was devastating their hearths and homes; they descended the right bank of Beaver Dam Creek, they even essayed to cross the stream, although the waters were waist-high, they were within one hundred yards of the enemy's batteries, but even those brave troops could not stand against the storm of shot, shell, canister, and rifle bullets which was poured down on them from the breastworks crowning the left bank. The brigades were repulsed from the attack, but occupied a position along the right bank of the stream, supported by a battery of D. H. Hill's division which had succeeded in crossing the broken bridge over the Chickahominy; night closed in on the combatants, and about 9 P.M. the battle ceased. The action of the 26th had terminated so far in favour of the Federals, inasmuch as they had repulsed the attack made on their lines; and General M'Clellan in the evening, from Porter's head-quarters, telegraphed to his chief of the staff the following message;—

'Tell the divisions that M'Call is worthy to belong to the army of the Potomac, and that Morell has done as well as at Hanover Court-house.'

Notwithstanding this announcement, there was much anxiety on the night of the 26th in the Federal army. It was known that the troops engaged on the previous day were not those of General Jackson, and it was even supposed that the attack had been made in order to cover the entry of that general into Richmond.

In reviewing the action, it appears strange that the attack should have been made without the co-operation of General Jackson's division, and on the strongest part of the Federal line. It may however have been General Lee's intention to have cut off the portion of the Federal army holding the left bank of the Chickahominy from that encamped on its right bank, and thus to have enabled his own troops to advance along its left bank, and as they had already uncovered Meadow and Mechanicsville Bridges, to open New Bridge, and the direct communication with Richmond. If this had been his purpose, it so far failed on the 26th, inasmuch as the Federals held their lines at Beaver Dam Creek after the action.* Owing however

* In Federal accounts the loss in the action of the 26th is said to have been 80 killed and 150 wounded.

to the advance of General Jackson, and owing also to the alteration made in General M'Clellan's plan of operations, the Federal troops were withdrawn during the night to a position about two miles lower down the Chickahominy, from whence they could more effectually cover the bridges, and where also they would be in closer communication with the main body of the army. During the same night the stores, teams, waggons and cattle belonging to Porter's corps, together with some of the heavier artillery, were brought over the several bridges, and were concentrated in the large fields adjoining the Chickahominy, and directly below the head-quarters camp. It was a striking scene which the army presented on the morning of the 27th. Everyone was astir. Slocum's division of Franklin's corps was marching towards Sumner's Upper Bridge to reinforce General Porter; the entrenchments facing Richmond were lined with troops expecting an immediate attack, and the supports and reserves were under arms. Every spot of open ground unoccupied by troops was covered with waggons, and their attendant horses and mules, whilst large droves of oxen sought pasturage amidst the young corn. Overlooking this animated and extraordinary scene were the white tents of the head-quarters camp, shaded by two conspicuous trees, and decorated with bowers erected to afford shelter from the sun.

In the meantime Colonel Ingalls had not been idle at the White House, the gunboats were ready for action, the trees in the vicinity of the depôt were cleared away to afford range for their artillery, the transports and other ships were laden with stores, and bales of hay were piled round the buildings, from which the contents had not yet been removed, in order that they should burn well should they be set on fire. Frequent telegram from head-quarters proved that the line had not as yet been cut, but the anxiety was very great, and every preparation for an immediate and rapid retreat down the Pamunkey was made. Fortunately an able man was in command at the White House, and Colonel Ingalls fully justified the trust reposed in him.

General M'Clellan, who had returned to head-quarters during the night, was himself uncertain from which quarter the attack would be made; whether a direct advance against his lines would be attempted from Richmond, or whether his right wing would have to bear the brunt of the engagement. He supposed that not only had Jackson joined Lee, but that a portion of Beauregard's forces, under that general in person, had also entered Richmond. He therefore estimated the whole force which could be brought against him at 200,000 men, whilst in reality not more than half that number was really opposed to him. As at York Town, so on the Chickahominy, did he over-estimate the numbers of his opponent, and consequently based his plans on false data.

Before describing the battle of the 27th, and the subsequent events, it will be well to recapitulate the exact position of the Federal army. On the extreme left, guarding the approaches from the White Oaks Swamp, was Keyes's corps. Continuing the semicircle on the Williamsburg Road and Railway was Heintzelman; to his right, opposite the old tavern, was Sumner; and on the right of the semicircle, on the right bank of the Chickahominy, was the corps of General Franklin. Connecting his right with Porter's left, and commanded by his guns, was Woodbury's Bridge, lower down Sumner's Upper Bridge, then

Sumner's Lower Bridge, below that the Railway Bridge, and still farther down Long Bridge.

Such was the position of the main body of the army on the left bank. On the right, General Porter occupied a smaller arc of a circle, of which the curve may be said to have extended from a strip of woods on the hills which sloped towards the Chickahominy, on the left of the small stream of Gaines' Mill, about a mile south of Dr. Gaines' house, to the open ground in rear of Coal Harbour. The left and left centre of the line was held by General Morell's division of three brigades, the right and right centre by General Sykes' division, also of three brigades. Each brigade was supported by two of its own regiments.* A second line was formed of General M'Call's division, with one brigade in reserve. Thus Porter's corps consisted of nine brigades, with the proper complement of artillery belonging to the divisions, in addition to four squadrons and a half of regular cavalry and three of volunteer lancers, under General St. G. Cooke, and two batteries of horse artillery from the artillery reserve. The main body of the cavalry under General Stoneman had received orders from General Porter, after the action of the 26th, to retreat to the White House, and to rejoin the main army as they best could, as he feared lest they should be cut off. On the early morning of the 27th, as the rear of General Porter's corps was withdrawing from the position it occupied on the 26th, it was closely pressed by General Longstreet, whilst the division of General D. H. Hill advanced along the Coal Harbour Road to effect a junction with General Jackson. It was not until about noon that the several Confederate

* General M'Clellan's official report.

divisions were in their proper positions. As the Federals may be said to have occupied the convex of the curve, so did the Confederates occupy the concave, embracing in their attack the country lying between the Chickahominy and the fields adjoining the road leading from Coal Harbour to Bottom's Bridge. The right of the line was formed of Longstreet's division, which had advanced along the slopes of the hills overlooking the Chickahominy. On his left was the division of A. P. Hill, which had crossed at Mechanicsville Bridge; then Whiting's and Ewell's divisions under General Jackson's command; and on the left of the whole line the division of D. H. Hill, which had effected a junction with Jackson in the morning, and, crossing his line of march, had moved to the extreme left.

The action commenced soon after twelve o'clock noon, by an artillery engagement on the left of the Confederate line, intended to divert attention from General Longstreet's attack. The Federal artillery were more powerful than that of their opponents, and succeeded in silencing General D. H. Hill's batteries. In the meantime Longstreet advanced, supported by the division on his left. Leaving the shelter of the woods in the vicinity of Dr. Gaines' house, the advancing brigades entered on an open undulating country, sloping downwards on their right towards the Chickahominy, and in front towards the little stream of Gaines' Mill, along the opposite side of which, and covered by a belt of woods, was the Federal army. Terrible was the loss of the attacking force as they marched over this open ground, exposed to the fire of the powerful and numerous Federal artillery, an arm which had attained greater excellence in General M'Clellan's army than either the infantry or cavalry. Men and officers fell by hundreds; the mounted officers soon lost their horses, and the generals led their men on foot.* The undulations of the ground afforded a partial cover from the fire; the loss was notwithstanding very great, and the Federal batteries from the opposite side of the Chickahominy—where Smith's division of Franklin's corps was posted—poured in shell at long range. General Porter, seeing that the enemy was advancing against him in force, applied for assistance, and about 2.30 P.M. Slocum's division, which had been detained when the real point of attack seemed doubtful, was sent over the bridges to his support. It arrived on the ground at a critical time; the second line had been engaged and was hardly pressed, and General Porter divided General Slocum's division, and sent it by separate regiments to reinforce the weaker points. The total number under Porter's command amounted now to 35,000, and he was probably opposed to about 54,000, under General Lee in person; he had, however, the advantage of position, and of an artillery stronger than his adversary, and, if properly posted, sufficient to sweep the approaches to his lines.

During the whole afternoon the combat raged along the strip of woods near Gaines' Mill Creek. The greater portion of the Federal artillery was in rear of their line of infantry and fired over their heads, receiving but little reply from the Confederate guns. As the right of the Confederate line was struggling in vain to overcome the opposition offered to their advance at the strip of woods, Generals Jackson and D. H. Hill pressed forward on the left, and succeeded in driving

* The *Seven Days' Battles in front of Richmond*, published at Richmond.

back the forces opposed to them; the right renewed its efforts, and about 6 P.M. a general advance was made along the whole Confederate line. The Federals were weary with fighting; there had been little system in relieving the regiments or supplying them with ammunition; the several commands, in order to meet the exigencies of the day, had been divided; above all, except in some regiments, especially in the regulars, there was not that *esprit de corps*, or that feeling of confidence between man and officer, and comrade to comrade, which induces to prolonged resistance against superior odds and under disadvantageous circumstances: there was also a want of instructed staff officers, and when the crash came no one could stop the current of fugitives. The retreat or flight commenced on the right; large numbers of men without order, with arms in their hands, left the ranks and walked to the rear; officers were intermingled with them, in some instances leading their companies away from instead of towards the enemy. There was little or no panic; the men said they were weary, had had enough fighting for the day, or were in want of ammunition; thus the crowd swept onwards, covering the open country, and ascending the hill immediately overlooking Sumner's Upper Bridge. Here some squadrons of cavalry attempted to stop the fugitives, the officers threatening them with their revolvers; but all in vain; they continued their flight over the hill towards the bridge. In the meantime General Longstreet pushed on, and the front line of the Federal infantry engaged on the left broke. Then General St. G. Cook, perceiving the Confederate infantry debouching from the wood, and conceiving the time come for the cavalry to act, led his small force bravely on. The regular regiments advanced to the charge, but in place of riding in with their sabres they, 'following the traditions of Indian warfare,' drew their pistols and carbines. The Confederate infantry poured in a volley which emptied many saddles, and the remainder of the cavalry galloped back to the bridge. In their headlong career, they passed through their own artillery, which was in rear of the line of infantry, and the gunners, mistaking them for the enemy's cavalry, fled. Some however stood steadily to their guns through the panic caused by the cavalry, and until the Confederate infantry shot them down. At their posts, conspicuous among these brave men, were the artillerymen of the German batteries. The regular infantry regiments preserved their discipline better than the volunteers, and many, without yielding to the influence of the now widely-spread panic, fell, disdaining to fly. General Porter's staff, to which were attached some of General M'Clellan's aides, endeavoured in vain to rally the men, and the French princes were especially distinguished, as they exerted themselves to the utmost to stem the torrent of the fugitives.

At this moment two brigades of Sumner's corps, under Generals French and Meagher,* having, owing to the crowd, with difficulty crossed the bridge, ascended the hill overlooking the scene of action. Their presence served in some measure to restore order, and this fresh line of troops drawn up on the brow of the hill and in the dusk of the evening, having the appearance of a larger body than they really were, checked the pursuit. The fugitives pressed onwards to the bridge, and the majority effected a passage over it, but more than twenty pieces of artillery were left on

* The same who was notorious in the disturbances in Ireland.

the field of battle, and on the following morning fell into the hands of the enemy; the wounded also were for the most part abandoned, and sad indeed was their fate. The succeeding battles taxed all the energies of the Confederates, and they had neither time nor a sufficient medical staff to afford the requisite assistance. Many must have fallen in the woods and swamps, and it is terrible to think of their sufferings.

As the stream of fugitives, of ambulances, or caissons (the guns themselves abandoned) arrived on the other side of the Chickahominy, they were halted, and formed into some sort of order, by a line of sentries and strong patrols which guarded the bridge. The regular infantry formed the rear-guard, and about 6 A.M. on the 28th crossed the bridge and then destroyed it. The Confederates, possibly from fatigue, possibly from the loss they themselves had sustained, had missed the opportunity of almost annihilating General Porter's corps. If they had followed up the pursuit, nothing could have saved the Federal right wing, and the mass of men crowded in a contracted space, and engaged in forcing a passage across the narrow causeway extending for about three-quarters of a mile over the Chickahominy swamp, would have easily succumbed to their fire.

The tactics displayed by General Lee on the 27th were very bold. He had divided his army, bringing the greater portion to the left bank of the Chickahominy, and actually at a greater distance from Richmond than the main body of General M'Clellan's army. He trusted, however, to the caution of his adversary, and to the exaggerated opinions he had formed of the Confederate numbers, and the strength of their position. During the whole day, feints of attack had been made on Generals Sumner and Franklin's positions, and thus additional reinforcements, which would otherwise have been sent to General Porter, were detained to guard the lines. Even on the night of the 27th and morning of the 28th, the position of Richmond was critical; but slight fortifications had been thrown up round the town, and these were guarded by the troops under General Magruder (consisting of his own and General Huger's and M'Law's divisions), which were far inferior in numbers to the Federal army, whilst the main body of the Confederate force was still on the further side of the river.* The Confederate general was uncertain as to the movements of his opponent; that he would retreat he had little doubt, but by what line was as yet unknown; he therefore retained the bulk of his army on the left bank of the river.

During the night of the 27th and 28th, General

* That the idea of attacking Richmond after the battle of Gaines' Mill had been considered by General M'Clellan is apparent from the following extract from his report:—

'It may be asked, why, after the concentration of our forces on the right bank of the Chickahominy, with a large part of the enemy drawn away from Richmond, upon the opposite side, I did not, instead of striking for James River fifteen miles below that place, at once march directly on Richmond. It will be remembered, that at this juncture the enemy was on our rear, and there was every reason to believe that he would sever our communications with our supply dépôt at the White House. We had on hand but a limited amount of rations, and if we had advanced directly on Richmond it would have required considerable time to carry the strong works around that place, during which our men would have been destitute of food; and even if Richmond had fallen before our arms the enemy could still have occupied our supply communications between that place and our gunboats, and turned their disaster into victory. If, on the other hand, the enemy had concentrated all his forces at Richmond during the progress of our attack, and we had been defeated, we must in all probability have lost our trains before reaching the flotilla.'

M'Clellan moved his head-quarters to Savage's Station on the Richmond Railway; and all day on the 28th he made arrangements for the retreat or change of base, as he himself denominated it, to the James River. The Confederates were slow to avail themselves of their success. Early on the 28th, an A.D.C. of General M'Clellan, having crossed the Chickahominy, reported that the guns abandoned on the field had not been appropriated, and it was not until 12·30 P.M. that the railway line to the White House was taken possession of. In the morning, about daybreak, General Smith, of Franklin's corps, became engaged, and again later in the day, as he was withdrawing from his more advanced position; but the day passed comparatively quietly. All the bridges, excepting the Railway Bridge and Bottom's Bridge, were destroyed; and these were guarded until the 29th, when they were also burned. During the same day the long line of baggage waggons and the siege train were collected on the roads leading to the White Oak Swamp, and the corps of General Keyes was sent forward to watch the Charles City Road leading direct from Richmond. Fortunately for the Federals the weather was fine, and the roads hard and dry, otherwise very different might have been the subsequent fate of the army. The troops were much demoralised, and the mere rumour of Confederate cavalry was sufficient to cause a panic.

During the 28th the stores were finally removed from White House, Colonel Ingalls having been apprised of the capture of the telegraph station by an uncomplimentary message despatched along the line by some of the enemy. General Stoneman's cavalry passed the White House, and continued their retreat to York Town. As the fleet was leaving, either accidentally or by the unauthorised act of some miscreant, the White House caught fire, and the former residence* of Washington was burned to the ground. The greater portion of the stores were removed, a small amount only falling into the enemy's hand.

During the 28th, and night of the 28th and 29th, Porter's corps, together with M'Call's division, was moved over the White Oak Swamp and placed in a position to guard the roads leading from Richmond to the Long Bridge; whilst the corps of Generals Sumner and Heintzelman, together with Smith's division, were withdrawn from their former lines and ordered to cover Savage's Station and the roads leading from thence to the White Oak Swamp; Slocum's division being held in reserve at Savage's Station. Preparations were at the same time made to abandon the hospitals at Savage's Station, containing the wounded, and to destroy the vast amount of stores and railway material collected there and at Fair Oaks Station. General M'Clellan was most desirous of saving his train, but, in view of eventualities, orders were given, even to the head-quarters staff, to be prepared for the burning of their baggage. At 1 A.M. on the 29th, the head-quarters baggage moved to the rear, and the staff was ordered to be in readiness to march. All that night they stood holding their horses, whilst the one remaining tent still standing contained General M'Clellan, who was engaged in consultation with Generals Heintzelman and Porter.

At daybreak, M'Clellan mounted, and rode to the rear over the White Oak Swamp, in order to superintend the retreat, as he was anxious lest the enemy should have forestalled him and occupied the roads

* The White House was either the house of Washington, or was erected on the site of the older building which was his home.

between his position and the James River. It was a sorrowful day for the Federal army; and their General, although kind and considerate as he always was,* could not help showing the grief and disappointment that weighed on him. As he rode down the long lines of the retreating army, the men took little notice of him, and, contrary to their usual custom, they allowed their favourite General to pass with scarcely any recognition; they were weary and dispirited; and it was only when he arrived opposite Porter's corps,† which had suffered so severely on the previous day, that he was received with anything like his usual greetings. The men of that corps alone cheered as he went by. Having passed the whole army on the line of march, the General rode forward to the out-pickets, and received the reports from Colonel Averill, who had reconnoitred the Charles City Road and surprised a Confederate picket, thereby proving that the Federal army was not expected in that direction. The head-quarters halted for the night about half-way between their former camp and the James River; the whole of the baggage and artillery had safely passed the White Oak Swamp, and so far the retreat had been successful.

In the meantime, Longstreet's division had crossed the Chickahominy, whilst the divisions of Generals Magruder, Huger, and M'Laws were advancing from

* During the day, as the General was halting at a small farm-house, the mistress of the house complained that the men were picking her cherries, and the General personally interfered and prevented the soldiers from taking them. The very next day the same house was set on fire by a shell from the Confederate guns, and burned to the ground.

† Of which the regulars formed a part.

Richmond. Cautiously, but without opposition, they passed the Federal entrenchments near Fair Oaks Station, and continuing along the Williamsburg Road and the railway they encountered Sumner's corps and Smith's division drawn up in the open fields near Savage's Station. Accompanying, or rather preceding their line of march, was an engine as yet untried in war. It was termed the Railway Merrimac, and consisted of a battery propelled by steam on the line of railway and coated with iron; as it moved down the line it poured shot and shell into the Federal divisions; these, however, stood firm and bore the brunt of an attack with fewer numbers than were anticipated either by General M'Clellan or their own commander, General Sumner. It had been arranged that General Heintzelman should guard the Williamsburg Road until nightfall, but, owing to a mistake in the orders, he had withdrawn across the White Oak Swamp, and by the evening of the 29th was on the Charles City Road. General Sumner, however, repulsed the attack. Later in the night, Sumner retired, leaving a vast amount of stores collected at Savage's Station smouldering in the flames. General French commanded the rear-guard, and by 5 A.M. the whole Federal army was on the further side of the White Oak Swamp. During the day, Slocum's division had relieved Porter at the Charles City Road, and Generals Porter and Keyes were on their march to the James River.

The Confederates had suffered severely in the action at Savage's Station, and General Griffiths, who had in the previous year distinguished himself at Leesburg, was killed.* During the night of Sunday the 29th

* *The Seven Days' Battles.* Confederate accounts.

and Monday the 30th, the divisions commanded by D. H. Hill, Whiting, and Ewell, the whole under the command of General Jackson, crossed the Chickahominy and advanced on Savage's Station; the other portion of the army, consisting of General Magruder's, Huger's, M'Law's, Longstreet's, and A. P. Hill's divisions, of which the three first-named were under General Magruder and the other two under General Longstreet, were ordered to pursue the enemy by the Charles City Road. Jackson's corps encountered the rear-guard, commanded by General Franklin, near the White Oak Swamp, about 12 noon, but was hindered from assaulting the Federal position, as the bridge over White Oak Stream had been burned. However, an artillery duel commenced, which continued with increasing fury until dark; finally, the Federals retired, abandoning some of their guns, a portion of the pontoon train, and the balloons. On the same day, the two divisions of Generals Longstreet and A. P. Hill came up with the Federals on the Charles City Road, which crosses the mass of forest and swamps known as White Oak Swamp, nearly at right angles with the road pursued by the Federal army in its retreat. The action commenced about 3 P.M., and M'Call's division, which was guarding the road and occupied a pine wood on either side of it, was driven back with great loss both in guns and men, and also of the general, who was wounded and taken prisoner. General Heintzelman moved up to its support, and the divisions of Hooker and Kearney* succeeded in holding the Confederates in check, and even in regaining a portion of the ground lost by General M'Call. General Sumner also, who with Sedgwick's division was acting as the

* Belonging to General Heintzelman's corps.

reserve both to Franklin and to M'Call, contributed to the assistance of the hard-pressed troops on the Charles City Road. These reinforcements gave the advantage in numbers to the Federals, and A. P. Hill, who during the latter part of the day commanded the two divisions, with great difficulty held his position until Magruder's corps reached the ground. This was not until about 10 P.M., and as the divisions that had been engaged all day were wearied out, General Magruder was ordered to continue the pursuit.

The battle of Glendale, or Frayser's Farm, was fought in the presence of General Lee and President Davis, and, acting under the eyes of their President and of their Commander-in-Chief, the troops of the Confederacy had fought with desperate courage. But the delay in following up the battle of Gaines' Mill, and the loss of Saturday the 28th, in so far as no serious attack was made on the Federals on that day, allowed M'Clellan to outmarch his opponents; and although, on the 30th, portions of the Confederate army were brought up to harass his retreat, yet, acting as he was in a country most favourable for defence, and assisted by the weather, he was able to secure the safety of the greater portion of his baggage trains; and having by the rapidity of his march prevented an attack on his exposed flank, to guard his rear with a force superior to that which could successively be brought against him.

General M'Clellan was not personally present at these several actions; the machinery for working an American army at that period was not perfect; and the General-in-Chief was called upon to perform duties which in European armies fall to the province of the Quarter-master General and Chief of the staff. Indeed, so little were the duties of the several departments understood, that it happened more than once that generals commanding corps, in place of sending their aides-de-camp, were themselves seeking the commanding general, and wasting precious time at his temporary head-quarters, whilst their corps were engaged in the rear, and whilst General M'Clellan was superintending the arrangements of the baggage and the movements of the gunboats on the James River.

During the afternoon of Monday, the 30th, the long lines of baggage waggons, accompanied by innumerable stragglers, amounting to many thousands, reached the height called Malvern Hill, overlooking the James River. The line of waggons appeared interminable; happily the roads were firm and in good order, and they proceeded at a brisk pace, occasionally quickened by the sound of artillery in their rear, or by the rifles of detached parties on their flank; then the teamsters would urge their mules and horses into a gallop, giving some idea of the terrible confusion which would have arisen if an enemy had appeared on the flank.

At an old red-brick mansion, in a grove of ancient trees in the midst of cultivated land, and overlooking from steep heights the flat country bordering the James River, General M'Clellan established his temporary head-quarters about midday on the 30th; but at 4 P.M. he rode down the hill, and went on board Commodore Rodgers's gunboat, in order (to use General M'Clellan's own words) to confer with him in reference to the condition of the supply vessels, and the state of things on the river. General Porter established his head-quarters at the old mansion, and his corps, together with portions of that of Keyes, took up a position to defend Malvern Heights. The point threatened was on the left, supposing the army to have their backs to the James River; and along steep heights, which overlooked woods and forests, was the greater portion of the reserve artillery placed. A few cavalry, assisted by some of General M'Clellan's staff, endeavoured to stop the stragglers, and to form them up in some sort of order; but a portion of General Magruder's command, advancing by one of the roads from Richmond to the south of the Charles City Road, and bringing a battery to bear on Malvern Hill, fired a few shells which, bursting over the position, caused a panic among the wretched fugitives. Porter's corps, however, held their ground, although the general in person, who was ill, did not superintend its formation; at the same time the gunboats on the James River threw several large shells into the wood, and the noise they caused, together with the fear which the gunboats had inspired, sufficed to protect the flank attacked until night closed in.

Great was the despondency at head-quarters. General M'Clellan was on board the gunboats, and apparently the whole army were hurrying to the James River in confusion. The head-quarters tents were pitched close to its bank, opposite Turkey Island, and late in the evening the general having landed, rode up to Malvern Heights, and received the reports from his Adjutant-General, Colonel Colbourne. He sent orders for Generals Sumner, Heintzelman, and Franklin to retire; but Franklin was already falling back, and the three corps during the night retreated and took up the positions assigned to them on Malvern Hill. The Federal army was now in comparative safety, and the main bulk of the artillery and waggons had been saved. The latter were directed to Harrison's Landing, whilst the former were placed in favourable positions to cover the approaches to the plateau of open ground which was known as Malvern Hill. At daybreak, General M'Clellan, having returned to head-quarters during the night, proceeded to Malvern Hill to superintend the disposition of his forces. The position can be best described in his own words :—

'The position selected for resisting the further advance of the enemy on the 1st of July, was the left and centre of our lines resting on Malvern Hill, whilst the right curved back towards a wooded country, toward a point below Haxalls, on James River. Malvern Hill is an elevated plateau about a mile and a half by three-fourths of a mile area, well cleared of timber, and with several converging roads running over it. In front are numerous defensible ravines, and the ground slopes gradually towards the north and east to the woodland, giving clear ranges for artillery in those directions. Toward the north-west the plateau falls off more abruptly into a ravine, which extends to James River.

This formation of the ground afforded a very strong position for the Federal army, which by midday on the 1st of July had partially recovered from its fatigue, and had been refreshed by the issue of stores brought up by the supply vessels. Its flanks were protected by the gunboats, whilst the powerful field artillery, with a portion of the siege train, swept all the roads leading from Richmond. Supposing the army facing Richmond with their backs to the James, the left of the line was held by Porter's corps; on his right was Couch's division of Keyes's corps, then Sumner's corps, then Heintzelman's; and on the right of all, extending backward nearly to the river, the remainder of Keyes's corps, whilst the Pennsylvanian reserves were held in reserve between Porter's and Couch's position. The left flank, being the point on which the attack would most probably be made, was rendered as strong as possible both by the concentration of troops and of artillery; on the right, the line was guarded by proportionally fewer men, and was strengthened as far as time would admit by abattis. In this disposition the army awaited the enemy, should he be bold enough to attack so strong a position.

About 10 A.M. skirmishers from General Magruder's corps commenced feeling the whole of the left and left centre of the Federal line, but it was not until 3 P.M. that the artillery opened on Kearney's division of Heintzelman's corps, and on Couch's division. The men lay down to avoid the fire, and prepared to meet the infantry columns which were forming in the woods below and beyond the open ground. Gallantly did the Confederates advance, passing through at a run the storm of shell and canister which swept the slope of the hill. But the Federal infantry reserved their fire until their opponents had arrived within short musketry range; they then poured in a destructive volley, and drove the Confederates back to the shelter of the woods. Again and again was the assault renewed, but the more powerful artillery of the Federals silenced the opposing batteries, and the strong position occupied by the infantry allowed them to inflict far greater injury on the attacking force than they themselves incurred. Between 4 and 6 P.M. there was a cessation in the attack; but as fresh divisions arrived at the front, General Magruder renewed the engagement, and directed his columns against the part of the line held by Porter and Couch. General M'Clellan about 7 P.M. relieved these troops by portions of Sumner's and Heintzelman's corps, under

Generals Meagher and Sickles, and the battle still continued. The Confederates, although suffering terribly, yet persisted in their unavailing attacks, after each repulse falling back on the woods to re-form. During the engagement the gunboats shelled the woods, and protected the flanks of the Federal line. Towards the close of the day, General Jackson brought up his divisions from the White Oak Swamp, and engaged the Federal right; but the reinforcements arrived too late to be of much service, and the Federals held their own until darkness ended the battle.

The loss on the side of the Confederates was very great—far greater in proportion to that incurred by their adversaries. They had attacked the whole of General M'Clellan's army, posted in a peculiarly strong position, with but portions of their own; the several divisions of the Confederate army having been brought into action as they arrived on the ground, only to be beaten back in detail. At Malvern Hill, General M'Clellan reaped the advantage of the care he had taken to secure his artillery during the difficulties attending the retreat; for not only had he preserved his field artillery, but the greater portion of his siege guns, under Colonel Tyler, had also been saved, and performed good service during the action.

On the next day General M'Clellan prepared to retire to Harrison's Bar, which had been selected as the most convenient place for landing stores, and also as affording a secure position for the camps, the country near the river being flat, and easily swept by the fire of the gunboats. The retreat was effected with scarcely any molestation from the enemy; the rear-guard was formed of Keyes's corps, together with the cavalry under General Averill. A great portion of the waggons had already reached the landing-place on the morning of the 1st, and by the night of the 3rd the whole were in safety, and M'Clellan's army, after some loss and great hardships, had gained a comparatively secure position on the James River, from which their commander thought that another series of operations against Richmond might be conducted.

The battle of Malvern Hill had retrieved the *morale* of the men; and the reinforcements which arrived shortly afterwards in some measure recruited their numbers. M'Clellan estimated the total losses, from the 26th of June to the 1st of July, at 15,249 men, and only twenty-five guns; but the Confederates gave a different account, and placed the loss much higher.*

Notwithstanding the joy felt in Richmond at the raising of the siege, and the departure of the army of the invader, there was likewise some disappointment. The destruction of the Federal host had been expected; as it was hoped that the retreat would have been cut off, and that M'Clellan, hemmed in within his lines on the Chickahominy, and severed both from his old depôt on the Pamunkey and the proposed new depôt on the James River, would have been forced to surrender. The loss also of the Confederates had been very heavy, especially at the battle of Malvern Hill; and in some quarters great blame was attached to General

* General Lee, in the General Order dated Richmond, July 9, thus summed up the results of the seven days' battles:—'The immediate fruits of our success are—the relief of Richmond from a state of siege; the rout of the great army that so long menaced its safety; many thousand prisoners, including officers of high rank; the capture and destruction of stores to the value of millions; and the acquisition of thousands of arms, and fifty-one pieces of superior artillery.'

Magruder,* for what was termed the hopeless butchery to which he had urged on his troops. Notwithstanding these drawbacks, the exultation at Richmond and through the Confederacy was very great. It was felt that the tide of success had turned in favour of the South, and that the losses of the earlier campaigns of the year had been retrieved. The trophies exhibited in the city excited the populace; and conspicuous among them was the great flag which had been destined to wave over their State House. On the other hand, during the progress of the seven days' battles, the North had been depressed by the most gloomy forebodings. For some days there had been no communication with the army; and, although General M'Clellan's splendid strategy was talked of, yet it could easily be seen that the greatest uneasiness was felt, and it was a relief not only to the Government, but to the whole of the Northern people, when a telegram was received from M'Clellan announcing his arrival at the James River. In answer to this communication, Mr. Lincoln sent a telegram to this effect:—

'Washington, July 5th, 1862, 9 A.M.

'A thousand thanks for the relief your two despatches of 12 and 1 P.M. yesterday gave me. Be assured, the heroism and skill of yourself, officers, and men is, and for ever will be, appreciated. If you can hold your present position we shall have the enemy yet.

'A. LINCOLN.'

The President at the same time promised that, in addition to the reinforcements already sent, 'about ten

* That the services of General Magruder were subsequently appreciated by his Government, is proved from the high commands which have since been assigned to him.

thousand' other forces from General Burnside in North Carolina, and from General Hunter in South Carolina, should be forwarded to the James River as soon as possible. But, although M'Clellan's telegram may have calmed the anxiety of the North, yet his defeat was productive of gloom and doubt as to the early termination of the war. The money market was violently agitated, and the price of gold went up to 10½ premium; in fact, since the battle of Bull Run, the reverses on the Chickahominy were far the most serious that the North had sustained.*

* After the army had reached the James River, the French princes took leave of General M'Clellan and departed for Europe. For this they have been much censured in Europe, although not in America, and reasons have been adduced for their conduct calculated to prejudice their character as soldiers. The true facts of the case are as follows:—Previous to General Jackson's arrival on the flank of the army of the Potomac, when everything appeared as prosperous as was possible for the Federal arms, the princes, for private reasons, were anxious to return to Europe, especially as the Duc de Chartres had for some time been suffering from illness brought on by the climate. General M'Clellan begged the Count de Paris to remain for a few days longer to witness the attack on Richmond, whilst his younger brother, in consequence of his illness, returned to Washington. This the Count de Paris agreed to do, and most unwillingly the Duc de Chartres made preparations for his departure. But on the very day he had arranged to go, news arrived that General Jackson had attacked the right wing, and the Duc de Chartres refused to leave the army. Notwithstanding his severe illness, he with his brother acted as A.D.C. to General Porter at Gaines' Mill, and were distinguished by their gallantry; afterwards, during the trying days of the retreat, they performed most efficient service in their capacity of aides-de-camp to the General Commanding-in-Chief; and it was only when he himself reached the James River that they carried out their previous intention of departing for Europe. They were much beloved and respected at the head-quarters of General M'Clellan, and by those officers with whom they had served in other divisions.

CHAPTER V.

INTERIOR STATE OF THE COUNTRY.

A SECOND time since the commencement of the war had the anniversary of the birth of the American Republic recurred; and again had the fourth of July dawned in the northern portion of the Union on a people suffering from reverses in place of, as in former years, rejoicing over a course of prosperity. The fourth of July of the preceding year had followed soon after the great defeat of Bull Run; and that of the year 1862 had been almost contemporary with the still more terrible reverses on the Chickahominy. Notwithstanding these causes tending to depression, the day was observed outwardly in the usual manner. Fireworks, were let off in the streets, and speeches, resembling the fireworks in their characteristics and results, were delivered to the populace of the great cities. In the army of the Potomac, a review was held; and the troops, although thinned in numbers, yet recruited in body by rest and refreshment, and in *morale* by the action at Malvern Hill, were drawn up for the inspection of their General. On the same day he issued a congratulatory address, which, however, received a severe comment from the proclamation put forth by the President of the Southern Republic at Richmond. In these words did M'Clellan address his army:—

'Soldiers of the Army of the Potomac!—Your

achievements of the last ten days have illustrated the valour and endurance of the American soldier. Attacked by superior forces, and without hope of reinforcements, you have succeeded in changing your base of operations by a flank movement—always regarded as the most hazardous of military expedients. You have saved all your material, all your trains, and all your guns, except a few lost in battle; taking in return guns and colours from the enemy. Upon your march you have been assailed day after day with desperate fury, by men of the same race and nation, skilfully massed and led. Under every disadvantage of number, and necessarily of position also, you have in every conflict beaten back your foes with enormous slaughter. Your conduct ranks you among the celebrated armies of history. No one will now question that each of you may always with pride say—"I belong to the Army of the Potomac." You have reached the new base complete in organisation and unimpaired in spirit. The enemy may at any moment attack you. We are prepared to meet them; I have personally established your lines. Let them come, and we will convert their repulse into final defeat. Your Government is strengthening you with the resources of a great people. On this our nation's birthday, we declare to our foes, who are rebels against the best interests of mankind, that this army shall enter the capital of the so-called Confederacy; that our national constitution shall prevail; and that the Union, which can alone ensure internal peace and external security to each State, must and shall be preserved, cost what it may in time, treasure, and blood.'

These were brave words to utter to an army which had suffered so severely, and had met with such serious disasters; but even if they were not in character with the man who gave vent to them, they were suited to the 4th of July, and in accordance with the description of manifesto popular with the Americans of the Northern States. A somewhat similar congratulatory address, but couched in different terms, was about the same time issued by President Davis. He wrote as follows:—

'Soldiers!—I congratulate you on the series of brilliant victories which, under favour of Divine Providence, we have lately won; and as the President of the Confederate States, I do hereby tender you the thanks of the country whose just cause you have so skilfully and heroically saved. Ten days ago, an invading army, vastly superior to you in numbers and materials of war, closely beleaguered your capital, and vauntingly proclaimed its speedy conquest. You marched to attack the enemy in his entrenchments. With well-directed movements and death-dealing valour, you charged upon him in his strong position, drove him from field to field over a distance of more than thirty-five miles, and, spite of his reinforcements, compelled him to seek shelter under cover of his gunboats, where he now lies, cowering before the army he so lately derided and threatened with entire subjugation. The fortitude with which you have borne the trials and privations, the gallantry with which you have entered into each successive battle, must have been witnessed to be fully appreciated; but a grateful people will not fail to recognise your deeds, and bear you in loved remembrance. Well may it be said of you, that you have done enough for glory; but duty to a suffering country, and to the cause of constitutional liberty, claims from you yet further efforts. Let it be your pride to relax in nothing that can promote your own future efficiency, your one great object being to drive the invaders from your soil, carrying your standard beyond the outer boundaries of the Confederacy, to wring from an unscrupulous foe the recognition which is the birthright of every independent community.'

In comparing these two addresses, so different in character, it will be observed that the same word, 'Constitution,' is made use of. In the address of General M'Clellan, he puts forward, as an object of the war, that *our national constitution shall prevail*; whilst in that of President Davis the cause of *constitutional liberty* is said to claim the further efforts of the army. That the latter—*i.e.* the constitutional liberty of the South—was an object of attainment always upheld by the leaders of the Confederacy, there can be little question; but with reference to the former—namely the preservation of the national constitution of the United States—there were signs that the restoration of the Union, even at the sacrifice of the constitution, was rapidly becoming the aim of a large majority of the people of the Northern States. The Republican party was fast adopting abolition principles, and throwing themselves more and more into the arms of what had been at the election of Mr. Lincoln only a minority of the party.

From various causes—partly from the clearer aim proposed by this faction, partly from the weakness of the Democratic party in attempting to wage a war of coercion and invasion on constitutional grounds, partly also from the exigencies of war and the want of men to supply its losses—the Abolition party was able not only to strengthen the ground it already held, but to recruit its ranks, and to push forward its schemes for the future. To counteract the influence of these principles, and at the same time to declare its own opinions, and to collect its forces, the Democratic party assembled a meeting at the Cooper Institute, in New York, on the 1st July. There the cry was, *The Union as it was, the Constitution as it is*; and the speeches of the leaders clearly pointed to the good policy of conciliating the South, and reconstructing the Union on its former basis. But the time had passed for such measures. As in all periods of revolution, the more ultra party had taken the lead, and the Democrats were not only looked on with suspicion by a large mass of the Northern people, but even incurred contempt from those of the South, who regarded them as men compromising their principles* for the sake of personal security and motives of interest.

The failure of General M'Clellan to conquer Richmond also tended to weaken the party, and his method of waging war, and treating his enemies as if ultimately they might become his friends, was condemned by the leaders of the Republicans, who advocated more stringent measures and greater severity towards the conquered territories. In addition to these reasons for the increase of power of the Abolition faction, there was another which weighed greatly with a large body of the American people. As in the South, so in the North, had the first war fever passed away; the portion of the population willing to embrace the profession of arms had been exhausted, and the earlier enthusiasm of the struggle had evaporated. The President, in order to reinforce the army, had made a call for 300,000 men, and the question arose, how were these men to be obtained? General Hunter had set the example of employing negroes in South Carolina; and although his conduct had not met with the direct approval of the

* By the denial of State rights.

Government, yet it induced many to conceive the idea of partially replacing the white soldiers by blacks. In a debate on the subject in the Federal Congress, the arming of the slaves of rebels was advocated by more than one member. Various motives for so doing were urged. One senator contended that the Federals could not wage war against savages unless they became in part savages themselves; another, that, owing to the unhealthiness of the climate, the men from his State were not willing to enlist, and to perform services which could be better done by blacks; whilst, on the other hand, the senators from the Border States advocated the employment of slaves only in the trenches and for fatigue duty, saying that the States they represented would *resist to the death the plan to arm the slaves.** The Government was in difficulties as to the

* See quotations from Messrs. Sherman and Fessenden's speeches on the Republican side, and Mr. Davis on that of the Border States.—*Times' Correspondence, New York, July 10th.* The debate arose on the report of the Military Committee advocating a bill for the employment of persons of African descent for building entrenchments and for other war purposes. On the bill to amend the Militia Act of 1795, Mr. Gaines proposed that the militia should include men without reference to colour.—Mr. Saulsbury was at once on his feet. This was an attempt to elevate the 'miserable nigger.' 'It would not restore the Union.'—Mr. Carlisle fell back upon the constitution. 'It didn't recognise nigger militia;' the constitution was immaculate; hence Congress could not make a militiaman of a black.—Mr. King tried to steer a middle course. He would not let Sambo have a gun; but if he delved diligently with a spade, his mother, wife, and children should be free.—Mr. Saulsbury thought this was a general scheme of emancipation.—Mr. Sherman took a diametrically opposite view. He said the slaves had hitherto worked only for the rebels: he would have their services for the Union. He would compel officers to take their services. Rather than this Union should be destroyed, he would organise a great army of black men, and desolate every Southern State. He would, if necessary, pass a

course of action it should adopt, and hesitated before it gave up the constitutional grounds on which it had at first professed to conduct the war, and threw itself into the plans of the more violent portion of the Republican party.

The indecision of the ruling powers is sufficiently clear from the correspondence held on the subject of slavery, at various times, between the Secretary of War and the several generals. On July 3, 1862, the Secretary of War wrote in these terms to General Butler:—

'The President is of opinion that, under the law of Congress, they (slaves) cannot be sent back to their masters; that in common humanity they must not be permitted to suffer for want of food, shelter, and other necessaries of life; that to this end they should be provided for by the Quartermaster and Commissary Departments, and that those who are capable of labour should be set to work and paid reasonable wages. The President indicating this, does not assume to settle any general rule at present with regard to the States.'

The President himself, in a letter to Horace Greely, dated August 22nd, 1862, defined in clear terms the motives which actuated his line of policy. He wrote:—

'As to the line of policy I "seem to be pursuing" as you say, I have not meant to leave anyone in doubt. I would save the Union—I would save it in the shortest way under the constitution; the sooner the national authority can be restored, the nearer the Union will be—the Union as it was. If there be those who would not save the Union unless they could at the same time save slavery, I do not agree with them. If there be those who would not save the Union unless they

Conscription Act; and we might, if necessary, as well draft niggers as white men, etc. etc.

could at the same time destroy slavery, I do not agree with them. My paramount object is to save the Union, and not either to save or destroy slavery. If I could save the Union without freeing any slaves, I would do it. If I could save it by freeing all the slaves, I would do it. If I could save it by freeing some and leaving others alone, I would also do that. What I do about slavery and the coloured race, I do because I believe it helps to save the Union; and what I forbear, I forbear because I do not believe it would help to save the Union. I shall do less whenever I shall believe what I am now doing hurts the cause, and shall do more whenever I believe doing more will help the cause. I shall try to correct errors when shown to be errors, and I shall adopt new views as fast as they shall appear to be true views. I have here stated my purpose, according to my view of official duty, and I intend no modification of my oft-expressed personal wish, that all men everywhere could be free.'*

This letter sufficiently defines the object of the Government as represented by its head, and shows that the aim of both its civil and military measures was not the preservation of the Constitution, advocated by the Democratic party, or the freedom of the slaves, demanded by the Abolition party, but the restoration of the Union. It also sets forth with sufficient clearness that the provisions of the Constitution, equally with the schemes of Emancipation, would be disregarded so long as they hindered the restoration of the United Sovereignty of the American people.

A short time previous to the issue of this letter, on

* See page 334, M'Pherson's *Political History of the United States during the Great Rebellion.*

July 17, a Bill passed the Senate at Washington, decreeing the infliction of additional penalties to those already in force, against persons either in arms against the United States, or in any way engaged in assisting (what was termed in the Bill) the so-called Confederate States in the prosecution of the war. Among other penalties attached to those guilty of the crime of treason, it was decreed that all the slaves possessed by such criminal should be free. To this President Lincoln objected, on the ground that it was beyond the power of Congress to free a slave within a slave state; but, at the same time, he suggested that the difficulty might be overruled by an alteration in the wording of the Act, so as first to transfer to the nation the ownership of the slave, and thereby bring it into the power of Congress to declare him free. No change was however made in the wording of this section of the Act; and on a second objection urged by the President being allowed, and a clause inserted that 'no punishment or proceeding under said Act be so construed as to work a forfeiture of the real estate of the offender beyond his natural life,' President Lincoln approved and signed the Act. The plan for arming the blacks was for the time put aside, and the ordinary method continued, of recruiting the army by the offer of a bounty for enlistment, with the threat of conscription* unless the quota of men allotted to the several states should be supplied. The Government set the example of bounties by the offer of $40 per man; and the several states and cities increased this offer by additional sums, in order to make up the number of men demanded from them.†

* Termed a draft in America.

† On the 4th August, 1862, an order was issued by the President for a draft of 300,000 to serve in the militia for nine months, unless

Another difficulty, besides the want of soldiers, also beset the Administration. The absence of specie was becoming severely felt, especially as regarded the smaller coins necessary for daily use. The Financial Minister, Mr. Chase, in proposing his new issue of $150,000,000 of Treasury Notes, asked permission of Congress to print off a few millions for sums under five dollars. After some discussion, this application was granted, and $25,000,000 were permitted to be issued in bills of one, two, and three dollars each. Even this concession did not afford sufficient assistance to the requirements of trade, and all sorts of expedients were tried to remedy the great deficiency of small-change. I O U's, in the form of notes, were issued by many of the hotels and drinking-saloons. Orders on shops were given in exchange for larger sums tendered in purchases of small value. Omnibus tickets, theatre tickets, tickets for ferries, postage stamps, all came into circulation as small-change, and passed current in the localities in which they were issued.* Various plans for the remedy of this evil were proposed, but it continued to increase; and the ever-changing value of the precious metals had the effect of augmenting the

sooner discharged. The same order directed that, should any state not furnish its quota of the 300,000 volunteers, the deficiency should be made up by a special draft from the militia. The volunteer force to serve against the South must not be confounded with the militia forces of each separate state, organised for the defence of the state, and under the control of the state governor.

* In Chicago, barber-shop tickets for the amount of a dollar were in circulation; the ticket depreciating 10 cents each time the holder was shaved, when the barber would punch a hole in the ticket to mark its depreciation of value. The plates held in the churches presented curious specimens of circulating mediums, filled as they were with every description of I O U.

spirit of speculation, only too much developed in the great trading cities of America.

If we turn to the Confederate States, and watch the line of conduct advocated by President Davis, as set forth in his Message to Congress on the 16th August, we shall see success borne with equanimity, and the passions fiercely excited in the breasts of the Southern people, by such acts as the Confiscation Act, and by proclamations issued about this time by the Northern Generals, calmed down and guided into proper channels by the head of the Government. President Davis, in his message, alluded to the gallantry of the army: he showed 'that it had not faltered in any of the various trials to which it had been subjected; and that the great body of the people had continued to manifest a zeal and unanimity which not only cheered the battle-stained soldier, but gave assurance to the friends of constitutional liberty of the final triumph of the South in the pending struggle against despotic usurpation.' He pointed out how the malignity of the North against the South had been augmented by defeat, and instanced, as proofs, the passing of the Confiscation Act, and the open forgery and sale in the Northern cities of the Confederate paper-money. He spoke of Butler's proclamation at New Orleans, and the orders of other military commanders; and although he deprecated retaliatory measures, yet he considered that stern justice should be meted out to those whom he termed 'murderers and felons,' in the event of their coming within the power of the Confederate laws. President Davis then drew attention to the internal condition of the States. He begged Congress to endeavour, as far as was possible, to give complete efficiency to the Conscription Act, and to devise the best means for securing the entire co-operation of the State and Confederate Governments. He also congratulated the country, that at length an arrangement had been effected with regard to the exchange of prisoners, which would, it was hoped, speedily restore many brave and unfortunate men to the ranks of the army. He concluded as follows:—'We have never-ceasing cause to be grateful for the favour with which God has protected our infant Confederacy, and it becomes us reverently to return our thanks, and humbly to ask of His bounteousness that wisdom which is needful for the performance of the high trusts with which we are charged.'

The Congress commenced its sittings, and confined itself generally to the consideration of questions bearing more immediately on the conduct of the war. It gave additional powers to the President in matters relating to the promotion of deserving officers and men, providing at the same time against undue jobbing and the effects of political interest, by decreeing that the advancement of all officers, unless in special exceptional cases, should be by seniority. With reference to the blockade of the ports of the Confederacy, it passed a Bill permitting vessels to unload their cargoes on any part of the coast of the Confederate States. The blockade of the coast had not been very effectual, and even at the ports at which the Federal ships-of-war had been stationed, the swift steamships, built for the purpose of running the blockade at some of the shipyards of England and Scotland, succeeded frequently in effecting an entrance.

At Mobile, a port more easily watched than many of the others, the steamer Oreto, subsequently named the Florida, having run the gauntlet in broad daylight of the whole blockading squadron, lay at anchor, awaiting her armament and stores to issue forth to prey on the Federal commerce. Trusting to her speed to escape destruction from the Federal artillery, she had boldly steamed through the fleet, passing within easy range of grape and shrapnel, of which her sides showed the marks, but unhurt in any vital point by the heavier shot. Captain Maffitt and many of the crew were at the time ill with fever, but, undermanned as she was, and totally devoid of weapons, offensive or defensive, she had boldly faced the Federal fleet, and was now reaping the reward of her enterprise in the admiration which her bold exploit had excited among the Southern people.

CHAPTER VI.

CAMPAIGN BETWEEN WASHINGTON AND GORDONSVILLE.

IN the meantime energetic measures were taken on the part of the North for the prosecution of the war. On July 11, by order of President Lincoln, General Halleck was appointed General-in-Chief of the whole land-forces of the United States. General Burnside, with a large portion of his army, was recalled from North Carolina, and despatched to the James River to reinforce General M'Clellan, and plans were considered for another advance on Richmond under the guidance of the officer who had been so successful at Island No. 10.

General Pope, who had been appointed to the command of the forces in the vicinity of Washington and in the Shenandoah Valley, was an officer of the regular army, and previous to the war with the South had performed various services, more especially connected with engineering, on the south-western frontier. When the war of Secession broke out he was employed in Missouri, and acquired some renown at Island No. 10, and much notoriety from his despatch announcing the capture of 10,000 men of General Beauregard's army on the retreat from Corinth. On his arrival at Washington he was warmly welcomed by the personal and political opponents of General M'Clellan, as well as by the great majority of the common people, who were ready to receive with favour a new man, especially if by any peculiarities he gave promise of the brilliant talent which had been long looked for and eagerly expected in the many generals whom the war had raised to eminence if not to fame. In every way General Pope proclaimed himself as opposed to the policy of General M'Clellan. He disapproved of his retreat to the James River, and, in ignorance of the circumstances of the case, impressed upon the President that he ought, at any sacrifice, to have withdrawn in the direction of Hanover Court-house.* With regard to his method of treating belligerents and the unarmed population of the South, he advocated an entirely different line of conduct: and whilst General M'Clellan was urging upon President Lincoln the policy of conducting the war *on the highest principles known to Christian civilisation*—saying 'that it should not be a war upon population, but against armed forces and political organisations, and that neither confiscation of property, political executions of persons, territorial organisation of States, or forcible abolition of slavery should be contemplated for a moment†—General Pope issued orders that his troops should live on the country in which they campaigned, and directed that subscription to the oath of allegiance, or banishment beyond the lines of the army to the South, should be the choice of the farmers of Eastern Virginia and of the Shenandoah Valley. In his notorious address to the Army of Virginia, he evidently aimed a blow against the strategy of General M'Clellan; and although no soldier can approve of the bombastic tone of the order, and few

* General Pope's official report; *Rebellion Record*, vol. v. p. 342. Documents.

† Vide General M'Clellan's letter to Mr. Lincoln, July 7th, 1862.

can restrain a smile at the results of the campaign which immediately followed its issue, yet under its boastful tone there are some grains of truth. In these terms did Pope announce his appointment to the command of the Army of Virginia :—

'By special assignment of the President of the United States, I have assumed command of this army. I have spent two weeks in learning your whereabouts, your condition, and your wants; in preparing you for active operations, and in placing you in positions from which you can act promptly and to the purpose. I have come to you from the West, where we have always seen the backs of our enemies—from an army whose business it has been to seek the adversary and to beat him when found—whose policy has been attack and not defence. In but one instance has the enemy been able to place our Western armies in a defensive attitude. I presume that I have been called here to pursue the same system, and to lead you against the enemy; it is my purpose to do so, and that speedily. I am sure you long for an opportunity to win the distinction you are capable of achieving; that opportunity I shall endeavour to give you. Meantime I desire you to dismiss from your minds certain phrases which I am sorry to find much in vogue amongst you. I hear constantly of taking strong positions and holding them—of lines of retreat, and bases of supplies. Let us discard such ideas. The strongest position which a soldier should desire to occupy is one from which he can most easily advance against the enemy. Let us study the probable lines of retreat of our opponents, and leave our own to take care of themselves. Let us look before us, not behind: success and glory are in the advance—disaster and shame lurk in the rear. Let us act on this understanding, and it is safe to predict that your banners shall be inscribed with many a glorious deed, and that your names shall be dear to your countrymen for ever.'

Such was the proclamation of July 14! It was received with favour by the people of the North: its swagger was pleasing to their ears, and its tone gave promise—to the too easily credulous—of a brilliant campaign, fought, *more Americano*, on principles of strategy unknown to the generals of the Old World. The shadow of truth which lay under its bombastic nonsense was the check it gave to the ignorant use of phrases relating to the art of war, too common among the civilian soldiers of the North.

The first object of General Pope after taking command was to concentrate the scattered corps under the respective commands of M'Dowell, Sigel (formerly Fremont), and Banks. The total strength he estimated at 38,000, and he formed the design of so placing his force as to cover Washington, and at the same time to draw away troops from the Confederate army which was pressing General M'Clellan. His line of operations was the Orange and Alexandria Railway—the same that had been used in the advance preceding the Battle of Bull's Run, and again when the Army of the Potomac marched on Centreville. His objective point was Gordonsville, on the Virginia Central Railway, although prospectively he looked for a farther advance on Richmond. In order to carry out these plans, he concentrated the corps of Banks and Shields and one division of M'Dowell's army at Sperryville, east and at the foot of the Blue Ridge Mountains, whilst he left the other division of General M'Dowell at Falmouth to watch the lower fords of the Rappahannock, and to protect the Aquia Creek

Railway. On the 14th of July, General Pope pushed forward his cavalry towards Gordonsville, and ordered General King, at Falmouth, to make a reconnaissance in force along the Richmond and Fredericksburg Railway. The former accomplished nothing, as General Ewell had been detached from Jackson's corps,* and on the 16th of July reached Gordonsville, and prevented any attack on the line of rail. King's reconnaissance was also productive of little result.

The Federal cavalry were now stationed along the line of the Rapidan river, and in the beginning of August the outpickets reported that the enemy was advancing, both in the direction of Madison Court-house, and also from Gordonsville towards Culpepper Court-house. Uncertain by which line the attack would be made, and jealous of his communications with Fredericksburg, Pope moved his infantry and artillery from Sperryville to Culpepper Court-house, and ordered Banks to occupy a strong position at Cedar Mountain, a few miles in advance; at the same time telegraphing to M'Clellan that the force in his front was reduced in numbers, and leading that General to push forward Hooker's division to Malvern Hill. On the 8th of August Jackson crossed the Rapidan, and took up a position in the wooded and hilly country in the vicinity of the main road from Gordonsville to Culpepper. His force consisted of about 15,000 men, and was composed of his own division under General Winder, with General Ewell's and a portion of General A. P. Hill's divisions.

On the afternoon of the 9th August, the skirmishers of the two armies came into collision, and soon afterwards the artillery opened on both sides. The Confede-

* About this time the Confederate army was organised in *corps d'armée*.

rates occupied a strong position on the wooded slopes of a sugarloaf hill called Cedar or Slaughter Mountain, and it was General Jackson's object to induce his opponent to attack him.

Gradually as the supports to the skirmishers became engaged, and the reserves suffered from the fire of the enemy's guns, Banks advanced his divisions, and attempted to capture the batteries. Each attack was repulsed with considerable loss, and the action, which commenced at 5 P.M., was carried on until late in the evening. About 7 o'clock Pope arrived on the field, bringing up with him Ricketts' division, under the command of M'Dowell, who took up a position on the left of Banks. But the Federal line had been driven back about a mile, and as night closed in the troops bivouacked on the ground they occupied.

About midnight, by the light of a bright moon, the Confederate artillerymen discovered that the enemy was within range of their guns, and opened on them as they lay tired and wearied with the battle of the previous day.* Great confusion ensued, and a panic spread through a portion of General Banks's corps. Some of the Confederate cavalry taking advantage of the occasion charged, and nearly succeeded in capturing General Pope and his staff.

The loss on the part of the Federals in this battle was very great. General Pope himself acknowledged to 1,800 killed, wounded, and prisoners, and states that fully 1,000 more straggled back to Culpepper Court-house and beyond, and never entirely returned to their commands.† On the Confederate side General Winder

* *Review of the Recent Campaigns of Virginia.*—Chesney.

† General Pope's official report.

was killed, and the loss in killed and wounded was about 800 or 900.

On the following morning General Sigel's corps arrived on the ground, making up the numbers of the Federals to about 22,000 men,* exclusive of the corps of General Banks, which, in consequence of having been so cut up in the action of the previous day, was ordered to Culpepper.

General Pope made no attempt to renew the battle, but sent for King's division from Fredericksburg, which joined the main army on the 11th. Thus reinforced Pope determined to attack on the 12th; but it was no part of General Jackson's plan to engage the whole Federal army with his single corps. He had succeeded in inflicting a serious check on its advanced divisions, and in saving Gordonsville, and he now proposed to defer operations until the arrival of the main army from Richmond, set free by the withdrawal of General M'Clellan's army from Harrison's Landing. He therefore retreated during the night of the 11th, and recrossed the Rapidan, the Federal cavalry again advancing as far as that stream.

The action of Cedar Mountain† alarmed the Federal Government, and General Halleck telegraphed at once to M'Clellan, repeating an order previously given, to send Burnside to Aquia Creek, and at the same time directing him to retreat to York Town and Fortress Monroe. This was accordingly done. General Burnside, with 13,000 men, was sent to Aquia Creek, and the stores, baggage, and sick were shipped on board the transports at Harrison's Landing, their se-

* General Pope's official report.

† Called also Cedar Run and Slaughter Mountain.

curity from the Confederate batteries having been insured by the previous occupation of the opposite shore of the James River.

On the 17th, 18th, 19th, and 20th of August, the army marched by Williamsburg to York Town and Newport News. The defences of York Town were strengthened under the direction of General Keyes, and the several corps of the Army of the Potomac prepared to embark for the Rappahannock.

The campaign of the York Town peninsula had now terminated, and the only fruits of the advance on Richmond, the only result of the many battles and the terrible losses of the four-months' campaign, were the capture and occupation of York Town and Gloucester Point. The interest of the war was now centred in General Pope's army, which, it was thought by many, would soon have to struggle not for victory but for existence, and for the safety of Washington.

In order to form anything like a clear idea of the approaching campaign, it is necessary to bear in mind certain features of the country in which the opposing armies were about to manœuvre, and also the objects aimed at by their respective generals. General M'Clellan's scheme had been to protect Washington by an attack on Richmond, to disregard the enemy's aggressive movements in the Shenandoah Valley and towards Centreville, and to devote the whole energies of the country to the reduction of the Confederate capital. For this plan he had never received the cordial support of the President, who, anxious for the safety of Washington, preferred the Shenandoah Valley, or the route by Centreville or Gordonsville, for the scene of operations.

After General M'Clellan's defeat, and the accession

to power of General Pope, the last-named plan was adopted. Pope considered that the presence of a large army on the Rapidan would prevent any advance by the enemy into the Shenandoah Valley, and at the same time would lead to the capture of Gordonsville, the severance of Richmond from Western Virginia, and the ultimate investment of the city on its eastern side. He hoped to be able to advance along the Orange and Alexandria Railroad, and, whilst driving back the enemy in his front, to protect his own long lines of communication. The distance from Washington to Richmond in a straight line is about 110 miles, by Gordonsville 150 miles. The direct route lay through Fredericksburg, of which the greater portion is by water, to Aquia Creek, and thence per rail for about 60 miles to Richmond. Although this route offered the advantage of a shorter distance, yet the movement of the army by Fredericksburg would not (it was considered) so directly cover Washington as an advance on Gordonsville; whilst the country between Fredericksburg and Richmond, being thickly wooded and intersected with streams, was unfitted for the march of any large force, and favourable for purposes of defence. For these reasons General Pope preferred the latter plan of operations. But at the same time that he covered Washington and marched on Gordonsville, he was anxious, and indeed was commanded, to keep open his communications with Fredericksburg, in order to receive reinforcements from the Army of the Potomac, arriving by Aquia Creek.

On turning to the map it will be seen, that the distance to Fredericksburg from the point where the road to Gordonsville crosses the Rapidan is about thirty-five miles. Not only had General Pope to protect this line, but he had also to watch lest the enemy, who had the advantage of a rail running direct from Richmond to Gordonsville, should turn his right flank. He was therefore forced to extend his right wing to the foot of the Blue Ridge Mountains, which separate the Shenandoah Valley from the country bordering the Rapidan and Rappahannock Rivers; whilst he was also obliged to guard the lower fords of the Rapidan, and keep open communications with Fredericksburg. These two streams—they can scarcely be dignified by the name of rivers—rising in the Blue Ridge Mountains, unite about fifteen miles above Fredericksburg, the Rapidan flowing in a north-easterly, the Rappahannock in a south-easterly course. They are crossed in many places by fords, and also by a few bridges. Along the left banks of each, the Federal army, as it advanced or retired, took up its position. Running at nearly right-angles with these streams is the Alexandria and Orange Railroad, and the direct road from Washington to Gordonsville. The earlier actions of the campaign, embracing the battle of Cedar Mountain and the events which immediately followed it, were fought in the vicinity of the Rappahannock and Rapidan Rivers, and between the Blue Ridge Mountains and Fredericksburg, where the character of the country is woody and undulating, but more open than that to the south-east of Richmond or in the neighbourhood of Fredericksburg. The later battles were fought nearer Washington, and immediately adjoining the stream of Bull Run, which likewise intersects at nearly right-angles the Orange and Alexandria Rail. Here the Bull Run Mountains, running parallel with the Blue Ridge, narrow the theatre of operations, and in their passes afford means of attack or defence

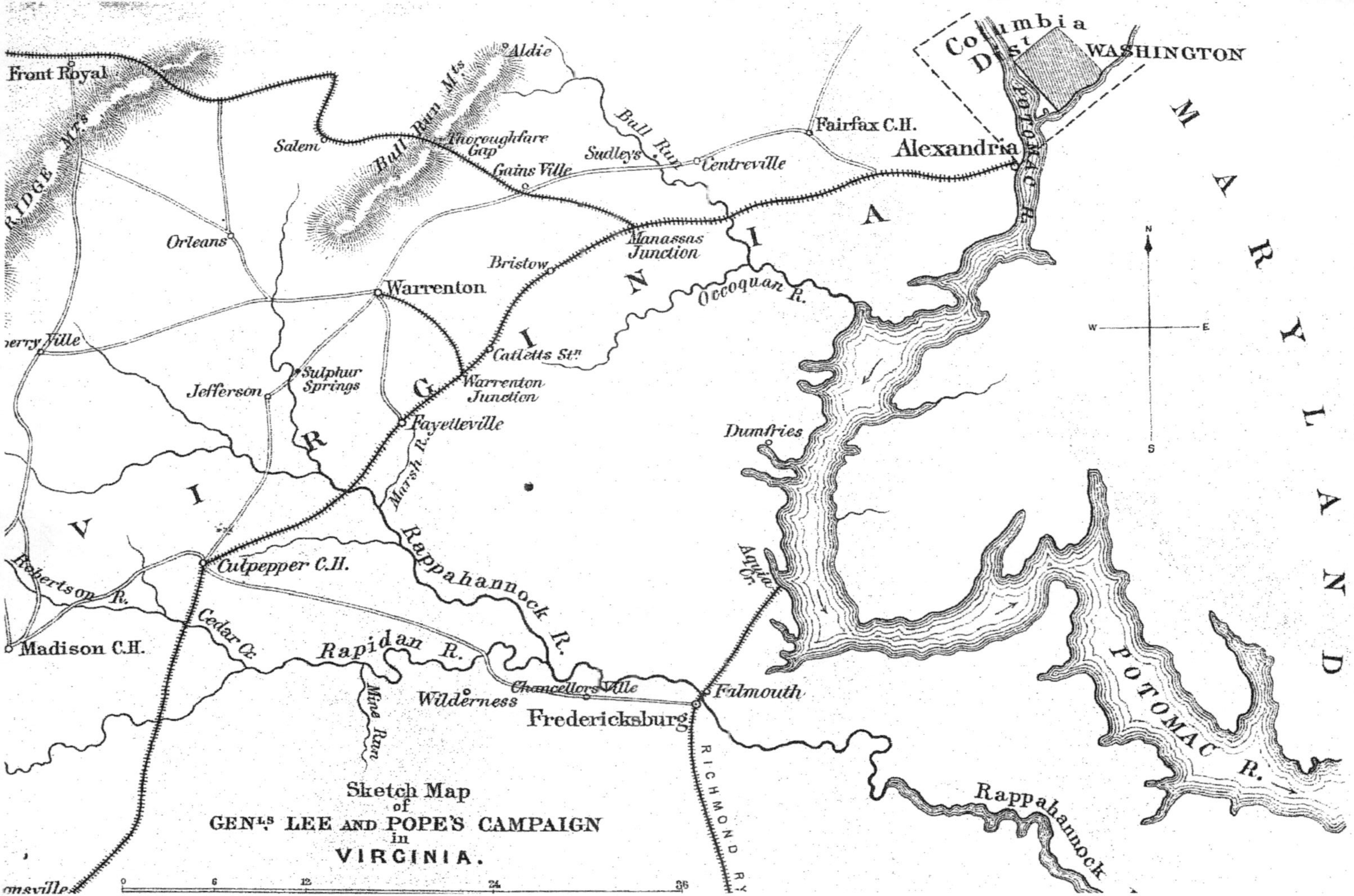

Sketch Map of GEN^LS LEE AND POPE'S CAMPAIGN in VIRGINIA.

in regard to the army occupying the valley of Bull Run. This country is also intersected by the rail, which, running from Manassas Junction to the Shenandoah Valley, had played so considerable a part in the battle of Bull Run, but had since been so much injured as to be nearly worthless except as a road. The principal natural features to be borne in mind, in considering the campaign of General Pope, are the three streams of Bull Run, the Rappahannock, and the Rapidan, the Blue Ridge Mountains, and the Bull Run Mountains; whilst the artificial features are the rail and road from Alexandria to Gordonsville, and the rail from Gordonsville to Richmond, the several stations on the former being the scenes of many of the subsequent engagements.

By looking at any map which embraces the whole theatre of the war in Virginia, it will be easily perceived that the Confederates had the advantage of acting on interior lines with respect to the armies of General Pope and General M'Clellan; and, having once determined on which army to bring the bulk of their forces, by using the rail to Gordonsville, they were able to forestall their opponents, who were forced to make a long detour by land and water from the James River to the Rappahannock. When General M'Clellan was ordered to retreat from Harrison's Landing, it was felt to be doubtful whether General Lee would follow and harass the retreating army, or whether he would bring the main body of his forces against General Pope, and during the uncertainty as to the course his adversary would pursue, Pope remained on the Rapidan, anxiously awaiting reinforcements, until the 14th of August, when he was joined by Reno's division of General Burnside's army, numbering according to his estimate 8,000 men. He now occupied the line of the Rapidan, from Robertson's River on the right, where Sigel's corps was posted, by Cedar Mountain, where M'Dowell was, to Racoonford, held by General Reno, whose duty it was to cover the road to and keep open communication with Fredericksburg.

A few days after the arrival of Reno, Pope received intelligence, which was further confirmed by a letter taken from a Confederate courier, that General Lee was rapidly transporting his army to Gordonsville, and was preparing to attack him. Feeling that he was not sufficiently strong to resist the whole army of Richmond, exaggerated by rumour to far more than their real numbers, and being desirous of effecting a junction with the reinforcements which were rapidly arriving from the army of the Potomac, Pope decided on retreating to the Rappahannock. Then were found the ill effects to his own army of his previous order,* which virtually had almost sanctioned plundering and depredation. The troops had become demoralised, the country on the line of march had been devastated, and the country people embittered to the highest degree against the army at whose hands they had received such injuries. General Pope was forced for the well-being of his own forces to explain more fully his former order, and to take measures to prevent depredations on the property of the inhabitants. On the 18th of August, having previously sent his waggon trains to

* Referring to the orders of July 18—'General order, No. 5. Hereafter, as far as practicable, the troops of this command will subsist on the country in which their operations are carried on, &c., &c.' This order, and others which related to the treatment of the inhabitants, resulted in plundering, although such was not the probable intention of General Pope.

the rear, Pope ordered a retreat to the Rappahannock by *echellon* of corps from the left, General Banks still continuing to form a reserve. This was accomplished on the night of the 18th of August, and on the 19th his army held the line of the Rappahannock from Sulphur Springs to the Marsh River, still keeping open communication with Fredericksburg. On the 21st he was joined by the division of Reynolds, and that of Kearney * from the army of the Potomac.

General Lee, who had arrived with the bulk of the army of Richmond, followed him as far as the Rappahannock, where during the 20th, 21st, and 22nd he made feints of attempting to force a passage with Longstreet's corps, in order to cover a flank march of Jackson's corps round the Federal right wing. That corps was concentrated at Jefferson, and taking advantage of the hilly and wooded country forming the spurs of the Blue Ridge Mountains, and availing itself of bye roads well known to many of the officers and men, and willingly indicated by the Virginian farmers, it commenced on Monday the 25th of August its flank march to Thoroughfare Gap. In the meantime a small force of Confederate cavalry under Stuart, imitating their former exploit on the Chickahominy, passed round the right of Pope's army, and on the night of the 22nd suddenly galloped into Catlett's Station, where were concentrated the greater portion of the head-quarters baggage, together with the spare horses belonging to General Pope and his staff. The baggage guard, completely surprised at this unexpected appearance of the

* General Pope estimates these reinforcements at only 7,000 men. The number is probably rather under than over stated, as the report was written after his defeat.

enemy,* made little or no resistance, and the greater number of the waggons were burnt. Many of Pope's plans and letters were captured, and among other things *his uniform* coat, which was exhibited in Richmond as a trophy of the raid.† Great was the excitement at Washington at this unexpected appearance of the enemy in rear of the army, and between it and the city. Notwithstanding the newspapers spoke confidently of the result of the campaign, and, together with General Pope's despatches, tended to keep up expectations of final victory in the minds of the populace. It was known that the greater portion of M'Clellan's army had joined Pope, that the remainder would soon be pushed up to the front, and it was concluded that the united armies of the Potomac and Virginia would more than counterbalance any number of troops which Lee could bring from Richmond. In fact, the junction of the armies had by this time been nearly completed. The left of the Federal army, occupying Fredericksburg, was commanded by Burnside; Heintzelman and Porter had marched to the front, and Franklin and Sumner would soon be in readiness to follow them.

Large, however, as the army was, and better provided with war material than their opponents, whom the Federal journals represented as half-starved and worse equipped, there were yet elements in its composition which militated against its efficiency. General Pope was unknown to the eastern armies, and he does not appear to have been a man who either possessed

* It was said that their rifles, in place of being in their hands, were on the baggage waggons.

† A label was attached to the coat with this inscription:—'Taken from the man who said he never expected to see anything but the backs of the rebels.'

the respect or gained the cordial co-operation of his subordinates, even of those in the army of Virginia;* whilst by his open criticisms on General M'Clellan, and by his evident desire to supplant him in the chief command, he offended many of the generals of the army of the Potomac,† and failed to inspire the men with the personal confidence and affection they felt for their former commander. The army of the Potomac thought also that it had been slighted by the President, and that no commendation had been bestowed on it for the many hard battles and wearisome marches of the peninsular campaign.‡ In addition to these elements of weakness, the very abundance of the supplies tended to the tardy movements of the divisions; the long lines of waggons blocked up the roads, and impeded the celerity of the march; and the men, accustomed to competence both in matters of food and also in respect of ammunition and stores, were not, when deprived of these accessories, fit to compete with the less well-equipped but more self-reliant soldiers of General Lee. Has not this frequently been the case, and has not history more than once recorded that the most completely furnished troops have been defeated by men possessed of little except the arms they carried? The earlier wars of the French Revolution afford parallel examples, and the troops who fought the first campaign of Italy under General Bonaparte, both in the want of what may be termed the *luxe* of war, and also in the success which attended them in the field, may be compared to those who contended, under Lee,

* See General Pope's official despatch, containing frequent complaints of the mistakes and want of co-operation of his subordinates.

† See the court-martial on General Porter.

‡ General M'Clellan's letter to the President, August 18, 1862.

Jackson, and Longstreet, in the campaigns of Virginia. But such men must be roused to exertion by more than ordinary impulses, and to the motives which actuate them must be added confidence in the chiefs who command them. The spirit of the man must triumph over the hardships and sufferings of the body.

Such was the case with the veterans who, under Stonewall Jackson, were marching through the woods and thickets of the Blue Ridge Mountains. Badly clothed and badly shod, they did not lag on the line of march; ill-fed, subsisting on the grain they plucked, and on the scanty food willingly furnished by the scattered population, which watched them with surprise as they passed the farmhouses of a district as yet untouched by the war, they hastened on, buoyed up by the sanctity of their cause, and in full confidence in the general who commanded them. They expected to replenish their haversacks and their ammunition pouches from the stores of the enemy; and, ignorant of the object of their march, they yet knew that it led them nearer to the foe. In these expectations they were not disappointed.

Whilst Pope was watching Longstreet's corps on the Rappahannock, and making plans of attack, which either the rise of the stream or the want of intelligence of the movements of his opponents prevented him from executing,* Jackson was marching through Orleans and Salem; and on the 26th of August debouched through Thoroughfare Gap, directly in the rear of the Federal army. Although ignorant of the exact movements of his adversary, Pope had acquired sufficient information to make him aware that his right flank had been turned,

* See General Pope's official report.

and that he must either give up his base of communications at Fredericksburg or at Alexandria. He determined on the former, and resolved to retreat towards Warrenton, and to yield the line of the Rappahannock.

On the 25th, the army, which may be divided into three columns, was marching respectively on the following points:—M'Dowell and Sigel were directed on Warrenton, with Banks at Fayetteville in support, forming the left wing, supposing the army to be facing westwards; Reno and Porter were advancing by cross roads towards the high-road between Warrenton and Alexandria; and Heintzelman was in the vicinity of Warrenton Junction. But the several divisions of the army had been marched separately to the front; many of them were not under their respective generals of corps; and their position, means of transport, and numerical strength were not understood by the general commanding-in-chief; consequently, there was a want of unity in their movements; and the better handled, although far less numerous, army of General Lee was enabled to inflict defeat on them in detail.

General Pope states, in his report, that the troops from Alexandria, including the cavalry, were according to his intention to have watched Thoroughfare Gap, and to have prevented any advance of the enemy on his line of communication; but it does not appear that he had any grounds for such a conclusion, and it is probable that he was unaware of the bold scheme of his opponent. The army of the Potomac had been pushed to the front as soon as it had arrived, and the newly raised regiments which were gradually arriving at Alexandria were so completely without organisation as to be quite unfitted for a campaign. Of cavalry there was little or none;

that belonging to Pope's own army had been completely worn out in picket duty, and the force at Alexandria consisted of little else than the small escort which M'Clellan had brought with him from the Peninsula. For these reasons Jackson met with no opposition in his passage through the defile of Thoroughfare Gap, and on the evening of the 26th August he cut the line of rail directly in Pope's rear at Bristow Station.

Great was the astonishment and delight of the inhabitants of the villages as they recognised the Confederate troops; greater still was the amazement of the Federals when a detachment of cavalry of Stuart's force, on the evening of the 26th, stopped the train and burnt the waggons at Bristow Station. Even then, however, the reality of the presence of any large body of the enemy was not recognised; and on the following day, when the great depôt at Manassas Junction was captured, the newspapers of the North spoke of the misfortune as the result of a bold and desperate raid unparalleled in the history of any war; but assured their readers *that it was a raid, and nothing else, from the fact that it would have been impossible for any considerable force to have got in rear of General Pope's army*. The Federal generals were not better informed. The commanders of corps and divisions were unaware from what direction to expect an attack; they were ignorant of the position of headquarters, were embarrassed by a variety of contradictory orders, and, with men dispirited by retreat and disheartened by hardship and the want of supplies, marched and countermarched the troops under their command, and by want of organisation neutralised the advantage of their superior forces.*

* See General Sigel's report; also General Porter's courtmartial.

On the evening of the 27th, Hooker's division engaged that of Ewell, forming Jackson's rear-guard, at Bristow Station; and as the latter followed the main body of the corps on the night of the 28th to Manassas and Centreville, Hooker claimed a success. The Confederate general thought otherwise, and whilst Pope was hastening the movements of M'Dowell on Gainesville and Porter on Bristow, General Jackson with the divisions of A. P. Hill and Taliaferro, fell upon the immense depôt of stores at Manassas Junction. These were guarded by a brigade under General Tyler,* who, *it is said*,† at first supposed the advancing force to be a small body of the enemy cut off from the main army, and summoned it to surrender. If such was the case, soon was he undeceived; the divisions moved rapidly on to the attack, Manassas Junction was captured, a great portion of its defenders taken prisoners, and the remainder driven across Bull Run and through Centreville, which was also occupied by the Confederates.

The immense accumulation of army stores and sutlers' depôts fell into the hands of the hungry and ill-provided Confederate soldiers. They had no means to convey away the plunder, but each man seized on what he could find, and those who had for weeks been living on parched corn regaled themselves on all the luxuries accumulated for the Federal troops.‡ At night what was not consumed was burnt, and by the light of the

* Of Slocum's division of Franklin's corps.

† See an account by a combatant. *Rebellion Record*, vol. v. p. 402, Documents.

‡ An eye-witness wrote thus:—'To see a starving man eating lobster-salad and drinking Rhine wine, barefooted and in tatters, was curious; the whole thing was incredible.'

vast conflagration the Confederate divisions marched from Manassas Junction, that under General Taliaferro* to the old battle-ground of Bull Run, the other two to Centreville. Not only had vast stores been destroyed, but the line of rail and telegraph had been cut, so that neither could reinforcements be sent to Pope, nor could any news from the army reach Halleck at Washington, or M'Clellan, who commanded at Alexandria.

Notwithstanding these successes, the position of General Jackson was very critical; he was between the fortified lines of Alexandria and a superior force under General Pope in person, who was marching by the Orange and Alexandria Railroad; whilst another large force, under M'Dowell, was moving from Warrenton, with the intention of cutting him off from Thoroughfare Gap, and thus separating him from the other portion of General Lee's army, which, following in his footsteps, were still in the defiles of the Blue Ridge Mountains.

So far Jackson's position was one of great danger, but the want of unity in the Federal army stood him in good stead. Sigel's corps, which with that of M'Dowell formed the left wing of the army, was so harassed by attempts to obey contradictory orders during the night of the 27th and the greater portion of the 28th, that it was of little use in even endeavouring to cut off General Jackson from Thoroughfare Gap; the services of M'Dowell's own corps were in like manner neutralised; and out of the whole great army under General Pope, Kearney, commanding a division, was the only general who at all pressed Jackson on the 28th. He, after a skirmish with the rear-guard, occupied Centreville, and re-opened the communication with Alexandria.

* The old Stonewall division.

General Jackson in the meantime crossed Bull Run with the two divisions of Ewell and A. P. Hill, and effected a junction with Taliaferro on the right bank. He drew up his army on the 29th in a diagonal direction, his left resting on a ridge of hills near Sudley Springs, which he had gained after an engagement of two hours on the previous evening with a portion of Sigel's corps, his right stretching along the Manassas Gap Railroad towards the main road from Warrenton. General Pope, who hoped that he should be able to crush him before the arrival of Longstreet's corps, ordered an advance on the morning of the 29th. Sigel's corps was the first engaged, but was defeated in every attempt to drive the enemy from his strong position, who in turn threatened to overwhelm him. Reynolds came up about twelve o'clock, and took up a position on his left; Reno formed a reserve; and the two divisions of Heintzelman's corps, under Kearney and Hooker, likewise came into line on his right. General Pope, in person, arrived on the field about the middle of the day, but hesitated to direct a determined attack with forces which had already been severely handled. He awaited M'Dowell and Porter, and precious time was lost, for on that day the head of Longstreet's corps debouched through Thoroughfare Gap; the leading division had been retarded in its march by the force detached to defend the pass, but towards sunset came into line, and Jackson knew that the crisis of the battle was over. General M'Dowell brought up his corps late in the day, but that of Porter was not engaged, whether owing to miscarriage of orders or other causes.*

* General Porter was tried for disobedience of orders, and dismissed the service; but so great appears to have been the confusion with regard to the issue of orders by General Pope, that possibly there might have been some excuse for his conduct.

Such was the battle of Friday, fought between Sudley Springs and Thoroughfare Gap. The Confederates acted on the defensive, and, although far inferior in numbers to their opponents, yet had the advantage of a strong position, selected by a general who well-knew how to avail himself of the advantages of ground. They, under well-tried leaders and commanded by such men as Jackson, acted in concert, and beat back in succession the several divisions which came forward separately to the attack. General Pope estimated his loss at 8,000, but claimed a victory, telegraphing the same to Washington by the line which had been repaired on that morning. Even in the North men doubted the correctness of his despatch, and the events of the succeeding days served to increase the panic which his retreat had already given rise to in Washington. During the night of the 29th and morning of the 30th the whole of the Confederate army became united, and on the 30th prepared for a renewal of the engagement on the scene of the first great battle of the war.

The line of battle stretched for a distance of about five miles from Sudley Springs on the left to the Warrenton Road, and thence in an oblique direction towards the south-west; it formed an oblique angle, of which the apex faced westwards. The left wing was under Jackson, the right under Longstreet, who during the previous night, and early morning of the 30th, had brought his division through Thoroughfare Gap. A great portion of the artillery was placed in position on some commanding ground between the two wings.

Both armies had suffered severely in the previous actions. The Federals, however, were nearer their supplies, and anticipated fresh reinforcements; the Confederates were, on the other hand, at a great distance from their base of operations, but had the prestige of success, and the knowledge that, to replenish both their ammunition and commissariat waggons, victory was a necessity.

As the Confederate right was thrown forward, so was the left of the Federals drawn back. Porter's corps formed the left of the line; in the centre was Heintzelman, and on his right Reno; whilst King's division of M'Dowell's corps, together with the corps of General Sigel, supported the left and centre; and Ricketts, of M'Dowell's corps, supported the right. Banks' corps was still at Bristow Station, guarding the railway.

Porter's corps commenced the action by an attempt to clear the enemy out of the woods in his front, but was driven back with considerable loss; and as it was thought that the enemy, pressing his advantage, threatened to turn the Federal left, Ricketts' division was marched to the point of danger. For a considerable time the action was fought principally with artillery. Then followed an advance in three lines of the Federal infantry, which was repulsed with great loss by the concentrated fire of some batteries of artillery posted on a commanding position. It was now evening, and General Lee perceiving that there was confusion in the enemy's lines, ordered an advance. Jackson on the left, and Longstreet on the right, pushed forward, and Beverley Robinson advanced with his brigade of cavalry. The Federals were driven back in confusion over the old battle-ground of Bull Run; a large number of prisoners were captured on the field,* and the remains of the army, during the night of the 30th, crossed Bull Run

* General Lee is stated to have parolled 7,000 on the field of battle.

stream, and took refuge behind the field-works at Centreville, where Sumner and Franklin's corps, which had arrived from Alexandria and the lines round Washington, were drawn up.

These reinforcements, according to Pope's account, only made up for the losses of the previous day. Not only had the Federals suffered in killed, wounded, and prisoners, but vast crowds of stragglers and fugitives had fled to the rear, seeking shelter in the lines round Alexandria.* The march of Franklin's corps to the front had been greatly retarded by the mass of fugitives. He had done what lay in his power to rally them, and on the road from Centreville to Alexandria had collected from six to seven thousand.† On the morning of the 31st, the whole Federal army was collected behind the entrenchments at Centreville. Banks, after destroying vast quantities of stores and railway stock, crossed Bull Run during the night, and the beaten army contented itself, on the 31st, with occupying the field-works at Centreville and guarding its right in the direction of Cub Run. General Lee, with an army fewer in numbers, and harassed by the long marches and severe fighting of the previous weeks, was unwilling to attempt a direct attack on an enemy newly reinforced and occupying so strong a position. His soldiers needed rest, and in regard to ammunition, clothing, and stores were glad to avail themselves of the captured spoils.‡

* General Pope, in his official report, used these words:—'At least one-half of this great diminution of our forces was occasioned by skulking and straggling from the army.'

† See General Franklin's evidence before the Court of Inquiry.

‡ It has been alleged as a reproach to the Confederates that they plundered the dead of their clothing; but, when men want boots and clothes, surely it is better to rob the dead than to stint the living.

But, if General Lee was unwilling to attack the enemy in front, he accomplished his purpose no less effectually by operating against his flank. On the morning of the 1st September, General D. Hill brought his corps on the right flank of the Federal army, threatening Fairfax Court-house and the direct road to Washington; and Pope, unable to give battle on account of the demoralisation of his troops, was forced to make dispositions for retreat, his right flank covered by Heintzelman's corps. Towards evening the retreat commenced. D. Hill, in the midst of a severe storm of thunder and lightning, made a vigorous assault on the Federal right.* Kearney and Stevens exerted themselves to rally the men, and whilst doing so fell mortally wounded. The main body of the army hurried on, and night closing in, and the rear-guard fighting with determination, protected it from greater misfortune. So closed the 1st day of September. On the 2nd, the Federal army was still outside the lines of fortification, but it was apparent to every general that the succession of defeats had so demoralised the troops that the risk of again meeting the enemy in the open would be too great. If defeat should occur, the victorious troops would possibly enter the lines with the defeated, and Washington would fall. Therefore, on the morning of the 2nd of September, the combined armies of the Potomac and of Virginia re-entered the lines of fortification around Washington. At Upton Hill they were met by M'Clellan, who in an order of the previous day had been appointed to the command of the army for the defence of Washington. The general who had commanded the army of the Potomac, who

* Or left, supposing the army in retreat to Washington.

had measured his strength with the great leader of the Confederates, who had lost prestige and sustained defeat on the banks of the Chickahominy, who had been deprived of his army and put aside whilst a more presumptuous but far less able man occupied his place, was now reinvested with command, and sought for as the last resource of a government driven to desperation, not to lead the armies to conquest, but to protect the very capital of the nation.

The new man, the great hero of the West, had been found wanting. Opposed to a master of the art of war, he had, in defiance of the caution of his predecessor, attempted a campaign on principles which only success could justify. In this he had been worsted, by an enemy far inferior in numbers, but rich in qualities which conduce to efficiency.

First among the advantages possessed by the Confederates must be numbered the presence of such a man as General Lee to command the armies. It is indeed but seldom that so many noble qualities are found united in the same person. He evinced talents both for organising and moving armies; he excelled in council and in the field. Irreproachable in character, a deeply religious man, even his enemies could not attribute motives to his conduct other than those which actuate good men, whilst among his companions in arms he was not only respected and obeyed, but deeply beloved. Jealousy against such a man as Lee could find no place among the other leaders of the war. Jackson and Longstreet, his two most able lieutenants, supported him, not only as generals under his command, but as men actuated towards himself by the deepest admiration and warmest personal friendship. Like all truly great men who have risen to successful pre-eminence, General Lee had the faculty of imbuing his subordinates with his own spirit, and, as the limbs of a body are governed by the head, so were the leaders who directed the movements of the several parts of the army in complete accord with the general commanding-in-chief.

If the Confederate army was fortunate in possessing a head like General Lee, so was General Lee especially happy in the men who acted under him. The campaign of the Shenandoah Valley in the previous March, followed by the attack on the Federal right on the Chickahominy, sufficiently established General Jackson's fame; but the climax of his glory was reached when, by the bold and almost unprecedented flank march round Pope's army, he cut it off from its supplies, and not only compelled a retreat, but so completely confused its commander as to render the retreat disorderly, and to neutralise the benefits of the reinforcements which were continually arriving.

If to Jackson the more brilliant strategy is to be attributed, yet the able manner in which General Lee's plans were carried into execution by Longstreet must not be forgotten in the history of the campaign. The personal friendship between these two men, and the mutual confidence of each in the other, sufficiently testify to the noble qualities of both.

The army was also greatly indebted to the young cavalry general who knew how to utilise the bold riders of the South, and to employ them in services for which they were peculiarly fitted, directing their energies to the efficient performance of picket duty, and to dashing raids on the enemy's lines of communication. General Stuart had succeeded to the reputation of Turner Ashby as the best cavalry general in Virginia, and both in chivalrous character and in daring exploits emulated the renown of those cavaliers from whom it is the boast of the Virginian gentleman to have descended. Led by such men, the Confederate army had carried the war from the gates of Richmond to those of Washington.

Would the North at length be taught to feel on her own soil the presence of the enemy? Such was the hope of the people of the South; they knew that their army was few in numbers, but the triumphs of the past week led them to anticipate continued success, and even to look forward to peace dictated in the enemy's country. At this dark hour for the North, when General Pope was returning to Washington, having failed not only to secure victory, but even to acquire the respect of his troops, to whom could the Government turn for aid? Mr. Lincoln knew that the only hope of reconstructing an army out of the disorganised force defiling into Washington was again to place M'Clellan in chief command. He knew that men would work for him when they would work for no one else, and that, although defeated, he still retained a hold over the affections of the army who had fought under him on the Peninsula.

During the retreat of the Federal army, M'Clellan had been retained at Alexandria, and it had been one of General Pope's grounds of complaint that reinforcements had not been sent forward with sufficient rapidity; but although shorn of authority, and acting oftentimes without distinct orders, M'Clellan had done what lay in his power to push forward the several corps as they arrived from the Peninsula. That of General Franklin was delayed for want of artillery horses and transports as—considering the position of the Federal army, cut off by General Jackson from Alexandria—it was thought inadvisable to push forward infantry without a proper force of artillery, or to send waggon trains without escort. Sumner's corps was likewise hindered from marching to the front, by the fear lest the enemy, having turned the right of Pope's army, should force the passage of the Potomac, and attack Washington on the side of the Chain Bridge. General M'Clellan was in a position of no ordinary difficulty, and attended with no common amount of trial. He, the general of the army of the Potomac, was virtually deprived of his command; his troops were taken from him; he was invested with little real authority, being under the orders of General Halleck; yet he was often required to act on his own responsibility; and when defeat and its attendant terror and anxiety had awakened the President and his advisers to a sense of their danger, he was begged informally to resume command, and to succour, at their utmost need, the men who were only too anxious to supplant and supersede him. That he was a man actuated by motives of patriotism, and not influenced by selfish considerations, is apparent from the readiness with which he came to the rescue of his country, and his abstaining from any stipulation with regard to his own personal position.

Great was the consternation in the North when the true results of Pope's campaign became known. Many had believed his despatch claiming victory on the 29th, and, of those who had doubted its accuracy, few were prepared to hear of the retreat and total demoralisation of the army on the three subsequent days. In order to raise a sufficient force for the further prosecution of the war, the President had issued a call for an additional 300,000 men, and it became apparent that there would be great difficulty in raising the required number. Measures were taken by the wealthy in the several large cities to procure volunteers, by the offer of high bounties, so as to avoid the necessity of a conscription. Whilst, therefore, the crowd of demoralised fugitives were pouring into Washington, whilst the bridges over the Potomac were blocked with long lines of ambulances, whilst the streets and squares of the city were rendered hideous by the sight of the halt and lame and still untended sufferers from the recent battles, New York was streaming with flags, was gay with bands, and eagerly enthusiastic to welcome the men who offered themselves to fill up the quota of troops demanded to replace the victims of the last campaign. Not only was every inducement held out to enlistment, but severe measures were adopted to check expressions of discouragement. A strict censorship was placed over the press, and many men for apparently slight causes were incarcerated in Fort Lafayette and other prisons.

The people meanwhile cried out for a victim on whom to vent their anger for the late misfortunes. Most unjustly General M'Dowell was selected, and an outcry raised against him as the traitor at whose door many of the defeats were to be laid. To their credit be it said, that neither Mr. Lincoln or his advisers would yield to this outcry. General M'Dowell was sent away on furlough, and General Pope removed to Minnesota to wage war against the Indians; but no blood was shed; and, in this respect, not only in the present instance but in many others, have both the Northern and Southern Governments and people afforded a pleasing contrast to the violence and cruelty of European nations in times of revolution and public misfortune.

Amidst all the pomp of war, the excitement of victory, and the confusion of defeat, followed by fresh efforts to create armies, the victims of the many days' battles remained for the most part uncared for. Thickly were the dead and wounded strewed over the field of Bull Run, and for some time little or no means were taken to relieve them. The Confederates were unable to furnish either medical comforts or attendants for their own men, and such was the confusion among the authorities at Washington, that even the materials at their disposal were not utilized. Great quantities of stores were willingly and quickly sent from the several Northern cities, and many surgeons volunteered to proceed to the scene of the recent battles, but little good was effected for some time, and many valuable lives were lost which might have been saved if proper care had been bestowed on them. In every way were the resources of the North taxed to the utmost, for not only in Virginia had the tide of victory turned against her, but in the West likewise her armies had been driven back, and the successes of the previous spring counterbalanced by reverses which threatened to snatch from her the fruits of the campaigns of Kentucky and Tennessee.

For a short period following the entrance of Pope's army into Washington there was a pause in active operations. Lee was not sufficiently strong to attempt the siege of the long lines of entrenchments, which every day became more numerously garrisoned by recruits pouring in from the North; and although the Southern people, through the organs of the Richmond press, cried out for a change in the scene of operations and an invasion of the enemy's country, it was yet doubtful whether such a course could be pursued, and, supposing it should be decided on, to what point the advance of the Confederate army should be directed. The river below Washington was guarded by gunboats, whilst an invasion of Maryland or Pennsylvania involved the risk of a movement in the presence of a superior army strongly entrenched on the flank. It could only be alleged in favour of such a proposal, that bold operations will oftentimes succeed when the right moment is seized, and that possibly the population of Maryland would be induced by the presence of the Confederate army openly to declare itself in favour of the South.

Such a march required some days for preparation, and whilst General Lee was collecting the necessary stores for a new campaign, General M'Clellan was as diligently engaged in reorganising his army. Several changes were made in the commanders of corps and divisions, and care was taken to intermingle the new regiments with those who had acquired the experience, if not the prestige, of more than one hard fought campaign.

CHAPTER VII.

CAMPAIGN IN MARYLAND.

FOR some few days after the entry into Washington of General Pope's army, a variety of rumours purporting to indicate the destination of the Confederates were circulated through the city. The numbers under General Lee's command were very much exaggerated; and so greatly had he and his subordinates, especially General Jackson, risen in the opinion of their enemies, that no project was thought too extravagant, or enterprise too daring, for the adoption of such successful generals. Lee knew better his position, and the means at his disposal and at that of his Government; but even he, who hitherto had acted almost entirely on the defensive, having been driven in the last campaign to adopt offensive movements only as a means of protecting Richmond, was tempted to carry the war across the Potomac, and to endeavour to prove how far the reported enthusiasm of the Marylanders would urge them to rise in his favour and recruit his army, almost cut off as it then would be from communication with Richmond. Doubtless there would be some risk attending this movement. The strongly fortified city of Washington would be in close proximity to the right rear of the invading force, and almost between it and its base of operations. That city was garrisoned by an army already far larger than the force which Lee could bring into the field, and one which was receiving daily reinforcements from the populous States of the North. The portion of Maryland most favourable to the South lay between the Potomac and the Chesapeake, and would therefore be removed from the immediate theatre of operations; whilst, by the movement across the Potomac, Lee's own army would be threatened by the garrisons of Washington and Baltimore on its right, and the thickly-populated State of Pennsylvania, strongly Union in its sentiments, on its left. Such were the dangers and difficulties of an advance into Maryland.

On the other hand, it could be alleged in favour of the plan, that the main army of the North was completely demoralised; that it was commanded by generals who did not possess the confidence of their men, and who had shown little military capacity; that after such a succession of victories the Confederate troops and people would be greatly disappointed and disheartened if the army should retreat to Richmond without accomplishing anything beyond the repulse of the enemy; that the siege of Washington could not be attempted with any prospect of success; and that, owing to the devastation of the country in its immediate vicinity, the army could not long remain in the position it at present occupied. It might also be urged, that so much had been said of the enthusiasm of the Marylanders for the South, and their hatred of the tyranny of the North, that now was the time to try whether that enthusiasm would be shown in deeds, as well as in words and patriotic songs; whilst, should the army be joined by large reinforcements from that State, the invasion of Pennsylvania might be attempted, and peace obtained more speedily by thus bringing home to the people of the North the evils and misery of war than by acting entirely on the defensive, and trusting to her exhaustion by the successive repulse of her invading armies.

The time seemed favourable for converting a defensive into an offensive war. The West was not in a position to send reinforcements, trembling as she was lest the great city of Ohio should fall, and the Eastern States were thus left entirely to their own resources to fight their own battles. Influenced by these considerations, President Davis sanctioned an advance into Maryland, and General Lee, almost within sight of his own house on Arlington Heights, turned his horse's head northwards, and marched towards the fords* of the Potomac. One thing he does not appear to have sufficiently calculated, and that is the influence which the change of commanders would exercise on the troops. M'Clellan's name seems to have possessed at that time a peculiar power in raising the confidence of those under his command, whilst his talents were especially adapted for the organisation of an army. In a few days the army of Virginia regained in a great measure its *morale*, and afforded an additional proof how quickly American soldiers recover from the most disastrous defeats. Stringent orders respecting the sale of spirits were issued, strong provost-guards were organised, and every means taken to reform the army under its several brigade, division, and corps commanders. General M'Clellan was for some short time ignorant of the plans of his opponent; the Government still trembled for the safety of Washington; and, until the 6th of September, the army remained in close vicinity to the lines of fortification.

* Fordable in some places at this time of year.

In the meantime Lee had crossed the Potomac; his army still continued to be divided into three commands —viz. the corps of General Jackson, consisting of the divisions of Generals A. P. Hill, Ewell, and his own division;* and that of General Longstreet, composed of the divisions of Generals M'Laws, Walker, Anderson, and Hood, and a division under General D. H. Hill, which usually acted independently of either of the generals commanding corps. The cavalry, under General Stuart, continued to cover the advance of the army, and was generally attached to the corps of Longstreet and D. Hill, a small number only acting with Jackson. The scene of operations selected was the country between Washington and the range of hills bearing the name of South Mountain, and forming a continuation of the chain of the Blue Ridge on the northern side of the Potomac.

On the 5th September the army crossed the fords of the Potomac, and on the 6th Jackson's corps entered Frederick City (Maryland), situated on the right bank of the Monocacy River, a tributary of the Potomac. The march was in some degree one of triumph. The soldiers of the Confederate army fully believed in the enthusiasm of the whole of Maryland for the South, and looked forward to a campaign in a rich and friendly country. The song most popular in the ranks was that in which Maryland invoked Southern aid to free her from Northern tyranny, whilst the presence in the army of many of her sons appeared to afford proof of the truth of her professions. It was therefore with much disappointment that the men perceived that the people of the State whom they first encountered were content

* Commanded successively by General Starke and General Jones.

to gaze with wonder on the ragged and poorly-equipped army, but showed little disposition to join its ranks. From contact with Pennsylvania they had imbibed many of the sentiments of their neighbours, and, accustomed as they had been to the well-clothed and well-fed Federal troops, they could scarcely believe that the men, so devoid of all the pomp of war, whom they saw defiling along the roads and through the streets of their villages, could be the army which had defeated in so many engagements the apparently splendid troops of the North. There was little in the appearance of Jackson's veterans to entice the recruit, uninfluenced by other motives than that of a vague idea of obtaining military glory, the service seemed to offer plenty of hardships and hard blows; but, stripped of the externals which he had hitherto associated with a soldier's life, there was little to induce him to leave his comfortable farm and to embark in a cause for which he had possibly no deeply-seated attachment. The case would probably have been different if the Confederate army had reached Eastern Maryland, or if Baltimore had been free from the pressure put on her by the guns of the forts and gunboats commanding her streets; but, from whatever cause it originated, the fact remained that Western Maryland afforded but slight assistance to the Southern cause, and little response to the proclamation issued by General Lee on his entry into Frederick. The divisions of Longstreet and that of D. Hill followed Jackson's corps across the Potomac, and the line of the Monocacy River was for a short time occupied by the Confederate forces.

Irrespective of the army in Washington, a garrison of about 9,000 Federals, under Colonel Miles, occupied a strong and entrenched position on heights overlooking Harper's Ferry, commanding the main road from the Shenandoah Valley to Frederick and Baltimore; this garrison was numerically too considerable to be passed unnoticed, even if the position, forming as it may be said to have done, a door of entry from Virginia to Maryland and Pennsylvania, could be disregarded.

Whilst, therefore, General Lee, with Longstreet's corps, continued his march into Maryland, Jackson received orders to advance up the left bank of the Potomac, and, crossing the river in the vicinity of Martingsburg, to occupy that place. This was accordingly done, and a large quantity of stores collected at Martingsburg fell into the hands of A. P. Hill, whilst the remaining two divisions seized on North Mountain Depôt, nearer to Harper's Ferry.* The Federal force garrisoning Martingsburg retreated to Harper's Ferry,† and General Jackson proceeded to invest the place on the western angle formed by the Shenandoah and Potomac Rivers, whilst detachments from Longstreet's command closed the approaches from Washington. On both sides of the Potomac squadrons of cavalry guarded the direct road to Pennsylvania.

Whilst these operations were in progress, it became known to General Lee that the Federal army, reorganised under M'Clellan, was marching from their lines with the intention of offering battle and of relieving Harper's Ferry. The numerical strength of the Confederate army was about seventy or seventy-five thousand men, whilst M'Clellan had under his command at least one hundred thousand men, irrespective of the garrisons

* See General Jackson's official despatch. *Second Year of the War*, by Pollard, page 128.

† This force had retreated from Winchester on September 3.

of Washington and Harper's Ferry, numbering over eighty thousand, exclusive of the sick and absent. Lee had therefore the difficult task before him of conducting a siege against a force posted in a strongly entrenched position, and of concentrating his army to meet the attack of vastly superior forces marching to relieve the place.

To fulfil these two objects, he abandoned the line of the Monocacy River, and moving a portion of his force under Longstreet, with the supply train, to Boonesboro,' he directed D. Hill with his division to guard the passes through South Mountain, and to cover the siege of Harper's Ferry. To ensure a distinct understanding of this plan of operations, he sent written orders to D. Hill; and this document, detailing with exactitude the proposed movements of the several portions of the army, fell into the hands of General M'Clellan. It had been conveyed to D. Hill, who, after reading it, either through a feeling of impatience at its contents, or through carelessness, threw or let it fall on the ground, and, lying there forgotten, it was picked up by a soldier of the Federal army, and forwarded at once to M'Clellan, who thus became possessed of the exact detail of his adversary's plan of operations.* This knowledge enabled General M'Clellan to direct the movements of his army with certainty.

Since the crossing of the Confederates into Maryland he had been preparing to meet them in the field, with all his disposable force. He was obliged to leave a very strong garrison in Washington, far more than was necessary, in order to allay the fears of the President

* For this curious incident see General M'Clellan's report to Congress, page 353; and the article, in the *Quarterly* of April 1864, on America.

and his advisers, who were anxious lest General Lee, having by a feint of an advance into Maryland drawn the army from Washington, should turn round and capture the city by a *coup de main.* As, however, Lee's plans developed themselves more fully, and it became evident that the garrison and stores at Harper's Ferry were in danger of being cut off from the main army, General M'Clellan received the sanction of the President to move to its relief. Leaving, therefore, Banks to command at Washington, with Heintzelman to superintend the defences around Alexandria, General M'Clellan, having divided his army into three columns, marched on the Monocacy River. The right column, under Burnside's command, and consisting of the 9th corps, under Reno, and the 1st (formerly M'Dowell's), under Hooker, was directed to march by the road leading from Washington to Brookville and Frederick City. The centre, under Sumner, comprising his own corps, the 2nd, and the 12th corps under Mansfield, by the direct road through Rockville and Middlebrook, also on Frederick City; and the left under Franklin, consisting of his own corps, the 6th, and Couch's division, was ordered to keep near the left bank of the Potomac, and march by Poolesville towards the Monocacy River.

In addition to this force, General Porter followed the main army, with a corps of 20,000 men, on the 12th of September. On the same day, the right column having crossed the Monocacy, occupied Frederick City, the remainder of the army being still on the left bank of the stream, near Urbana and Barnesville. M'Clellan was as yet uncertain of his adversary's movements, and kept his army well in hand, so as to be able to concentrate it quickly for the purpose of delivering battle at the same time that he covered the approaches to Wash-

CAMPAIGN OF ANTIETAM.

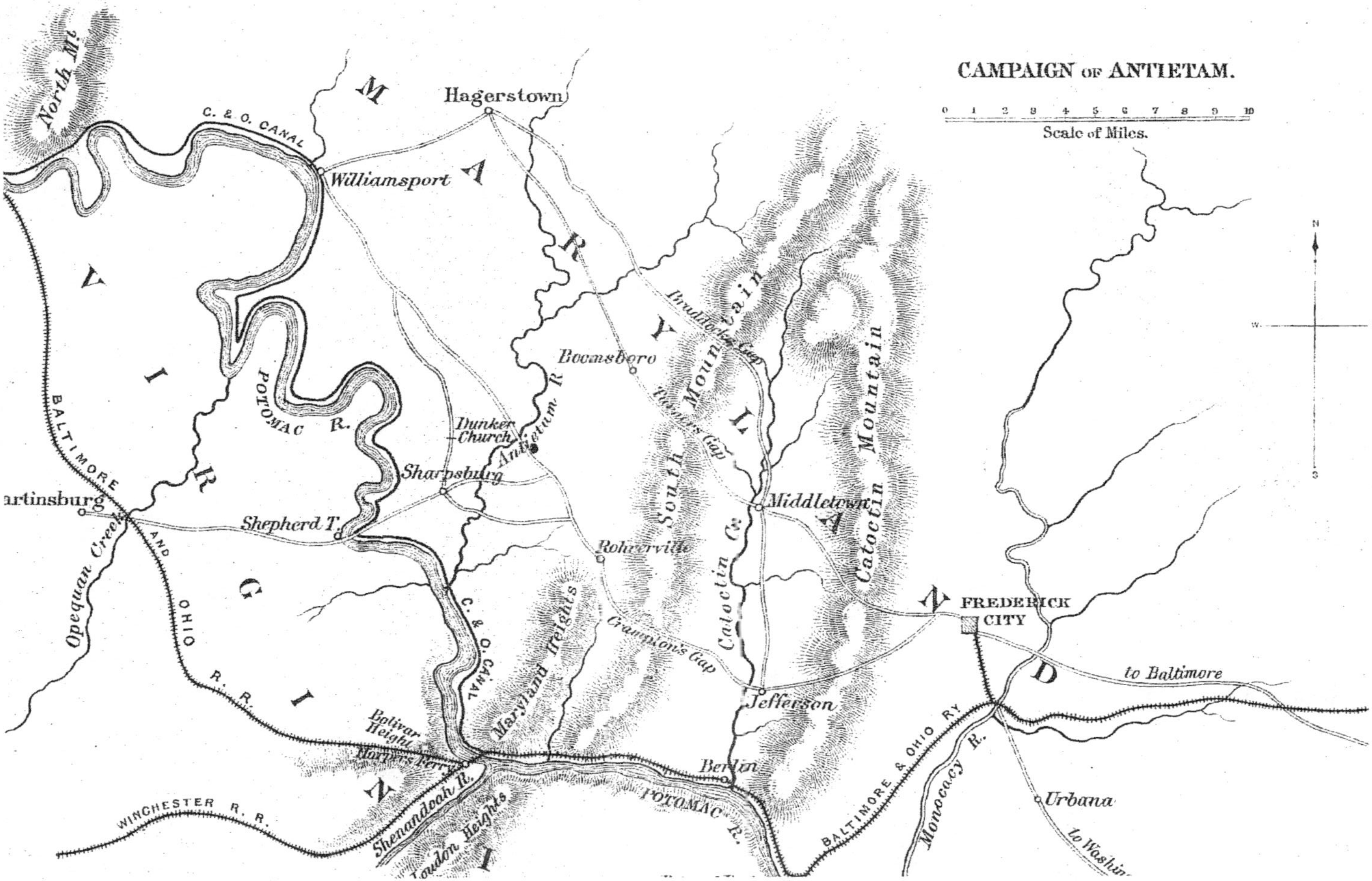

ington or Baltimore. On the 13th of September the above-mentioned order from General Lee fell into his hands, and he was thus fully possessed of the intentions of the enemy, and enabled to shape his movements accordingly.*

As the possession of Harper's Ferry appeared by this order to be the principal immediate aim of General

* A copy of this order is given in General M'Clellan's official report to Congress.

'Head-quarters, Army of Virginia, Sept. 9, 1862.
'Special Orders, No. 19.

'The army will resume its march tomorrow, taking the Hagerstown Road. General Jackson's command will form the advance, and after passing through Middletown, with such portion as he may select, will take the route towards Sharpsburg, cross the Potomac at the most convenient point, and by Friday night take possession of the Baltimore and Ohio Railroad, capture such of the enemy as may be at Martingsburg, and intercept such as may attempt to escape from Harper's Ferry. General Longstreet's command will pursue the same road as far as Boonsboro', where it will halt with the reserve, supply, and baggage trains, of the army. General M'Laws, with his own division and that of General R. H. Anderson, will follow General Longstreet. On reaching Middletown, he will take the route to Harper's Ferry, and by Friday morning possess himself of the Maryland Heights, and endeavour to capture the enemy at Harper's Ferry and vicinity. General Walker, with his division, after accomplishing the object in which he is now engaged, will cross the Potomac at Cheek's Ford, ascend its right bank to Lovettsville, take possession of Loudon Heights if practicable, and co-operate with General M'Laws and General Jackson in intercepting the retreat of the enemy. General D. H. Hill's division will form the rear-guard of the army, pursuing the road taken by the main body. The reserve artillery, ordnance, and supply trains, &c., will precede General Hill. General Stuart will detach a squadron of cavalry to accompany the commands of General Longstreet, Jackson, and M'Laws, and with the main body of the cavalry will cover the route of the army, and bring up all stragglers that may have been left behind. The commands of General Jackson, M'Laws, and Walker, after accomplishing the objects for which they have been detached, will join the

Lee, no time was to be lost in endeavouring to succour Colonel Miles and its defenders; and as the main body of the Federal army was within one day's march of the place, there seemed every prospect of relief reaching them. By an accident General M'Clellan had been made aware of the exact disposition of the several divisions of the army opposed to him, and although he probably over-estimated their strength, yet he must have known that, on the direct road to Harper's Ferry, he would be able to bring superior forces to bear on the covering army occupying the passes through South Mountain. Immediately, therefore, on the receipt of the intelligence furnished by Lee's intercepted order, he directed Franklin to force a passage through South Mountain at Crampton's Gap, whilst Burnside received directions to co-operate with him by an attack on Turner's Gap; and as the columns advanced, warning of the approach of relief was to be given to the garrison by the frequent discharge of artillery.

If M'Clellan appreciated the importance of time, his opponent was equally aware of its value; and the celerity of General Jackson's former movements in the Shenandoah Valley was equalled by the rapidity with which he effected the disposition of his troops for the purpose of speedily reducing the garrison of Harper's Ferry to the necessity of surrender. The intense interest of the campaign had now reached its climax, and the little corner of Maryland, so long remarkable for

main body of the army at Boonsboro' or Hagerstown. Each regiment on the march will habitually carry its axes in the regimental ordnance waggons, for use of the men at their encampments to procure wood, etc. By command of General R. E. Lee,

'R. H. CHILTON, A. A.-General.

'Major-General D. H. Hill, Comdg. Division.'

its picturesque beauties, had become the centre on which the attention of all, both in North and South, was concentrated. The excitement of the immediate presence of the enemy had for the first time become known in the Northern States. In Pennsylvania there was alarm and terror; preparations were made to remove the State archives and money from Harrisburg, the capital, and even the quiet citizens of the Quaker city did not feel secure from a visit from Stuart's troopers.

As men reached Washington, Baltimore, and New York from the places occupied by the Confederates, they astonished their hearers with accounts of the discipline maintained among their ragged and shoeless legions. They had seen men who had long fed on nothing but the roughest and most scanty fare, enter towns and refrain not only from pillage, but even from the harshness of authority common to soldiers. They had beheld the gentlemen of the South, changed indeed in outward appearance, and as poorly clothed as their men, yet retaining their courtesy and refinement, and combining deep-seated hatred to the Northern nation with kindness and forbearance toward individuals composing it.

It was not without mixed feelings that the better classes in the North heard of the exploits of their former fellow-countrymen. They could not but admire the military qualities and personal character of the leaders of the Confederate armies; and although feeling the reproach that their own well-equipped troops had been beaten by men who possessed few of their advantages, yet they received some comfort from the fact that their opponents were Americans. Even if a portion of the Democratic party could scarcely refrain from the opinion that a Union under President Davis and General Lee would be preferable to discord under President Lincoln and Mr. Stanton, few can blame them.

Whilst men's attention was eagerly fixed on the two armies, and every day news of some important battle was expected, General Lee made preparations to hold the passes of South Mountain, whilst Jackson pressed the siege of Harper's Ferry. He (General Lee) was unaware whether the attack would be made on his left (supposing his army to be facing Washington), or whether the passes nearer the Potomac would be selected. He was also forced to keep a considerable portion of his troops to watch lest an attempt should be made from the Pennsylvanian side to succour the garrison of Harper's Ferry, or to harass his large supply train. For these purposes a portion of Longstreet's corps was retained near Boonsboro', whilst General M'Laws, with two divisions, was detached to seize the Maryland heights, and General Walker was directed to cross the Potomac below Harper's Ferry, and marching up the right bank to take up a position on the Loudon heights, overlooking the junction of the Shenandoah and the Potomac.

All was accomplished according to orders; and it argues good organisation in the army that the three generals commanding the columns of attack should each have reached his destined point at the required time, viz. Jackson from the west, M'Laws from the north, and Walker from the east. Communications by means of courier and signal were established, and on the evening of the 13th September, General M'Laws drove the Federals, after a feeble resistance, from the Maryland heights, forcing them across the river to the western angle formed by the Shenandoah and Potomac.

There, on Bolivar heights, Colonel Miles made a stand, but his indefatigable antagonist gave him but little respite. On the afternoon of the 14th, the morning having been occupied in perfecting the arrangements with Generals M'Laws and Walker, the three divisions of Jackson's corps moved forward to the attack. Hill was ordered to keep near the left bank of the Shenandoah, and endeavour to turn the enemy's left, and so enter Harper's Ferry; Lawton was directed to march by the turnpike immediately against his centre; whilst Jones, now in command of the Stonewall division, was ordered to make a demonstration against his right. The three columns advanced and occupied, with little resistance, some heights near the Shenandoah, which had been left almost unguarded, whilst M'Laws and Walker watched the avenues of escape.

During the night of the 15th, General Jackson's chief of artillery transported ten guns across the Shenandoah, and placed them in position to take in reverse the batteries on the left of the Federal line, whilst the other batteries of Lawton's division, on rising ground on either side of the road, prepared to cover the advance of the infantry. At dawn the whole of the batteries were ready to open fire; and from the opposite side of the Potomac, from the east bank of the Shenandoah, and from the heights gained on the previous day, a cross fire of artillery poured into the Federal entrenchments. In an hour the enemy's guns were supposed to be silenced, and preparations were made to storm the works. As the leading brigade was moving forward, the Federals again opened fire, and again was the bombardment renewed. Then the Federal commander, despairing of being able to hold out until reinforcements should arrive, and cut off from communication with the relieving army, hoisted the white flag. Before it could be perceived, a shell bursting near Colonel Miles mortally wounded him, and he fell; spared by his death the disgrace which awaited the garrison for their too easy surrender. Eleven thousand men,* the whole garrison, excepting a small body of cavalry which effected their escape into Pennsylvania, were made prisoners of war, and 73 pieces of artillery, 13,000 small-arms, and other stores, became the prize of the captors.

Short time had General Jackson to enjoy the fruits of his conquest; the guns of the relieving army had been heard distinctly on the previous day, and he well knew that the commander-in-chief would be hard pressed by the far superior forces of General M'Clellan.

As has been previously mentioned, orders had been issued on the evening of the 13th for Franklin to force a passage through South Mountain at Crampton's Gap, whilst Burnside attacked at Turner's Gap; the shorter road to Harper's Ferry along the Potomac being considered impassable, owing to the Confederate guns, which commanded it from the opposite bank.

The action commenced at about 6 A.M., with skirmishing on the direct road from Frederick to Boonsboro', but the whole of the Federal forces were not in position to attack before noon. The Confederates under General D. Hill, from ten to fifteen thousand strong, occupied the eastern slopes and crest of the range of the South Mountain, availing themselves of the shelter of the woods and of the stone walls which formed the boundaries of the fields, their artillery being placed in such positions as would command the roads. Imme-

* The original garrison of 9,000 had been strengthened by Col. White's force from Martinsburg.

diately on its becoming apparent that the Federals were preparing to attack in force, Lee was advised of the movement, and he at once directed the remainder of Longstreet's force—still at Boonsboro', excepting one brigade—to proceed to the scene of action.* Until their arrival D. Hill had to bear the brunt of the enemy's attack. Well was it for him that M'Clellan and his subordinates were unaware of the small force which presented so bold a front. As usual, delay occurred in the attack until the divisions in rear had come up, and it was not until the afternoon that the main body of the Federals attempted to assail the position. Franklin pressed forward on the left, Reno in the centre, and Hooker on the right; whilst the two corps under Sumner's command were moved up in support. The main brunt of the action fell on Franklin† and Reno, but the battle was fought in a great measure with artillery, and took place under the eyes of Generals M'Clellan and Burnside, who were in rear of the centre column. Gradually the Confederates, overwhelmed by superior forces, were driven, after a stout resistance, from the slopes of the mountain. They retired through the woods towards the higher ridge, and many an anxious look was directed to the quarter from which Longstreet was expected. At length, about 4 P.M., the heads of his columns were perceived, and soon afterwards his troops got into position, and a contest ensued for the crest of the ridge. Neither side obtained any advantage, and when the Confederates, after nightfall, attempted to regain some of the ground they had

* This force of course excludes the three divisions detached to Harper's Ferry.

† General Franklin's command consisted of his own corps and Couch's division.

lost in the earlier part of the day, they were repulsed. Franklin on the left, as night closed in, was within three miles of the Maryland Height, and within six miles of Harper's Ferry, whilst Burnside was still below the crest of the ridge of hills.

General Lee had gained his point. The position had been held until Jackson had completed the capture of Harper's Ferry; and as the Federals prepared to renew the attack on the following morning, they were startled by the cessation of the firing in that direction, proclaiming, as they well knew, the surrender of the place. Each side had lost a distinguished officer. General Garland, of Virginia, commanding one of D. Hill's brigades, fell, pierced by a rifle bullet; whilst later in the day, as the sun was setting, the Federal general Reno was killed whilst reconnoitring the enemy's position.

The results of the action could not justify the accounts telegraphed by General M'Clellan to Washington, announcing a glorious victory, and citing a report from Hooker, alleging that *the enemy was making for the river in a perfect panic.** On both sides the loss was nearly equal, numbering about twenty-five hundred, and whilst allowing that General M'Clellan had forced the enemy to withdraw from South Mountain, and had won a

* A military man must condemn the tone of the following despatch which, indeed, almost savours of absurdity:—

'Head-quarters of the Army of the Potomac, Sept. 15, 1862, 8 A. M.

'To Henry W. Halleck, Commander-in-Chief.

'I have just learned from General Hooker, in the advance, who states that the information is perfectly reliable, that the enemy is making for the river in a perfect panic; and General Lee stated last night, publicly, that he must admit they had been shockingly whipped. I am hurrying everything forward to press their retreat to the utmost.

'GEORGE B. M'CLELLAN.'

passage through the line of hills, it must be admitted that he had failed in one of the objects of his advance, which had been to prevent the surrender of the garrison of Harper's Ferry.

On the morning of the 15th Franklin found himself opposed by a strong force of the enemy, in apparently so great strength that he was unwilling to attack without reinforcements; whilst on the other hand Burnside informed General M'Clellan that the pickets opposite to him had disappeared, and that the Confederates were in retreat. Both accounts were true; the troops opposed to Burnside at Turner's Gap had been withdrawn during the night in the direction of Rohrerville, and had thus strengthened that portion of the army facing Franklin, showing a bold front in order to cover the retreat to Antietam Creek.

It was now fully apparent to General Lee that he would be obliged to fight a battle against superior forces, not for conquest but for safety; that a united army, far larger than his own, was marching against him, and that he would be forced in all probability to meet that army with a portion only of his own force. On the morning of the 15th, General Jackson with four divisions was still on the opposite side of the Potomac, and M'Laws and Anderson were separated from D. Hill and Longstreet by Franklin's corps, whilst the whole army of M'Clellan was pressing forward by the Boonsboro' road on the right, and by the Rohrerville road on the left. It remained for General Lee to select a position where he could hold the enemy in check until his scattered divisions were reunited. Having therefore issued orders for Jackson to join him as quickly as possible, he withdrew the troops under his immediate command from the western slopes of South Mountain across the valley and creek of Antietam, and took up a position on a range of low heights, extending in a semicircle of about four miles from the point of entry into the Potomac of Antietam Creek to a re-entering angle of the same river a short distance higher up. The stream of the Antietam, on which rested the right of the line, is deep and impassable for troops at this part of its course, but is crossed by four bridges—the three upper ones on the direct route by which the Federal columns would advance, the lowest one on the road from Sharpsburg to Harper's Ferry. The upper course of the Antietam was fordable, but was not included in the line of the Confederate position, which before reaching the bridge farthest from the mouth of the creek or stream, bent in a westerly direction towards the Potomac. Almost in the centre of the Confederate line was the small town of Sharpsburg.

During the nights of the 14th and 15th of September, General Lee withdrew the left wing of his army across the Antietam, his retreat covered by the cavalry, between whom and the Federals there was skirmishing at Boonsboro'. Nothing further occurred on the 15th. General Jackson, after receiving the surrender of the garrison of Harper's Ferry, marched with the whole of his corps, excepting A. P. Hill's division, to join Lee. Generals Anderson and M'Laws also moved from the Maryland Heights in the same direction, having crossed the Potomac by the railway bridge.* General A. P.

* These divisions could not join General Lee by the left bank of the Potomac, as General Franklin's corps was on the immediate right of the road; they therefore crossed by the railway bridge, which, although it had often been rendered partially unfitted for use, was now in working order, and was subsequently destroyed by Gen. A. P. Hill.

Hill was left to receive the parole of the prisoners and to collect the vast mass of captured stores, with directions to follow the main body as soon as might be possible. But General Jackson's troops were weary with their previous exertions; and whilst the heads of the column hastened on, the rear straggled, many men fell out, and although on the 16th Stonewall Jackson himself joined Lee at Sharpsburg, yet a great portion of his force, irrespective of the division of A. P. Hill, was still on the road from Harper's Ferry. On the other hand the Federal troops did not prove themselves good marchers; their advance from South Mountain was slow, and General M'Clellan, with characteristic caution, did not venture to engage the enemy, posted apparently in a strong position, with only a portion of his force. He knew how raw many of his troops were; he also knew that some of the divisions had been but recently disorganised by defeat, and he felt that another defeat or even repulse at this critical moment, might not only endanger the army, but even result in ruin to the Federal cause. Possibly a greater man might have risked all and attacked; but General M'Clellan's character was notably cautious, and if he failed in achieving great victories, he in this campaign avoided defeat, and checked in its career of conquest the main army of the Confederacy.

In person he superintended the movements of the several corps as they arrived on the banks of the Antietam, massing them on either side of the Sharpsburg main road. General Lee, as the Federal columns appeared, carefully concealed the position and strength of his army, availing himself of the undulations of the ground and of the thick masses of wood which clothed the hill sides. Skirmishers along the right bank of the Antietam prevented the too near approach of reconnoitring parties, and batteries commanded the bridges over the stream. Such was the position of affairs on the night of the 15th and early part of the 16th. During the 16th, General Jackson, with a great portion of his corps, arrived as before stated at Sharpsburg, and was immediately pushed forward to the left of the line with orders to relieve Hood's division of Longstreet's corps. This division, previous to his arrival, had been warmly engaged with Hooker's corps, which had crossed the upper fords of the Antietam, and had succeeded in establishing itself within a short distance of the Confederate line of pickets.

Thus, on the night of the 16th, General Jackson held the left of the Confederate line, extending from near the Potomac to the Sharpsburg and Boonsboro' Road; in the centre was D. Hill's division, and the right was but thinly occupied by what remained of Longstreet's corps. General Hood supported Jackson, as the left, being the weakest part of the line in regard to the advantages of ground, required more troops than the centre and right. There were also other reasons which led General Lee to concentrate a stronger force on his left than on the other portions of his line; against the left General M'Clellan seemed to be massing the larger portion of his forces, and whilst it thus appeared more exposed to attack, it was also farther removed from the reinforcements which were hourly expected to arrive from Harper's Ferry. On the night of the 16th, neither had M'Laws, Anderson, Walker, or A. P. Hill effected a junction with General Lee; and on the morning of the 17th, not more than thirty-five thousand men were in line of battle.

It was indeed an anxious night for the leaders of the Confederate army. General Lee's tactics had been very bold, and it remained to be seen whether calculations based on the success of combined movements would prove correct, and whether his scattered army would be reunited in time to meet M'Clellan's onslaught. The men slept on their arms, frequently disturbed during the night by picket firing, and immediately on the appearance of the first dawn of light the skirmishing between the two armies commenced.

Before the smoke from the artillery had clouded the prospect it was a grand scene that dawned upon the eyes of those who stood on the hills overlooking the Antietam. In front was the wooded line of low heights, partially cultivated, on which were posted the several divisions of the Confederate army—the brown uniforms of the soldiers scarcely showing against the ground. Below lay the stream of the Antietam, flowing through a rich valley, and crossed by bridges carefully watched by advanced skirmishers, and commanded by guns whose muzzles gleamed from among the woods. Beyond rose the smoke from the numberless picket fires which marked the bivouacs of the Federal army, extending in a semicircle and enclosing on two sides the Confederate position; whilst in the background the wooded heights of South Mountain, stretching away southwards until they connected with the chain of the Blue Ridge, showed distinct outlines against the clear sky. Soon, however, was this scene hidden from view. As the sun rose the batteries on either side opened fire; the smoke hung heavily over the woods, and the stillness of the morning air was rudely broken by the boom of the artillery and the sharp rattle of musketry.

The action commenced by an artillery fire from the batteries in the centre of the Federal line posted on the left bank of the Antietam, which enfiladed and caused some loss to Jackson's division. Under cover of this fire, Hooker with three divisions, viz. Rickett's, Meade's, and Doubleday's, advanced to the attack, supported by Mansfield's corps of two divisions (Williams' and Green's), which had followed Hooker across the stream during the previous night. It was M'Clellan's intention to make the principal attack on Lee's left as being his weakest point, and to delay the assault on his right until he (General Lee) had drawn away forces from that portion of his line to strengthen the flank attacked. For this purpose M'Clellan had concentrated Hooker's, Mansfield's, and Sumner's corps on the right of his army. He held Porter's corps in reserve in the centre, and Burnside with one corps on the left, in readiness to advance when the order should be given. He had also ordered up Franklin's corps from Crampton's Gap, where it had been retained to watch the Maryland heights, and to prevent an attack on the left rear of the Federal army from Harper's Ferry, and directed it to march as rapidly as possible on the upper bridge and fords of the Antietam. Irrespective of the artillery which accompanied the several corps and divisions, he had placed several batteries on the low hills in the centre of his line to play on the Confederate position, and to distract attention from the attack directed against the left. Such were General M'Clellan's dispositions previous to the battle. His own statement shows that the numbers in the field on the morning of the 17th September were from ninety to ninety-five thousand; he had thus a large numerical superiority over his opponent, even if the whole Confederate army had been united; but, as has been before stated, some of the divisions had not arrived on the ground, and when the action commenced only thirty-five thousand men were in line of battle under General Lee.

Against the left wing of this army Hooker's corps advanced, and entering the woods immediately in its front succeeded in driving back the skirmishers and occupying the belt of wood; here he placed his field batteries, and a contest ensued for the possession of the open ground between the wood he now held and another belt of trees near Dunker Church. The old Stonewall division opposed him, and under a terrible fire of shot, shell, canister, and musketry, held its ground. General Jones was wounded, and his place occupied by General Starke, who was killed almost immediately after he had taken the command. This was about 7 A.M., and the second line of the Federals, under General Mansfield, came up in support—Williams's division on the right, and Green's on the left. Still the Confederates held their ground, and the battle raged with varying success until 9 A.M., each side trying alternately to defend or possess themselves of the belts of wood. The Confederates had suffered terribly; more than half the brigades forming the first line had been either killed or wounded, together with nearly every regimental commander.* The Federals at length pressed forward and drove their opponents from the woods, taking possession of Dunker Church. About this time General Mansfield was killed, and his place taken by General Williams; General

* See General Jackson's report. Pollard's *Second Year of the War*, page 132.

Hooker was also wounded, and compelled to leave the field, but the position of the Confederates was very critical, as already was the leading division of Sumner's corps approaching the scene of action, and no reinforcements had as yet reached them. Then General Early, taking the place of Lawton (wounded), put himself at the head of Ewell's* old division, and with the remainder of the Stonewall division withstood the enemy; the artillery also, under General Stewart, was concentrated in rear of the line, to support the infantry. Converting the defence into attack, Early led forward his brigades; the Federal line was shaken; but large reinforcements appeared coming up. At this juncture, portions of Anderson's and M'Law's divisions reached the field. Inspirited by this addition to their force, the Confederate line rushed forward. They drove back Hooker's corps from Dunker Church; they followed the fugitives across the open, and nearly regained the position they had held in the morning. Hooker's corps were completely demoralised and put to flight,† and portions of Sumner's (under Sedgwick) considerably shaken; but the retreat of the infantry unmasked the powerful artillery in the first line of woods, and the fire from these batteries checked the Confederate pursuit. Then were Richardson's and French's divisions of Sumner's corps brought forward, but did little more than hold the line of woods. In doing so Richardson was mortally wounded, and succeeded by Hancock. Franklin's corps also came up

* General Ewell was badly wounded, and lost a leg at the second battle of Bull Run.

† General Sumner, in his evidence before the Committee on the Conduct of the War, stated that Hooker's corps were dispersed and routed; and subsequently he added, 'I sent one of my staff officers to find out where they were, and General Ricketts, the only officer we could find, said that he could not raise 300 men of the corps.'

on the left of Sumner's, but by order of General Sumner abstained from attack, and remained under a heavy artillery fire during the day, not, however, actively engaged.* General M'Clellan in person visited this portion of the field, and concurred in Sumner's opinion. In fact he felt much uneasiness with regard to the position of affairs. The attack made by the right had been unsuccessful, and the several corps had been so severely handled, that at one time he considered it necessary to strengthen them with two brigades from Porter's reserve; however, fearing that the enemy in turn might attack his centre and pierce the line, he countermanded the order.

During the time occupied by the attack on the Confederate left, General Burnside was engaged in endeavouring to obtain possession of the lower bridge over the Antietam. His operations had been much slower than was pleasing to M'Clellan, who sent repeated orders to him to carry the bridge at all hazards. This was not effected until 1 A.M., and content with the success, Burnside halted until 3 P.M. Then, urged by an imperative message from M'Clellan, he pressed forward to the attack of the batteries on the heights in his front, and at one time succeeded in advancing almost to the village of Sharpsburg; but at this critical moment General A. P. Hill arrived on the ground from Harper's Ferry, and took up a position on the right of the Confederate line, and opposed to Burnside. This reinforcement was most opportune; it enabled the Confederates to resume the offensive, and Burnside was driven from

* General M'Clellan alludes to Franklin's arrival in these terms—'The advance of General Franklin's corps was opportune. The attack of the enemy on the position, but for the timely arrival of his corps, must have been disastrous had it succeeded in piercing the line between General Sedgwick's and French's divisions.'

the heights he had carried, and with some difficulty maintained his hold of the bridge. Fearful of bringing into action his last reserves, General M'Clellan abstained from employing Porter's corps; and although he sent the most urgent orders to Burnside to hold the bridge at all risks, he yet refrained from furnishing him with fresh troops, still fearing that an attack might be directed against the centre of his line.

It was now dark, and the battle terminated. Burnside held the bridge he had won, and the divisions on the Federal right bivouacked on the ground they had held during the day. General M'Clellan claimed a victory, and telegraphed to that effect to Washington; but, in truth, the battle of Antietam was only another of the many indecisive battles of the war.

In reviewing its incidents, few can refrain from being struck with the manner in which the Federal attack was conducted. Corps after corps and division after division were pushed forward, but no simultaneous movement of the whole line was attempted. From whatever cause it arose, the delay of Burnside's attack on the Confederate right was most detrimental to the success of the Federals. General Lee was able to concentrate a large portion of his artillery to repel the advance of the Federal right wing, and was also in a position to avail himself, for a similar purpose, of the divisions of Anderson and M'Laws. When the attack on his own right wing was made, the Federal right had been repulsed, and the opportune arrival of General A. P. Hill enabled the Confederates to attempt an offensive movement against Burnside's corps.

No doubt the Federal army was composed of very heterogeneous elements, as intermixed with the older soldiers of the Peninsula were many raw levies, which could scarcely be trusted to manœuvre under fire, but there seems to have been little method in bringing the several divisions into action, or in supplying them with ammunition on the field. Each successive line moved to the front, fired as long as the ammunition lasted, and then gave way to a fresh line—unless pressed by the enemy, when, as was the case with Hooker's corps, it broke and fled. The power of the great army of the Federals was frittered away in successive attacks by driblets, and General M'Clellan, over-estimating the strength of his adversary, refrained from employing his reserve at the decisive moment. From 15,000 to 20,000 of his best troops, under Porter, were not engaged; nor did the division under General Couch reach the field until the following morning. Over-caution and exaggeration of the power of his opponent prevented General M'Clellan from availing himself of the opportunity which the bold if not rash tactics of General Lee had presented to him. He cannot plead the excuse of want of information of the movements of the enemy, as the unexpected and singularly-acquired possession of Lee's orders had furnished him with full details. He knew of the division of the Confederate army; he also must have been aware that, by the occupation of South Mountain after the action of the 15th, his own army was between Lee's main force and the divisions under General Jackson, and, indeed, was moving upon their direct road of communication; and yet he did not press forward with sufficient vigour to attack Lee before Jackson's arrival; and, when the action had commenced, allowed it to linger on during a long summer's day, until successively his adversary's troops had all arrived on the field. Why was Burnside so slow in his advance on the bridge? Why were two battles fought consecutively by the two wings, in place of a combined attack by the whole united force? Why was not the reserve employed? All these questions naturally suggest themselves; and a European critic may possibly find their solution in other causes beside those which may have been occasioned by the character of the general commanding.

It requires long practice and much training to enable a general to manœuvre with advantage large bodies of men. Lieutenant Burnside, of the regular army, could have had little opportunity before the war in even handling a company; and, although he might have acquired some experience in command in North Carolina, yet the nature of the country admitted of few operations on a grand scale by masses of troops. The dispositions for the attack of a bridge and a strong position, even if held by far inferior numbers, require powers of combination usually only to be obtained by practice; and when it is remembered that not only he himself, but his staff, and generals of divisions and brigades, were equally inexperienced, the delay in making the attack at Antietam may be partially understood. A somewhat similar answer may be given to the second question. The country on the banks of the Chickahominy allowed of little supervision, on the part of the general commanding-in-chief, of the movements of his troops in action; and General M'Clellan had had little or no opportunity of directing the tactics of an army in the field. The machinery of his army was not in such perfect order as to ensure the efficient working of each separate part after the directing impulse had been given; and the Commander-in-Chief was often required to bestow his attention on details of execution when his mind should have been concentrated on supervising the whole plan of action. The training of the men had likewise been necessarily very imperfect. Many were mere recruits, others had been demoralised by defeat, and even the best were not equal to the armies of Europe in the performance of the details of discipline. The men wasted their ammunition in firing into the woods, and there were no sufficient means of furnishing them with a fresh supply on the field. With respect to the non-employment of the reserve, could General M'Clellan have been thinking of a similar instance in the history of Napoleon,* and did he consider the occasion parallel? It would almost seem that such was the case. He knew that he commanded the last army of the Union, and possibly the only barrier between Lee and Washington. He thought of the morrow, and of the battle which he might be required to fight with the concentrated Confederate force, and he feared to employ his reserve.† Want of energy and of combination characterised the operations of the Federals during the campaign and battle of Antietam. There seems to have been indecision regarding the employment of Franklin's corps, and after the rout of Hooker's corps the attack on the right degenerated into an effort to hold the ground already gained. Well may General Lee point to Antietam as one of his most brilliant achievements. He had played a game so bold as almost to amount to rashness; he had calculated too much upon the demoralisation of the Federal army consequent on the defeats of Pope, and also on the known caution of General M'Clellan. The reorganisation of that army, and the advance of M'Clellan on South Mountain, had

* At the battle of Borodino.

† Not his last reserve, as Couch's division was not on the field. Vide General Franklin's evidence before the Court of Inquiry.

taken him by surprise, and, in conjunction with the possession by his opponent of the important order to General D. Hill, had almost proved fatal, not only to his plans of conquest, but even to his safety.

For the earlier part of the campaign, high praise should be awarded to General M'Clellan. He evinced to a great degree the qualities he possessed, of organisation, and the power of securing the attachment of his men; by his efforts he probably saved the Union from terrible disaster if not utter defeat; but at the same time, by his over-caution and want of enterprise, he failed in availing himself of the rare opportunity of crushing his antagonist.

On the day following the battle neither side was prepared to resume the offensive. General Lee's plans for the invasion of Pennsylvania had been thwarted by the resistance he had met with; and although determined, by the offer of battle, to prevent M'Clellan from claiming the honour of driving him across the Potomac, he yet found himself compelled to make preparation for retreat, content with the prestige and the material results of his campaign on the enemy's soil. The capture of Harper's Ferry furnished him with large supplies, and although it cannot be believed (as stated in some of the Confederate journals) that the campaign was undertaken for that object, and was therefore successful in so far as it was gained, yet the amount of arms and stores obtained was of great assistance to troops so poorly provided as those of the Confederacy. On the other hand, General M'Clellan's army had been so severely handled on the previous day, one corps having been completely shattered,* that he refrained

* That of General Hooker.

from making a fresh attack until the arrival of expected reinforcements of 15,000 men, with which he hoped *to make all safe.**

The losses of the Federal side, according to General M'Clellan's report, were 12,460, whilst those of the Confederate army were about 9,000.† On both sides distinguished generals had fallen. The Confederates had to mourn the deaths of Generals Branch, Jones, Starke; and the Federals that of General Mansfield killed, and many others wounded. On the morning of the 18th, the Federal army, in the opinion of General M'Clellan and of many of the superior officers, was not in a condition to make another attack. The troops were greatly overcome by fatigue and exhaustion, the supply trains both of food and ammunition were still in rear, and one division of Sumner's and the whole of Hooker's corps were shattered and demoralised. General Burnside

* In his evidence before the Committee of Inquiry on the conduct of the war, General M'Clellan made the following statement regarding the condition of his army on the morning following the battle:—'The next morning (the 18th) I found that our loss had been so great, and there was so much disorganisation in some of the commands, that I did not consider it proper to renew the attack on that day, especially as I was sure of the arrival on that day of two fresh divisions, amounting to about 15,000 men. As an instance of the condition of some of the troops that morning, I happen to recollect the returns of the first corps (General Hooker's), made on the morning of the 18th, by which there were about 3,500 men reported present for duty. Four days after, the returns of the same corps showed 13,500.' In General M'Clellan's report the numbers are differently stated, the first number being 6,729, the last 13,093. Now, if this latter statement be taken as correct, 6,364 men must have absented themselves during the action, a sufficient demonstration of the demoralisation of the corps.

† See Captain Chesney's estimate of the losses in the battle of Antietam, vol. i., *Review of the Recent Campaigns in Virginia*, page 137.

reported that he was unable, without reinforcements, to hold a position on the further side of the stream, and on Morell's division of Porter's corps being sent to reinforce him, withdrew his own men to the left bank. Couch's division had arrived on the ground, and a division of raw troops under General Humphries also reached the army in the course of the day; but, to counterbalance these reinforcements, M'Clellan's aide-de-camp reported that fresh troops were crossing the Potomac to join the Confederate army. Taking all these facts into consideration, and remembering that possibly the safety of Washington, the maintenance in its allegiance to the Union of Baltimore, and the security of Pennsylvania, rested on the efficiency of the army under his command, General M'Clellan considered that he would be wrong in risking a battle on the 18th.

General Lee was willing to fight again on the defensive; he had received no reinforcements, but his whole army was now concentrated, and the troops seen by General M'Clellan's aide-de-camp were the stragglers from Jackson's corps, which had joined since the action, and were being marched to the front. On the night of the 18th and 19th, he crossed the Potomac under cover of batteries posted on the right bank, his rear protected by the division of A. P. Hill. He did not move far from the river, and a strong reconnaissance pushed forward from Porter's corps on the 20th was driven back across the river with considerable loss. No further attempt was made for some time to molest the Confederate army. General Lee established his headquarters between Martingsburg and Shepperds Town, where he maintained a sufficiently threatening attitude to prevent the attempt by the Federal army of any except defensive operations.

M'Clellan, knowing the defects of the force under his command, feared to cross the Potomac by the fords, and to hazard a battle with a river subject to sudden floods in his rear. He contented himself with defensive measures, detaching General Couch to Williamsport, and General Williams to the Maryland Heights, to guard against any attempt on the part of the enemy to cross in force to the Maryland side of the river. His cavalry, which had not recovered from the hardships of Pope's campaign, were not sufficiently numerous or efficient to prevent raids on the part of the indefatigable General Stuart, and Washington was again forced to submit to the insult of the presence, between her and her main army, of the enemy's cavalry, which, after destroying and capturing stores, effected a safe retreat almost unmolested across the Potomac.

The Government at Washington, having recovered from its panic, urged an immediate advance against the Confederate army, and refusing to be convinced by M'Clellan's demonstrations of the inefficiency of his forces, used the weapon which his supposed dilatory conduct had placed in their hands to vilify him in the eyes of the people, and to sap the influence which he had regained over their minds.

Although there may doubtless be some truth in the conclusion of the report of the committee on the conduct of the war, relating to the character and conduct of General M'Clellan, yet a careful perusal of the despatches which passed between him and General Halleck will lead to the opinion that personal or party enmity influenced some members of the Cabinet as much, or more, as desire for the public weal. In closing the report on the campaign of Maryland, the committee above alluded to used the following expressions, of which it would perhaps be difficult even for General M'Clellan's warmest admirers wholly to deny the truth:

'Your committee, having gone so fully into the details of the Peninsular campaign, do not deem it necessary to devote so much space to the campaign of Maryland. The same mind that controlled the movements upon the Peninsula controlled those of Maryland, and the same general features characterise the one campaign as characterised the other. In each may be seen the same unreadiness to move promptly and to act vigorously, the same desire for more troops before advancing, and the same reference to the great superiority of numbers on the part of the enemy.'

CHAPTER VIII.

CAMPAIGN IN THE WEST.

OWING to several causes, the campaigns of Virginia had gradually assumed the characteristics of the more regular operations conducted by European armies; the desultory and detached movements which had tended to confuse the history of the earlier periods of the war had given place to combined operations of large bodies of troops, based on rules in conformity with the laws of strategy. The great battles had been fought by opposing armies, and the sympathies of the population of the country in which the campaigns had been conducted had not directly influenced their results. For these reasons, as well as from the fact that the geography of Virginia and Maryland is far better known than that of the Western States, the campaigns around Richmond and Washington present more objects of interest than those waged in the West and South. There the vast distances which separated the several objective points, the scattered positions of the forces, the desultory warfare waged by guerillas, and the combined political and military objects aimed at by the several generals, tended to confuse the movements of the armies, at the same time that it renders the task of presenting a connected narrative of events especially difficult.

As we have seen, the possession of the great rivers of the West enabled the Federals to penetrate far into the interior of the country, although in doing so they left in their rear an unfriendly population, ready at any moment to assist the efforts of a Confederate force, however small, or to harass the communications of the invading army by guerilla warfare.

Having, however, secured the course of the Mississippi and Tennessee Rivers, the Federal generals had been able to concentrate their forces about midway between the two, and even to advance beyond the great southern line of rail which connects Memphis with Corinth. They held the strategical point of Grand Junction with a detached force as far south as Holly Springs. But whilst with the assistance of the rivers they had reached the confines of the State of Mississippi, they had yet left a large extent of country in their rear avowedly hostile to the Union cause.

In order to comprehend the operations of the summer and autumn campaign of the West, a clear notion should be arrived at of the principal positions of the contending armies. As will be remembered, the impossibility of holding Memphis, the fall of New Orleans, and the passage both up and down the Mississippi of the Federal gunboats, together with the advance on Corinth of the main army of the West, had forced General Beauregard to retire about fifty miles south of Corinth, and to take up a position among the forests and swamps of Mississippi. As, therefore, Columbus, Island No. 10, and Fort Pillow had in succession formed the left of the Confederate line of defence in the West, so may Vicksburg be now considered as holding the same position. Owing, however, to the capture of New Orleans and the passage up the river of the

Federal ships of war, the trans-Mississippi department had been partially cut off from the States on the east of the river, and the Confederate line of defence was bent southwards from Vicksburg to the neighbourhood of Lake Pontchartrain and New Orleans.

The nature of the country in the State of Mississippi rendered the advance of an invading army extremely difficult, therefore a comparatively small force was necessary to guard the great Southern rails which intersected the State, and consequently the Confederates were able to assemble an army for the purpose of acting on the left rear of the Federal lines.

Following the course of the Confederate line of defence from Mississippi, we find that it passed along the Tennessee River south of Florence to Chattanooga, and then extended northwards through Eastern Tennessee, embracing Knoxville, to the Cumberland Mountains. Thus, although the Federals had possessed themselves of Kentucky, of the greater portion of Western Tennessee, and of a part of Mississippi, yet the Confederates were able to menace the left rear of their line by operations against Eastern Kentucky, and were much assisted in such operations by the possession of the railway from Chattanooga to Knoxville, and so westwards to Virginia. As, therefore, with regard to the campaign in Mississippi, the Federals had the advantage of possessing two sides of the square, and could press the Confederates from a line drawn from Memphis to Corinth, and on another line from Memphis down the Mississippi, so, on the other hand, the Confederates, with respect to the campaign in Kentucky and Tennessee, could either make their attack directly from the vicinity of Chattanooga, and from thence to Corinth, or from Knoxsville and the Cumberland Mountains.

The difficulty of procuring men to reinforce the armies, and subsequently the necessity of devoting its energy to the defence of Virginia, had prevented the Federal Government from prosecuting the war in the West with the vigour which had characterised the campaigns of Fort Donelson and Shiloh. For which reasons, after the occupation of Corinth, no great aggressive movement excepting the siege of Vicksburg had been undertaken. The heroic defence of that town, and their successes in Virginia, had, on the other hand, inspirited the Confederates, and a grand scheme was organised for an aggressive campaign, embracing the whole theatre of war in the West, and extending for a distance of between seven and eight hundred miles, from Cumberland Gap, on the borders of Eastern Tennessee and Kentucky, to the vicinity of the Lower Mississippi. It was proposed to assault Batôn Rouge at the lower extremity of this line, to manœuvre against the Federal army in the vicinity of Corinth in the centre, and to operate from its extreme right against Eastern Kentucky. With these objects in view, a small army under General Breckenridge was assembled in Louisiana, a larger force under Van Dorn in Upper Mississippi, whilst a still more formidable army under General Bragg, who had succeeded Beauregard in the command of the West, was organised in Eastern Tennessee for the invasion of Kentucky.

As the geography of Mississippi was especially favourable to the Confederates for purposes of defence, so was that of Eastern Tennessee well-adapted for those of attack. The long line of rail, of which the whole extent from Chattanooga to Western Virginia, and so to Richmond, was in their hands, afforded means for the concentration of their forces. The country had been as yet unhurt by the war, and was able to furnish supplies; and the range of the Cumberland Mountains, stretching from the confines of Eastern Virginia to Chattanooga, covered the approaches to Eastern Tennessee, and, whilst they furnished a screen behind which the Confederates could concentrate their forces, did not present a barrier to aggressive movements.

In addition to its strategical importance, the possession of Eastern Tennessee was of great consequence to the Confederates from its mineral wealth, and from the quantity of saltpetre or nitre which is found in some parts of the State, as also from the fact that the great salt works at Abingdon, Virginia, were immediately on the line of railway which intersects it.

To secure the possession of this country, and at the same time to have the means of attacking the western part of the State and Kentucky, it was necessary to hold the passes through the Cumberland Mountains. Through this range there are several passes or gaps, of which the principal and most northern is Cumberland Gap, on the direct road from Knoxville to Kentucky; whilst about halfway between Cumberland Gap and Chattanooga, over more broken and less high ridges, runs the road from Knoxville, by Kingston and Murfreesboro', to Nashville. Previous to the autumn campaign of the West, both of these routes had been threatened by the Federal forces from Kentucky and from Eastern Tennessee; indeed the pass of Cumberland Gap had been seized on the 18th June by the Federal General Morgan, and detachments from General Buell's army occupied Murfreesboro' and M'Minnsville, on the road to Kingston; at the same time that a Federal force under General Mitchell threatened Chattanooga, and the country lying between that town and Corinth.

To sum up the positions of the contending armies of the West :—In the south, General Butler occupied New Orleans, whilst Admirals Farragut and Porter guarded the Lower Mississippi and bombarded Vicksburg. Opposed to them was the Confederate General Breckenridge in Louisiana, and General Smith at Vicksburg. Commanding the army of Tennessee, in the neighbourhood of Corinth, with his advance as far south as Holly Springs and his right at Memphis, was General Grant, with Generals Sherman, Rosecrans,* and M'Clernand under his command. In his front was the army of the Mississippi, under Generals Van Dorn, Price, and Lovell. Further east was the Federal General Mitchell, between Corinth and Chattanooga, opposed to a small force under General Adams, whilst threatening Eastern Tennessee was Buell's army, and occupying Cumberland Gap was General Morgan. In their front, holding Knoxsville, Kingston, and the line of rail, was the force under General Kirby Smith, prepared by means of this railway either to succour Chattanooga, defend Kingston, or move northwards into Kentucky, the whole Confederate army of the West being under the command of General Bragg,† who had taken the place of General Beauregard.

Having thus arrived at a distinct idea of the positions of the several armies, and (as in the Virginian campaign) bearing in mind the strategical value of the

* General Rosecrans had been transferred from the army of Western Virginia.

† General Bragg had been an officer of the old regular army, and carried with him when in command of the army of the West the strict notions of discipline which he had imbibed in his earlier military career, perhaps somewhat too strict for the volunteer force which he was called upon to form and to lead.

rivers, especially the Mississippi, and of the railways, particularly the great trunk line running from Memphis to Virginia, and the several rails which connect it with Nashville and with the Ohio, and southwards with the cities on the sea-coast, we will next proceed to follow up in order the various movements which culminated in the battles of the autumn campaign of the West.

Intermixed with the military motives which actuated the Confederate Government in deciding on an offensive campaign were certain political considerations. It was known that a large portion of the population of Kentucky looked favourably on the Confederate cause; and although, at an earlier period of the war, Generals Buckner and Johnston had been disappointed in the help which they had anticipated, yet it was hoped that the advance of another army would raise the spirits of the people, and would lead them to throw off a yoke found by a great majority to be sufficiently galling. In addition to this inducement for an advance into Kentucky, the expectation of recruiting the army, and obtaining a large supply of horses from the Blue grass country, was another motive which prompted an offensive campaign, whilst it was hoped that a threatening movement on the Ohio would relieve the pressure of the invading armies on the Mississippi and Tennessee Rivers.

As, on a minor scale, the cavalry reconnaissance of General Stuart in Virginia had preceded the attack on M'Clellan by General Lee, so did the extended raids of Generals Morgan and Forrest into Kentucky and Tennessee inaugurate the advance of the main armies. The former of these officers had received no military education prior to the war, but very soon after its commencement had distinguished himself as a captain of irregular cavalry, in which capacity he had attracted the especial notice of General Beauregard, who, appreciating his rare genius for that description of warfare, and anxious to avail himself of his services on a larger scale, prevailed on him, with great difficulty, to accept a Brigadier-General's command, assigning to him as Assistant-Adjutant-General, Colonel Grenfell (an Englishman).* His force, numbering less than two entire regiments of cavalry, was composed of volunteers raised principally among the gentry of Kentucky and Tennessee, and armed with shot guns and pistols, few only using the sabre. With this small force, Morgan, trusting to the rapidity of his movements and to the

* The following description of Colonel Grenfell appeared in the Louisville Journal, and may be taken as a specimen of the writing of a portion of the American press. Col. Grenfell is designated as a big bully, devilish-looking blackguard, whiskey bloat, unmerciful, degenerate puppy—an Englishman. The real history of his life, mentioned in Lieut.-Colonel Fremantle's interesting account of the Southern States, is so curious that we must be pardoned for quoting it:—'A member of a well-known English family, he seems to have devoted his whole life to the exciting career of a soldier of fortune. He told me that in early life he had served three years in a French lancer regiment, and had risen from a private to be a sous-lieutenant. He afterwards became a sort of consular agent at Tangiers, under old Mr. Drummond Hay. Having acquired a perfect knowledge of Arabic, he entered the service of Abd-el-Kader, and under that renowned chief he fought the French for four years and a-half. At another period of his life, he fitted out a yacht and carried on a private war with the Riff pirates. He was brigade-major in the Turkish contingent during the Crimean war, and had some employment in the Indian mutiny. He has also been engaged at Buenos Ayres and the South American Republics. At an early period of the present troubles he ran the blockade, and joined the Confederates. Even in this army, which abounds in foolhardy and desperate characters, he has acquired the admiration of all ranks by his reckless daring, and gallantry in the field.'

sympathy of the population, undertook the invasion of Kentucky. Irrespective of his cavalry and two howitzers, he took with him an engine, hitherto unused as an offensive weapon in war, but in this expedition of the greatest value. Attached to Morgan's staff, and carrying a portable electric battery, was Mr. Ellsworth, the telegraphic operator, and the extraordinary use which he made of this seemingly harmless weapon, forms one of the most curious features of modern irregular warfare.

The expedition left Knoxville on the 4th July, and advancing by Monticello, after a skirmish at Thomkinsville, captured the town of Glasgow,* about halfway between Nashville and Louisville, where Morgan collected arms, which he distributed among such of his force as had not as yet received them, and, after burning the commissariat stores, marched towards the main line of railway. There, Mr. Ellsworth, having taken down the telegraphic wire and connected it with his pocket instrument, proceeded to read off and answer the several despatches passing between Louisville and Nashville. He represented himself as the telegraphic operator at Louisville, and General Morgan and himself, seated on a heap of stones by the side of the railway, received reports, despatched information, and ordered and counter-ordered the movements of the Federal troops and stores for many hours. Often the messages sent from Louisville were very amusing to those into whose hands they had thus unexpectedly fallen. They frequently contained warnings of the presence of Morgan in the country, and consequently countermanded all previous orders respecting the transmission

* See page 204 for Map.

of money and valuables. On arriving at Lebanon, which General Morgan captured, the same course was adopted. The telegraphic office having been seized, Mr. Ellsworth personated the operator,* and despatched messages to General Boyle, commanding the Federal troops at Louisville, and received his answers; General Boyle supposing that he was in communication with Colonel Johnson, who had commanded the Federal garrison at Lebanon, but was then a prisoner in Morgan's hands.

Marching eastward from Lebanon, Morgan passed through Harrodsburgh, and threatened Lexington, tearing up railways, destroying bridges, and burning government stores on his way; but treating the inhabitants of the country with courtesy and kindness. At Cynthiana he encountered a considerable force of infantry, cavalry, and artillery, mostly composed of raw

* Some of these dialogues are amusing, and afford a contrast to the usual serious business of war. Mr. Ellsworth reports the following incident:—'At 7·30, an operator, signing Z., commenced calling B., which I had ascertained by the books in the office was the signal for the Lebanon office. I answered the call, when the following conversation between Z. and myself ensued:—"To Lebanon: What news? Any more skirmishing after the last message? —To Z.: No. We drove what little cavalry there was away.—To B.: Has the train arrived yet?—To Z.: No; about how many troops on train?—To B.: Five hundred, 60th Indiana commanded by Col. Owens." My curiosity being excited as to what station Z. was, and to ascertain, without creating any suspicion, I adopted the following plan:—"To Z.: A gentleman here in the office bets me two cigars you cannot spell the name of your station correctly.—To B.: Take the bet. L-e-b-a-n-o-n J-u-n-c-t-i-o-n. Is this not right? How do you think I would spell it.—To Z.: He gives it up. He thought you would put two b's in Lebanon.—To B.: Ha-ha-ha! he is a green one.—To Z.: Yes, that is so.—To Z.: What time did the train with soldiers pass?—To B.: 8·30 last night.—To Z.: Very singular where the train is," &c., &c.'

troops. These he defeated, taking many prisoners, and continued his march to Paris. From thence he proceeded to Richmond, where he had thought of making a stand, and endeavouring to raise the population; but hearing that large bodies of cavalry were moving towards him with the intention of surrounding his force, he retreated to Crab Orchard, and from thence to Somerset. At Somerset he took possession of the telegraphic office, and countermanded all the orders which General Boyle had sent to intercept him. Before leaving the place he despatched the following messages, the first to Mr. Prentice, at Louisville, the second to General Boyle, and the third to a resident in Washington city:—

'Good morning, George D. I am quietly watching the complete destruction of all of Uncle Sam's property in this little burg. I regret exceedingly that this is the last that comes under my supervision on this route. I expect in a short time to pay you a visit, and wish to know if you will be at home. All well in Dixie.

'JOHN H. MORGAN,
'Commanding Brigade.'

'Good morning, Jerry. This telegraph is a great institution. You should destroy it, as it keeps you too well posted. My friend Ellsworth has all the despatches since the 12th of July on file. Do you wish copies?

'JOHN H. MORGAN,
'Commanding Brigade.'

'To General J. T. Boyle, Louisville.'

'Just completed my tour through Kentucky—captured seventeen cities—destroyed millions of dollars worth of United States property—passed through your country, but regret not seeing you. We paroled fifteen hundred rebel prisoners. Your old friend,

'JOHN H. MORGAN,

'Commanding Brigade.'

'Hon. Geo. Dunlap, Washington City.'

From Somerset, Morgan continued his retreat to Monticello, and from thence to Sparta, where he encamped. In his official report to General Kirby Smith, he thus summed up the results of his expedition:—'I left Knoxville on the 4th day of this month (July), with about nine hundred men, and returned to Livingston on the 28th instant, with nearly twelve hundred, having been absent just twenty-four days; during which time I travelled over a thousand miles, captured seventeen towns,* destroyed all the government supplies and arms in them, dispersed about one thousand five hundred home-guards, and paroled nearly one thousand two hundred regular troops. I lost, in killed, wounded, and missing, of the number that I carried into Kentucky, about ninety.'

This expedition tended to raise high the fame of Morgan. His name became a bugbear to the Federal officers and to such Union men as resided in Kentucky. The rapidity and secrecy of his movements, the swiftness of his attacks, and the originality of his schemes, excited the alarm of his enemies as they gained the admiration of his friends; far North, even in Ohio, did men tremble at the name of Morgan, and the exaggerated tales of his exploits tended to increase his success in subsequent raids.

Competing with him in fame, and engaged in a similar description of warfare, was General Forrest,

* In size, probably more resembling English villages than towns.

who, simultaneously with Morgan's raid into Kentucky, had marched with a cavalry force into Western Tennessee. He surprised and captured the garrison of Murfreesboro', taking prisoner Brigadier-General Crittenden, who had lately been appointed to the command. The slight resistance offered by the garrison, and the want of precaution against surprise evinced by the senior officers, called forth a strong order from General Buell, reflecting on the conduct of both officers and men. Forrest did not retain possession of Murfreesboro', but having paroled* the prisoners, marched from place to place with his cavalry—falling on detached posts, and capturing convoys, thereby weakening the main armies by creating a necessity for strong guards for their communications.

When this irregular warfare was conducted by such men as Morgan and Forrest, who preserved discipline among their troops, there were few of the horrors which usually accompany what may be termed guerilla warfare; but when partizan corps sprang up in the unsettled country, and when enterprizes were undertaken less with the object of forwarding the operations of the main armies than with the desire of gratifying private revenge or of the acquisition of plunder, deeds were committed and misery inflicted on non-combatants which frequently called forth measures of retaliation,

* A peculiar feature of the American war is the extent to which the system of granting paroles is carried. Owing often to the want of means of transport and power of guarding prisoners, there would be no means of conveying them to secure places, therefore they would be paroled and allowed to return to their own country, awaiting a regular exchange before serving again. Much suffering must have been spared to prisoners by this arrangement; and as neither side has made much complaint that paroles have been broken, we may infer that they were usually kept.

sometimes more reprehensible than the deeds themselves.

About this time, the death of General M'Cook excited a strong feeling of animosity in the North, whilst the undisciplined acts of retaliation which followed it called forth a still more deep-seated spirit of hatred in the South. The general was marching with his brigade from Athens (Alabama) towards Tennessee, and in consequence of sickness was travelling in an ambulance, about three miles in front of his men. The ambulance was suddenly attacked by a small band of guerillas, and the general either accidentally or purposely shot in his waggon. Immediately on the alarm being given, the brigade hurried up, but too late to capture the guerillas. The men of M'Cook's former regiment, exasperated at the death of their commanding officer, spread themselves over the country, burning and destroying all descriptions of property, and shooting many whom they merely suspected to have been implicated in the deed, including a Confederate lieutenant who was on furlough, and whom they supposed to have been connected with the guerillas. There can be no excuse for such acts of barbarity, even if the assassination had been proved. But, judging from the report of the officer who succeeded General M'Cook in command of the detachment, there was evidently a doubt whether the general was not shot whilst attempting to escape.*

For a short period following the raids into Kentucky and Tennessee of Generals Morgan and Forrest, there was a pause in the operations of the armies of the North-

* Colonel Vanderveer's Official Report, *Rebellion Record*, vol. v. page 572, Documents. Correspondent of the *Philadelphia Press*.

western States, whilst General Bragg was engaged in collecting his forces for a campaign on a more extended scale. During this time an attempt was made by the Confederates to regain their hold on the Lower Mississippi, and by establishing themselves in one of the towns above New Orleans, but below Vicksburg, to protect the line of the river between these places and to reopen communication with the western banks, which had been hindered, although not stopped, by the Federal gunboats. With this object in view, General Breckenridge collected an army at Camp Moore (near Tangipanoa), eighty miles from New Orleans and sixty from Batôn Rouge, and dividing it into two divisions, under Generals Ruggles and Clarke, prepared to march on Batôn Rouge. It was proposed that the expedition should act in conjunction with the ironclad Arkansas from Vicksburg, which, having been repaired after her engagement with the Federal gunboats, was ready for a fresh descent on the enemy's fleet. After receiving a telegraphic message that the refitting of the Arkansas was complete, Breckenridge marched on the Comite River. The heat was intense, water was scarce, and the men fell out along the sandy roads faint with fatigue; every farmhouse was converted into an hospital; but the troops pressed on, and a simultaneous attack by land and water was arranged for the 5th August. In the meantime, the Arkansas had left Vicksburg, and had steamed leisurely down the river; but on arriving at a point about fifteen miles above Batôn Rouge her starboard-engine broke down, and repairs causing delay became necessary. This accident was fatal to her cooperation in the attack about to be made by the land force, and Breckenridge was deprived at a most critical time of the ally on which he had depended. In the meantime, the Federals, although unaware of the exact nature of the expedition which was about to attack them, were yet on the alert, expecting the advance of the enemy. Their commander, General Williams, had drawn up his force, consisting of infantry and artillery, outside the town, the left flank resting on the river, and embracing within its lines the two roads which approached the place from the east. The position does not appear to have been well selected, as in front of the centre of the line, between the two roads, was a large cemetery overgrown with high grass, and affording both cover for an advancing enemy and, when occupied, a strong offensive position. The Federal force numbered about 4,000, having been much reduced by sickness.*

At daybreak on the 5th August, the Confederate skirmishers were perceived pushing their way rapidly through the Indian corn and the sugar-plantations in front of the line, and driving back the Federal pickets. The Western regiments, veterans of Shiloh under General Clarke, were on the right, and the Louisiana troops, under General Ruggles, on the left, General Breckenridge in person leading the right wing, and his young son acting as aid-de-camp.† With a yell, the Confederates rushed on; they overwhelmed the first of the Federal lines, forcing it back on its supports, and capturing the camp. The batteries checked their advance, but again, led by their respective generals, they moved forward from the cemetery, and drove back

* There were eight regiments and three and a half batteries, and a small detachment of cavalry. Gen. Butler's Order, *Rebellion Record*, vol. v. page 304, Documents.

† The numbers on both sides were probably about equal. The Confederates had lost considerably during their 70 miles march.

their opponents within shelter of the houses of Batôn Rouge. General Williams (commanding the Federals), an old and distinguished officer, was killed whilst, at the head of the 21st Indiana regiment which had lost its field officers, he was endeavouring to rally them for a charge.

Thus far the Confederates had been completely successful; however, in the midst of his victory, Breckenridge listened anxiously for the guns of the Arkansas. Already were his men suffering from the fire of the Federal gunboats, and the rifles of the troops posted in and among the houses, and no signs could be perceived of the ironclad. Then the Confederate General seeing the hopelessness of contending against an equal force supported by gunboats, ordered the recall to be sounded; slowly and reluctantly his troops fell back, and after setting fire to the Federal camps, retired to the Comite River, losing in the retreat General Clarke, wounded and a prisoner.

The action had lasted four hours, and the loss on either side amounted to about three hundred. Vain had been the advantage gained by the Confederates; the land operations had indeed been successful, but the failure to cooperate on the part of the Arkansas had rendered nugatory the gallantry of the troops. The career of that renowned vessel had terminated far otherwise than was expected; her engines were not in proper order, and although the first breakage had been remedied, and she had attempted to descend the river, yet on her other engine failing, she was forced again to stop for repairs. All night had her crew worked, and on the morning of the 6th, when the Federal gunboats were perceived moving up the river, she cleared for action, and attempted to run down the Essex. Again her engines stopped, and her commander seeing her helpless condition ran her ashore, and abandoned her, having first set her on fire. She soon afterwards blew up in mid-stream, and thus freed the Federal fleet from its most alarming opponent.

For a time the course of the Mississippi, from New Orleans to Vicksburg, was clear from other obstructions than the guerillas on the banks, and from field artillery, which was often brought to bear on transports and storeships. To put an end to this practice, and to make an example which should serve as a warning to others, Admiral Farragut bombarded and partially destroyed the town of Donaldsonville, between New Orleans and Batôn Rouge. The course of the Mississippi was however so tortuous, and its bluffs so thickly covered with woods, that notwithstanding the vigilance of the Federal gunboats, the Confederates succeeded in establishing batteries, and ultimately in fortifying a position at Port Hudson, between Batôn Rouge and Vicksburg, destined to play a considerable part at a subsequent period of the war.

On the Lower Mississippi the summer operations of 1862 may be said to have terminated; higher up the river, below Memphis, at Helena, General Curtis had established himself, having succeeded in traversing Arkansas. This was the lowest station on the upper river which the Federals possessed, and proved of little importance as a military post, although it furnished a depôt for cotton and a means for annoying and ruining many of the rich Southern planters.

We must now return to Eastern Tennessee, where General Bragg was concentrating his army preparatory to the invasion of Kentucky. The object of his campaign was to relieve Western Tennessee and Alabama from the presence of the Federals by an advance against Kentucky, with possibly the ultimate object of capturing and holding Louisville on the Ohio, and occupying permanently the eastern portion of the State. The plan of operations which he adopted, was to distract the attention of the Federal commanders by guerilla warfare in the western parts of Tennessee and Kentucky, and by the more important cavalry movements of General Forrest, whilst he pushed forward a strong force under General Kirby Smith through the passes west of Cumberland Gap to menace Cincinnati, and at the same time threatened both Nashville and Louisville with the main army under himself in person.

Early in August, Kirby Smith, with the divisions of Generals Churchill and Cleburne,* issued from the passes of the Cumberland Mountains, and hurrying forward by forced marches through a wild and mountainous country, appeared in front of the town of Richmond on the 29th of August.

* Spelt Claibourne in Pollard's *Second Year of the War*. The following extract from Lieut.-Colonel Fremantle's *Two Months in the Southern States* will be interesting to Englishmen:—'Major-General Cleburne is the son of a doctor at or near Balincolig. At the age of seventeen, he ran away from home and enlisted into Her Majesty's 41st regiment of Foot, in which he served three years as private and corporal. He then bought his discharge and emigrated to Arkansas, where he studied law, and eschewing politics, he got a good practice as a lawyer. At the outbreak of the war he was elected captain of his company, then colonel of his regiment, and has since, for his distinguished services in all the Western campaigns, been appointed to the command of a division; the highest military rank which has been attained by a foreigner in the Confederate service. He told me that he ascribed his advancement mainly to the useful lessons which he had learnt in the ranks of the British army, and he pointed, with a laugh, to his general's white facings, which he said his 41st experiences enabled him to keep cleaner than any other Confederate general.

The Federals had had warning of his approach; the invasion of Kentucky had been for some time expected and even announced in the Northern journals, and the small cavalry force which watched the roads to Richmond, and which galloped back to the town on the approach of Kirby Smith's advanced guard, only corroborated previous rumour. General Manson, the Federal general, had collected at Richmond a force of about 8,000 men, mostly from the Western States, and determined to offer battle to protect the town. His army, although more numerous than that under Kirby Smith, consisted almost entirely of raw levies; the majority of the men had never been under fire, and had only recently received arms. His cavalry were worthless, and his artillery inexperienced.

In order to oppose the advance of the Confederates, Manson led his troops about six miles from Richmond, and took up a position on rising ground, on either side of the Barboursville and Richmond Roads. There Kirby Smith, who had previously sent forward a cavalry reconnaissance to report on the enemy's position, determined to attack him on the following morning. Soon after daybreak on 30th August, Cleburne's division of about 2,500 men advanced. The battle, as usual, commenced with the artillery, under cover of which Churchill moved his division to the enemy's right, with the intention of falling on that flank. This movement gave General Manson an opportunity of pressing hard on Cleburne's division, which suffered severely, the General himself being wounded, and delegating the command to Colonel Preston Smith. But the Federal artillery had by this time almost exhausted their ammunition, and the excitement caused by the removal of the guns to the rear, joined to the attack made on the right flank by Churchill,

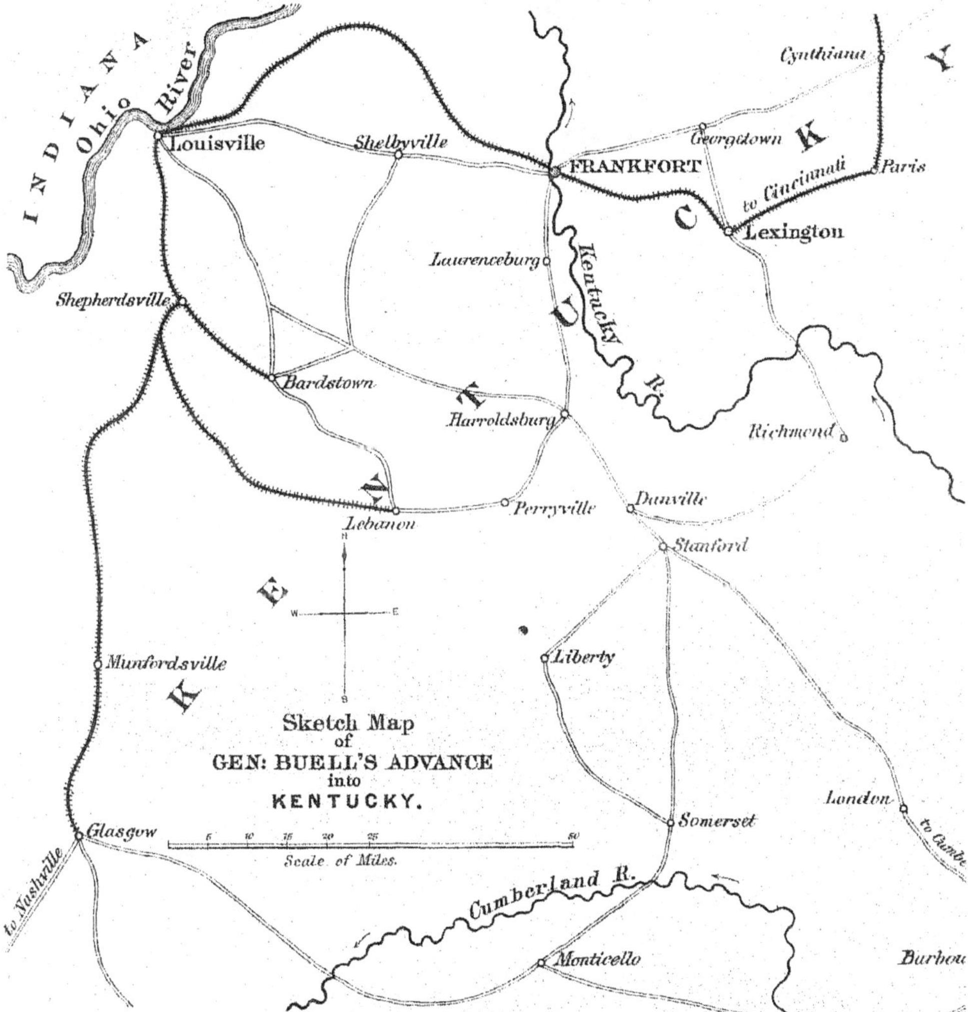

Sketch Map of GEN: BUELL'S ADVANCE into KENTUCKY.

created some confusion, and Manson ordered a retreat to a position nearer the town. The brunt of the action now fell on Churchill's division, which with some difficulty held its ground until the arrival of Preston Smith, who drove the Federals back in great confusion through their camp, to a line of hills in close vicinity to Richmond. There General Nelson, who had arrived during the battle, assisted by General Manson, rallied the retreating regiments, and the artillery having received a fresh supply of ammunition were brought to the front, and posted in an advantageous position. All was in vain; the Confederates, flushed with victory, pressed forward rapidly to the attack, and drove their opponents headlong into Richmond. Nelson received a wound, and leaving the army in charge of General Manson, effected his escape. In the meantime, the Confederate cavalry having marched round Richmond, attacked the long line of waggons already sent to the rear, and captured almost the whole of the train. The confusion caused by this unexpected hindrance to the retreat spread to the troops: the cavalry jumped off their horses,* and ran into the woods, and the greater portion of the entire force, including General Manson, surrendered as prisoners. Nine pieces of artillery, 10,000 stand of arms, 5,000 prisoners, and a vast amount of supplies, rewarded the conquerors, and General Kirby Smith entered Richmond amid the ac-

* The correspondent of the *Cincinnati Gazette* (Federal) thus reports the circumstance:—'In a few minutes the squadron of cavalry returned flying, announcing that the enemy were in our advance, and ordering all the cavalry, of which there was quite a number near us, to the front. The effect of this intelligence can be imagined. The cavalry, instead of obeying the order, dismounted, and took to the fields—an example which was speedily followed by the teamsters, and everybody else.

clamations of many true Southern sympathisers, and of others who had been converted by the result of the battle. Pushing forward from Richmond, the Confederate force entered Lexington on the 2nd September, and Frankfort on the 17th, and was thus in a position to threaten either Cincinnati, about eighty miles, or Louisville, about fifty miles distant.

Great was the excitement at these places. General Wright, commanding the department of the Ohio, used every exertion to prepare to meet the invading force. He collected and endeavoured to organise the raw regiments hastily forwarded from the Western States; he employed negroes to work at the fortifications of Louisville and of Cincinnati; he organised volunteer corps at the latter, and took measures to keep down the Southern sympathisers at the former place; but he much doubted his power of meeting Kirby Smith's victorious troops in the field, and looked anxiously for the approach of succour from the South.

As Kirby Smith was threatening Louisville and Cincinnati, so was the main army under General Bragg marching either with the intention of attacking Nashville, or of cooperating in the reduction of Louisville. The situation of the Federal cause in the West seemed as critical as in the East, and the invasion of Kentucky appeared fraught with as much danger to the Union as the invasion of Maryland.

General Buell, who with his army was between Murfreesboro' and Chattanooga, hurried by forced marches to the North, and General Jeff Davis, with 6,000 men, detached from Rosecrans's army, hastened to garrison Nashville; but it appeared very doubtful whether Louisville, or even Nashville, could be saved, for not only were the Confederates strategically in a better position than their opponents, but the Federal garrisons offered little resistance to their onward march.

About 4,000 men surrendered to General Bragg's advanced divisions at Monfordsville on the 17th September, and thus his whole army was on the road between Nashville and Louisville, i. e. on the road by which Buell would be forced to march if he sought to interpose his army between the Confederates and the Ohio. There appeared to be an opportunity of striking not only a military but a political blow against the Federal cause in Kentucky. It seemed optional to General Bragg either to press on, and in conjunction with Kirby Smith to capture Louisville, or with equal forces to meet General Buell in the field, and force him back to Nashville.

Neither course was adopted. Buell, without opposition and almost within sight of the Confederate army, effected his march to Louisville, recapturing Monfordsville on the way, whilst Bragg, marching first to Bardstown and then to Frankfort, contented himself with inaugurating a provisional governor of Kentucky. Thus Buell entered Louisville, and General Morgan,* who had, by Kirby Smith's advance, been cut off with his detachment at Cumberland Gap, effected his retreat to Cincinnati; the first road between Nashville and Louisville having been left open by Bragg's march to Frankfort from the west, the second between Cumberland Gap and Nashville by Kirby Smith's march to the same point from the east.

The opportunity was lost, and the Federals resumed the offensive. In both the Eastern and Western States had the crisis of the danger past; the battle of Antietam

* Not to be confused with the Confederate General John Morgan.

and the entry of Buell into Louisville were the two turning-points of the autumn campaigns of 1862, and as General Lee had been forced to retreat across the Potomac, so was General Bragg obliged to retire through the Cumberland Mountains.

Buell, reinforced by the army under Wright, advanced from Louisville on October 1st, and after skirmishing with Polk's division at Bardstown, encountered the greater portion of the main army on the road from Lebanon to Harrodsburg. The battle of Perryville or Chaplin Hills followed. It would appear that General Bragg having ascertained that, owing to the junction of General Buell with the army of the Ohio, the Federal force in Kentucky was superior to his own, and perceiving also that he could expect little real aid from the population, resolved to retreat. In order to do so with credit, and to secure the large amount of captured stores accumulated by the army during its successful advance, he considered it necessary to fight a battle. It was, however, doubtful by which road the main Federal army was marching, and whether their advance might be expected by the Louisville and Lawrenceburg Road, or by the Bardston and Lebanon Road. The former road was watched by Kirby Smith, the latter by General Polk. From information which he received, General Bragg arrived at the conclusion that a heavy column of the enemy was marching against Kirby Smith; he therefore, on the 7th of October, detached Wither's division to his assistance, leaving only three divisions under the command of Polk to watch the Bardston and Lebanon Roads. Bragg's army was thus divided into two portions, separated from each other by a distance of about twenty miles, the small town of Harrodsburg being at the point of junction of the two roads. At this place on the 6th of October, Bragg had fixed his head-quarters, and hearing that the force in front of Kirby Smith was not large, whilst heavy columns were marching on Harrodsburg from the west, he desired Polk with the three divisions under his command to offer battle at Perryville, at the same time sending orders to Kirby Smith and Withers to march with all haste on Harrodsburg. On the morning of the 8th, he inspected the proposed field of battle, and examined and approved of the disposition of the troops made by Polk.

The action did not commence until late in the morning. The Confederate right was formed of Cheatham's division, the centre of Buckner's, the left of Anderson's, the two latter under the command of General Hardee.

After some skirmishing and artillery firing, in which the longer range of the Federal guns gave them the advantage, General Bragg perceiving that the enemy was receiving reinforcements, resolved to attack, and issued the necessary directions to that effect to General Polk. In the meantime, the Federals under General Buell had marched in three columns, consisting of as many corps, from Louisville and Munsfordville, and were converging on Perryville. The right corps was under General Crittenden, the centre under General Gilbert, the left under General M'Cook, the whole army numbering not less than 45,000 men.* Of these two divisions of M'Cook's corps and Gilbert's corps were the only troops present in front of Perryville on the 8th of October, M'Cook's third division, under Sill,

* Calculating three divisions of 5000 men each to a corps, which number corresponds with other accounts.

having been sent to threaten Frankfort,* and Crittenden's corps being too far to the right rear to be of service. The brunt of the action fell on the two divisions of M'Cook's corps, under Generals Jackson and Rousseau. They formed the left of the line, which extended across the Perryville Road, of which the southern or right side was occupied by Gilbert's corps.

The earlier part of the day was consumed in skirmishing, the Federals being content to act on the defensive, until the whole of their large force should reach the field. It was not, however, the intention of the Confederate general to await this event; and before Crittenden's corps had come into position, Polk ordered the attack to commence. Cheatham's division endeavoured to turn the Federal right flank, and falling with great impetuosity upon the raw troops of General Jackson, drove them back, capturing some of their artillery. Whilst endeavouring to rally his men, Jackson fell, and soon afterwards General Tirrell was killed. The troops re-formed under cover of their artillery, but Rousseau's division was hard pressed, and notwithstanding the reinforcements sent from Gilbert's corps, was forced to yield ground. The Confederates still advanced, but night put an end to the engagement. During the night the Confederates retreated, carrying with them a vast amount of stores and artillery, which had been further increased by the capture by General Withers of Sill's artillery train.

The battle of Perryville was as usual indecisive; it had been fought by the Confederates to cover their retreat; and with inferior numbers they had attacked,

* This division formed the force which had threatened Kirby Smith, and caused the detachment of General Withers from General Polk's corps.

and had driven back the Federal left wing with great loss. Both Generals Buell and Bragg were on the ground, but the former seems to have exercised little direct supervision over the army, and to have allowed a portion of his force to be compromised, whilst large numbers were not engaged; the latter, as has been already said, had delegated the command to General Polk. Rousseau's division received high praise from the general of the corps, who, however, reflected strongly on the conduct of some of the officers commanding the more inexperienced troops, whose misbehaviour he attributed to a want of discipline, and of confidence in the field and line officers. The loss of the Federals in killed, wounded, and missing, was over 4000 men; that of the Confederates was estimated at about 2,500, of which more than half were of Cheatham's division.*

General Bragg has been blamed for having failed to bring all his force into the field at this battle, in which case, it is alleged, he might have crushed the enemy; but the crisis of the campaign was not the battle of Perryville, which was obviously fought to cover the retreat of the army, but the junction of Buell with Wright at Louisville; it was at Munfordsville, or in its vicinity, that General Bragg should have concentrated his army for the decisive battle, and should have fallen on Buell during his march to Louisville, forcing him either to accept battle on his adversaries' terms, or to have fallen back on Nashville, and left Louisville and even Cincinnati to their fate.

The battle of Perryville in some respects resembles

* *Knoxville Register Account*, October 18th, 1863, quoted in *Rebellion Record*. For Federal loss, see the Official Reports, *Rebellion Record*, vol. v. Documents.

that of Antietam; it was fought to cover a retreat after a series of successes; it terminated in favour rather of the Confederates than of the Federals, yet it resulted in the continued retreat of the former; whilst in both instances the commanders of the Federal armies, although so far successful, in that they delivered a large territory from an invading army, yet failed to satisfy their government, and consequently incurred disgrace. General Buell was soon afterwards removed from the command of the army of the Cumberland, and was replaced by General Rosecrans; whilst, on returning to the campaign of Virginia, it will be seen that General M'Clellan was similarly rewarded.*

From Perryville the Confederate army retired to Cumberland Gap, the line of march resembling a vast immigration rather than the retreat of an army. Long lines of waggons laden with plunder, vast herds of cattle and horses, private carriages and coaches, containing families who, with their negroes, were seeking safety from Northern tyranny, blocked up the roads and encumbered the movements of the troops. The Federals had, however, received a severe lesson at Perryville, and Wheeler's cavalry closed in the rear, and effectually prevented the too near approach of the enemy's advanced guard. The army passed through Cumberland Gap, and the campaign of Kentucky was ended.

The high hopes of the South were disappointed; the easy successes of the first month of the campaign had excited expectations of the permanent possession of Western Kentucky, and the change of the scene of war from Tennessee to Ohio; these hopes had now passed away, and the barren victories and accumulated spoils

* In both instances political motives possibly influenced the Government.

but feebly compensated for the anticipated results of the campaign. General Bragg, whose severe discipline had produced murmurs among the troops, incurred renewed unpopularity from his failure to arrest the march of General Buell, and the rapid movements of Kirby Smith were compared favourably with the slow march of the main army under the Commander-in-Chief. Disappointment was likewise felt at the apathy of the Kentuckians. No doubt Southern sympathy had been shown in abundance as the conquering armies of the Confederacy advanced, but the people had not risen in favour of the South, and although some recruits had been enlisted, yet there had been no decided action on the part of the mass of the population; probably, as in Maryland, the near vicinity of the Union States and the facility with which overwhelming forces could be poured in to repress insurrections tended to keep down the spirit of the people, and caused them to hesitate before they openly embraced a cause of which the success, so far from the heart of the Confederacy, might be ephemeral. The tide of Southern conquest, both in the Eastern and Western States, had turned, and the aggressive operations in the State of Mississippi, although they tended to increase the respect already felt for the troops of the Confederacy, yet ended in discomfiture, and proved that the Federal soldiers of the West were no mean antagonists.

It will be remembered that General Grant, commanding the Federal army in Northern Mississippi, occupied, in the latter months of the summer of 1862, Corinth, Memphis, and Holly Springs; he had since withdrawn from the last-named place, and having assigned Sherman to the command at Memphis, had directed Rosecrans to guard Corinth and to watch lest the Confederate army of the Mississippi should endeavour to cross the Tennessee river and harass Buell in his march towards Kentucky. Rosecrans, in compliance with these orders, drew in his advanced detachment and encamped about seven miles south of Corinth. Price, who commanded the Confederates in his immediate front, occupied the villages he had evacuated, and on the 18th September concentrated his force at Iuka, about thirty miles south of Corinth. There Rosecrans, having obtained the cooperation of a portion of Grant's army, under General Ord, decided on attacking, and, if possible, overwhelming him with superior forces before he could receive assistance from Van Dorn. For this purpose, he concentrated his force at Jacintho; and marching from thence on the morning of the 19th, at about 5 P.M., reached the front of General Price's army near the village of Iuka. Hamilton's division, supported by Stanley's, immediately attacked; but Ord failing to cooperate, the Federals were held in check until darkness prevented the continuance of the engagement. On the following morning the Confederates retreated, their rear-guard holding in check Rosecrans's cavalry.

The lawless and cruel character of the war in the West is sufficiently indicated by incidental occurrences during and after the engagement at Iuka. A Federal officer, in describing the action, announces with glee that a house in which a dinner was found, which was supposed to have been prepared for the Confederate officers, was sacked and burnt, to punish the owner for giving aid and comfort to the enemy; whilst, on the other hand, the correspondent of a Southern journal indicates the want of discipline, showing itself in deeds of pillage and destruction, which characterized the retreat of Price's army. The repulse of the Confederates did not prevent a second and more important attempt to drive the Federals from Mississippi, and by efficient cooperation to assist Bragg in his operations in Kentucky.

Pending the result of the operations of General Buell, the Federals were content to remain on the defensive, and Rosecrans, from whose command a division had been detached to reinforce Buell, took measures to fortify his position at Corinth. The natural features of the ground gave him great facilities; the various streams and swamps, which shut in the town on the south and west, prevented approach from these quarters, and thus the lines of defence were confined to the north and east. The old earthworks, constructed by General Beauregard, furnished an outer line of defence; but as they were too extended for the smaller force under Rosecrans's command, an inner line was selected, in which redoubts, strengthened by abattis, were erected. The undulations of the ground, broken by ravines thickly clothed with brushwood, afforded strong positions for defence, although in some cases they furnished the means of approach for an attacking force.

After the repulse of Price at Iuka, the Confederates did not resume the offensive until the junction of Generals Van Dorn's and Lovell's commands; they then concentrated their army at Ripley, under Van Dorn, threatening Bolivar on the left and Corinth on the right.

The Federal line of defence of the country from the Mississippi to the Tennessee rivers may be considered to have extended from Memphis on the right, held by Sherman, through Bolivar (Tennessee), garrisoned by Ord's and Hurlbut's divisions, to Corinth, held by Rosecrans in command of four divisions, under M'Kean, Davies, Hamilton and Stanley. The reserve, under

General Grant in person, occupied Jackson at the point of junction of the two rails running from the south through Corinth and Bolivar. It was uncertain on which place the principal attack would be made: in the event of operations being conducted against Bolivar, Rosecrans was prepared to fall on the Confederate right rear, whilst if Corinth should be attacked a similar duty would devolve on the garrison of Bolivar.

On the 2nd October, the Federal pickets in the neighbourhood of Corinth were rapidly driven in, and on the morning of the 3rd General Rosecrans became aware that the bulk of the Confederate army was in his front. His forces occupied a position outside the defences of the town, three divisions forming the first two lines, and one division slightly in rear as a reserve. General Rosecrans was anxious to retire slowly within the inner line of works, and gave orders to that effect; but Price's troops, flushed with the excitement of an attack, and anxious to wipe out the recollection of their repulse at Iuka, advanced rapidly, and pressed hard on the Federal centre, capturing two guns from Davies' division, and driving the Federals within their inner line of redoubts. Van Dorn anticipated an easy success on the following morning, and telegraphed to Richmond the announcement of a great victory; but Rosecrans thought otherwise, and whilst many in Corinth were anxious and perturbed, he maintained his equanimity and even cheerfulness, carefully arranging his troops for the battle expected to commence at dawn on the following morning. By 3 A.M. all the dispositions were complete, and for two hours the troops slept on their arms.

The Federal army fronted towards the north, the right resting on high ground, covering the Pittsburg-landing road, the centre on a ridge north of the houses of the town, the left on batteries and redoubts, near the Corinth and Memphis Railroad. The Confederates had marched round the position, avoiding the defences both natural and artificial on the southern side, and hoping to enter Corinth from the direction supposed to have been less exposed to attack and therefore less carefully protected. During the night both sides were engaged in erecting batteries: two new redoubts were completed by the Federal engineers, whilst on the Confederate side batteries were prepared to throw shells into the town, as soon as daylight should afford opportunity.

At dawn the bombardment commenced, but the heavier guns of the Federals silenced those of their opponents: at 7 A.M. there was a pause, the infantry columns were preparing to storm the works, and about 8 A.M. Price's division rushed impetuously on the Federal right centre, capturing the redoubts, driving the defenders from the batteries, and pushing them into the town. Where, in the meantime, was Van Dorn? His attack on the Federal left should have been simultaneous with that on the right; but the country in his front was much broken, and the thick brushwood and deep ravines impeded and delayed his advance; therefore, unsupported as it found itself to be, Price's division, when opposed to fresh troops and confronted at close range by a new battery, reeled, was shaken, and gave way. As it retired, followed by the now victorious Federals, Van Dorn's columns, twenty minutes too late, marched to the assault. As they advanced on the right, Price's division retreated, and the Federals retook their batteries and regained their lines. Still Van Dorn, probably unaware of Price's repulse, leading forward his men, pushed his way up a rugged ravine, his flanks impeded and detained under the fire of the forts by abattis; notwithstanding these obstructions, he continued to advance and formed two brigades of Texan and Louisiana troops for the assault of the most destructive of the forts that were playing on him. The brigades moved up the face of the hill on which stood Fort Robinette; the heavy guns made great gaps in their ranks, but steadily, and to the admiration even of their enemies, did the troops continue their advance. They reached the edge of the ditch; the Federals, amazed at their intrepidity, abated their fire; they paused before the final rush, and the defenders, regaining their courage, poured in a destructive volley. In vain Captain Rogers, revolver in hand, and holding the colours of his regiment, leapt into the ditch. He fell dead—his men hesitated; the Missouri and Ohio regiments garrisoning the work followed their volleys by a charge; and the Confederates were driven down the face of the hill followed by the victorious Federals through the woods and over the ground they had gained by such desperate courage. By noon the battle of Corinth was ended, and both sides completely exhausted; and, encumbered with wounded, paused ere they renewed the work of destruction. The Confederates had suffered fearfully: General Rosecrans reported their loss at 1,423 killed, about 5,000 wounded, and 2,248 prisoners; whilst he estimated his own at 315 killed, 1,812 wounded, and 232 prisoners. Even if the Confederate accounts of their loss are received as correct,* those killed and wounded numbered 3,000, and the prisoners 15,000.

On both sides great courage had been shown, the Confederates failed by a want of combination in achiev-

* Vide Pollard, *Second Year of the War*, p. 171.

ing victory, and, foiled successively in their assaults, were forced to retreat. The two divisions under Ord and Hurlbut from Bolivar were threatening their left flank, and were with difficulty held in check, whilst it was known that Rosecrans was preparing to sally forth from his entrenchments and take an offensive attitude; nothing therefore remained for Van Dorn but to withdraw to his former position, behind the lagoons and swamps of Mississippi, and this he accomplished in good order and with little loss; Rosecrans * followed him forty miles with his infantry, and sixty with his cavalry, but subsequently retired to his old position at Corinth, where he remained until October 26th, when he was appointed to replace General Buell in command of the army of the Cumberland.

The Western Campaign of the year 1862 closed with the battle of Corinth. We have seen how, at its commencement, the Confederates had been successively driven back from Fort Donelson, had been forced from Kentucky, had made a bold stand at Pittsburg and a prolonged defence at Corinth; how, ultimately, the line of the Cumberland River and of the trunk rail through Kentucky had been replaced by the line of the Upper Tennessee River, and the Memphis, Chattanooga and Western Tennessee rail; how, taking advantage of the impulse given to the Confederate cause by the victories in Virginia, the Western army had resumed the offen-

* General Rosecrans had been an engineer officer of the regular army. He was born in 1819, was educated at West Point, and served in the army until 1854, when he resigned and practised as an architect at Cincinnati. In Western Virginia he served with distinction at the commencement of the war, both under M'Clellan and in an independent command. He had since been moved to the army of the Mississippi. General Rosecrans is a Roman Catholic.

sive, had again threatened Kentucky, and had sought to recover its former strong position at Corinth, threatening in the South the Lower Mississippi and even New Orleans. We have followed out this short, brilliant, but in the main unsuccessful campaign, and, at the close of the autumn of 1862, we find that the opposing forces have almost resumed their former positions, excepting that the country between Nashville and Chattanooga had been reoccupied by the Confederate forces, the Federal out-pickets extending only for a short distance south of Nashville.

Notwithstanding the failure of the Western Campaign, the position of the Confederates in the autumn of 1862 was very different from what it had been in the spring. Then a succession of defeats in the West had tended to shake the confidence of even their warmest adherents, whilst the advance of the grand army of the Potomac almost to the gates of Richmond made men tremble for the safety of the capital. Now, on the contrary, the troops of the South-west had regained their morale, had forced their enemy to fight, not for conquest, but for existence; had carried the war from Chattanooga to Louisville, had caused the merchants of Cincinnati and the farmers of Ohio to arm for the defence of their own city and state; and, although forced ultimately to retire, had sufficiently proved that the subjugation of the West was a task far more difficult than, after the spring campaign, the Federals had been accustomed to regard it. In Virginia the change in events had been even more remarkable: army after army had been defeated by General Lee and his Lieutenants; and Washington, in the autumn of 1862, was in as great, if not greater, danger than had Richmond been in the summer of the same year. If, however, the success of the South had raised the hopes of her friends ; and the gallantry of her armies and the ability of her chiefs had gained for her the respect of even the most apathetic of European nations, so had her failure in offensive campaigns, and her weakness in men and material, as compared to her opponent, cast a doubt on her power to demand peace at the sword's point, and to do more than to wage a successful defensive war.

CHAPTER IX.

MINOR OPERATIONS OF THE WAR.

It is only by searching out the details of the American war that the real misery inflicted on so large a portion of the human race can be fully comprehended. The eye wearies as it seeks to mark on the map the various places where battles have been fought; the hand falters as it endeavours to narrate the details; and, above all, the heart grows sorrowful as the mind meditates on the accumulation of misery resulting from a war, so fearful in its character and accompaniments. Great campaigns, leading to bloody but indecisive battles, follow each other in rapid succession; cavalry raids and detached expeditions, having for their objects the destruction of all that makes life pleasant or endurable, fill up the necessary intervals between the movements of the larger armies; guerilla warfare on the frontiers of civilization equals in ferocity the battles of the but recently dispossessed Indians; whilst occasionally some deed of especial cruelty, or some crime peculiarly striking in its features, for the moment attracts observation, soon to be forgotten in the constant recurring horrors of the strife. Wars waged by opposing armies are indeed sufficiently productive of misery; but when the struggle is between whole populations,—when the lesser and weaker is so resolute in its spirit, so unbending in its courage, so self-sacrificing in its conduct, as to give up all that men hold dear, rather than to yield, then the misery of war seems to have reached its climax.

Spread out the map of the thirteen Southern States of America, and in succession, putting aside the great campaigns of the West and of Virginia, follow out the various minor operations of the belligerents. See Missouri, a prey to the most savage of guerilla wars; the partizan leader, Quantrel, standing pre-eminently forward in this species of strife, now attacking detached bodies of Federals, now destroying and capturing convoys, or burning houses and towns suspected of leaning to the Union cause; and, on the other hand, the jay hawkers from Kansas retaliating on the farms and villages of Missouri, and yet equalled in their unbridled deeds of ferocity by the Federal General, M'Neil.*

It was on the 18th of October that an officer and nine soldiers of the Confederate Colonel Joseph Porter's guerilla force were lead forth from the town of Palmyra, Missouri, by orders of General M'Neil, to be executed in retaliation for a Union man who was missing from the town, and who was supposed, on but slight evidence, to have been either killed or carried away by guerillas.† His body had not been found, and no proof was received that the notification addressed, but not sent, by M'Neil to Colonel Porter, accusing him of the deed, and proclaiming retaliation, ever reached its destination.

After the lapse of ten days, during which time no communication arrived from Porter, Captain Thomas Snider and nine private soldiers were driven from the gaol at Palmyra in government waggons, each seated

* Formerly a hatter at St. Louis.

† It is said that, soon after the execution of the Confederate soldiers, the man, who had been absent on his own business, returned unhurt to his own home; but this report lacks confirmation.

on his coffin, and at a short distance from the town shot with circumstances of great barbarity. The firing party failed to execute its work properly, and a reserve having been called up, despatched the wounded men with revolvers. Nobly did these Confederate soldiers meet their death,—all but two refused to allow their eyes to be bandaged; and Captain Snider, by his remarkable equanimity and more than ordinary courage, showed that he had well merited the honour of commanding such brave men.

Even in the North was detestation expressed at so foul a deed; but the Federal Government, by allowing M'Neil to retain his command, made itself responsible for the act. On the facts becoming known in the South, President Davis issued orders to General Holmes, commanding the Confederate forces in the trans-Mississippi department, to demand the surrender of M'Neil, and failing compliance with this demand to execute the first ten United States officers who might fall into his hands. Happily for the future conduct of the war, the Confederates showed themselves more noble and more merciful than their opponents; and although no satisfaction was given by the Federal authorities, retaliation was not exacted.

Such was one of the many deeds of horror perpetrated in the wilder states of the West. As a sample of the lawlessness and ferocity that prevailed even in the regular armies, the death of General Nelson, shot by his brother-General, Jeff Davis,* affords a striking instance. General Davis had received great provocation from General Nelson, who had not only treated him arbitrarily and unjustly, but, on his applying for explanation,

* No relative of the President.

had assailed him with opprobrious epithets, and even struck him, in the presence of several officers. Goaded to revenge or excited by passion, General Davis either borrowed or snatched a pistol from a bystander and shot General Nelson dead on the spot. The provocation he had received was allowed to palliate the offence, and not only was no punishment inflicted on General Davis, but he was allowed to retain his command.* Deeds such as these evince the demoralisation of society, whilst they caused the belligerents to cease from wonder or to feel pity for the woes inflicted on the enemy.

Along the course of the Mississippi river guerilla operations were rife; steamers were frequently fired on from the banks, and in retaliation plantations were destroyed and houses burned. In Arkansas, there were several engagements, dignified by the names of battles, on the north-western frontier in the vicinity of the former battle-field of Pea Ridge, where the Federal army of the frontier, under Generals Blunt and Herron opposed to that of General Hindman, fought successively the actions of Fort Wagner, Cross Hollows and Cane Hill, near the frontiers of Arkansas, Missouri, and the Indian territory. No results followed these engagements; the Federals usually claimed victories, and then retreated to the camps they had previously occupied.

The last battle of the year, of more importance both as regarded the numbers engaged and the loss on either side, received the name of Prairie Grove, and was fought about ten miles south of Fayetteville. The circumstances which led to it were as follows:—General Blunt

* See the account given in the *Times* newspaper of October 14, 1862, in the Letter from their Correspondent, dated New York, September 30.

having advanced by the Fayetteville and Van Buren Road, and having, after a slight engagement with General Marmaduke towards the end of November, crossed the Boston Mountains, halted and encamped about fifteen miles north of Van Buren. There General Hindman, who had effected a junction with Marmaduke, ventured to attack him, with the intention of overwhelming his single division before the arrival of the force under Herron. Suspecting this plan, Blunt telegraphed to Herron, directing him to push forward as rapidly as possible to his relief. Herron received the message on the 3rd December, at his camp at Wilson's Creek on the frontier of Missouri, and advanced by rapid marches on Fayetteville. Until his arrival, Blunt determined to retain his present position, acting on the defensive. On the 6th December he received a reinforcement of 1,600 cavalry sent forward by Herron. Owing, however, to the negligence of his out-pickets, the Confederates succeeded in turning his left flank, and marched directly towards Fayetteville, and towards the depôts of the waggon-train belonging to the Federal army. Blunt did not discover this movement until it was too late to prevent it; he therefore, on the morning of the 7th December, retreated and sought to effect a junction with General Herron, whom he knew to be advancing to his assistance. But Hindman had forestalled him, and had attacked and driven in Herron's advanced guard, forcing him to accept battle.

A beautiful valley of the Boston Mountains, partially cultivated and partially of wooded and prairie land, was the scene of the engagement. The Federals maintained a defensive attitude, and repelled General Hindman's attacks until the arrival, about 1 P.M., of General Blunt; the forces were then more evenly balanced, and the action continued until night closed in, neither side having gained a victory, although the loss of both Federals* and Confederates had been severe. During the night and the following day the Confederates retreated to Van Buren, and for some time the campaign of the Trans-Mississippi department, except so far as regarded the usual guerilla warfare, may be considered to have ceased. The Federals had secured to themselves the possession of the north-western corner of Arkansas, and the freedom of Missouri from the presence of any regular Confederate force.

On the Mississippi a strong force held Helena, subject to frequent attacks, and in return forming the depôt from which expeditions were sent forth to burn, plunder, and destroy in what was formerly the fertile cotton districts of Mississippi and Arkansas. It is alleged that not unfrequently the capture of that valuable commodity rather than the furtherance of purely military operations was the object for which these expeditions were undertaken, and that officers of high rank were sometimes mixed up in trading speculations which it would have been better that they should have avoided.

On the Lower Mississippi little of importance occurred after the action at Batôn Rouge. In the vicinity of Donaldsonville there was a slight engagement between the Federal troops under General Weitzel and a small force of Confederates, proving that although the Federals might hold the banks of the Mississippi, they would be unable to penetrate the interior without meeting determined opposition.

At New Orleans the reign of General Butler was drawing to a close; his tyranny had not only provoked

* The Federal loss, according to their own account, was 1,145 killed, wounded, and missing.

the most deadly hatred in the South, but had even kindled a feeling of shame in the hearts of many of the more respectable of the Northern people, whilst his illegal acts in regard to a foreign nation had called forth a strong remonstrance from the French Government. His removal was determined on, and General Banks, who although he had shown little military capacity, was yet esteemed as a gentleman and an able administrator, was appointed to succeed him.

In his farewell to the people of New Orleans, General Butler sought justification for his own acts of tyranny, which he termed merited severity, by a category of charges against European nations, ransacking their history for a period of two centuries to find instances of cruelty which he could contrast with his own mild exercise of authority. His proclamation contains the following paragraph, which may be read as a specimen of the writings of some of the civilian generals of America:—'I do not feel that I have erred in too much harshness, for that harshness has ever been exhibited to disloyal enemies of my country, and not to loyal friends. To be sure I might have regaled you with the amenities of British civilisation, and yet been within the supposed rules of civilised warfare. You might have been smoked to death in caverns, as were the Covenanters of Scotland, by the command of a general of the royal household of England; or roasted like the inhabitants of Algiers during the French campaign. Your wives and daughters might have been given over to the ravisher, as were the unfortunate dames of Spain in the Peninsular War; or you might have been scalped and tomahawked, as our mothers were at Wyoming by the savage allies of Great Britain in our own revolution; your property could have been turned over to indiscriminate "loot," like the palace of the Emperor of China; works of art which adorned your buildings might have been sent away like the paintings at the Vatican; your sons might have been blown from the mouths of cannon like the sepoys of Delhi; and yet all this would have been within the rules of civilised warfare, as practised by the most polished and the most hypocritical nations of Europe. For such acts the records of the doings of some of the inhabitants of your city towards the friends of the Union, before my coming, were a sufficient provocation and justification. But I have not so conducted.' General Butler then enumerates the mild punishments he was forced to inflict, and also the great benefits he had conferred on the city of New Orleans—benefits which were certainly not appreciated by its inhabitants.

His successor, General Banks, brought with him large reinforcements with which to inaugurate a fresh campaign in Louisiana; but his operations belong to the year 1863, and before commencing their history, it will be well to glance at some of the events which signalised the autumn of 1862 on the sea-coast.

The blockade had become more strict and more efficient; many vessels had been captured, and the fast steamers seized as blockade runners had been converted into ships of war, and performed the duties of blockaders more effectually than the regular ships of the line of the Federal navy. As a counterpoise to this injury to trade inflicted on the Confederates, the steamer Alabama had become the terror of the Northern merchants; she burnt and captured their vessels almost without molestation, and the insurance on traders in New York consequently rose considerably. To her was now joined the Oreto, rechristened the Florida. This vessel had effected her escape from Mobile in defiance of the blockading squadrons, and soon equalled the Alabama in the mischief she inflicted on the Northern commerce. A large reward was offered for her capture, but during a considerable time she continued to prey upon her enemies, and her subsequent fate belongs to a much later period of the war.

Along the southern coast the Federal fleet was not idle; expeditions detached from Admiral Farragut's fleet captured with little resistance Galveston and Sabine Pass, thereby closing two important inlets for the blockade-runners from Havana, whilst combined naval and military operations from Hilton Head were sent up the rivers of Florida, where they encountered little resistance, and captured a few unimportant works.

Farther to the north, on the coast of North Carolina, a more important expedition was organised under General Forster. There had been during the autumn months several skirmishes between the Federal force occupying Washington and other towns on Pamlico Sound and the Confederates engaged in protecting the interior of the country, but as General Forster had under his command an army of sufficient strength to warrant more important operations, he determined to advance in force from Newberne, and endeavour to destroy the line of railway between Wilmington and Weldon and Richmond. Having therefore collected a force of about 15,000 infantry, a regiment of cavalry, and three batteries of artillery, he moved on the 11th of December along the railroad track to Kingston. He found the road obstructed with trees, the bridges over the streams burned, and the banks defended by skirmishers from General Evans's brigade of 2,000 men. Notwithstanding the delay caused by these impediments, Forster continued to advance, and on the 14th drove the enemy across the Neuse River, and following rapidly before he had had time to burn the bridge, occupied the town of Kingston. From thence expeditions were detached to destroy the rail and occupy a deserted fort near the mouth of the river. In the meantime General G. W. Smith, commanding the department of North Carolina, having become aware of the intentions of the enemy, reinforced Evans, and ordered him to take up a position to cover Goldsboro'. This he accordingly did, and on the 17th December stationed himself on the left bank of the Neuse, awaiting the approach of the Federal force. Forster had in the meantime advanced by the road on the right bank of the river, and becoming aware that the Confederates were in force near Goldsboro', determined to destroy the bridges over the river, and so protect his right flank. The railway bridge was burned, but the county bridge still remained; and late in the afternoon Evans, supported by three brigades which had arrived as reinforcements, moved rapidly across it, and drove the Federals from the railway track. Forster, who appears to have undertaken the expedition with little other object than that of impeding and partially destroying the Weldon Railway, withdrew during the night and retreated to Newberne, the Confederates reoccupying the country and repairing the railway, which was shortly afterwards in working order.

With the exception of some unimportant operations in the Kanawha Valley in Western Virginia, we have now glanced rapidly over what may be termed the minor operations of the war, and shall soon pass to the consideration of campaigns presenting features of greater interest. It is however well to pause for a moment to realise what these comparatively unimportant operations mean: the details of the movements of a few thousand troops or of the exploits of gunboats against small and hitherto to Europe scarcely known towns, are soon read and passed over; but the real misery inflicted on the unfortunate inhabitants, the many homes broken up, the families reduced from great wealth to as great poverty, the sufferings of the unfortunate negroes from their reputed friends—all these terrible realities of war are scarcely thought of, or if thought of are frequently put aside without meeting with the sympathy or consideration which they merit. The possession by the Federals of the sea-coast and great rivers enabled them to inflict these miseries on the population of the South, miseries which Southern men and more especially Southern women endured without a murmur. The men were away serving in the armies on some far-distant frontier; the women, the ladies of the South, brought up and educated in the greatest refinements of luxury, were left to manage the large plantations and rule and provide for the numerous families of slaves. Possibly a Federal force would land on some remote part of the coast, and hasty flight into the interior would necessarily follow; the negro families and such of the household property which could be collected together would be placed on the waggons, the cattle would be driven in, and the whole population leaving their homes, and burning their wealth stored up in the shape of cotton, would seek some fresh shelter in districts more remote from the enemy's attacks. Often the deserted houses would be occupied and afterwards burned and plundered by Northern soldiers, and all the home relics and associations tracing back frequently to the times of the first settlements from the mother country would be scattered or carried off to deck the houses of their plunderers in the New England States.

England has been so long free from the scourge of war on her own soil, that it is difficult for her people to appreciate the horrors, the miseries, and the desolation which the presence of an invading army entails. It can scarcely be a matter of wonder that some of the more violent of the Confederates should at this period have advocated retaliatory measures; and it ought to be a cause of gratitude to all lovers of humanity that such men as President Davis and General Lee headed the political and military governments of the Confederacy, and restraining their own feelings of anger, dared to withstand popular clamour, and to hold a steady, consistent, and humane bearing towards their enemies.

President Lincoln's emancipation proclamation, in which he declared that on the 1st day of January, 1863, all persons held as slaves within any state, or any designated part of a state, the people whereof should then be in rebellion against the United States, should be then henceforward and for ever free, provoked intense anger in the South. It was looked on as a direct invitation to a Servile war; and whilst the Southern Press stigmatised it as the production of a man who was willing to encourage every species of atrocity, which would attend a rising in revolt of the slaves, a great portion of the Northern people and of the press were opposed to the proclamation on political grounds. They alleged that it was illegal, that it could be of no value, and that it would only tend to inflame the passions of the South, and to close the door to every attempt at reconciliation and reunion. The Abolition party, although better pleased, regarded it only as the thin end of the wedge, and, consistent in their principles, looked forward to the time when slavery should be abolished in every part of the Union.

As an acknowledgment of the concession to their party, the friends of emancipation serenaded Mr. Lincoln, Mr. Chase, and Mr. Cassius M. Clay, and the three speeches of these men give an index of their character and of the feelings of the party of which they were the representatives. Mr. Lincoln spoke as if doubtful of the effects of his own act; the weakness of an honest but second-rate man showed itself in the words he uttered. Mr. Chase, having less responsibility, was more fluent and more hopeful, but mixed up principles of action with the requirements of military exigencies, both of which, according to his speech, were the motives which influenced the proclamation. Mr. Clay based his commendation of the proclamation entirely on the principles it enunciated, and uttered a great deal of what in America would be termed 'buncumbe.' He said that the entire question of freedom and self-government was involved in the great act, which he assured his hearers would make Abraham Lincoln immortal among men, and he pronounced that the man who did not stand by the President's proclamation was a traitor to his country and an enemy to his race.

The Proclamation was in fact of little real value, the slaves in the States in arms against the Union could only be freed by the success and advance of the armies, whilst the fear of a servile insurrection proved to have been needless, as the blacks remained quietly on the plantations, and showed no inclination to change their lot by violent measures. As a political measure it tended to evince the bias of the Government, and to prove that unless a vigorous effort was made, the Democratic party which held to the constitution would be for a long period excluded not only from direct power, but from any voice in the Government. The leaders of the party were well aware of this, and during the autumn of 1862 strove to gain the election of Democrats as members of Congress for the States where seats were vacant, and especially devoted their energies to the furtherance of the election of Mr. Seymour in opposition to General Wadsworth, for the office of Governor of the State of New York.

In Europe as well as in the North the result of the elections was looked forward to with great interest, as it was supposed that the question of peace or war might be involved in it. In the South, men judged more truly in depreciating the value of its importance and mistrusting the Democratic party both in respect to its principles and to its civil courage. The progress and results of the draft were watched with greater interest. At one time it seemed that violent opposition might be expected to its enforcement, but owing to the large bounties paid by the States for volunteers, the required quota of men within a small number was generally procured, and the drafting in all the States with few exceptions was carried on without violent opposition. Measures were taken by the introduction of passports to prevent the escape from the country of men subject to the draft, whilst all means were tried by speeches and even sermons to inflame the spirit of the people for the prosecution of the war. To the Irish, Archbishop Hughes spoke from the pulpit, whilst Colonel Corcoran, captured at Bull Run, and for a long time a prisoner in the South, after an ovation on his return to New York such as no one had before received, was employed with General Meagher to rouse his fellow-countrymen to a sense of the duty of fighting the battles of their but recently adopted country.

In the meanwhile the result of the elections terminated generally in favour of the Democrats, and owing possibly to fear, possibly to the fact that freedom of discussion had been necessarily permitted during the period of the elections, and could not again be totally repressed, the severe and illegal system adopted by Government officials towards political offenders was in some degree modified. The gates of Fort Warren, M'Henry, and Lafayette were thrown open, and many persons who had been imprisoned without trial, or even without any specified charges having been preferred against them, were allowed to go free.

There was much at this time calculated to cause alarm and disquietude in the North: the armies had not been successful, the pressure of the war was severely felt by some portions of the people, there were strikes among the labouring population of the large cities, the currency was in a most unsatisfactory state, great frauds and peculations had been discovered in some of the Government departments, and rumours of foreign intervention, which it was believed would not be unpalatable to certain classes, were in circulation. A proposal of mediation had indeed been made by the French Government to those of England and Russia, but declined by both, for the reasons, as stated by Lord Russell, that there was no ground at that time to hope that the Federal Government would accept the proposed suggestions, and as set forth by Prince Gortschakoff, that a combined step between France, England, and Russia, no matter how conciliatory or how cautiously made, would run the risk of causing precisely the very opposite of the object of pacification. Thus the Americans were left to fight out their own quarrel.

In the South, although the results of the summer

campaigns had partially compensated for the losses in the spring, there was still much suffering, and new causes of sorrow and anxiety. Provisions were dear, the currency was depreciated so as scarcely to serve the purpose of a medinm of exchange, forgeries of the badly executed notes were common, and among a portion of the commercial population, immorality in their dealings with the Government was rife. The conscription pressed heavily on the people, the price of substitutes was very high, and the crime of desertion was only too common among the newly raised troops,—desertion, not to the enemy, but to their own homes.

In October, the Confederate Congress passed a bill to authorise President Davis to suspend the writ of habeas corpus, and in the House of Representatives the punishment of death was decreed to Union soldiers who might have in their possession, or might endeavour to pass, counterfeit Confederate treasury notes. The Military Exemption Act was also passed, decreeing that the police for sections of the country with dense negro population should be exempt from conscription; also editors of newspapers, *employés* of telegraphs and transportation companies, ministers of the gospel, physicians, shoemakers, tanners, blacksmiths, waggon makers, millers, superintendents and *employés* of Government works, overseers of plantations, and one man to every five hundred head of cattle.

The labours of the white troops were in a great degree lessened by the employment of negroes to work on the fortifications, obtained either by impressment, or by the voluntary contributions of their owners, although there is evidence in the Governor of Georgia's proclamation of November 3rd, that some of the wealthy planters did not show sufficient readiness in affording this assistance to the State. This was, however, an exception to the usual patriotism of the Southern people: their unanimity in supporting their Government cannot be sufficiently admired; they had imbibed fresh confidence from the results of the autumn campaigns, and were now bracing themselves up for the renewed struggle which on all sides appeared imminent.

Neither did the heat of summer nor the cold of winter bring any cessation to the war. As we have seen the battles of the Chickahominy fought under a sultry July sun, so shall we see the soil of Virginia stained with the blood of her children and her enemies contrasting with the white hoar frost which covered her fields.

CHAPTER X.

BATTLE OF FREDERICKSBURG.

SINCE the campaign of Maryland the army of the Potomac had remained encamped on the banks of that river, recruiting from the severe losses incurred in the several battles of the Chickahominy, of the second Bull Run, and of Antietam. Elated by the absence of defeat in the last of these battles, the President and his advisers urged General M'Clellan to an immediate recommencement of active hostilities; General Lee was to be driven back, forced to accept battle, and to be not only defeated but crushed. They ignored the demoralisation of the army consequent on the terrible campaigns in which it had been engaged; they showed little zeal in furnishing its general with stores, army equipments, and horses; but sending repeated orders for him to advance, seemed to seek an opportunity to represent him as slow and wanting in energy, and thus gradually to sap his greatly increased popularity. In all political principles M'Clellan was strongly opposed to the party to which the advisers of the President belonged and to which he himself inclined; and at a time when this party was incurring defeat in the elections, it appeared dangerous to allow a political opponent to possess the confidence and to hold the chief command of the main army. Thus whilst policy led many members of Mr. Lincoln's cabinet to wish for General M'Clellan's removal, his own slowness of action and perhaps over great caution gave them not only a handle which they could use in biassing public opinion, but also a cloak which would conceal from themselves their own motives.

The army under General M'Clellan continued to hold the left bank of the Potomac during the greater part of the month of October, whilst continuous correspondence passed between him and General Halleck, the commander-in chief; the latter urging an advance, the former repeating his requisitions for supplies and cavalry horses.

Two lines of march were open for the adoption of the general, either to advance up the Shenandoah Valley, in which case from 12,000 to 15,000 additional men would be furnished him, or crossing the Blue Ridge to interpose between the Confederates and Washington, when 30,000 would be sent as reinforcements. M'Clellan inclined to the first-mentioned plan, as by it he would cover Maryland, as well as have the advantage of the Harper's Ferry and Winchester rail for the conveyance of his supplies. The President was in favour of the latter, as he would then be relieved from all anxiety with regard to Washington. As however, from several causes, the army delayed its advance, and the fine weather of early autumn changed to the rain of a later period of the year, circumstances altered. The waters of the Potomac rose, the river became unfordable, and the roads into Maryland were rendered difficult for the movements of troops. These natural causes were considered sufficient to protect Maryland and the country bordering on the upper Potomac, and General M'Clellan therefore resolved to cross over to the south side of the Blue Ridge Mountains, and advancing parallel with the range and seizing each pass with detachments, to protect his own line of communications at the same time that he threatened those of the enemy in the Shenandoah Valley.

On the 25th of October the movement commenced, and by the first week in November the whole army was concentrated in the neighbourhood of Warrenton. General M'Clellan expressed his opinion that a general engagement would probably take place in a few days; he considered the troops under his command in admirable condition and spirits, and awaited the result with confidence. This was on the 7th of November, but in the evening of the same day, or rather during the night, a Brigadier General of the name of Buckenham arrived at the camp and delivered to M'Clellan an order to resign the command of the army to General Burnside, and to report himself at Trenton, a small town of New Jersey. The announcement was totally unexpected by both Generals M'Clellan and Burnside; it was evidently a *coup d'état* suggested by the fears of the dominant party in Mr. Lincoln's cabinet,—fears lest M'Clellan should use his vast influence in the army to assist with force the partial political triumph of the Democrats. That such a course had been thought possible by some members of the party, both civil and military, there is ground for believing; but M'Clellan himself had given no encouragement to such expectations: during his active career as a soldier he had never interfered in politics, and had always loyally supported the President and Government to whom he owed allegiance. His character as evinced by his conduct was as a citizen irreproachable, and considered merely in respect to his own feelings, the method of his dismissal was harsh in the extreme; but if his admirers may be inclined to pass judgment on his political opponents, and to cry shame on the ingratitude of the nation, those who carefully consider the circumstances of the case will possibly find that some excuse can be offered for the line of conduct adopted. The country, irrespective of the trials of war, was passing through a revolution, old landmarks were in course of removal, old restraints were being broken, and during such periods acts which might be termed violent in peaceful times must be excused, and a government and nation may even be commended which abstain from bloodshed, and refrain from the too common recourse to political executions.

General M'Clellan's ready compliance with the order he had received, his temperate address to his army, and his subsequent conduct in refusing to become the representative of a discontented party,* proclaim him to be a man actuated by higher motives than those of ambition; and if he cannot be numbered among the leaders of his age, he will yet be entitled to respect for his honesty of purpose, his moderation, and his capability for the organisation of an army; whilst his advance from Washington and the battles of South Mountain and Antietam will be considered as among the turning-points of the war, when defeat prevented was almost equal to victory gained.

His personal friend General Burnside was now invested with the command of the Potomac army. He was known as a man of high character, and although a Democrat, yet free from any decided political bias; he had been successful in North Carolina, and had distinguished himself at South Mountain and Antietam; he, moreover, possessed the confidence of General M'Clellan, and was on terms of personal friendship with his staff and with that of the army, thereby possessing

* No reference is here intended to General M'Clellan's subsequent constitutional opposition to Mr. Lincoln's re-election.

an advantage over the hero of the public prints—General Hooker.

The army was now divided into three grand divisions, each consisting of two corps, and commanded by Generals Sumner, Hooker, and Franklin; among the subordinate generals no change was made, excepting in the case of General Fitz John Porter, who was deprived of his command and placed under arrest, to await trial on charges resulting from occurrences connected with Pope's campaign.

It was Burnside's plan to make a demonstration on the Rappahannock, and then rapidly marching down the left bank of that river, to cross by means of pontoons at Fredericksburg, and depending on the Potomac and on the Aquia Creek rail for his supplies, to advance on Richmond by Hanover Court-house. He considered that he would thus avoid the evil of having to protect long lines of communication necessitated by a movement against Richmond by Gordonsville, and, on the other hand, would defeat the objection raised to the adoption of the line of the Pamunkey and James Rivers, by his ability to cover Washington from Fredericksburg almost equally well as from Warrenton and Gordonsville. He depended for success on the rapidity of his movements; he supposed that General Jackson was still west of the Blue Ridge, and that by a rapid march he might cross the Rappahannock, and advancing on Richmond, might fall with his whole army on a portion only of that of his opponent.

Requisitions were sent to General Halleck for the movement of the pontoons and supplies to Aquia Creek, the former especially to be transported as speedily as possible, either by land or water, to Fredericksburg. Shortly afterwards General Sumner was ordered to march on the same point, followed by Franklin and Hooker; whilst to General Pleasanton, now in command of the cavalry, was assigned the duty of protecting the right rear of the army, and preventing the incursions of the Confederate troopers; and General Sigel, with an independent corps, was detached to guard the upper Potomac, as also the direct route between Gordonsville and Washington.

Such was General Burnside's plan of operations; but his adversary General Lee was well informed of all his movements, and as Sumner advanced along the banks of the Rappahannock to Fredericksburg, Longstreet moved in a parallel line on the same point. Thus, when Sumner reached Falmouth opposite Fredericksburg, he found that the enemy's batteries were facing him on the other side of the river, and that the pontoons on which he had depended for effecting a passage had not arrived. The plan of surprising the enemy, and establishing the army on the heights beyond Fredericksburg preparatory to an advance on Richmond, had miscarried, and it remained for General Burnside to concentrate his forces at Falmouth and attempt (if so disposed) by open force, what he had failed in accomplishing by strategy.

The time necessary to collect the Federal forces was equally sufficient to allow of the arrival of General Jackson, and thus by the 25th of November the whole Confederate army—augmented in numbers since the battle of Antietam—was in position on the heights overlooking the quiet little town of Fredericksburg and the Rappahannock River.

The fate of the town was singularly unhappy: under the guns of the Federal batteries, it was yet occupied by the out-pickets of the Confederate army, and its inhabitants were dependent for safety and for life on the forbearance of the Federal general, whom any belligerent act on the part of the advanced pickets might provoke to wreak vengeance on the helpless population. There were associations connected with Fredericksburg similar to those which formerly attached to the banks of the Pamunkey. It had been the scene of the earlier portion of Washington's life; here his mother had dwelt; and in the neighbourhood of the town much of his boyhood had been passed. As Fredericksburg resembled the White House in its associations, so did it partake in its fate.

For nearly three weeks the two armies remained confronting each other, the Confederate pickets holding the town of Fredericksburg and the right bank of the Rappahannock; the Federals the left bank and the small town of Falmouth. The inhabitants had removed from Fredericksburg, and the trains from Richmond—which ran regularly to the head-quarters of the Confederate army—stopped two miles outside the town. The breaking up of the weather, and the imposing position occupied by Lee, made the Federal general hesitate before ordering an attack. At length, owing possibly to the pressure put upon him by the Government, or by *public opinion*, Burnside took measures for a general advance against the Confederate position. He determined to cross the river by means of pontoon bridges, constructed in front of his centre, opposite to the town of Fredericksburg, and also to effect a passage at a point about a mile and a half lower down the river, where the conformation of the ground on the right bank afforded play for the guns posted on the higher ground on the left bank. His army, consisting of three grand divisions, held the heights immediately overlooking the Rappahannock, and extended for a distance of about four miles along its left bank. The right grand division was under the command of General Hooker, the centre under General Sumner, the left under General Franklin; the total numerical strength being about 150,000 men. A more than ordinary powerful artillery was attached to the army, of which no less than 143 guns, overlooking the town of Fredericksburg, commanded the course of the river and the opposite bank.

The Confederate army under General Lee, numbering about 80,000 men, was drawn up along the heights, which, retiring in a semicircle from the river, embrace within their arms a plain six miles in length, and from two to three in depth. These heights, or bluffs, rise higher and steeper immediately in rear of the town of Fredericksburg than those which stretch away towards the East; they are also almost bare of trees, whilst, on the contrary, the hills receding from the river are thickly covered, and their lower ridges, or spurs, clothed with brushwood. This semicircle of hills terminates at Massaponax River, about five miles below Fredericksburg. The right of the Confederate army, extending nearly as far as the Massaponax, comprised the cavalry and horse artillery under General J. E. B. Stuart, posted on the only ground at all suitable for that arm of the service. On his left was General Jackson's corps, of which Early's * division formed the right, and A. P. Hill the left, the divisions of Generals Taliaferro and D. H. Hill being in reserve. The left wing of the army under General Longstreet comprised the division of General Hood on the right, next to it that of General Pickett, then those of Generals

* Formerly General Ewell's.

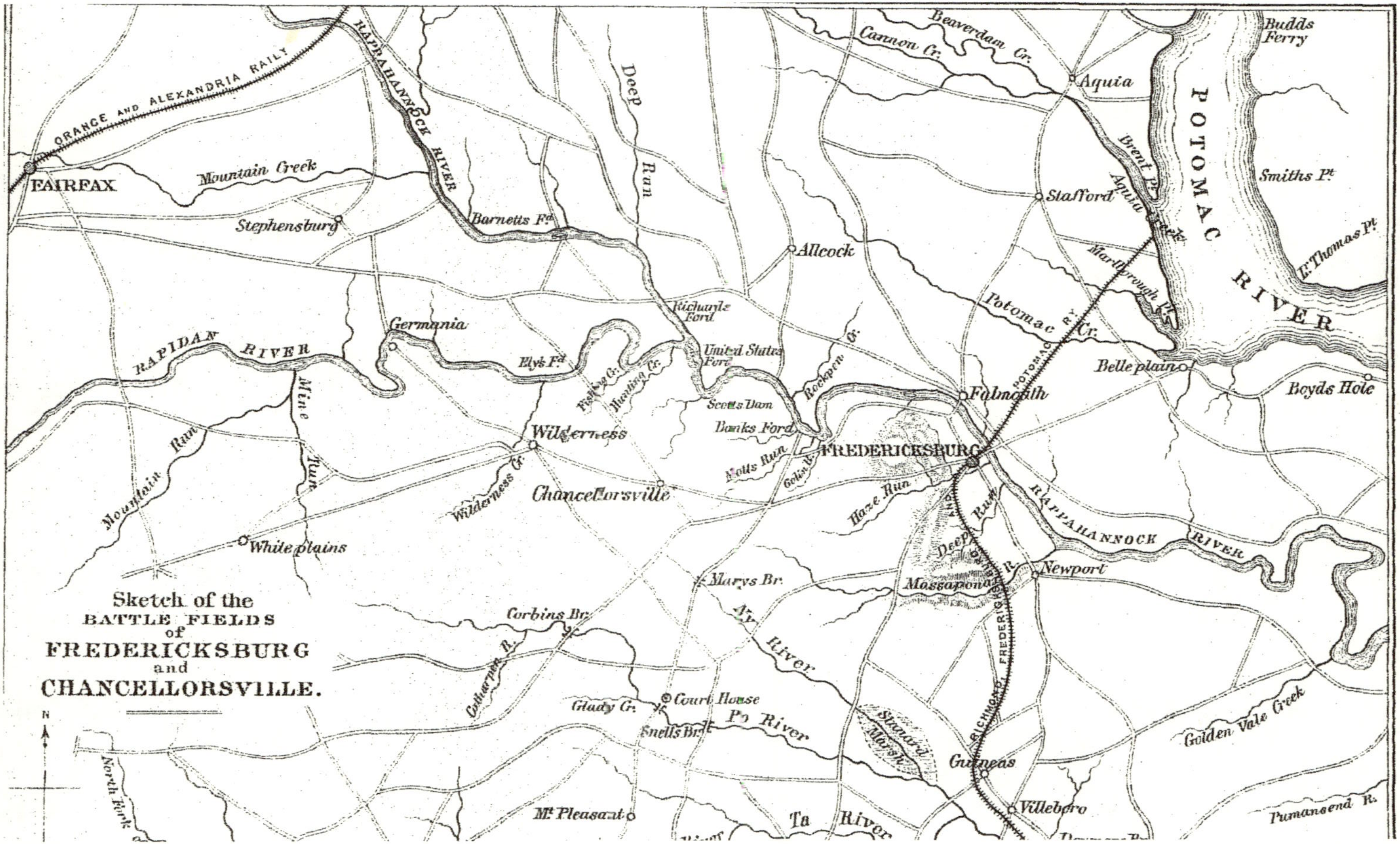

Sketch of the
BATTLE FIELDS
of
FREDERICKSBURG
and
CHANCELLORSVILLE.
POTOMAC RIVER
RAPPAHANNOCK RIVER
RAPIDAN RIVER
ORANGE AND ALEXANDRIA RAILY
POTOMAC RY.
FAIRFAX
Mountain Creek
Stephensburg
Barnetts Fd.
Deep Run
Allcock
Stafford
Aquia
Aquia Creek
Brent Pt.
Beaverdam Cr.
Cannon Cr.
Budds Ferry
Smiths Pt.
L. Thomas Pt.
Marlborough Pt.
Potomac Cr.
Belle plain
Boyds Hole
Falmouth
FREDERICKSBURG
Germania
Elys Fd.
Richards Ford
United States Ford
Scotts Dam
Banks Ford
Motts Run
Hazel Run
Deep Run
Massaponax R.
Newport
Wilderness
Wilderness Cr.
Chancellorsville
Mine Run
Mountain Run
White plains
Marys Br.
Ny River
Corbins Br.
Court House
Glady Cr.
Snells Br.
Po River
Stanard Marsh
Guineas
Villeboro
Golden Vale Creek
Pumansend R.
Mt. Pleasant
Ta River
North Fork
N

M'Laws, Ranson, and Anderson. The artillery, according to General Lee's practice, was massed together, and not dispersed among the divisions, and was so posted as to sweep the front of the position—the semicircular formation of the hills favouring this disposition. Few stronger positions have ever been occupied by an army; a direct road running in rear of the crest of hills connected its two wings, and the minor features of the country were favourable to troops acting on the defensive. The Confederate army, confident in their leader, and flushed with success, awaited without anxiety, and almost with exultation, the anticipated attack.

On the 11th of December the Federal engineers commenced the construction of the pontoon bridges on which it was proposed that the army should cross the river. Franklin, on the Federal left, completed his bridge without opposition, and requested leave from General Burnside to commence at once the passage of the river; he was desired to await the construction of the bridges opposite the centre, attended with greater difficulties, as Barksdale's Mississippians, holding the houses on the right bank, opened a brisk fire on the bridge builders, and even in the darkness of the early morning succeeded in killing and wounding several of the engineers. The men were driven from their work, and operations were at a standstill. News that such was the case was brought to Burnside, who was precluded, by a thick mist which hung over the valley, from watching the operations; he therefore gave orders that the whole of the artillery should open on the town. For two hours the bombardment continued, the mist concealed its effects, and only a black cloud of smoke rising from the valley marked the probable result of the terrible fire. At noon the curtain rose, and the town of Fredericksburg, or rather its ruins, became apparent to both armies. Many of the houses were in flames, many had been battered down, but the object of the bombardment remained unfulfilled. Barksdale's Mississippians still held their position, concealed in the houses facing the river, which were comparatively secure from the artillery, as the guns could not be sufficiently depressed to play on them.

During this time scarcely a shot had been fired from the Confederate batteries, as General Lee was unwilling to indicate their position. Finding the artillery unavailing, two regiments of infantry were ordered by General Burnside to cross by means of the pontoon boats, and to drive off the enemy's riflemen. This was successfully accomplished, and on the evening of the 11th, one corps from Sumner's command, and one from Franklin's, crossed the river. During the 12th Burnside massed the greater portion of his army near the pontoon bridges, in readiness to advance when the attack should commence. He endeavoured also to move Stoneman's corps across the river, but the fire of the Confederate batteries, which commanded the slope of the road leading to the pontoons, delayed the attempt till after dark. Nothing occurred during the 12th, excepting skirmishing between the advanced pickets, which now on either side formed a continuous line, Franklin's right being connected with Sumner's left in the town of Fredericksburg. An artillery duel across the river was likewise kept up with energy by the Federals, and replied to sparingly by the Confederates, who were still careful to conceal the position of their batteries. Thus passed the 12th of December; and it was known in both armies that dawn on the following day would inaugurate a battle which must be desperate, and which might prove fatal to one of the armies engaged.

There was quiet during the hours of darkness: the Confederates, appreciating the advantage of their position, confident in their general, and enthusiastic for their cause, awaited the morning's light in full expectation of victory, their sanguine spirits seeing an omen of success in the beautiful aurora which illumined the winter's night. The Federals, inspirited by the success of their attempt to cross the river, by the grand spectacle of their enormous army, by their numerous and powerful artillery, and under the guidance of regimental, brigade, and division leaders whom they had learned to trust, likewise awaited, but not without feelings of anxiety, the approach of dawn. Few among either officers or men could fail to appreciate the task which awaited them; they were fully aware of the gallantry of their opponents; they could see their strong position, and estimate their strength; they appreciated highly General Lee's qualities, and knew full well that they themselves were commanded by a general who had not as yet gained their confidence, and between whom and some of the superior officers there was not complete accord. Many of the men and officers regretted *little Mac*,* and his health was drunk, and his speedy return looked for, around many a camp-fire, on the night preceding the battle of Fredericksburg.

The morning of the 13th of December dawned bright and warm, contrasting with the cold of the previous days; and as soon as there was sufficient light the Federal columns on the right prepared for the attack. Even at the commencement of the day there

* M'Clellan's name among the soldiers.

seems to have been a want of unity in the operations of the Federal generals. Franklin—on whom General Burnside intended the brunt of the action should fall, and who, by carrying the less strong position in his front, was to allow of a decisive attack on the steep heights held by the Confederate left—failed to comprehend his orders; he supposed that he was intended only to make a feint, and although in command of two *corps d'armée*, comprising six divisions, he yet engaged in the attack with but three divisions, the remainder being so placed as to be unavailable even if required.* The Federal army was too large for the capacities of the men who commanded it; it was unwieldy, its strength was frittered away in dribbles, and it suffered defeat in detail.

Burnside, who appears to have supposed that a feint made by him of crossing the river some miles below Fredericksburg had so far deceived General Lee as to have led him to extend and weaken his line, proposed first to attack and carry the low wooded hills in the vicinity of Deep Run, and thus, having separated the Confederate army, to storm the heights immediately south of Fredericksburg, and to overwhelm the Confederate right wing.

About 9 A.M. the advance commenced, and the Federal columns moved forward, under cover of a fog which concealed them from their opponents. General Stuart was the first to notice their movements, and hastened forward a section of a horse artillery battery, under a very gallant young officer of the name of Pelham. For two hours these two guns sustained the heavy

* See General Franklin's evidence before the Court of Inquiry. He said, Meade, Gibbon, and Doubleday were actually engaged. It would have taken from four to five hours to bring up the remainder.

fire directed against them by the Federal supporting batteries, whilst the columns of infantry moved forward. As the sun obtained strength the mist rose, and the Confederates were enabled to direct their musketry fire with more deadly effect. The first shock of the action fell on A. P. Hill's division, and two brigades of North Carolina troops for the moment gave way, but part of Early's division coming up in support, the attack was repulsed. Vainly did the Federal officers endeavour to deploy their men under fire; twice indeed did they advance, but A. P. Hill and Early drove them back, the latter following them across the plain, until the supporting artillery opened on and repulsed the pursuers.

On the right of the left Federal attack, Hood, with his Texans, became engaged shortly after A. P. Hill's division had commenced the action. Franklin's right and Sumner's left advanced against that part of the line, and for a short time a body of Federals succeeded in occupying a small copse in front of Hood's position: but the Texans rushed forward, and with little difficulty drove their opponents from the shelter they had gained.

During the advance of the Federal left, fresh divisions had crossed the river at Fredericksburg, and the mass of Burnside's army was concentrated in front of Longstreet's strong position. Sumner's grand division formed the column of attack, assisted by a part of Hooker's command. But in this portion of the line General Lee in person superintended the operations of his troops, and by his calm presence gave confidence to those who may be excused if they watched with anxiety the masses of the enemy gathering on the plain, and the long lines of men pouring continuously across the bridges and through the streets of Fredericksburg. In the morning, before the attack had commenced, he had ridden from one end of the position to the other, and had seen with his own eyes that every preparation had been made for the approaching battle. He had then stationed himself on a hill to the south-east of the heights overlooking the town, from which he could command the whole field of battle, and could watch with more direct supervision the preparations to receive the successive columns of attack as they marched out of Fredericksburg and dashed vainly against Marye's Height, held by M'Laws' division and the Washington artillery. In vain Sumner pushed forward French, Hancock, and Howard; each division was repulsed with terrible loss; the Irish brigade advanced impetuously and perished within a short distance of the Confederate guns; all was in vain, and General Burnside saw the successive defeat of each assaulting column. He then called on Hooker to hasten his men over the bridges, and endeavour to retrieve the day. Hooker crossed the river, but hesitated to make the attack, and sent an aide-de-camp to General Burnside, to say that he considered that the heights could not be carried. Burnside reiterated his orders, and Hooker got on his horse, recrossed the river, and remonstrated in person. Again he received the command to advance, and this time he directed General Humphries' division to form up for the attack; he made them take off their knapsacks, haversacks, and overcoats, and with unloaded muskets to advance to the assault. All proved futile: the men rushed forward; they arrived within twenty yards of the stone wall held by Colonel Alexander's battalion, they wavered, a third of their number fell, and the remainder fled.

The town of Fredericksburg was full of wounded and stragglers: the guards on the bridges prevented the latter from escaping; but hiding among the houses, and in many instances engaged in plundering, the men refused to be led forward to what they regarded as certain death. All day the action continued: the simile so often used—of waves breaking against cliffs—can be truly taken as representing the successive assaults of the Federal divisions; with comparatively little loss to the defenders each wave was shattered and hurled back, and as night closed in the battle ceased, and both armies held the ground they had occupied in the early morning. Then appeared an opportunity of driving the demoralized Federals into the river, and inflicting on them not only defeat but destruction. But General Lee did not order an advance; content with the victory he had gained, and knowing the inferiority in numbers of the troops under his command, careful of the lives of his soldiers, and possibly fearful of exposing them to the fire of the batteries on the left bank, he maintained a defensive attitude, and allowed the Federals to occupy unmolested the plain and the town. Indeed, General Lee and other Confederate officers appear to have expected a renewal of the assault on the following day, and instead of preparing for an advance, employed the men in throwing up fresh works.*

* The reasons which prevented General Lee from assuming the offensive have never been satisfactorily accounted for. The able correspondent of the *Times*' newspaper, to whom the author is much indebted for his account of the battle, seems at a loss fully to explain them. He writes in his letter dated Richmond, Dec. 20, 1862—'How perilous that position (that of the Federal army) was, it is obvious that the Confederate generals, who hoped against hope that the 14th and 15th of December would witness a renewal of the Federal attack, did not at the moment fully realise. But summing up the results of the late battle, it is sufficient to say that enough has been gained by it; and, although it is conceivable that on the night of the

Sunday, the 14th, dawned; Burnside wished to renew the attack, but his subordinate generals, who knew better the temper of the troops, begged him to desist, and the day passed in comparative quiet, broken only by skirmishing, and an occasional shot from the heavy guns. All day the wounded and dead lay intermingled in front of the Confederate lines; Burnside refused to acknowledge his defeat by sending a flag of truce, and Lee, resolved to maintain his privilege as the victor in the battle of the 13th, awaited its arrival, and refused to listen to any terms proposed by the subordinate generals of the advanced divisions. On Monday, the 15th, most of the wounded were removed; and during the night, under cover of the darkness, the Federal general withdrew his forces across the river: a high wind blowing from the south prevented the noise of the wheels of the guns and the tramp of the men from reaching the Confederate camp, and on the morning of the 16th General Lee looked down with surprise on the deserted plain, and the town unoccupied, except by the wounded, too badly injured to bear removal.

Such was the battle of Fredericksburg. With but the comparatively slight loss of 1,800 men, General Lee had repulsed his opponent, and diminished the Federal army by 13,771 men killed, wounded, and missing.*

13th, or the afternoon of the 14th or 15th, a general advance of the Confederate lines might have turned the Federal rout into what is known on this continent as "a Ball's Bluff affair," still it is more in accordance with the well-known humanity of such men as Generals Lee and Jackson that not one life, even the life of an enemy, should be unnecessarily sacrificed, when already a sufficient lesson had been taught to the foe.'

* See General Lee's official report, and the estimate of the Federal losses in the report of the Committee of Inquiry into the conduct of the war.

Through bad generalship, confusion in orders, and want of unity, the strength of the Federal army had been wasted. The assault on so strong a position as that held by General Lee may have been rash, but having been decided on it ought to have been carried through with unanimity and vigour. A large portion of the Federal army was not engaged, and vast numbers of troops not belonging to the Army of the Potomac, but within a short distance of the battle-field, lay idle and unemployed, when every serviceable man was in the ranks of the Confederate army. What was Sigel doing during the battle of Fredericksburg, and why were large bodies of men encamped near Alexandria, whilst Richmond was almost destitute of defenders? There was no lack of men in the Federal armies, but there was an absence of talent to command them. The Northern Americans —unread in history—failed to appreciate the lesson so often taught by its pages, that large armies are not the only requisites for victorious campaigns.*

For the passage of the river, and for the failure of the attack, General Burnside took the whole responsibility, thereby relieving the Government of much anxiety and securing the gratitude of the President. But he had lost the confidence of his officers and men; and on a plan of another advance having been formed, a series of remonstrances were addressed not only to him, but to the President in person. General Burnside expostu-

* About the time the battle of Fredericksburg was fought, the author travelled from Richmond to Washington; he saw only a few irregular troops of cavalry and a small detachment of infantry belonging to the Confederate army, whilst in the vicinity of Alexandria and between it and Bull Run there were many thousands of Federal troops in continual expectation of attack by some large and unknown Confederate force.

lated, and issued a stringent order, dismissing and removing several general officers of high rank from their commands, and decreeing death as a punishment for the crime of desertion, which had much increased, and threatened considerably to reduce the army. The President, to whom this order was referred, refused to sanction it, but was yet unwilling to accept Burnside's consequent resignation. When, however, he found that the army was in a complete state of demoralisation, and that he must either punish the malcontents—of which General Hooker was among the most conspicuous—or remove General Burnside, he decided on the latter course, and Burnside was relieved of his command, and Hooker appointed to succeed him. This change was pleasing to the Republican party and to a portion of the army, but there were men who doubted whether so loud a talker as General Hooker was known to be would prove a discreet commander, and not a few entertained a personal dislike against him on account of the discourtesy and absence of good feeling which he had shown in his conduct towards M'Clellan.

Thus terminated for the present the winter campaign of Fredericksburg. Seldom have so many lives been so fruitlessly sacrificed, and seldom has a nation been called on to bear with equanimity misfortunes occasioned by so great mismanagement. Commencing with the miscarriage of the orders relating to the pontoons,* and

* Captain Chesney, in his review of the recent campaign of Virginia, thus refers to the mistakes which occurred in reference to the transport of the pontoons. 'And it should be noted that these blunders were not made—as in the Crimean war, so sharply criticised by American officers—at the commencement of hostilities, but at the end of eighteen months of war conducted on the very largest scale.'

continuing during nearly the whole campaign, the general mismanagement of its conduct was redeemed solely by the masterly manner in which the retreat of the Federal army was secured during the night of the 15th—a retreat which might have been rendered disastrous if the Confederate General had been aware that it was in progress. It is indeed difficult to read the account of the battle of Fredericksburg without counting it as another among the many lost opportunities of the war. Had the Federals been followed after their last repulse, or had they been pressed during their retreat, the Rappahannock might have been more fatal to their army than was the Elster at Leipsic to the rear-guard of Napoleon.

For several months the two armies continued to watch each other across the Rappahannock, nor was it until the spring that active operations were resumed in Virginia. The Campaign of the West, less influenced by weather, continued during the winter months, and in that direction, although gallantly opposed, the Federal armies pursued a steady but not uninterrupted advance.

CHAPTER XI.

THE WINTER CAMPAIGN IN THE WEST.

THAT the importance of the Western Campaign was fully appreciated by the Government of the Confederate States is clear both from the words and acts of the President. During the month of December he undertook the long and tedious journey from Richmond to Chattanooga, and after passing in review the army of General Bragg near Murfreesboro, proceeded onwards to his own state, Mississippi. There he addressed the State Legislature, urging the people of the West to renewed exertions, and putting before them the sufferings of those who had been brought under the power of the Federal armies, drawing a vivid and perhaps highly coloured picture of the savage character of the war, and showing how re-union with such a race as the hated Yankee was impossible. He pointed out that there were two prominent objects in the programme of the enemy,—one to get possession of the Mississippi River and to open it to navigation, in order to appease the clamours of the West, and to utilize the capture of New Orleans, which had thus far rendered the Federals no service; the other to seize the capital of the Confederacy, and to hold it, if only as a proof that the Confederacy had no existence. 'We have recently (said the President) defeated them at Fredericksburg, and I believe that, under God and by the valour of our troops, the capital of the Confederacy will stand safe behind its wall of living breasts. Vicksburg and Port Hudson have been strengthened, and now we can concentrate at either of them a force sufficient for their protection. Let every man (he added) hasten to defend these places, and thus hold the Mississippi River, that great artery of the Confederacy, preserve our communications with the Trans-Mississippi departments, and thwart the enemy's scheme of forcing navigation through to New Orleans. By holding that section of the river between Port Hudson and Vicksburg, we shall secure these results, and the people of the West, cut off from New Orleans, will be driven to the East to seek a market for their products, and will be compelled to pay so much in the way of freights, that those products will be rendered almost valueless. Thus (he concluded) I should not be surprised if the first day-break of peace were to dawn upon us from that quarter.'

Such were the opinions uttered by President Davis, and his words will serve as an indication of the objects of the Western Campaign. The heroic defence of Vicksburg and the repulse in the previous summer of the Federal fleet, encouraged the Confederates to fortify Port Hudson some distance further down the Mississippi, and to endeavour to hold the river between those places. On their possession rested in a great measure the safety of the State of Mississippi, as the left flank and lines of communication of the army defending its Northern extremities depended for their security on immunity from attack from the river. The army of Mississippi, including the garrisons of Vicksburg and Port Hudson, was placed under General Pemberton, an old West Point officer, but the whole command of the West was given to General J. Johnston, the hero of Bull Run and the Seven Pines.

His command included the army of Tennessee, still under General Braxton Bragg, who although he had disappointed the hopes of his fellow-countrymen in the campaign of Kentucky, was yet supported by the President, who did not desert those whom he deemed meritorious even when unsuccessful. To him was allotted the task of defending Southern Tennessee, and if possible, when the communications of the Federal armies should have been sufficiently harassed by the cavalry of Morgan and Forrest, of advancing on Nashville and the line of the Cumberland.

As was indicated in President Davis's speech, there were hopes in the South that the West, viewing her own interests, might separate her policy from the Northern and Eastern States, and either force them to agree to peace, or conclude a separate treaty. This hope had been long encouraged among the Confederates, but proved equally fallacious as the expectation of European intervention. The West was the most formidable antagonist with which the South had to contend; her troops were accounted to be the bravest in the Federal armies, and it was from her that the most terrible blows were to be received.

Two main armies were now threatening the Confederacy from the West, of which one was moving from Western Tennessee into the State of Mississippi, whilst a strong detached force which may be called its right wing, was organising for a separate expedition down the Mississippi River against Vicksburg. This army was under General Grant, and the detached expedition, under General Sherman. It was opposed by Generals Pemberton, Van Dorn, and Price, who defended the lines of the Tallahatchie River, the approaches by the rail into the State of Mississippi, and the fortifications at Vicksburg. The other army, now under General Rosecrans, had received a severe check in its onward progress by General Bragg's campaign in Kentucky, and in the autumn of 1862 maintained itself with some difficulty at Nashville and on the line of the Cumberland. In its front, on the main line of railway south of Nashville, lay the Confederate army of Tennessee under General Bragg in cantonments at Murfreesboro, active operations being confined to the expeditions of the indefatigable partizan leaders Morgan and Forrest.

These two officers with comparatively small bodies of men, reinforced by the inhabitants of the country through which they marched, made continual inroads into Kentucky, and fell unexpectedly on the enemy's detached posts. No difficulties seemed to daunt them; along roads rendered impassable for regular troops, through snow, ice, and mud, they forced their way, dependent on the country for supplies, often on their enemies for ammunition, and on the peculiar description of their force, infantry mounted on horses, for celerity of movement and for the performance of the various duties required from men in guerilla warfare. The Federals occupied certain strategical positions and fortified towns, but the country was not conquered, and the condition of Kentucky seemed to afford a proof of the difficulties which would accompany an advance into the more Southern States.

General Rosecrans's position was one which many men would regard as unenviable; he had been appointed to succeed an able general, superseded and disgraced, not for the crime of incurring defeat, but for failure in securing a decisive victory; it was clear therefore that he was expected to resume with little delay an offensive campaign. The States north and west of the Ohio formed his original base of operations, but his intermediate base was Nashville, between which town and the Ohio lines of railway brought up reinforcements and supplies, and these lines, subject to interruption by the Confederate cavalry, required guards to protect them. In Nashville he had not only to organise his own troops but to exercise a careful supervision over the inhabitants, many of whom were known to be strong sympathisers with the South. He had also to fortify the town, and watch the line of the Cumberland River, where his detached posts, often commanded by most inefficient officers, were constantly exposed to surprise. Nashville itself was threatened, and shortly previous to General Rosecrans's arrival, a combined movement of Forrest and Morgan, the former from the South and the latter from the North, had with some difficulty been repulsed by General Negley.

A month later, General Morgan again distinguished himself by his successful capture of a Federal detachment holding Hartsville, a small town on the right bank of the Cumberland, about equidistant from the Federal head-quarters at Nashville and those of the Confederates at Murfreesboro. After a march of about forty miles, through snow and ice, Morgan, with a combined infantry and cavalry force, succeeded in the darkness of the night, on the 6th and 7th of December, in crossing the Cumberland River at a point seven miles below Hartsville, and between it and Nashville. So difficult or rather impossible did the Federals consider the passage of the river at this point, that they had neglected to watch it, and Morgan was thus able to surprise their pickets on the right bank. At daybreak on the 7th, he moved forward against the main body, which hastily seized its arms, and, drawn up on the farther side of a ravine, endeavoured to oppose his advance. Little judgment was shown by the Federal commander, the orders given to the troops were confused and contradictory, and after but a slight resistance the greater number, about 1,800, surrendered. They were immediately marched as prisoners to Murfreesboro, as a large body of Federals was known to be in the neighbourhood, and after paying toll to their captors, in arms, blankets, and overcoats, were parolled and sent back to Nashville.

The success of these detached expeditions appears to have created a belief in the minds of the Confederate Generals that Rosecrans, unable to undertake offensive operations, was only intent on holding his strong position at Nashville, and that it would be necessary to force him to leave his entrenchments by operating on his lines of communication. With this object Morgan was again detached to Kentucky to cut off the Federal detachments and seize the rail between Nashville and Louisville, whilst Forrest was sent with a somewhat similar design into Western Tennessee to menace Grant's communications with Columbus, and to prevent reinforcements from reaching the Federal army of Tennessee from the army of Mississippi.

Whilst these expeditions were undertaken by the cavalry, the main body of the Confederate army, unsuspecting any movement on the part of the enemy, and cheered by the visit of the President and by the more favourable aspect of affairs, remained within their cantonments, enjoying as far as was possible the hospitality of the inhabitants of Murfreesboro,—a hospitality which received an increased impulse from the season of the year. Christmas-day in 1862 was passed in serenity and such festivity as circumstances would admit, by the Confederate army of the West, but, on the following day, news reached General Bragg which changed the aspect of affairs. The enemy was reported to be advancing in force and a general engagement appeared imminent.

The front of the army was covered, and the roads and rail watched by three brigades of cavalry under Wheeler, Wharton, and Pegram, so that no movement of the Federals could take place without due notice being received at the Confederate head-quarters.

In three columns on the 26th December, General Rosecrans advanced, M'Cook with three divisions forming the right column, Thomas the centre with two divisions, and Crittenden the left with three divisions; numbering in all about forty thousand infantry and artillery and a small force of cavalry.* The roads were good, but the country, undulating and wooded, afforded cover for the Confederate skirmishers. The columns marched slowly, and time was thus allowed for Bragg to concentrate his forces and to choose the ground on which he intended to give battle. His army consisted of two corps of two divisions each, under Generals Hardee and Polk, with a detached division under General M'Cowen, and comprised about 30,000 infantry and artillery, in addition to the three brigades of irregular cavalry, numbering about 5,000. The distance from Nashville to Murfreesboro was under forty miles, but the Federal army, advancing very slowly and cautiously feeling its way, did not reach the neighbourhood of the latter town until the 30th. On that day one of Crittenden's divisions made a reconnaissance on the left,

* There were about twenty-four infantry brigades (Federals), and nineteen brigades (Confederates), engaged in the battle of Stone River or Murfreesboro.

crossing the Stone River by a ford, and forcing back a regiment belonging to Breckenridge's division, at the same time that M'Cook pushed forward on the right, shelling the woods in his front and driving in Polk's pickets. The Confederate guns replied, and there was a warm artillery engagement, interspersed with heavy skirmishing and an attempt to capture one of Polk's batteries, which was repulsed. During the night the two armies bivouacked within a very short distance of each other, and the watch-fires of each were distinctly visible to the other as they gleamed through the forest. Both armies knew that on the following day a battle which might decide the fate of the West would be fought, and each general made his preparations accordingly.

General Rosecrans disposed the mass of his troops on his left, prepared to force the passage of the Stone River on the north of the Murfreesboro rail; whilst his right, more extended and more advanced, formed an angle with the centre and left, and faced in an almost due easterly direction. Crittenden's corps formed the left of the line, Thomas's the centre, of which Negley's division was drawn up in advance and Rousseau's in reserve, and M'Cook's corps the right. The pioneers were employed during the evening of the 30th in cutting roads through the frequent cane brakes and cypress woods, to connect the several corps and divisions. The woods which clothed the country rendered the disposition and supervision of an army by the General in command extremely difficult; divisions and corps were hidden and almost lost in the forests and undergrowth, and the undulations and low hills concealed the enemy's forces, and made it difficult to ascertain his intentions. Nearer Murfreesboro the land was more cultivated, and therefore more open, and several roads converging from various directions led to the town. The principal of these was the turnpike from Nashville, running almost parallel with the railway, and for a short distance with the Stone River, which it crossed about one mile and a half from Murfreesboro. This road and the river divided both armies into two wings; of these the Federal left was considerably the stronger, whilst, on the other hand, the Confederate right which faced it was much weaker than the left, on which General Bragg judged, from the engagement of the 30th, that the brunt of the action would fall.

He had previously drawn up his army in two equal wings on either side of the Stone River, but after the engagement of the 30th, he had moved one division of Hardee's corps from the right to the left of the line, and had thus on the left bank of the Stone River, Cleburn's division, supported by M'Cowen under General Hardee, and Withers' division, supported by Cheatham under General Polk, whilst on the right bank of the river General Breckenridge alone opposed the main body of the Federal army. During the night General Bragg directed Wheeler's brigade of cavalry to move round the enemy's rear and assail his waggon trains; this duty was efficiently performed, and after capturing many baggage and supply waggons, he joined the army on the flank opposite from which he had started.

On the morning of the 31st, whilst General Rosecrans was leisurely preparing for an attack on the Confederate right, General Bragg ordered his left wing to advance. This order was carried out with energy and alacrity, and the right division of M'Cook's corps under Johnston was driven back in great confusion, guns were captured before the horses could be harnessed to them, and even the breakfasts prepared by the Federal soldiers furnished a meal for their less well supplied antagonists. Johnston's division having been put to rout, Davis's division was next assailed with the same result, and thus two out of the three divisions of M'Cook's corps were driven back. Aides-de-camp were sent in all haste to General Rosecrans to inform him of the advance of the enemy, followed by others to announce the repulse of his right wing; indeed, of this he was himself an eye-witness, as the numerous fugitives rushing through the cane brakes sufficiently attested the calamity. In the meantime, Sheridan's, the third and left division of M'Cook's corps, throwing back its right, maintained a stout resistance, while Rosecrans hurried forward Rousseau's division from the centre, and sent orders to Crittenden to abandon all idea of an advance, and to march as quickly as possible two out of his three divisions to support the right wing. Rousseau was too late to enable Sheridan to hold his ground; he retired, and Rousseau finding that he could make no use of his artillery in the thick woods, in which he found himself enclosed, withdrew to some rising and more open ground in rear, where he repulsed the still advancing enemy. His retreat necessitated the retirement of Negley, and the whole of the Federal right and centre, on the afternoon of the 30th, was drawn up nearly at right angles with the position it held in the morning; the right of the left wing alone maintaining its ground, and holding the angle of high ground between the rail and river.

The Federals had suffered severely; and the Confederates, although successful, had also lost heavily. In the attack of Sheridan's division, a brigade of General Polk's corps lost a third of its number, and almost every field and staff officer was dismounted. The left of the Federal line still occupied a strong position, and to dislodge it there were no reserves. To remedy this defect, Bragg sent orders for Breckenridge's division to move from the right to reinforce Polk, but there was a considerable delay in carrying out this order, owing to a threat of an advance of the Federal left, and a rumour of fresh forces appearing on the Lebanon Road. Late in the afternoon two brigades of Breckenridge's division arrived on the ground, and formed up for the assault of the hill held by the Federal left. Soon afterwards the remaining two brigades followed, and under General Breckenridge in person advanced to the attack; but the Federals who had recovered from their reverses, and knew the advantages of the ground, poured in so heavy a fire from their powerful artillery, that the Confederates, although evincing great bravery, could not stand against it, and retired. Partly owing to the exhaustion of the troops, partly to the closing in of the day, the attack was not renewed, and the two armies bivouacked on the ground they occupied at the termination of the action.

The Confederates had captured many prisoners and from twenty to thirty guns, they had forced back the whole of the Federal right wing, and their cavalry operating on the flanks and rear had taken waggons and prisoners, but they had failed in driving their opponents from the key of the position. Steadfastly holding the hill near the river, the Federal left had maintained its ground, and prevented a repulse from degenerating into a disastrous defeat. As in nearly all the battles of the American war, few tactics had been used on either side. The men fought in the dense thickets and cane brakes, under but little supervision from the generals, and it sometimes happened that the troops were so inter-

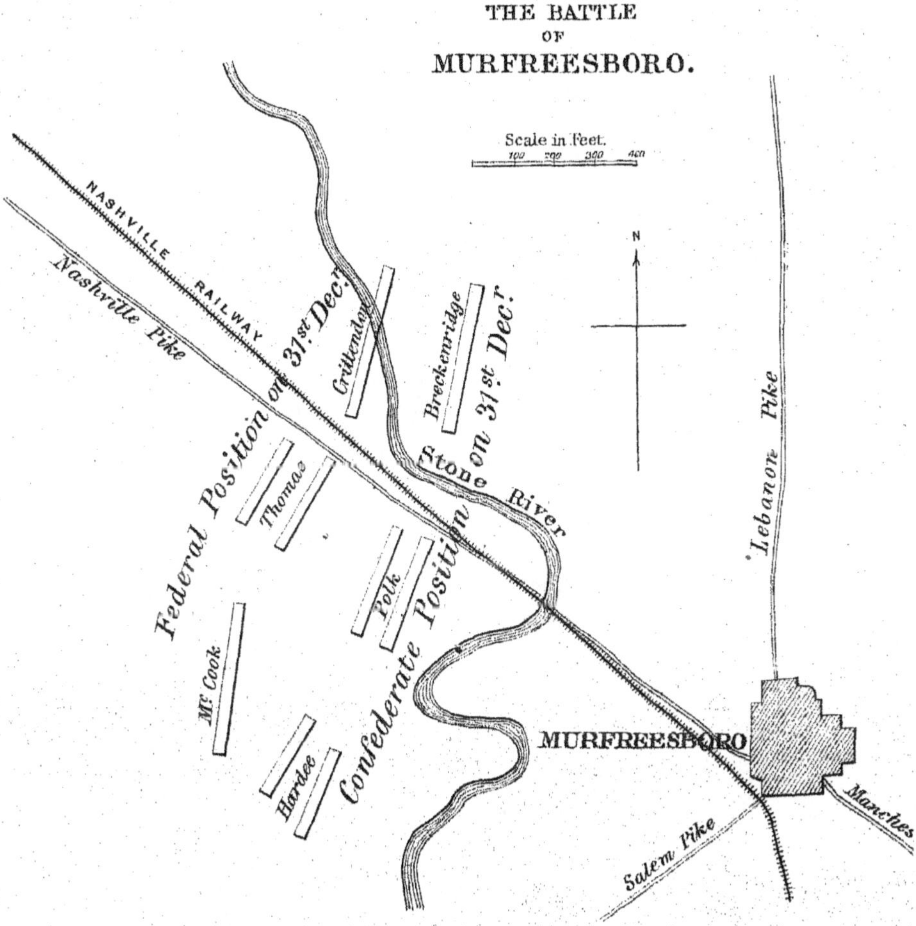

THE BATTLE
OF
MURFREESBORO.
Scale in Feet.
100 200 300 400
N
NASHVILLE RAILWAY
Nashville Pike
Federal Position on 31st Decr
Crittenden
Breckenridge
Confederate Position on 31st Decr
Thomas
Polk
Mc Cook
Hardee
Stone River
Lebanon Pike
MURFREESBORO
Salem Pike
Manches

mingled, and were so little distinguished by their uniform, that it became difficult to recognise friend from foe.*

On the following day, January 1, 1865, both armies remained quiet, exhausted by their previous efforts; Breckenridge was moved back to his former position, on the right bank of the Stone River, and the indefatigable Generals Wharton and Wheeler were sent to operate on the line of the Federal communications, to cut off and capture supplies, and to reconnoitre whether reinforcements were arriving from Nashville, or whether there were signs that a retreat had been decided upon. General Rosecrans finding that his position at the close of the action was of too cramped and narrow a frontage, and that there were great difficulties in bringing up ammunition through the thick cedar woods, withdrew his forces a short distance

* The following anecdote, narrated in General Polk's report, illustrates the peculiarities of American fighting, at the same time that it bears witness to the gallantry of two brave men:—

'A battery (writes the General) was pouring a murderous fire into the brigade of General Maney from a point which made it doubtful whether it was ours or the enemy's. Two unsuccessful efforts had been made by staff officers—one of whom was killed in the attempt—to determine its character. The doubt caused the brigade on which it was firing to hesitate in returning the fire, when Sergeant Oakley, colour-bearer of the fourth Tennessee Confederate regiment, and Sergeant M. C. Hooks, colour-bearer of the ninth Tennessee regiment, gallantly advanced eight or ten paces to the front, displaying their colours, and holding themselves and the flag of their country erect, remained ten minutes in a place so conspicuous as to be plainly seen and fully to test from whom their brigade was suffering so severely. The murderous fire instead of abating increased and intensified, and soon demonstrated that the battery and its supports were not friends, but enemies. The sergeants then returned deliberately to their proper positions in the line unhurt, and the enemy's battery was silenced, and his column put to flight.'

to the rear, leaving the ground between the river and the rail, so fiercely disputed during the evening of the 31st, to be occupied by General Bragg. From twenty-eight to thirty guns, great quantities of small arms carefully collected after the action, numerous colours, and many prisoners, remained with the Confederates as trophies of the battle and evidences of their success. But, notwithstanding his repulse, Rosecrans showed no signs of retreating, his troops busily entrenched themselves, two brigades came up as reinforcements, and although long lines of waggons conveyed the wounded to the rear and partially misled the Confederate cavalry officers, causing them to think that the enemy was about to retire, he continued to maintain his position, prepared to offer battle should General Bragg endeavour to push forward on the Nashville road. The courage and coolness of General Rosecrans in the battle of the 31st, and his firmness in continuing to hold his ground after the severe handling his army had undergone, earned the praise and secured the confidence of those officers who for the first time had served under him, and laid the foundation for the respect which the army of the Cumberland equally with the army of the Mississippi subsequently felt for his character.

Either late on the evening of the 1st, or early on the morning of the 2nd, General Rosecrans ordered Van Cleve's division of Crittenden's corps to recross the Stone River and take position on rising ground which enfiladed General Polk's line. This movement was perceived by General Bragg, and he made dispositions for defeating it by an attack on Van Cleve. He ordered Polk to distract the enemy's attention by artillery fire, whilst Breckenridge formed the column of attack in two lines of four brigades, with a proportion of artillery, the cavalry under Wharton guarding the right flank. The action commenced at 4 P.M., and was of short duration; the Confederates advanced confidently, and drove back Van Cleve's division, gaining the crest of rising ground overlooking the river. But the troops do not appear to have been well-handled; the second line was too close to the first, and, consequently, suffering much from the enemy's fire, returned it, and in some instances inflicted injury on the front line;* the left of the attacking force was also pushed forward in some disorder across the river, and encountered the remainder of Crittenden's corps, with a portion of those of Thomas and M'Cook, posted on commanding ground. The Federals in turn advanced, and drove back Breckenridge's division in considerable disorder, inflicting on it very heavy loss. Bragg perceiving the disaster, ordered up Anderson's brigade of Polk's corps in support. Advancing steadily through the broken infantry of Breckenridge's division, Anderson checked the pursuit and saved the artillery abandoned in the confusion, with the exception of four guns, which remained in the enemy's hands. Night put an end to the engagement, and the two armies reoccupied their former lines; Breckenridge's division (rallied after its repulse) and Cleburne's division, transferred from the Confederate left wing, supporting Anderson, whose brigade formed the right of the army.

Each general anticipated an attack from his opponent. Rosecrans was fearful lest his right wing, weakened by detachments, should meet with a disaster similar to that it had incurred on the 31st; whilst Bragg was alarmed lest his right, somewhat demoralized by the action of the

* See General Bragg's report. *Rebellion Record,* vol. vi. p. 170.

2nd, should be driven back on Murfreesboro. Rosecrans made demonstrations to deceive his adversary into the belief of the arrival of reinforcements on his right, and entrenched his left on the eminence regained at the close of the day. Bragg, on the other hand, misled by these demonstrations, and knowing how much his army had suffered, feeling also that on the maintenance of its efficiency the welfare of the Confederate cause in the West depended, decided on retreating beyond Murfreesboro.

During Saturday, the 3rd of January, the prisoners and baggage waggons were sent to the rear, and at 11 P.M. the army commenced its retreat. The march was conducted in good order, unmolested by the enemy, who was held in check by the cavalry acting as the rear-guard, and the army having retired about fifty miles, took up a fresh position south of Murfreesboro behind the Duck River. On the 5th the Federal army entered Murfreesboro, where fifteen hundred of the Confederate sick and wounded had been left in the hospitals, and thus swelled the number of prisoners to two thousand three hundred. About the same number were captured by the Confederates, and the loss in both armies must have been nearly equal; that of the Federals, according to General Rosecrans's report, numbering 8,778 men.

The three days' battle of Murfreesboro was one of the most hardly contested of the war; on both sides the troops had fought well, and if the surprise of the two divisions on the Federal right at the commencement of the action reflects some discredit on their discipline, the manner in which the centre held its ground, and the subsequent gallant conduct of the combined corps during the action of the 2nd, proves that the army was not deficient in admirable qualities. The Confederate troops of the West had also fully maintained their character; the impetuosity of their attack, their perseverance in overcoming the obstacles presented to their advance by the thick cypress woods, their endurance of cold, hunger, and fatigue, the energy of their cavalry, and the fact that they were fewer in numbers than their opponents, must ensure to them the respect and admiration of all who can appreciate soldierly qualities. The Confederates claimed the battle of Murfreesboro as a victory, on the ground of the advantage gained on the 31st December. The Federals recorded it among their successes, as the retreat of the enemy concluded the series of operations between December 26th and January 5th. It was in truth another of the many indecisive battles of the war, where the results were not commensurate with the terrible loss incurred by both sides.

For many months, what may be considered as the grand operations of war, ceased in Tennessee, and the interest of the campaign in the West centered in Vicksburg. There were indeed, during the winter, frequent engagements between the partisan corps of Morgan and Forrest and the detachments of the Federal army garrisoning Kentucky and Tennessee; as also were there raids made into southern and eastern Tennessee by Federal officers desirous of emulating the deeds of the Confederate cavalry. A few of these engagements may deserve notice, inasmuch as they illustrate the unhappy condition of the border States, and demonstrate the difficulty of holding a country of so great extent as that included in the States of the Confederacy, by armies however large, and however successful.

It will be remembered that, previous to the battle of Murfreesboro, General Forrest had been sent into

Western Tennessee, and General Morgan into Kentucky, the former to operate on the communications of General Grant's army in Mississippi, the latter on those of General Rosecrans in Tennessee. To accomplish the work assigned to him, General Forrest had crossed the Tennessee River, about the middle of December, and after destroying bridges, tearing up rails, and otherwise impeding communication on the Mississippi and Ohio, and the Columbus and Corinth railways, after having also captured and parolled numerous Federal detachments, including many of the convalescents and recruits of the army of the Mississippi, he prepared to return to the lines occupied by the Confederate army. General Sullivan, who commanded the scattered Federal troops in that department, was unwilling that he should escape, and took measures for intercepting his retreat. He concentrated two brigades at Huntington, and marched rapidly in the direction of Lexington. In the meanwhile General Forrest encountered a small detachment of Federals, under Colonel Durham, immediately on his line of march towards the Tennessee River, and after demanding its surrender, which was refused, attacked it with vigour. The Federals stood their ground until General Sullivan, coming up with a considerable force from Lexington, and assailing the Confederates in flank and rear, routed them with considerable loss, capturing many prisoners, including Forrest's adjutant-general. The remainder forced their way to the Tennessee River, which they crossed, the Federals not venturing to follow them, and returned to their position on the left front of the Confederate army, holding the line of the Duck River

Similar in its character, undertaken with the same object and by the same description of force, was Morgan's raid into Kentucky, on the lines of rail connecting Nashville with the Ohio. Possibly considerable inconvenience and some loss may have resulted to the Federal army of the Cumberland from this raid; but it may be a matter of doubt whether the troops so scattered might not have been of more service had they been present at the battle of Murfreesboro.

The whole front of the Confederate army was covered by the irregular cavalry, and continual engagements were fought between them and detachments of the Federal army: sometimes occasioned by the former advancing from their cantonments and attacking posts far in rear of the main body of the enemy's forces; sometimes by the latter endeavouring to find a weak place in the Confederate line, and coming in contact with detached bodies guarding the rails and roads to the South. Engagements would then ensue, dignified in the newspaper accounts by the name of battles, but uninstructive in their details, and unimportant as affecting the course of the war.

The interest of the struggle in the West, after the battle of Murfreesboro, culminated in Vicksburg, and the campaign in the State of Mississippi was chiefly important, in so far as it affected the operations for the reduction of the hitherto insignificant town which closed the course of the great river to the Federal fleets, and, as it was then believed, formed the only obstacle which prevented the renewal of commerce between the corn-growing states of the Ohio and their natural port at New Orleans.

There seems little doubt that a combined movement had been arranged between the expeditionary force under General Sherman, organised at Memphis about the middle of December, 1862, the army of General Grant advanced as far as Oxford, Mississippi, and the military and naval force collected at New Orleans under General Banks and Admiral Farragut. The object in view was to open the Mississippi, and to obtain possession of the Great Trunk line of railway running through the state of the same name. To frustrate these plans, General J. Johnston, commanding in the West, had organised but a small force, but he had the advantage of direct lines of rail connecting the several places he had determined to defend, and was operating in a friendly country, where every inhabitant was willing to furnish intelligence of the enemy's movements, and where the swamps and forests afforded natural lines of defence. Port Hudson had been fortified, Vicksburg strengthened, and a strong cavalry force—or rather of infantry on horseback—under General Van Dorn, defended the swamps and bayous of Northern Mississippi and continually harassed the lines of communication of the invading army, acting in this respect in combination with General Forrest, who about the same time was engaged in destroying the railways in Western Tennessee.

In the third week of December General Grant's head-quarters were at Oxford, and he was preparing to advance on Grenada, the point of junction between the Memphis and Mobile and the Corinth and Mobile Railways. The great depôt of his stores was at Holly Springs, and on it he in a great measure depended for the supply of his army, as Northern Mississippi was far too poor a country to afford subsistence for so large a force. The command at Holly Spring had been given to Colonel Murphy, and a force of cavalry and infantry left in the town to guard the stores. No steps were, however, taken to protect the place by means of field-works, however slight; the roads into the town were open, and the troops were encamped more with regard to personal convenience than with reference to mutual support. All seemed tranquil. Grant was supposed to be driving the enemy before him, and availing themselves of the prospects of a trade in cotton, many commercial men from the West had taken up their residence in the small town of Holly Springs. Such was the aspect of affairs on the 19th of December, and little did either the military or civilians think that within eight miles was Van Dorn and his Texan cavalry. On that very night he approached the town; the pickets, if there were any, gave no alarm, and whilst a brigade stationed on rising ground acted as a reserve, Van Dorn dashed into the place at the head of his cavalry. Little resistance was attempted; a few of the Federal cavalry escaped, but the majority of the garrison of upwards of a thousand men surrendered. Colonel Murphy was taken prisoner, and most of the Federal officers—surprised in the houses in which they were lodging—were marched off in succession to Van Dorn's temporary headquarters, and with their men were parolled. Then commenced the work of destruction; vast accumulations of flour, cotton, and stores of all sorts were burned, the railway was torn up, the station and locomotives set on fire, and at length, the flames spreading to a building used as a magazine, caused it to blow up, and led to the demolition of a considerable portion of the town. After completing the work of destruction, Van Dorn—knowing that a considerable force would soon be concentrated for the purpose of cutting him off—abandoned the place and retreated.

The destruction of the great depôt at Holly Springs, the expedition of Forrest into Western Tennessee, and the failure of Sherman's attack on Vicksburg, compelled

General Grant to abandon his advance into Mississippi, and left the country between the Upper Tennessee and the Duck River open for fresh incursions from Van Dorn and his cavalry. There he signalised himself in the early spring by the capture of between one and two thousand men of General Rosecrans's army, who under Colonel Coburn were on the march from Franklin to Columbia. This affair received the name of the battle of Thompson's Station, and is only remarkable as being one of the most successful of the minor operations engaged in by the Confederate troops of the West.

Almost contemporary with the capture of Holly Springs was the repulse of Sherman from Vicksburg. The expedition under his command, consisting of four divisions, under Generals Steele, Morgan, L. Smith, and A. J. Smith, accompanied by several gunboats, had been organised at Memphis and Helena, and on the third week of December commenced the descent of the Mississippi River. The fleet reached Milliken's Bend, a short distance above Vicksburg, on the 24th December, without encountering any opposition excepting a few shots fired from the banks, revenged by the indiscriminate burning of houses; many of which, often the property of the rich planters, were destroyed wantonly and without provocation by the undisciplined soldiery.*

It was determined by General Sherman to attempt the capture of the town from the north-western side, making the Yazoo River the base from which the troops should advance. This river enters the Mississippi a few miles above Vicksburg, but making a bend in a north-

* Among others, the house which formerly belonged to General Sydney Johnston, who was killed at the battle of Shiloh, was burnt to the ground.

easterly direction, approaches the town within a still shorter distance, where a line of bluffs connects it with the hill on which Vicksburg stands. The north-eastern extremity of the bluffs overlooking the Yazoo is named Hayne's Bluff, and there a battery had been placed by the defenders, which barred the progress of the Federal gunboats up the Yazoo River. Not far from Hayne's Bluff, and between it and the mouth of the Yazoo, Chickasaw bayou enters the river, and along its right bank, and holding the line of low hills extending from Hayne's Bluff to Vicksburg, the Confederate forces belonging to General Pemberton's army were posted.

As soon as it appeared that a formidable attack was about to be made on the town, and that the Federal army had landed on the left bank of the Yazoo, the spade and axe were employed in raising batteries and preparing abattis, whilst the railway from Jackson brought up reinforcements to the garrison. The inhabitants, and even the ladies, crowded the higher bluffs, in order to watch the progress of the engagement which seemed inevitable, the Louisiana and Tennessee regiments lined the hastily constructed earthworks, and the artillerymen prepared to sweep with their fire the more open ground near the mouth of Chickasaw bayou. The disposition of the Federal force was as follows: General A. J. Smith on the right, next to him General L. Smith, and then General Morgan, whilst General Steele's division had been landed above Chickasaw bayou, in order to take in reverse the battery which enfiladed it from the right of the Confederate line of defence. The 27th was consumed principally in skirmishing, and in vain endeavours on the part of the Federals to capture the battery. At night both armies bivouacked in the woods, without fires and in silence, in order to conceal their position; the only noise which broke the stillness was the sound of the railway trains from Jackson bringing up reinforcements to the Confederates, and the only light which illumined the gloom was a rocket seen by the Federal troops, and supposed by the too sanguine to indicate the position of Grant's advance.

On the following day the action was renewed; efforts were made by the Federals to cross the bayou and to effect a junction between their left and centre, and it was whilst reconnoitring the swamp that General L. Smith was severely wounded, and was obliged to leave the field. This accident, together with the want of cooperation between the several divisions, occasioned possibly by the nature of the ground, prevented any concentrated attack on the Confederate position. At night the firing ceased, except from an occasional gun in the Federal batteries; the Confederates were better engaged in strengthening their position, and constructing a second line of breast-works, or, as the Americans term them, rifle-pits, in rear of the front line.

On the 29th a concerted attack was determined on by the Federal generals. With their usual engineering skill, the soldiers prepared bridges across the bayou, and two companies of the 6th Missouri regiment, who volunteered for the dangerous work, were pushed forward across the centre bridge, with the design of undermining the bank on which the Confederates were stationed. Gallantly did these brave men advance, encouraged by the loud cheers of their comrades, and vigorously with axe and spade did they commence their work. At the same time, the division on the right advanced to the assault of the bluffs beyond the bayou, whilst the artillery of those on the left attempted to drive away the defenders of the works attacked by the 6th Missouri. The opening of this heavy fire was intended to have been the signal for an advance over the centre bridge, but through some mistake the order was not given; the right division, of which General Blair commanded the leading brigade, was repulsed with great loss as they attempted to storm the hill, and the centre did not move forward until it was too late to render any material assistance. As night closed in, the rain fell in torrents; the ground on which the action had been fought, always low and marshy, soon became deep in mud and water, and many of the wounded are supposed to have perished, smothered in the swamp.

A curious incident is narrated in connection with the exploit of the 6th Missouri regiment. As the men were lying under the bank, the defenders, who could not depress their rifles sufficiently to command them, kept up a running conversation, questioning them as to what regiment they belonged, and complimenting them on their courage. The others replied, and even asked for a loaf of bread, which was thrown down to them, the fighting all the while continuing.* On the 30th the attack was not renewed, as the swamps were impassable, and the loss on the side of the Federals had been very severe, about 3,000. A project was indeed entertained of an assault on Hayne's Bluff, but its execution was prevented by a fog, and during the evening the troops re-embarked and returned to Milliken's Bend, where shortly afterwards Sherman was superseded in the command by M'Clernand, and the army, divided into two corps under Generals Sherman and Morgan, received the name of the Army of the Mississippi.

* See Missouri Democrat Account. *Rebellion Record*, vol. vi. page 316, Documents.

There were rejoicings at Vicksburg and throughout the Confederacy at this second repulse of the Federals, in their attempt to capture what may be termed the key of the Mississippi—rejoicings which were further increased by the almost simultaneous recapture of Galveston, on the sea coast of Texas. This feat was accomplished by General Magruder, who had recently been appointed to command that distant state. He had collected artillery at Houston, and marching from thence had occupied in force the works erected opposite the island on which the town of Galveston stands, and commanding the railway bridge which connects it with the mainland. At the same time he prepared two steam-packets to act as gunboats in cooperation with the land force. These vessels, strengthened and rendered almost shot-proof by means of bulwarks of cotton bales, were manned by volunteer Texan cavalry, and were ordered to proceed down the bay towards Galveston, and as the troops crossed the bridge, to attack the small blockading squadron. Accompanying the two armed vessels, were other tenders and yachts, filled with spectators and volunteers prepared to assist in the attack. It was arranged that the naval and military operations should be simultaneous, and should commence before daybreak on the first day of the new year. The action began with an artillery fire from the batteries commanding the bridge, which was replied to by the Federal gunboats, and shortly afterwards, as day commenced to break, the two Confederate steamers, the Bayou City and the Neptune, were seen coming down the bay. The Harriet Lane immediately prepared to engage them, and soon drove off the Neptune in a disabled condition; but the Bayou City steaming close alongside, swept her decks with the rifles of the men placed behind the cotton bales, whilst others jumping on board engaged the crew. The commander, Captain Wainwright, revolver in hand, fought to the last, but was killed with the larger portion of his men. The Federal flag-ship, the Westfield, had in the meantime grounded, as she was attempting to get into position, and the other gunboats, the Owasco and Clifton, were fearful of attacking the Bayou City, assisted, as she now was, by the guns of the Harriet Lane. During this action in the bay, the troops under Magruder had crossed the railway-bridge and occupied the town. The small Federal force held the wharf, but perceiving that the gunboats had been either captured or driven off, and that no retreat was open to them, being also unprovided with artillery, they surrendered as prisoners. The Westfield, hopelessly grounded, was blown up by her commander, and the explosion occurring prematurely, he, together with others of the crew, perished. Thus was Galveston recaptured, the blockade broken, and her port temporarily reopened to commerce, as announced by a proclamation put forth by General Magruder.

The adaptation of the packet-boats to act as gunboats, the motley crew who manned and worked them, the conversion of cavalry into sailors, all bear evidence to the versatile talent of Americans, especially characterising the population of the Border States, where every man is able, and often forced, to turn his hand to the most various, and, in civilised countries, the most opposite avocations.

The last few days of the year 1862 will be remembered as among the most fruitful of calamity to the Western portion of the human race. From Virginia to Texas, from Fredericksburg to Galveston, the country was wrapped in the smoke of battle, and its soil stained with the blood of those who had hitherto marked it out as the land of more than ordinary prosperity. The terrible repulse of Burnside at Fredericksburg, the retreat of the army of the Mississippi, the failure of the expedition against Vicksburg, and the recapture of Galveston, all bore witness to the talent, energy, and courage of the Southern race, but the indecisive and stubborn battle at Murfreesboro, the refusal to acknowledge defeat, the energy with which reinforcements and supplies were poured forward to restore the waste of war, the resolution of crushing their antagonists by force of numbers, and the lavish expenditure of labour, showed that the people of the North were terribly in earnest, and that although they might suffer defeat in the field, might see their armies led to destruction by inefficient generals, and behold their resources wasted and their wealth dissipated by a Government composed of men who would compare unfavourably with the statesmen of Europe, yet that they were possessed of resolution such as roused the nation after the disaster of Bull Run, and were determined to oppose to the chivalry of the South, the perseverance and activity which had created and had hitherto ministered to the prosperity of the Northern States. As the struggle continued, both sides learned by the teaching of actual experience lessons in the art of war. Lee's veterans became more amenable to discipline, and his army more manageable; but experience and discipline likewise influenced the hosts of the North, and did much to counterbalance the defects which gave to the people of the South the advantage in the earlier campaigns. The more warlike character of the Confederates, the deeper sentiments which inspired them, the more brilliant talent which led them, began to be opposed to the discipline of troops who had been taught its necessity in many defeats, and by the experience of officers who had profited by the lessons of adversity. The excitability of the American character had toned down, and a quiet determination to perform their duty, whatever it might be, and to lead their men wherever they might be ordered, characterised the officers of the Northern army. They were not actuated by those intense feelings and strong passions which animated their opponents, but they had become imbued with the *esprit de corps* of soldiers, and assisted as they were by almost unlimited supplies of men, and by inexhaustible stores of *materiel*, provided with the most approved arms, the most powerful artillery, and the fruits of the latest inventions, they organised, equipped, and disciplined powerful armies, which, if they did not achieve the brilliant fame of their less well-appointed antagonists, yet purchased with their blood solid advantages, and gradually, except in Virginia, rolled back the tide of war from the frontiers to the heart of the seceding States.

Before closing the narrative of the events of 1862, it may be conducive to a clear understanding of the position of affairs, to glance over the positions occupied by the several armies. In Virginia, either army watched its opponents from the heights overlooking the town of Fredericksburg, whilst the country between the Rappahannock and the Potomac was the scene of bold forays executed by Stuart's cavalry, which were beginning to be imitated by the Federals under Pleasanton. The Upper Potomac and Lower Shenandoah Valleys were watched by Sigel, and Western Virginia, which seemed as if destined to become the theatre of the war during its first year, had enjoyed comparative tranquillity in

1862. Kentucky was free from the presence of any large army, but was subject to the evils of guerilla warfare, as was also Missouri. The war had travelled southwards to Tennessee, Mississippi, and Arkansas. In Tennessee, Bragg opposed Rosecrans on the Duck River; in Mississippi, Johnston and Pemberton held the line of the Tallahatchie and the town of Vicksburg; whilst Grant still threatened the northern portion of the state, and M'Clernand menaced Vicksburg. In Arkansas a Federal force had reached the banks of the Arkansas River, and held Van Buren. Hindman and Marmaduke prevented a further advance, and occasionally converted defensive tactics into those of offence, threatening to carry the war back into Missouri. Texas was almost free from the presence of the Federals; but in Louisiana, the increased force brought thither by Banks, foretold a recommencement of active operations; and the presence of Farragut's fleet in the Lower Mississippi foreshadowed an attack on Port Hudson. Alabama had hitherto almost escaped the horrors of war, as had also Georgia; and Mobile and Savannah retained some appearance of their former prosperity. The inhabited portions of Florida had been desolated by incursions from the sea coast. Little, excepting the blockade of Charleston, claims attention in South Carolina, and General Forster's march into North Carolina had been productive of no change in the attitude of the belligerents.

The time of year was more favourable to the prosecution of the campaign in the south and south-west than in the northern states of the Confederacy. The deep mud of Virginia, and the rise of the rivers, presented obstacles to the renewal on either side of active operations, even if the severe struggles of the summer, autumn, and winter of the year 1862 had not entailed some necessity for rest and reorganisation.

Notwithstanding the loss of territory in the West, respect for the power and resources of the Confederacy had greatly increased among the European nations, and the brilliant campaigns of Virginia and Maryland had raised the reputation of her armies, and spread the renown of her generals among all nations and through all classes who could appreciate self-devotion and courage on the part of the soldiery, and brilliant military qualities exemplified in their several branches, by such men as Lee, Jackson, Longstreet, and Stuart.

CHAPTER XII.

OPERATIONS ON THE SEA COAST AND ON THE MISSISSIPPI.

As the termination of the year 1862 had been especially marked by important battles, and as reaction usually follows periods of more than common activity, so during the first two months of the year 1863, there were fewer of what may be termed the grand operations of war than in the preceding month which closed 1862. During this pause opportunity offers for noticing some political events which bear indirectly on the conduct of the war. On the 1st January 1863, Mr. Lincoln issued a proclamation designating the states and portions of states in which the emancipation proclamation of the 22nd September 1862, should take effect. These were the states wherein (to quote the words of the proclamation) the people thereof respectively are this day in rebellion against the United States, to wit: 'Arkansas, Texas, Louisiana (excepting certain designated parishes), Mississippi, Alabama, Florida, Georgia, South Carolina, North Carolina and Virginia (excepting the forty-eight counties of Western Virginia and certain others particularly specified).'

This proclamation was issued by Mr. Lincoln, by virtue of the power vested in him as commander-in-chief of the Army and Navy of the United States, and as a fit and necessary war measure for repressing the rebellion.

Its legality had been challenged in the House of Representatives, but was ultimately allowed.

That its expediency was questioned by Mr. Lincoln himself may be gathered from the answer he gave to the Chicago deputation, which presented a memorial to him on the 15th September, 1862, praying for the immediate issue of an emancipation proclamation. After alluding to the difficulties attending the subject he gave utterance to the following opinion on what he termed the merits of the case:—

'What good would a proclamation of emancipation from me do, especially as we are now situated? I do not want to issue a document that the whole world will see must necessarily be inoperative, like the Pope's bull against the comet! Would my word free the slaves, when I cannot enforce the constitution in the rebel states? Is there a single court, or magistrate, or individual that would be influenced by it there? And what reason is there to think that it would have any greater effect upon the slaves than the late law of Congress, which I approved, and which offers protection and freedom to the slaves of rebel masters who come within our lines? Yet I cannot learn that the law has caused a single slave to come over to us. And suppose they could be induced by a proclamation of freedom from me to throw themselves upon us, what should we do with them? How can we feed and care for such a multitude?'

Such were Mr. Lincoln's avowed opinions on the 15th of September; nevertheless, owing probably to the pressure put upon him by the Abolition party, he issued the proclamation of the 22nd September, 1862, followed by that of the 1st January, 1863.

The result, or rather absence of result, of these proclamations had been well-estimated by Mr. Lincoln, but he had not sufficiently calculated the influence they would exercise on the people of the South, by binding them more closely together for the prosecution of the war.

In this light the emancipation proclamation was regarded by the President of the Southern Confederacy, who in his message to the Senate and House of Representatives of the Confederate States on the 12th of January, 1863, gave a *resumé* of the military and political events which bore on the war. He spoke of the successes of the latter portion of the year 1862, as evinced by the battle of Fredericksburg, and the engagements at Vicksburg and Galveston: he acknowledged the joy with which peace would be hailed, but insisted on the unalterable decision of the people of the South to endure any sufferings and continue any sacrifices until the right of self-government and the sovereignty and independence of the states should have been triumphantly vindicated and firmly established.

Of the conduct of the great powers of Europe he spoke somewhat bitterly; he complained of the recognition of what Mr. Davis termed a paper blockade, and asserted that their neutrality had been one-sided, especially with reference to the prohibition of either party from bringing prizes into neutral ports, which had fallen with especial hardness on the South. After alluding in terms of detestation to the conduct of Generals M'Neil and Butler, and informing the Houses of Congress that he had branded the latter as an outlaw, and directed his execution in expiation of his crimes, if he should fall into the hands of any of the Confederate forces, Mr. Davis drew attention to the recently issued emancipation proclamation, the results of which he prognosticated as follows:—'The proclamation will have a salutary effect, in calming the fears of those who have constantly evinced the apprehension that this war might end by some reconstruction of the old Union, or some renewal of close political relations with the United States. These fears have never been shared by me, nor have I been able to perceive on what basis they could rest. But the proclamation affords the fullest guarantees of the impossibility of such a result. It has established a state of things which can lead to but one of three consequences—the extermination of the slaves, the exile of the whole white population of the Confederacy, or absolute and total separation of these States from the United States.'

Such were Mr. Davis's opinions, and taken in conjunction with those of Mr. Lincoln, it may be premised that even at the time of its issue, little ultimate good as a war measure was expected from the proclamation in the North; and that in the South, although its effects as regarded the action of the slaves were watched with some doubt and anxiety, yet that its tendency was held to be so far beneficial, inasmuch as it would strengthen the hands of those who were resolved never to re-enter the Union. In the conclusion of his message, Mr. Davis congratulated the Congress on the development of home industry and manufactures, whereby the country would be gradually rendered independent of European assistance. He drew a favourable picture of its internal state, both as regarded manufactures and agriculture. 'Our fields' (he said), 'no longer whitened by cotton that cannot be exported, are devoted to the production of cereals, and the growth of stock formerly purchased with the proceeds of cotton. In the homes of our noble and devoted women—without whose sublime sacrifices our success would have been impossible—the noise of the loom and the spinning-wheel may be heard throughout the land.' The last mentioned element in the strong determination and noble spirit of endurance shown by the Confederate States, must excite the admiration of all who value self-denial and patriotism, even if they should differ in opinion as to the cause which called them forth. The women of the South have afforded an example to the world of both these qualities, and have furnished an additional proof to the many which history has recorded, of the influence of women in stimulating a nation to great and heroic acts.

Notwithstanding the alteration in the agriculture of the country, and the substitution of the growth of corn in place of cotton, there can be little doubt that there was much misery and want among the Southern people: there were bread riots in Richmond, easily suppressed, and of no great importance in their consequences, but still evidencing scarcity and destitution. It can be no matter for wonder that such was the case, as irrespective of the actual scarcity of provisions excepting those of the very simplest kind, there was the difficulty of transporting to the cities the produce of the widely scattered farms. The railways evinced signs of the pressure put on them, by the transportation of war material and supplies for the troops, and their thin and well-worn rails, their old and rickety carriages, and the weakness of their engines, showed that they could scarcely endure the constant strain which taxed all their energies. Indeed few changes could be more striking than those which awaited a traveller who journeyed from Richmond to Washington. In the former city, poorly furnished shops, women clad in black, and engaged in tending the numerous hospitals which covered one of the hills on which the city stands; an absence of bustle and excitement, even of that occasioned by military displays, the air of business and anxiety of the inhabitants, and the want of the ordinary comforts and luxuries of a large city, proclaimed the sufferings and privations of a poor nation, contending with one far its superior in population, in wealth, and in all that wealth can produce.

How different was the sight that awaited him at Washington; notwithstanding the near presence of the army, notwithstanding the crowds of armed men, which thronged the streets, and of waggons and artillery which blocked up the squares, and covered the adjoining fields, the war was not the prominent object; luxury, pleasure, excitement, and vice were apparent everywhere; the struggle for wealth, the triumph of party, the excitement of pleasure, seemed to be the inducements which drew together a great portion of the population; the war was talked of, but usually only as influencing the gold market, or the prospects of some political faction, whilst the numbers of invalids and wounded which overflowed from the numerous hospitals, appeared out of place in a city such as Washington was in the commencement of 1863.

Farther north, the evidences of the great national struggle were even less apparent. At New York the population was more than ordinarily given up to pleasure. Never previously had the demand for luxuries been so great; the requirements of the families enriched by the war were insatiable, and the thirst for pleasure at the east end of the city was only equalled by the furor for speculation at its west end. The population which a year previously had been eager for military displays, had ceased to care for them, and the marriage of Tom Thumb created more attention and drew together far larger crowds than the march through the city of the soldiers proceeding to or from the war. It was not that there did not lie concealed under this gilded exterior deep earnestness and much suffering, but the outward aspects of the chief towns of the two nations * (for such they must be called) provoked comparisons, which although they might be favourable to the North in respect of her wealth and power, yet in deep determination and in heroic qualities gave the palm to the South.

Before again turning our attention to the seat of war, we must notice a bill, which after passing both Houses of Congress in December, 1862, received the sanction of President Lincoln in April, 1863; it is that which provided for the admission of Western Virginia into the Union as a separate state, and which thus sanctioned the secession of a part of a state, whilst the nation was fighting on avowedly constitutional principles to prevent the secession of entire states. No doubt arguments can be used to justify the expediency, if they cannot prove the rectitude of such apparently contradictory acts, but the formation of the separate state of Virginia, must stand as one of the many proofs that other reasons besides the maintenance of the constitution, actuated those who were most eager in the prosecution of the war.

To resume the narrative of military events; the winter and early spring months of 1863 passed with-

* Subsequent events may be pointed to by some in contradiction of this assertion; but it can scarcely be denied that, in 1862–63, the Southern Confederacy contained many, if not all, the elements of distinct nationality; *i.e.* if a unanimous people, a powerful government, disciplined armies, and a concentrated if not well-defined territory are taken as its indications.

out any movement of importance in Virginia or Tennessee, the heavy rains impeded land operations, and confined the invading forces to attempts against the towns on the sea coast, and to a renewal of the siege of Vicksburg. Savannah, Charleston, and the villages of Florida, successively witnessed and felt the presence of the enemy's fleets, and the coast of North Carolina became the theatre of an active campaign undertaken by the Confederates against the invaders. The main depôt for the fleet continued to be at Port Royal, and from thence the blockaders obtained supplies, and various expeditions were detached against places on the coast. The presence of the Confederate war-steamer Nashville in the Ogeechee River necessitated a close surveillance over its mouth, as the escape of the Florida from Mobile proved how a bold attempt at running the blockade might succeed. Her destruction was, however, at length accomplished. After receiving her guns and a cargo of cotton, the Nashville steamed down the Ogeechee River, but grounded near the mouth, within range of the artillery of Fort M'Allister; here she was pursued by the iron-clad Montauk (a Monitor), and her destruction was determined on. Disregarding the fire of the fort, the Montauk opened on the Nashville, and in a short time set her on fire, and passed unharmed down the river without injury from the enemy's shots, which were unable to penetrate her armour. Shortly afterwards, partly with the object of capturing Fort M'Allister, partly to test the fighting qualities of the Monitors, an expedition was planned to ascend the Ogeechee River. Obstructions placed in the stream prevented the near approach of the Monitors, three of which, assisted by two mortar boats, formed the attacking force. They opened fire on the fort at the distance of about one thousand yards, and continued the bombardment for the whole day; the fort replied, but finding that her antagonists were invulnerable except at the port holes of the guns, was sparing of its ammunition. Neither side inflicted injury on the other; whilst the armour proved a sufficient protection to the vessels, the earth and sand of the fort were equally indestructible, opposed to the heavy guns employed against them. The bombardment was not renewed on the following day, and the Federal naval officers, satisfied with the trial, withdrew to prepare for a more formidable enterprise, which was no less than the attack of the city, which more than any other had incurred the hatred of the people of the North.

The defences of Charleston had hitherto bade defiance to the Federal arms, and under General Beauregard, who was now in command of the department which included both Charleston and Savannah, had materially increased in strength. New forts had been built, and the lines of entrenchment removed to a greater distance from the city, in order to protect it from bombardment. A proclamation had been issued recommending the withdrawal of non-combatants, and calling on the population of South Carolina to volunteer for the defence of the principal city of their state. That an attack was imminent there was little doubt; a large force of iron-clads was known to be at Port Royal; and the rebellious city had lately given a fresh evidence of her malignity, and added another insult to the Federal flag by a bold enterprise conducted against the blockading fleet. Two rams (the Palmetto State and Chicora) built and equipped at Charleston, and under the command of Captain Ingraham, steamed out of the harbour on a dark night about the end of January. Concealed by the darkness, they continued on their course, and each vessel singled out her antagonist. The Palmetto State attacked the Mercedita, the Chicora the Keystone City. The former, unperceived until she was close upon her antagonist, so close as to be safe from her guns, which could not be trained sufficiently low to strike her, ran into her, at the same time firing her seven-inch gun; the shell passed through the boiler of the Mercedita, and caused it to explode, in its exit blowing a hole in her side, and so incapacitating her for further resistance. The Mercedita surrendered, and the Palmetto proceeded to assist her companion engaged with three of the blockaders; the Keystone City was disabled, and the remainder of the squadron driven off or scattered. The rams then returned to the harbour, and it was reported that the blockade had been broken. This was however denied by the Admiral commanding the Federal fleet, and even Confederate accounts acknowledge that the claim could not be sustained. The question was one of importance, as a blockade once broken cannot be renewed unless after due notice given to the neutral powers, and during such interval stores and munitions could have been imported into Charleston sufficient for the wants of the Confederacy for a considerable time.

The enterprise of the Confederate rams was a gallant attempt to combat the Federals on their own element, but was of no permanent benefit to the cause.

A large fleet, including many iron-clads built after the model of the Monitor, had been assembled with some difficulty at Port Royal, and preparations were in progress for the attack on Charleston from the sea. For its success it was necessary to await fine weather, as the iron-clads had not shown themselves good sea boats, the Monitor itself having foundered off Cape Hatteras, with many of her crew on board. Indeed few can read the accounts of the performances of her and her companions in a heavy sea, without pitying the brave men who formed their crews. Enclosed in an iron box, almost suffocated from a want of fresh air, the sea dashing over and hiding from view the deck, the turret alone protruding from the waves, and at times almost concealed by spray, their safety depending on the strength of the cable attached to the tug, perfectly helpless and without the light of day, and feeling that each of the plunges made by the vessel might end in her total submergence, the crew of an iron-clad may be excused if they felt nervousness if not alarm at their position during rough weather.

The voyage round Cape Hatteras proved that this description of vessel, as built by Americans at that period, might be calculated for harbour defences, but was not fitted for a rough sea.

Waiting therefore until spring had heralded in calmer weather, Admiral Du Pont deferred his attack until the first week of April. During the month of March the greater portion of the fleet was gradually transferred from Port Royal to North Edisto River, about half way between Port Royal and Charleston harbour; and on the 1st of April about one hundred vessels were collected at the mouth of that river.

It was a great object, besides securing fine weather, to have the benefit of the spring tides, in order that there should be sufficient water to enable the Ironsides, the largest of the iron-clad vessels, to cross without risk the bar at the mouth of Charleston harbour. Anxiously therefore did the Admiral await the cessation of a stiff breeze which was blowing from the east during the early days of April, and when, on the evening of the 5th, the wind and sea calmed down, he immediately issued orders for the fleet to sail for Charleston bar on the following morning. At dawn the fleet started, and in three hours lay to off Charleston bar, when steps were taken to buoy out the channel, and to select marks on the shore from which bearings could be taken to assist the navigation.

In the meantime, the people of Charleston were fully aware of the danger which menaced them; the masts and funnels of the Federal fleet could be distinguished from the quays which lined the harbour, and from the windows of the houses of the rich merchants which overlooked the bay. As yet, although her trade had been nearly ruined, and a portion of her buildings destroyed by conflagrations, the city retained a semblance of the luxury and comfort which characterised her in former days, and a traveller reaching Charleston from the south might still fancy himself in Europe, and free from the actual presence of war. A large portion of the population, unwilling to leave their homes, or confiding in the strength of the defences, continued to dwell in the city, and the esplanade facing the harbour was eagerly sought as the place from which the preparations for attack and defence could be best seen. As the enemy's fleet lay off the bar during Sunday, many anxious eyes were directed towards it, and many prayers were offered up in the churches, the steeples of which were marked out as bearings for the Federal pilots.

On Monday the 6th the iron-clads crossed the bar, and took up a position about a mile from the shore in the main ship channel, along the line of Morris Island, but a haze which concealed the forts and the more distant city precluded further operations.

It was not, therefore, until the 7th that the engagement actually commenced. The order of battle was as follows:—Leading the line of iron-clads, which were alone to join in the attack, was the Weehawken, to which was attached a raft destined to explode torpedoes and tear away obstructions; following her was the Passaic, then in successive order the Montauk, Patapsco, New Ironside, Cats-kill, Nantucket, Nahant, and lastly the Keokuk with the double turret; whilst the squadron of reserve, consisting of wooden vessels, remained outside the bar. The day was favourable for the operations; the haze had cleared off, there was no wind, and the sea was calm as glass. Both sides could see clearly the position of their opponents, the forts, batteries, and steeples of the city could be clearly descried from the ships, whilst with equal distinctness could the movements of the iron-clads be discerned from the ramparts of the outer line of the defences. There were however but few signs of life: the iron-clads seemed to be worked without human agency; not a man was seen on the decks, but quietly and accurately, by an invisible motive power, did each vessel take up the position assigned to her. Not a shot was fired, the batteries showed no life, but far away in the distant city, every steeple, every house, and the long line of wharves, were crowded by spectators eager to watch the commencement of the battle which was to decide their fate.

Standing on the ramparts of Fort Sumter in mid-channel, let us before the combat commences glance round at the numerous forts and batteries which were prepared to dispute the progress of the Federal fleet. Looking to the east, on Sullivan's Island, were the Beauregard Battery, Fort Moultrie, and Battery Bee, where General Ripley in person superintended the defence. To the south, on Morris Island, were numerous batteries erected along the shore, of which Fort Wagner and Cumming's Point battery were the principal. Turning towards the city, and between it and

Sumter, were Fort Johnson on the south side of the harbour, Fort Ripley and Castle Pinckney on islands in mid-channel, besides other batteries on the northern shore. In addition to these works of defence, obstructions to detain the iron-clads under fire, and to block up the channels, had been placed between Fort Sumter and Fort Moultrie; and also between Fort Sumter and Fort Johnson, piles had been driven in, and nets and other contrivances used with the object of entangling the screws of the steamers.

At ebb-tide (12.30 P.M.) the fleet was ordered to move forward, led by the Weehawken, but a delay occurred owing to the disarrangement of the raft attached to this vessel for the purpose of clearing obstructions, and it was not until 1.30 P.M. that the garrison of Fort Sumter noticed its approach. Even then calculations proved that an hour would elapse before the leading vessel would be well under fire, therefore the officers of the garrison concluded their dinner, the band played the National Anthem, the Confederate flag and the blue and white banner of the Palmetto State were hoisted, and not until 2.30 P.M. did the drums beat as a signal for the garrison to repair to the guns. Slowly and majestically did the line of iron-clads, comprising seven Monitors, the new Ironsides, and the Keokuk, more dreaded than any, enter the channel; slowly the leading vessels steamed past Fort Wagner, then Battery Bee, and so in turn along the front of Morris Island; no sound came from the batteries, no gun opened on them, and the whole line of vessels passed the outer batteries. But as the Weehawken turned the point to enter the harbour proper, a single gun was fired from Fort Moultrie; immediately from Sumter, from Battery Bee, from

Battery Beauregard the fire was taken up, at first somewhat too rapidly, but as the officers perceived the difficulty of hitting the vulnerable parts of the vessels, accuracy succeeded to rapidity. The Weehawken afforded a fair mark for the guns, for in attempting to gain the position assigned to her opposite the north-western face of Sumter, she came in contact with the hawser stretching across the channel from Sumter to Moultrie, to which were suspended nets and other contrivances for fowling the screws. This obstruction hindered her progress; the other iron-clads sheered off, and endeavoured to cover her misfortune by a brisk fire on the forts and batteries, which had hitherto directed their attention almost exclusively to the Weehawken. The huge Ironsides attempted to come to her assistance, but did not properly answer the helm, and fell foul of two of the Monitors. Admiral Du Pont then signalled the fleet to disregard the movement of the flag-ship, and the Monitors took up their position between Cumming's Point and Sullivan's Island, and opposite the north-eastern and eastern face of Fort Sumter; the firing became terrific; the Ironsides from her position engaged Fort Moultrie; the others principally directed their attention to Fort Sumter; then the Keokuk (Captain Rhind commanding), pushing ahead of her companions, placed herself within about 850 yards of the fort, and seemed to challenge it to combat. Not slow to recognise a worthy antagonist, Colonel Rhete ordered his Lieut.-Colonel (Yates) to take charge of a Brooke's gun,* and sight it carefully himself. The shots told, and the Keokuk disabled crept slowly out

* This gun, somewhat resembling an Armstrong, was invented by a Confederate officer, Captain Brooke, and was the product, with others of a similar description, of the Tradegar foundry, Richmond.

of fire, replying, even when forced to retreat to the batteries which concentrated their guns on her. The remainder of the fleet, more or less severely injured, withdrew, and in thirty minutes from the time when the first gun opened, the action terminated.

Artillery had overcome iron-plating, and the several descriptions of vessels exemplified in the Monitors, the Ironsides, and the Keokuk, had each sustained serious injury. The Nahant had been struck on her pilot house, the bolts had been driven in, and had wounded some of the crew. The Nantucket's turret had been so jarred, that the cover of one of her ports could not be opened, and consequently her fifteen-inch gun had been rendered useless. The Ironsides had been frequently struck, and her wooden bows penetrated by shell; the Keokuk was said to have been hit ninety times, her turrets (five and three-quarter inches of iron in thickness) were completely riddled, and during the night, as the sea became somewhat rough, and the water rushed in through the holes in her bows, she sank near Light House Creek. In the fleet many men were killed and wounded, but in the forts but two death casualties occurred. The action on the part of the Federals was confined entirely to the navy, the land force under General Hunter, considered to be too few in numbers to attempt any diversion, remained mere spectators of the battle. The triumph of the Confederates was complete, the iron-clad fleet so much dreaded had been driven off, and the prestige of the description of vessel named after the Monitor, the first of the class, had been much injured if not destroyed. The Federal Government had hoped that it would have been able on the second anniversary of the surrender of Fort Sumter, to have announced to the nation that the stars and stripes were again flying over its walls, and expected that the reverses of the winter would have thus been counterbalanced by a triumph peculiarly grateful to Northern pride. In this they had been disappointed, and from the reports of the naval officers, it became apparent that the capture of Charleston could only be effected by a combined force, assisted by all the accompaniments for a regular siege.

Thus terminated the first of the attacks directed against Charleston, and whilst we admire the energy of the Confederates in the erection of fortifications, and their courage in defending them, we must yet award some praise to the gallant men who commanded their hitherto almost untried vessels, under circumstances which tested their coolness and determination to an uncommon degree. In the magnitude of the operations, in the calm determination of the garrison, in the enthusiasm of the population, and in the gallantry of the attacking force, there is much that must strike the imagination, and even to those who most deprecate war and its attendant evils, features of grandeur present themselves in an engagement such as that which was fought at Charleston; but when history records the fate of the small but beautiful town of Jacksonville in Florida, and when a narrative of its wanton destruction is read, few can fail to appreciate the demoralising influence of war, and whilst detesting the authors of the calamity, thank Heaven that they are spared the misery of the conquered, and the temptations which beset the conquerors.

A comparatively small force of three regiments under a Colonel Higginson had been sent about the end of March to seize and occupy the town of Jacksonville. This place, better than many of the towns of the South, was known in the Northern States, as it had formerly been the resort of invalids, who sought the benefit of its genial climate. The almost tropical vegetation of Florida was here mingled with the foliage of more Northern climes, and the rose and the jessamine were planted side by side with the orange and the palmetto. Groves of magnificent oaks, from which the Spanish moss hung in long pendules, lined the streets and shaded the houses and scattered villas which formed the town. Among the inhabitants were many who by birth and commerce were connected with the North, and who, surrounded by Southern influence, had yet retained sympathy with the Union.

The first regiment that landed was composed of negro troops, who were soon afterwards joined by the 6th Connecticut and 8th Maine, when a reconnaissance was pushed forward into the surrounding country, resulting in slight skirmishing with the Confederate militia; no further operations were attempted, and hardly had the troops marched back to the town, when an order arrived directing that they should be re-embarked, and should return to take part in the operations against Charleston. Then seemingly without provocation, or any inducement except love of destruction and plunder, the soldiery applied torches to the houses, broke open and rifled churches, villas, and shops, carrying away all that they considered of value, and burning the remainder. The flames spread through the streets, the trees caught fire, and in the short space of a few hours nearly the whole of the beautiful town was reduced to ashes. The few inhabitants who had remained and had shown sympathy for the Northerners, embarked on board the transports with such of the furniture as they could save; but even these scant necessaries were ordered to be thrown overboard, to make room for the negro troops.

Few occurrences of the war have been more disgraceful to the Federal arms than the destruction of Jacksonville. No result followed the expedition, and the wanton devastation of private property, much of which belonged to men not unfriendly to their cause, alone marked the presence of the Union soldiers. It is said that the white troops even more than the negroes made themselves notorious by their shameful conduct, and although this statement* must be received with doubt, owing to the strong party bias which characterised all allusions to the newly raised negro force, yet it is evident that if the New England regiments did not surpass, they fully equalled, their black brethren.

Little more of importance occurred on the coast during the commencement of the year 1863. In North Carolina, where General Forster held command of the Federal forces, the Confederates resumed the offensive, and under General Pettigrew made an attack on Newberne, which was repulsed with little loss, although a more important movement conducted against Washington, N.C., nearly proved successful. For almost three weeks the Federal garrison under General Forster in person was besieged and cut off from communication with the sea; the General ultimately ran the blockade and reached Newberne, where he was preparing an expedition to relieve the place, when news arrived that the Confederates, for reasons of their own, had raised the siege, their services probably being required in other quarters.

* The author has taken the account of the destruction of Jacksonville from Northern sources, contained in the *Rebellion Record*, vol. vi. pp. 483, 484, Documents.

On two points were men's eyes directed; in the West the siege of Vicksburg, and the attempts to force a passage up the Mississippi past the batteries at Port Hudson, attracted the attention and alternately raised the hopes and excited the fears of North and South; and in Virginia, as spring and dry weather gave promise of firm roads, the expectations of the recommencement of the campaign under a new general roused the sanguine spirits of the Northern people, and led them to forget the disasters of the previous year.

After General Sherman's failure to capture Vicksburg from the Yazoo River, General M'Clernand, who succeeded him in command, wisely resolved to attempt an easier enterprise, whilst General Grant pushed forward preparations for a regular siege. To restore the morale of his troops and to prevent the evils of prolonged idleness, were his first objects; he therefore, in place of leading them back to their previous encampment, organised an expedition against Arkansas Post, a village on the Arkansas River, which had been fortified by the Confederates. This place, settled by the French as early as 1685, stands on the left bank of the river fifty miles from its mouth, and is surrounded by a country abounding in cattle, corn, and cotton. A fort named Fort Hindman had been erected to command the river, and lines of entrenchment covered by marshes, and protected by abattis, defended the village. The garrison, of between 3,000 and 4,000 men, was under the command of General Churchill, who had orders to hold the post as long as he possibly could.

The expeditionary force consisted of two *corps d'armée* under Generals Morgan and Sherman, the whole commanded by General M'Clernand, and a fleet of three iron-clads and several gunboats of lighter draught, under Admiral Porter.

As the gunboats and transports steamed slowly up the Arkansas River, Texan cavalry watched them from the banks, keeping out of range of the rifles, and the negroes from the plantations peered curiously at the concourse of vessels and men which crowded the usually almost deserted stream. The swamps, and gloomy forests covered with Spanish moss, presented no inviting spectacle to the invaders; nevertheless the men were in good spirits, and anxious to wipe out the stain of their repulse from Vicksburg.*

On the 9th of January the troops landed four miles below the fort, and on the following day steps were taken to invest it, and to prevent the retreat of the garrison. General Sherman's corps was marched round the entrenchments and formed the right of the line, his own right resting on the river above the fort. On his left was General Morgan, who had also detached a brigade to march up the right bank of the river and to protect the transports from an attack from that side. During the movement the iron-clads engaged the attention of the garrison by keeping up a heavy fire on the entrenchments. On the next day, the 11th, a combined attack was arranged between General M'Clernand and Admiral Porter. The action commenced with the artillery, the gunboats at the same time engaging the fort from the river, the iron-clads being pushed forward

* The following is an extract from the *Missouri Republican*, of Jan. 12, which, read by the light of subsequent events, is curious as showing how little General Sherman was appreciated at that time except by those who knew him well. 'There was one change for the better, however; the troops, although somewhat dispirited, were no longer under a leader whom they wholly distrusted. An alteration was needed, and General Sherman was not superseded a moment too soon.' General Sherman was no favourite with the press, owing to the strict discipline he enforced among the newspaper correspondents.

within four hundred yards of the enemy's works. Covered by the artillery, the infantry advanced and took possession of the outer lines of entrenchments, and under shelter of the woods were preparing for a final assault, when the garrison, finding themselves unable to reply to the fire of the gunboats, and greatly overwhelmed by superior numbers, hoisted a white flag and surrendered. The prisoners were then put on board transports and sent up to Cairo, the stores and trophies were collected, and the fort blown up and destroyed. The General, satisfied with his success, and doubtless perceiving that the evil effects of the disaster at Vicksburg were wiped out of remembrance by the victory at Fort Hindman, returned with his troops to Young's Point, a short distance above Vicksburg, on the right bank of the Mississippi, where he established a permanent camp, and where he was joined soon afterwards by General Grant, who assumed the chief command.

What may be called the third siege of Vicksburg now commenced, and taking warning by the previous repulse of General Sherman, General Grant adopted other plans to reduce the place. As the works facing the Mississippi and lower Yazoo River had proved too strong to permit of an attempt to capture them by storm, and as the river batteries had already successfully resisted the Federal gunboats, General Grant resolved by combined naval and military operations to endeavour to turn the rear of the line of defence; and whilst the gunboats, assisted by a strong land force, watched the Mississippi, to obtain an entrance into the upper waters of the Yazoo River, and so take in reverse the batteries at Hayne's Bluff.

Whilst therefore he sought information and made the requisite preparations for these expeditions, he anxiously awaited the cooperation of Admiral Farragut's fleet on the Lower Mississippi; and Admiral Porter, who ably seconded him in all his plans, despatched more than one of his iron-clads past the batteries at Vicksburg to open communications with the lower fleet, and at the same time to destroy the supplies collected in the various tributary streams of the Mississippi for the use of the garrison.

Gallantly did the Queen of the West run the gauntlet of the batteries. Her Commander, Captain Ellet, not content with merely passing them, attacked, even under the protection of the guns, a Confederate steamer, and after knocking a hole in her with his ram, only drew off when he found his own vessel was on fire. Shortly afterwards the Indianola followed in the same course, and the two steamers entered separately on their perilous career in the waters of the Mississippi and its tributaries.

The enterprises of the gunboats in the Mississippi and inland waters present much that is striking and adventurous. Forcing their way up creeks and bayous, exposed to the fire of artillery and riflemen from the banks, and to the unseen dangers of torpedoes from the waters; ignorant of the preparations made to receive them, and uncertain whether the turn of the river, or the dense foliage overhanging the bayou, might not hide some foe, either in the shape of a newly equipped gunboat or a battery of artillery; dependent on their own resources for provisions and for fuel, which latter the crew cut and collected from the forest, the men who commanded the gunboats made their way through narrow streams and cuttings, and, daunted by no difficulties, carried the war in a shape difficult to be encountered far into the enemy's country. Frequently their vessels would be so injured that the crew would be forced to abandon them, and seek a refuge in the woods until other gunboats appeared, or until they could seize some boat and rejoin their companions.

The career of both the Queen of the West and Indianola was short. The former, after destroying and capturing cotton, dispersing and burning army waggons and firing houses, was at length herself so injured by a battery in the Red River, that it was found necessary to abandon her. The Indianola's end was somewhat more glorious. Whilst returning from her predatory expedition, her commander discovered that he was chased by four vessels, and immediately cleared for action. The night was very dark, and the enemy's steamers gained rapidly on the Indianola. The leading vessel attempted to run her down, but the blow being broken by a coal-barge lashed to the port-side, did little damage. The Indianola then turned and met the next vessel in full career. The shock was sufficient to throw down the crew of both vessels, but inflicted little injury on the Indianola. The engagement then became general. The Queen of the West, repaired and refitted by the Confederates, and the Webb (for such the two steamers were found to be), ran into and struck the Indianola several times, bearing the brunt of the action, whilst the cotton-clad steamers poured in their fire from rifles and field-pieces. At length the Indianola was discovered to be in a sinking condition, and surrendered, but was so much injured as to be of no service to her captors.

Such was war in the inland waters, and although few can refrain from admiring the enterprise of those engaged in it, yet the accounts given of the devastation of the country, the ruin of property, and the burning of villages and houses, argue a sad reverse to the picture. An expedition undertaken by General Steel in

April, up Deer Creek, a tributary of the Mississippi, affords an instance of the method of waging war in the south-west. Federal vessels had been fired on by what the general was pleased to term guerillas, and in retaliation he advanced by land and water into the rich country hitherto spared by war, and teeming with agricultural wealth, where he burnt, plundered, and destroyed so that, to quote the words of one who accompanied the expedition and admired its results, *this succession of terrestrial Edens in which General Steel operated, by the aid of fire and other warlike instruments, was soon reduced to a level with common earthly dwelling-places.** Horses, mules, oxen, waggons, and all the produce of the farms, including the slaves, were carried away captive by the Federals in their retreat; the rich planters' houses were pulled down and burnt; and as the cotton had been already destroyed by the Confederates, the cotton gins were burnt by the Federals. The method of carrying on war in Mississippi resembled rather the devastation inflicted by the French in the Palatinate, or the invasion of Eastern hordes, than the operations of regular armies in the pay of a Government which claimed to rule one of the most civilised and enlightened countries of the world.

Whilst the Federal army lay encamped at Young's Point, the people of the North were amused and their imaginations excited by expeditions undertaken with

* The horrible account of the devastation of this beautiful country was given in the *New York Times*. The narrator states that only one plantation belonging to a Union family was found, and adds—'That cotton gins, mills, &c., belonging to this Union family were given to the flames the same as those of the others. In this case, as in nearly all others, the ardour of our soldiers carried them away so much that they never waited for orders to set fire to a corn-mill or haystack, but did it at once as a matter of course.'

the object of turning the defences of Vicksburg, either by means of the vast network of rivers, such as the Tallahatchie, Yazoo Pass, and Sunflower, which connect the Mississippi River with the Yazoo, or by magnificently destructive plans of inundation for the purpose of inundating great tracts of country, and uniting the waters of the Upper Mississippi with the tributaries of Red River. To carry out these schemes, two expeditions were planned. The first, of a combined naval and military force, entered the Tallahatchie by the Yazoo Pass, about fifty miles above Helena, and after descending those rivers for about one hundred miles, almost succeeded in reaching the point of junction of the Tallahatchie and Yallabusha Rivers, which uniting together form the Yazoo. Great quantities of cotton had been captured during the advance, and boats laden with this valuable commodity had been seen flying before the Federal gunboats. Little resistance, except from riflemen on the banks, had hitherto been encountered; but near the junction of the two rivers, obstructions were discovered placed across the stream, whilst a fort threatened the leading vessels with its guns. The place had been well chosen. The surrounding marshes prevented the near approach of the troops, and the brunt of the action fell upon the gunboats. After a bombardment which lasted for two days, the gunboats were repulsed, and the Federal expedition returned with some difficulty to the Mississippi, having accomplished nothing excepting the plunder and devastation of a rich country.

The second expedition, undertaken almost simultaneously, terminated with no greater success. Forcing their way through bayous overgrown with tangled vegetation, and through channels hitherto only used by canoes, and which, with great labour, were widened sufficiently to admit the iron-clads, the naval force endeavoured to discover a passage, by creeks scarcely distinguishable from the marshes, and hardly visible in the thick forests, to the Sunflower River. The advance was very slow, and the Confederates were enabled to concentrate troops, and to collect bands of negroes, who working diligently with the axe, soon rendered the channels impassable, and threatened to cut off the gunboats from their retreat. Riflemen constantly picked off the crews, and so close were the Confederate troops, that it was feared that the gunboats might be captured by boarding. Urgent despatches were sent by Admiral Porter to General Sherman, informing him of the danger which beset the fleet. The troops were hurried forward, and arrived only just in time to rescue the gunboats, which were hemmed up in a narrow creek, so close to the bank as to be unable to use their broadsides. Sherman's advanced brigades checked the Confederates, and disconcerted their plans. The fleet was rescued from its perilous position, and returned as rapidly as was possible to the Mississippi. The scheme of forcing a passage into the Upper Yazoo was abandoned, as was also that of cutting a canal through the point of land opposite to the town of Vicksburg, and the plan of inundating the country around Lake Providence, and creating a fresh channel for the great Mississippi River, met with no better success. Large tracts of country were indeed laid under water, by cutting the levees, and the Federals had the satisfaction of feeling that they had equalled, if not surpassed, some of the most famous nations of antiquity in the vastness of their schemes, if they had not rivalled them in successful results.

Contemporary with these operations at Vicksburg, the lower fleet, under Admiral Farragut, made an attempt to pass the batteries at Port Hudson, and so to cooperate with Admiral Porter's fleet on the upper waters. The rendezvous of the fleet was at Providence Island, about four miles below Port Hudson, and there, on the evening of the 13th of March, were the several vessels under Admiral Farragut's command collected. The fleet consisted of the Hartford (the flag-ship), Richmond, Mississippi, Monongahela, Genesee, Albatross, Kineo, the iron-clad Essex, the gunboat Sachem, and a mortar flotilla of six schooners.

It was designed to attack the batteries in the following order: the Hartford, with her consort the Albatross, was to lead the attack; after her were to follow the Richmond and the Genesee; then the Monongahela, with the Kineo on her port-side; and, last of all, the Mississippi. The Essex and Sachem were ordered to remain to protect the mortar-vessels, which were to cover the attack by their fire. Everything was in readiness on Sunday the 14th of March, and the vessels lay concealed by Providence Island, until night closed in, and darkness favoured the enterprise. The Essex and mortar-vessels threw a few shells during the afternoon to get the range, but otherwise all was quiet.

The Confederates, prepared for an attack, remained at their guns; their batteries lined the left bank of the river, and a look-out was also kept on the right bank. The gunners slept at their posts, and although it was not known that the attempt to pass the batteries would be made on the night of the 14th, yet the near presence of the enemy's fleet occasioned uneasiness.

The night of the 14th and 15th was more than usually dark, and as the Hartford, followed by the fleet, steamed slowly up the river, breasting with some difficulty the swift current, no sign showed that they were perceived by the Confederate artillerymen—such was the fact—until the leading vessel had already passed the first of the line of batteries; then the guard gave the alarm; a rocket was sent up as a signal of the danger, and a great fire was lighted on the river's bank, near one of the most formidable works, to throw light across the stream and to illumine the Federal vessels. Immediately the artillerymen repaired to their posts, and waited the signal to begin their work. The Hartford, as soon as it was ascertained that she had been seen, opened fire, which was taken up by the other vessels of the fleet; the mortar-boats also commenced to throw shells into the enemy's lines, and the Essex advancing nearer the batteries, opened on them with her heavy guns. For a few minutes no reply was made to this terrific fire, and the Federal shells fell wide, as the exact locality of the batteries was unknown. Then the Confederate guns opened; the Hartford was struck, but being a swift vessel, succeeded, with her consort the Albatross, in running past the batteries. The Richmond and the other vessels were less fortunate; the darkness was so great, that with difficulty they avoided firing into each other, and the smoke which hung round the guns, owing to the humidity of the air, prevented them from being worked with effect. The flashes of the guns from the batteries alone presented marks at which to aim, and often was the command given to cease firing, for fear lest other vessels rather than the enemy's works should feel the effects of the broadsides. No order could be preserved in the fleet, and there was great risk lest the vessels should run foul of each other. Finding the enterprise so much more difficult than was contemplated, the Richmond and the vessels following her turned round: in doing so the Mississippi ran aground on the right bank of the river, and her commander finding that it was impossible to get her off, resolved to abandon her and blow her up. The greater portion of the crew were landed, and afterwards picked up by the Essex, and the vessel was set on fire. In the meantime the Richmond, Monongahela, and their consorts, had returned to Providence Island, and the Hartford and Albatross had run past the batteries, and were in safety on the opposite side. Many of the vessels had sustained injury, and their crews had suffered in killed and wounded, whilst the casualties in the batteries had been comparatively few, owing to the inaccuracy of the fire from the ships. As the Richmond and her companion lay at anchor under the trees of Providence Island, the Mississippi was perceived approaching in a sheet of flame. Lightened by the departure of the crew, and influenced by the current, she had swung round into the stream, and was now floating stem foremost down the river. Her guns exploded, together with many of the shells which were lying ready for use on her deck, and when the flames reached the magazine she blew up, shaking by the concussion every vessel in the fleet, and sinking almost in the same spot where the Arkansas had perished in the previous year. The enterprise against Port Hudson had proved a failure, and the land force under General Banks, which was advancing from Bâton Rouge to take part in the anticipated siege, withdrew to its former lines.

Much anxiety was felt in the North for the safety of Admiral Farragut, who with the wooden frigate Hartford, and the iron-clad Albatross, was between the two fortresses of Port Hudson and Vicksburg, and in danger of attack from the Queen of the West and the Webb, which had already proved so destructive to the

Indianola. He, however, maintained his supremacy on the river, and cruising between the two fortified places, watched the Mississippi and blockaded the mouth of the Red River.

With the failure to turn the position of Vicksburg, and to capture Port Hudson, the third period in the operations to open the Mississippi may be considered to have closed. The next great attempt, although made with the same army, which retained its position at Young's Point, and with the same fleet, was yet formed on a different plan. The first attack on Vicksburg from the river, by a naval force alone, had been defeated; the second, by an army unsupported by ships, had proved a more disastrous failure; the third, where strategy was intended to take the place of an attack by open force, had also been unsuccessful, and the campaign which followed and continued during the early summer months, both in Louisiana and Mississippi, was undertaken on a scale more commensurate with the object in view, and was the precursor of events which belong properly to a later period of the war. The peculiar constitution of the American Western armies especially qualified them for warfare such as that which was waged on the Mississippi. The independent habits of the men fitted them for sharpshooters, and the aptitude (acquired in Western life) of turning their hands to various employments, enabled the soldiers to adapt themselves either to the ordinary requirements of infantry or artillery, or to the engineering works so necessary in campaigning in a wild country, whilst occasionally the ease with which soldiers were converted into sailors on the inland waters, proved the natural intelligence of the men, and their fitness for the many requirements of war.

CHAPTER XIII.

THE BATTLE OF CHANCELLORSVILLE.

LITTLE influence had the season of the year in causing a cessation of hostilities in the South-Western States; through the winter months, the rise of the rivers encouraged enterprises on the part of the fleet, and in summer the firmness of the ground and the growth of the crops, allowed of more extended operations by the troops. There was no intermission in the strife, and the naval and military forces along the eastern and southern boundaries of the Confederacy, looked in vain for relaxation, which in colder climates is necessitated by winter. But in Tennessee and Virginia, the heavy rains of January, February, and March prevented all attempts at movement on a grand scale. The cavalry and detached corps on either side made raids into the enemy's country, and in Virginia, an engagement of more than ordinary dimensions, fought between the Federal and Confederate cavalry, was the forerunner of the important campaign of the spring.

During the time that the two armies watched each other from either bank of the Rappahannock, Stuart's cavalry, under his lieutenants, made several incursions within the Federal lines. Captain Mosby, commanding a troop of irregular cavalry, had distinguished himself by more than one bold enterprise, and, among others, the feat of capturing General Stoughton within his own lines, and surrounded by a considerable force, was not the least remarkable. With less than a troop of horsemen, he rode boldly into Fairfax Court-house, surprised and took prisoner in his bed the general in command, beat up the quarters of Colonel Wyndham, commanding the cavalry brigade, who fortunately for himself had gone to Washington, and rode off without the loss of a man, and with a considerable number of captured horses.

To revenge such insults, and to infuse *esprit de corps* into his cavalry, which under a proper system of discipline was improving and becoming more equal to the better horsemen of Virginia, General Averill, who with General Stoneman had acquired the reputation of a good cavalry officer, made a reconnaissance in force towards Culpepper Court-house, where Fitzhugh Lee was reported to be encamped. With seven cavalry regiments and six guns Averill advanced, and on reaching the banks of the Rappahannock encountered a dismounted detachment of Fitzhugh Lee's cavalry, who behind the shelter of the woods offered a resistance to the passage of the river. A squadron of the 1st Rhode Island regiment gallantly rode into the stream, and ascending the opposite bank drove back the skirmishers. In the meantime Fitzhugh Lee had drawn up his brigade of about 800 men, and barred the road to Culpepper. The Federals formed in line, and, supported by their artillery, kept up the engagement for the greater portion of the day, their front covered with dismounted skirmishers who advanced firing through the woods. Finding, however, that the force opposed to them presented a firm front, and alarmed lest his retreat should be cut off, Averill ordered the cavalry to retire across the Rappahannock. This was accomplished with little loss, for although the Confederate cavalry attempted to charge more than once, they were prevented by the broken ground, the woods, and the fences, from crossing swords with the enemy. The skirmish was of little importance, except as exhibiting the improvement made by the Federals in the organization of their cavalry, for even if the accounts of the hand to hand combats described in the New York papers cannot wholly be credited, the dash across the Rappahannock, and the orderly method with which the troops were manœuvred, evince a considerable improvement in the constitution of the cavalry force. The wealth of the Northern States in men, horses, and arms was beginning to counterbalance the inferiority of the riders exhibited in the earlier periods of the war; and the raid of Stoneman, which followed soon after the skirmish on the Rappahannock, presented features worthy of comparison with Stuart's bold movements on the Peninsula and in Maryland.

As the month of May approached, rumour spoke of a fresh attempt on Richmond. Hooker, the new general, had been lavish in criticisms on his predecessors, and not sparing of praise of his own past acts and promises for the future. It remained to be seen whether he could redeem the disaster of Fredericksburg and justify the hopes of his admirers.

After consultation with General Halleck, a combined scheme of advance on the enemy's capital was planned. Political as well as military reasons necessitated the resumption of the campaign. It was felt that prolonged inactivity would strengthen the hands of the Democrats, and add to the ranks of the peace party: the term of service of many of the men of the army of the Potomac would shortly expire, and, before losing a large proportion of the veteran soldiers, it was thought advisable again to try the issue of battle, and endeavour by a victory to infuse spirit into the troops, and also to rouse the enthusiasm of the population from which recruits were to be drawn. Notwithstanding the numerous desertions and the difficulty of obtaining volunteers, the Federal forces were far superior in numbers to their opponents. Not only was the army of the Potomac kept up to a strength of about 150,000 men, but the several detached expeditions on the coast of Virginia and North Carolina threatened the Confederate capital from other directions, and necessitated counter detachments from General Lee's army, which he could ill afford to spare.

There is no clearer proof of the want of men in the Confederacy, than the position in which General Lee found himself in April, 1863. To protect Richmond and its vicinity from Forster in North Carolina, Peck at Suffolk in South-Eastern Virginia, and Key threatening to advance from the Pamunkey, General Lee had been obliged to detach nearly a third of the army with which he had fought at Fredericksburg, and to send Longstreet himself to command the department which included Richmond and its vicinity, together with the state of North Carolina, placed under the immediate supervision of General D. Hill. Thus the great Confederate commander, aware of the strength of his adversary, and of his anticipated advance, prepared to meet him with a force little if at all exceeding 50,000 men. But if his army was few in numbers, its *morale* was such that it justified the expectations of its commander. The men who composed it were of one nation, fighting for one cause, and bound together by more than ordinary ties; they were commanded by generals who had led them during all the great battles of the war, and under whom they had never yet sustained defeat; and, above all, there was that perfect confidence in the Commander-in-Chief, and complete accord between him and his subordinates, that rendered the well-handled and compact body which held the heights above Fredericksburg, more than a match for the heterogeneous masses which seemed to threaten to overwhelm them.

General Hooker's plan of attack was to divide his army into two portions, of which the stronger, having crossed the Rappahannock and Rapidan rivers, should advance against the Confederate left wing, whilst the Federal left wing, equal in numbers to General Lee's whole army, should attack and occupy the heights above Fredericksburg, and seize the Richmond Railway. At the same time that the bulk of the army should be thus occupied, the cavalry, excepting a small force under Pleasanton, was to move completely round the Confederate position, and whilst one body under Averill marched on Gordonsville, the other under Stoneman, interposing between General Lee's army and Richmond, was to cut the lines of rail, and burn the bridges over the North and South Anna Rivers.

Such were General Hooker's dispositions when he commenced his march on the 27th of April; his great numerical force enabled him to divide his army, and yet to maintain his superiority at all points. It was hoped that the Confederate cavalry, concentrated to swell the numbers of the main army, would be unable to offer resistance to Stoneman and Averill, and that General Lee, attacked by such overwhelming forces, would either be crushed or forced to retreat along a line of rail already occupied and rendered ineffectual for the conveyance of reinforcements by Stoneman's cavalry. As in all operations where armies are divided and act separately, some portion of their numerical power must be lost, and the advantage given to the smaller force acting on interior lines, and as the inability of Federal generals to bring the whole of their forces into action, and to manage them with effect, had been demonstrated in more than one action, it was hoped by the Confederate general that proper combinations would counterbalance, in the forthcoming battle, the evils attending the division of forces.

For a complete understanding of the plan of operations adopted by General Hooker, and of the several battles to which they led, a clear knowledge must be obtained of the country, south and west of Fredericksburg, and of the rivers and roads which intersect it. The scene of the battles which, under the names of the Wilderness and Chancellorsville, were fought between Generals Lee and Hooker, lay in the angle formed between the Rapidan and Rappahannock Rivers on the north and the Richmond and Fredericksburg Railway on the east, and comprised a thickly wooded and only partially cultivated country, known by the appropriate name of the Wilderness. The apex of the angle faced and overlooked the town of Fredericksburg, and its two arms extended southwards and westwards along the rail and the river.

Twelve miles above Fredericksburg, the Rappahannock receives as its tributary the Rapidan River, flowing from a westerly direction, the main stream of the Rappahannock having pursued a course from the north-west. On the upper Rappahannock, twenty-five miles above Fredericksburg, is Kelly's Ford, and below it Barnett's Ford. Corresponding with these and united to them by roads are Germana Ford and Ely Ford on the Rapidan, whilst below the point of junction of the two rivers is United States Ford and Banks' Ford, the last about four miles above Fredericksburg. Traversing the wooded country known as the Wilderness, is the high road from Fredericksburg to Orange Court-house, which runs nearly parallel with the Rappahannock, and crosses the hills or bluffs bordering on the river. To avoid this hilly country, another road, called the plank road, had been more recently constructed, which leaving Fredericksburg, unites with the high road at a solitary house known by the name of Chancellorsville. Two miles before reaching this house and eight miles from Fredericksburg, a by-road branches off to the southward from the plank road, and reunites with the main road five miles beyond Chancellorsville, and fifteen miles from Fredericksburg. From Chancellorsville a road leads direct to Ely's Ford, and, from this, another road connects the Ely Ford road with United States Ford. Such are the principal features of the country to which attention should be directed whilst studying the campaign of Chancellorsville.

On the 27th of April General Hooker commenced his advance. Taking with him three *corps d'armée*, viz. the 11th Howard's, the 5th Meade's, and the 12th Slocum's, he marched *en echellon* up the left bank of the Rappahannock until his leading corps, the 11th Howard's, was opposite Kelly's Ford. This ford had been watched during the past two weeks by a strong detachment, and pontoons were in readiness to assist the crossing. The three corps commenced the passage of the Rappahannock on the 29th, encountering no opposition, a few Confederate videttes, who boldly reconnoitred the advancing columns and rode off, being the only troops who showed themselves. During the

29th and 30th the march was continued from the upper Rappahannock to the Rapidan, and crossing that river by Ely's and Germana Fords, the three corps encamped at a short distance from Chancellorsville, at which place on the 30th and 1st of May, the 3rd corps Sickles's and the 2nd Couch joined them by United States and Bank's Fords. Simultaneously with the passage of the upper Rappahannock, General Sedgwick, in command of the left wing at Falmouth, made a demonstration of crossing the river below the town, near the point adopted by Franklin's corps previous to the battle of Fredericksburg. The pontoons were brought down to the river's bank on the night of the 28th, and on the 29th a portion of the 1st and 6th corps were thrown across the river, surprising and capturing the Confederate pickets on the right bank.

Up to this time General Lee was uncertain from which quarter to expect the real attack, he therefore drew back his army in the direction of Chancellorsville, leaving Early's division to guard Marye's Heights. At Chancellorsville he learnt from General Anderson, who for some weeks past had been engaged in watching the roads leading from United States Ford, Ely's Ford, and Germana Ford, and who had fallen back on the approach of Hooker's overwhelming force, that the main body of the Federal army was advancing from that direction and threatened his left rear.

On the night of the 30th of April, the Confederate army, consisting of Jackson's three divisions, and two of Longstreet's former corps, viz. M'Law's and Anderson's, were on the roads leading from Fredericksburg to Chancellorsville, Early's division being left as before stated to guard the heights above Fredericksburg. In order to delay the enemy's advance, General Lee threw up some slight earthworks on the Fredericksburg roads;

and General Stuart made a night attack with two cavalry regiments, resulting in little except skirmishing. Even among those who had served during the campaigns of Virginia, and who appreciated most thoroughly the qualities of the Confederate troops and the talents of the General, there was some uneasiness at the aspect of affairs. The Confederate army was outnumbered nearly three to one; from 90,000 to 100,000 men were on what had formerly been its left rear, but which was now the front, whilst a force equalling in strength the whole army, threatened, by an advance from Fredericksburg, either to crush it or force it to retreat with both flanks exposed, along the Richmond rail, a portion of which the Federal cavalry had already occupied and partially destroyed.

In these trying circumstances, General Lee's calm manner, the quiet and collected orders which he issued, and his tone of confidence, created a similar feeling among all who were brought in contact with him. He had even countermanded the orders he had issued to General Longstreet to join him with the troops from Suffolk, upon that General's representation of the difficulties attending the movement,* and satisfied that he could withstand with the small force at his disposal General Hooker's vast army and powerful artillery, prepared by a movement almost unexampled in its daring to defeat his opponent's schemes. On the other hand, so confident did General Hooker feel in the success of his operations, that on the 30th he issued a congratulatory order to his army, informing it that *the rebel army was the legitimate property of the army of the Potomac*, and on the 1st of May directed an advance to be made from Chancellorsville in the direction of Fredericksburg,

* Owing partly to the state of the roads, partly to General Peck's threatening attitude at Suffolk.

at the same time taking the precaution of strengthening the lines he already held by earthworks and abattis.

Sykes's division of Meade's corps, forming the right of the army, advanced, covered by cavalry skirmishers, and drove back the Confederate out-pickets nearly a mile, but was recalled by an order from head-quarters, as General Hooker, ascertaining that General Lee was marching against him with his whole army, drew back behind the line of works he had constructed in the forest, hoping to induce his opponent to fight him on his own ground. Such, however, was not the intention of the Confederate General. Seeing, and as quickly comprehending, his adversary's strategy, he formed his own dispositions to thwart his plans, and availing himself of the advantages which the country afforded of concealing not only the movements but the numbers of his troops, he determined to turn Hooker's flank by detaching Jackson's corps round his right rear, whilst he himself with only two divisions held in check and engaged the attention of the great Federal army.

During the 1st of May, in order fully to ascertain Hooker's exact position and to keep him amused whilst preparations were in progress for the flank march, he ordered several attacks and feints to be made along the turnpike and plank roads, which so far succeeded in their object as to lead General Hooker to believe that the Confederates were in force in his front, and that it would be well that every man should join him previous to the approaching engagement; he therefore ordered Reynolds' division to cross the Rappahannock and unite with the main army at Chancellorsville. Thus, on the evening of the 1st of May, whilst the 1st corps under Reynolds was preparing to cross the Rappahannock by United States Ford, the main army held the ground from the neighbourhood of Banks' Ford to Chancellorsville, and from thence, with the right thrown back, covered the road to Germana Ford. Meade's corps formed the left, Couch and Slocum the centre, and Howard the right rear, with Sickles in reserve. At the same time Sedgwick, with his own and one division of Couch's corps, continued to threaten Marye's Heights from the right bank of the Rappahannock.

During the night of the 1st of May and early morning of the 2nd, the flank march of General Jackson commenced, his corps consisting of three divisions, under A. P. Hill, Coulson, and Rodes. Diverging to the south from the plank road, and availing himself of the by-road through the forest, he marched round the right flank of Hooker's army, without that General having any knowledge of the important movement which was in progress almost within reach of his guns. Once was the march of the Confederates perceived, and a few shells were fired, but the destination and numbers of the column were not suspected, and by the morning of the 2nd of May, Jackson's corps found itself on the right rear of Howard's, which formed the extreme right of the Federal army.

During the night and morning of the 2nd of May, whilst this movement was in progress, Lee, with the two divisions of M'Law and Anderson, kept up a succession of feints in the Federal front, the men advancing gallantly almost up to the enemy's batteries, and creating by the boldness and frequency of their attacks the belief that the Confederates were in great force, and prepared to assume the offensive. So passed the night of the 2nd, and in the forenoon of the 3rd, whilst Jackson was forming his columns of attack, and steadily and unsuspected by the enemy approaching Howard's corps, Hooker contented himself with maintaining a defensive attitude, probably awaiting the arrival of Reynolds' corps.

And now, before the two armies join in battle, let us for a few moments review their position. Probably bolder tactics have never been attempted than those of General Lee at Chancellorsville. In presence of an army of at least 90,000 men, to which additional reinforcements were in the act of marching,* with a force of 20,000 men threatening his rear, he dared to divide his army into two portions, and with the weaker half to hold the enemy's enormous army in check, whilst the ablest of his lieutenants prepared, after a brilliant march, to inflict a blow which was to foil his great enterprise and lead to his final retreat.

About 4 P.M. on the 2nd of May, Jackson's guns announced that he had commenced his attack; Lee pressed forward his two divisions with even greater energy than during the morning, and Jackson, marching rapidly from the direction of Germana Ford, fell suddenly on Howard's corps bivouacking in the forest totally unprepared for attack, and undefended by any abattis or works. With a yell the Confederates rushed on; the Federal divisions on the right were completely surprised, and fell back without order in panic and confusion; some few regiments were formed up in line, but nearly the whole of the 11th corps was broken, and retreated in rout and dismay towards the United States Ford. In vain Howard attempted to rally them, in vain Hooker and his personal staff interposed to check the flight, the men with few exceptions could not be brought to face Jackson's terrible veterans,

* Viz. Reynolds' corps.

and hastened in disgraceful flight to the rear. Then Hooker ordered up Berry's division of Sickles's corps, and Sickles himself and Pleasanton with his cavalry, taking post near a stone wall directly in the line of the retreat, succeeded in rallying some of the artillery, but the infantry continued its flight. However, Sickles's guns and such of the artillery of Howard's corps as had not been captured, were turned on the advancing enemy, and the pursuit was checked. Then Jackson rode forward in person to reconnoitre, in front of his advanced skirmishers, and having seen with his own eyes the position of affairs, turned to rejoin his men, that he might order a fresh attack; but it was 6 o'clock, and the dusk of evening rendered objects indistinct. Seen through the foliage, a Confederate regiment from South Carolina mistook General Jackson and his staff for the enemy's horsemen, and poured in a volley with too fatal effect. Jackson fell, struck in the arm, shot down by the very men whom he had so often led to victory, and who would have given their best blood to have preserved the life of their beloved General. An aide-de-camp was immediately sent to A. P. Hill to communicate the sad intelligence, and some officers rode up to the spot; whilst, however, they were engaged tending the wounded General, the Federal videttes, followed by the advanced skirmishers of Berry's division, made their appearance, and the staff officers were only just able by leaping on their horses to save themselves from capture. Again was a similar mistake made by the Confederate skirmishers, a second volley was fired, which wounded and killed some of the staff, and one of the litter-bearers engaged in carrying General Jackson, who fell to the ground, and remained for a few minutes actually within the line of Federal skirmishers; but his men becoming aware of his danger, rushed forward, quickly repulsed the advancing column, and the wounded General, struck twice again whilst on the ground by Confederate bullets, was carried carefully to the rear. But with Jackson's fall the impetus of the Confederate attack ceased; his presence, his voice, his fiery energy, were needed at this critical moment to carry forward the troops against the new opposition which encountered them; they paused, reinforcements reached the Federals, darkness intervened, and what had threatened to become a terrible disaster, resulted in a severe but not irremediable repulse.

So ended the battle of the 2nd of May, and with it the career of the second greatest of the Confederate generals. Contrast with his energy the caution and absence of dash exemplified by the Federal General commanding at Fredericksburg; although within hearing of the guns, and knowing that the main army was engaged, he attempted no diversion, and his want of enterprise can only be justified by the supposition that he was restrained from action by the direct orders of the Commander-in-Chief. Dearly was the success of the 2nd of May purchased by the loss of General Jackson; it was indeed hoped that his wounds would not prove fatal, and that General Stuart who was sent by Lee to command his old corps would soon be able to return to his cavalry; but at this critical moment Lee felt that his right arm had been taken from him, and although the magnitude of the operations in which he was engaged did not allow time for the indulgence of personal grief, yet they augmented the loss which he had sustained in the man who above all others was able to carry through the bold schemes of the Commander-in-Chief. Forgetful of his own injuries, and thinking only of the public weal, General Jackson sent to urge General Lee to order a vigorous attack on the following morning. But now the great preponderance of force on the Federal side began to tell. During the night of the 2nd, Meade's corps was transferred from the left to the right of the army, reinforced by the fresh troops of the 1st corps (Reynolds'), whilst Howard's corps was sent to man the works raised by Meade's men on the left of the line. Sickles's corps was formed on Meade's left, on either side of the Chancellorsville and Orange Road, and Slocum occupied the apex of the triangle at Chancellorsville, Couch with the 2nd corps minus one division acting as a reserve in a central position. Thus the Federal army held the triangle of ground stretching from the Rapidan between Germana and Ely Fords to Chancellorsville, and from thence to United States Ford on the Rappahannock. Sedgwick in the meantime gave signs of an intention to attack Marye's Heights.

Against this enormous force Lee could only bring the divisions which had suffered so severely on the previous day; but with these, few in number, tired in body, but indomitable in spirit, he determined not only to engage the Federals, but to fight them on their own ground, and in spite of their powerful artillery (more powerful than any European army ever brought into the field), to drive them from their entrenchments, and force them back if possible to the rivers.

At daybreak on the 3rd, the three divisions of Jackson's old corps advanced to the attack; they issued from the woods, and as they crossed the open ground up which the Orange Court-house Road ascends, became exposed to a fierce fire of artillery and musketry from the works raised during the night. The first line wavered, the second failed to support, and it seemed that the famous corps would be repulsed, but General Rodes, commanding the 3rd division, urged his men forward, commanding them to advance over friend and foe until they had crossed the enemy's works; the men of the other divisions rallied, pressed forward with renewed energy, and forced back the Federals in the direction of Chancellorsville. During this attack by Jackson's corps, Anderson's division, supported by a concentrated fire of artillery from a commanding hill named Fair View, was pushed forward by General Lee to assault the strongly entrenched position held by Slocum in front of Chancellorsville. They rushed forward in two lines, a brigade of Georgians and Mississippians leading. Through the abattis which covered the front of the Federal lines, they forced their way, and disdaining alike the fire of the enemy and the obstructions which impeded their advance, they drove back the defenders, forcing them to take shelter behind a second line of entrenchments, in rear of Chancellorsville. The house itself which gave the name to the battle, was burnt by the Confederate shells, and General Hooker forced to transfer his head-quarters farther to the rear.

The battle of the 2nd, in so far as regarded the main armies, terminated about 10 A.M.; but in the meantime Sedgwick had attempted the assault of Marye's Heights, defended by two Mississippian regiments posted behind the same stone wall that had proved so fatal to Burnside's columns. Gallantly did this small force hold its ground against the far greater numbers brought against it, but at length the whole corps of Sedgwick, issuing from Fredericksburg, and surrounding the heights, cut off the brave defenders from their supports, who finding that their ammunition was expended, surrendered. General Early, seeing that the Federals had gained the heights on his left, and were pressing forward towards Chancellorsville, withdrew, and took up a position near Salem Church, about five miles from Fredericksburg, where he threw up some slight field-works. Thus on the evening of the 3rd, General Lee was between Sedgwick's corps and the main Federal army, strongly entrenched in his front.

Even after the successes of the 2nd and 3rd, the position of the Confederates was sufficiently critical; only a part of Hooker's army had been engaged, several divisions and even whole corps had scarcely lost a man, and the Federal accounts, written on the battle-field, spoke of the General's intention of exhausting his opponent and then crushing him by overwhelming numbers. The more the battle is studied, the more marvellous do the boldness and talent of General Lee and the courage and endurance of his troops appear. Men who met the General on the eventful day of the 3rd, say that his calm courteous demeanour was the same as on ordinary occasions; he spoke of his success without exultation, and of Sedgwick's advance without uneasiness; his clear comprehension seemed to foresee events, and his unshaken confidence in the endurance of his men appeared to assure him of an easy victory over Sedgwick's victorious column.

On the news of Early's retreat reaching him, he immediately sent M'Law's division to his support, and that General meeting Sedgwick's advanced troops on the Fredericksburg Road, drove them back without difficulty on the main body. On the following day, the 4th, the battle was renewed: Sedgwick's men showed little energy, and on Early's division moving towards their left, and threatening their communications with Fredericksburg, they retreated precipitately towards Banks' Ford, surrendering to the enemy large numbers of supply waggons, mules, and horses. At 5 P.M. General Lee arrived on the ground, and took command in person; he infused energy into the attack, and the retreating Federals were driven headlong towards Banks' Ford, where, on the night of the 4th and 5th, they succeeded by the aid of pontoons in recrossing the river, only too happy to escape the destruction which seemed to threaten them.

During the day which witnessed the discomfiture of Sedgwick's corps, Hooker remained idle in his entrenchments, hemmed in within his straitened lines by a few Confederate divisions, whilst one of his own corps was being overwhelmed and driven back in disgraceful confusion. Either totally unaware of the smallness of the force opposed to him, or completely cowed by the fighting of the two previous days, Hooker contented himself with strengthening his position, and during the 4th of May did not even send out skirmishers to engage the attention of the enemy.

The morning of the 5th was passed likewise in inaction; the Confederate troops were in the highest spirits, and unaffected by the sad sights with which they were surrounded. The woods were filled with the dead and wounded, and the horrors of the battle-field augmented by a slow fire, which, creeping through the underwood, entailed, it is feared, the most terrible death on many who were lying helpless from their wounds. In the afternoon, the weather, which had been hot and sultry, underwent a change, rain fell in torrents, and the noise of the thunder took the place of the war of the artillery. During the afternoon and night of the

5th, the deluge of rain continued, and the rising waters of the Rapidan and Rappahannock threatened to sweep away the bridges at United States Ford, which alone presented a way of retreat to the Federal army. Aware of the demoralized condition of his troops, knowing the difficulties of transportation from Falmouth, and perhaps fearing that this sole line of communication would be seized by the enemy, General Hooker, after holding a council of war, determined to carry his army across the Rappahannock. Taking advantage of the darkness and of the storm, which concealed his movements from the enemy, he ordered his waggons to cross the bridges at United States Ford, over which pine boughs had been thickly laid to deaden the sound, and whilst Meade held the lines of entrenchment surrounding the Ford, the several corps crossed the river, and at daybreak on the 6th the whole army had safely effected its passage, and was on the march to its former camps at Falmouth.

So ended the battles of Chancellorsville. The losses of the Federal army will probably never be accurately known: the Confederates claimed to have captured 7,650 prisoners; and their own loss in killed, wounded, and prisoners was about 10,000. In Sedgwick's force alone which attacked at Fredericksburg, Northern accounts state that 5,000 men in killed, wounded, and missing were *hors de combat.* These numbers will probably throw some doubt on General Hooker's computation, that 10,000 would cover all his losses.*

On the 6th May, after the return of the beaten army to its former encampment, General Hooker issued a

* Captain Chesney, in his *Review of the Campaign of Virginia,* computes the Federal loss at about 18,000, and that of the Confederates at about 10,000.

congratulatory order, on which the terrible events of the previous days were a sad comment, and which failed even to serve its purpose in blinding the eyes of the North to the true state of affairs.* The President

* On the 6th of May General Hooker issued the following order:—

'General Order, No. 49.

'The Major-General Commanding tenders to the army his congratulations on its achievements of the last seven days. If it has not accomplished all that was expected, the reasons are well-known to the army. It is sufficient to say, that they were of a character not to be foreseen or prevented by human sagacity or resources.

'In withdrawing from the south bank of the Rappahannock before delivering a general battle to our adversaries, the army has given renewed evidence of its confidence in itself and its fidelity to the principles it represents.

'By fighting at a disadvantage we would have been recreant to our trust, to ourselves, to our cause, and to our country. Professedly loyal and conscious of its strength, the army of the Potomac will give or decline battle whenever its interests or honour may command it.

'By the celerity and secresy of our movements, our advance and passage of the river was undisputed, and on our withdrawal not a rebel dared to follow us. The events of the last week may well cause the heart of every officer and soldier of the army to swell with pride.

'We have added new laurels to our former renown. We have made long marches, crossed rivers, surprised the enemy in his retrenchments, and wherever we have fought we have inflicted heavier blows than those we have received.

'We have taken from the enemy 5,000 prisoners and 15 colours, captured seven pieces of artillery, and placed *hors de combat* 18,000 of our foe's chosen troops.

'We have destroyed his depôts, filled with vast amounts of stores, damaged his communications, captured prisoners within the fortifications of his capital, and filled his country with fear and consternation.

'We have no other regret than that caused by the loss of our brave companions, and in this we are consoled by the conviction that they have fallen in the holiest cause ever submitted to the arbitration of battle.

'By command of Major-General Hooker,

'S. WILLIAMS, Assistant-Adjt.-General.'

and General Halleck about the same time visited the General at his camp, but even their assurance, as published in a semi-official paper on their return to Washington, that *the demonstration of General Hooker had proved no disaster but simply a failure*, was productive of little more effect. The letters from individuals in the army, the accounts of the numerous deserters who sought refuge in their homes in the Northern States, and the details of the several engagements which found their way into the papers, were sufficient to clear away the halo, which official publications sought to throw over the defeats at Chancellorsville.

Affording as it did some counterpoise to the week of disasters incurred by the army of the Potomac, General Stoneman's raid in rear of the Confederate army, and up to the very gates of Richmond, was exalted beyond its intrinsic value. The operations were well-planned and efficiently carried out, evincing a marked improvement in the discipline and organisation of the cavalry, and bringing to the front officers who subsequently greatly distinguished themselves in that arm. Simultaneously with the crossing of the Rappahannock by the leading corps of General Hooker's army, General Stoneman, with Generals Averill, Buford, Gregg, Colonels Kilpatrick and Wyndham, led over a large body of cavalry, with which it was intended to cut the communications of the Confederate army, and if possible to injure the James River Canal, and the rail to Lynchburg. Separating into three divisions after crossing the river, Averill marched on Gordonsville, Stoneman with the main body to Yancyville on the South Anna River, detaching regiments in different directions, even as far as Columbia, on the Upper James River, and Gregg, with Colonel Kilpatrick, moved towards Richmond, and the rail from thence to Fredericksburg. Little opposition was encountered; the Confederate cavalry, reduced in numbers and efficiency by the active operations of the autumn and winter, were with the main army, and the people were so surprised at the sudden presence of the Federal troops, far from what they conceived to be the seat of war, that they could do little else than wonder, often mistaking the enemy's troopers for those of Stuart. Moving secretly and yet rapidly, the several detachments captured and destroyed Government stores, secured provisions and horses, tore up railways, burned depôts, and liberated negroes. Kilpatrick moved round the Confederate army, and marching within three miles of Richmond, actually captured and parolled prisoners within the lines of defence, ultimately effecting his retreat by the Peninsula over the well-known country bordering the Chickahominy, and after a slight skirmish joining the Federal force at Gloucester Point, on the York River.

The remainder of the force retreating towards Kelly's Ford, rejoined Hooker's army in the neighbourhood of Falmouth. Had that General been successful in his movement across the Rappahannock, and had he defeated the Confederates at Chancellorsville, Stoneman's operations might have entailed serious consequences on General Lee's army; but as the reverse had happened, and as the Federal army, in place of the enemy, had suffered defeat, the damage inflicted proved to be of little injury to the Confederates, and was quickly repaired. The bridges and culverts on the railways were rebuilt, and in a few days the trains were running as usual between Richmond and the army before Fredericksburg. Nevertheless General Stoneman and the officers under his command deserved the credit which was awarded them for a hazardous and in the main successful enterprise.

During these eventful days which witnessed the failure of the fifth great attempt on Richmond, the man who more than any other, excepting the Commander-in Chief, had acted as the shield and sword of the Confederacy, and who by talents, character, and indomitable courage had gained a peculiar and wonderful influence over those with whom he had been more especially brought in contact; who by the boldness of his schemes, the swiftness and energy of his movements, and the impulsive character of his attacks, had gained a name in Europe greater than any of the generals of the American war; who had successively by rapid combinations surprised and fallen on M'Clellan's flank on the Chickahominy, on Pope at Manassas, on Miles at Harper's Ferry; who had brought up the reserves at Antietam, and assisted materially to push back the Federals from the heights at Fredericksburg, the great general of division to whom Lee looked for the execution of his most daring plans, lay at a small farmhouse a few miles from where he had led his last and perhaps most famous attack, dying from the wounds received from his own men. At one time it had been hoped that his life might have been spared, but his constitution, always feeble, was unable to bear up against the shock it had sustained, and the loss of blood caused by his wounds and by the amputation of his arm: he himself had from the first doubted his own recovery, but when his friends expressed hopes and expectations, he exclaimed with emphasis, 'If I live it will be for the best, and if I die it will be for the best; God knows and directs all things for the best.' In these few words he gave evidence of the devout trust and confidence in God which had so strikingly marked his life for many years, and which, carried into all the details of private and public business, influenced his course of action, equally when a professor at a college as when in command of an army. On the 9th of May he died, and his death was felt to be one of the greatest blows that had fallen on the Confederacy: by no one was he more lamented than by General Lee, who, ever unmindful of his own merits, is said to have exclaimed, 'That it would have been better for the country if he had fallen rather than Stonewall Jackson.'*

In the bitterness engendered by war, it is pleasing to notice that even among his enemies Jackson's worth was acknowledged and admired. The North was proud America should have produced so great a man, and owned that his only crime was that of fighting against the Union. In the height of his career, at the moment of one of his greatest achievements and most brilliant successes, Jackson fell, and, since his death, no general has been found who could thoroughly replace him. For a time General Stuart held the command of his old corps, but shortly afterwards returned to the

* The following conversation is given in the letter of the Special Correspondent of the *Times*, which letter details with great accuracy and in a manner which brings the events of the battle before the reader, the incidents of the great days at Chancellorsville. Speaking of General Lee, the Correspondent writes:—'But most interesting of all was his conversation about Stonewall Jackson. Had I been able (said General Lee) to dictate events, most gladly would I have been disabled in my own person, if he had been spared. Such an executive officer the sun never shone on. I have but to show him my design, and I know that if it can be done it will be done. No need for me to send and watch him. Straight as the needle to the pole, he advances to the execution of my purpose. Pure, high-minded, unselfish, he has no earthly thought of himself or his own advancement. The sole aim and object of his life is the good of his country.'

arm of the service for which he was especially qualified, and to General Ewell was allotted the honour of leading the divisions who more than any others in the army, had acquired renown under their great commander.

On the 11th of May, two days after General Jackson's death, an order announcing the event was issued by the Commander-in-Chief; in it, whilst alluding to the loss which the army had sustained, he bore testimony to the great worth of the deceased in terms befitting the occasion:—

'The daring skill and energy of this great and good soldier, by a decree of an All-wise Providence, are now lost to us; but while we mourn his death, we feel that his spirit lives, and will inspire the whole army with his indomitable courage and unshaken confidence in God as our hope and strength. Let his name be a watchword for his corps, who have followed him to victory on so many fields. Let officers and soldiers imitate his invincible determination to do everything in the defence of our beloved country.'

At Richmond, when the news of General Jackson's death reached the city, all business was suspended, and the arrival of the special train which conveyed his remains was awaited by large and sorrowing crowds. On the following day the body lay in state, in the Hall of Representatives, where the citizens of Richmond thronged in countless numbers to see once more the face of their beloved hero, before he was consigned to the earth at the place were he had expressed a wish to be buried, in Lexington, Virginia.

With the battle of Chancellorsville began and ended the spring campaign in Virginia; the Federals, weakened by their losses, and by the departure of many regiments whose term of service had expired, were in no position to resume the offensive; the Confederates were not sufficiently strong to follow up the beaten army, and refrained from any decisive movement until later in the year. There were numerous cavalry skirmishes in the country between Alexandria and Gordonsville, and, in the passes of the Blue Ridge Mountains, Mosby's black horse cavalry became a terror to Federal detachments, and their incursions often provoked retaliatory expeditions. Sometimes success inclined to one side, sometimes to the other, but the unfortunate inhabitants of that almost desolated country always suffered.

During the spring months energetic measures were taken to recruit the armies, and, in the North, to replace the regiments who refused to renew their terms of enlistment. A negro regiment had been raised in Massachusetts, and the first troops of that description enlisted in the North left Boston amid some excitement at the end of May.

In the South, the President in a speech delivered at Richmond, admonished the people not to be deceived and rendered careless by their successes, but to prepare for fresh sacrifices and renewed efforts. He exhorted them to continue to cultivate corn, oats, beans, etc., in place of cotton and tobacco, and to sow corn broadcast by the sides of the lines of rail and roads, in order to afford fodder to the animals required for the service of the troops. The want of sufficient means of transport pressed heavily on those whose duty it was to furnish stores to the large armies fighting so far from each other, and from their basis of supply, and the vast distances and scanty population of the South, although adding to the difficulties of an invading army, were yet an element of weakness to the defenders. Irrespective of the numerous garrisons along the coast, and without reckoning the armies of the Trans-Mississippi department engaged in separate operations, three large armies taxed the resources of the South both in men, supplies, and arms; that of Virginia under General Lee, that of Tennessee under General Bragg, and that of Mississippi under Johnston, including the garrison of Vicksburg under Pemberton. The constant drain of war conducted on so large a scale necessitated the utmost exertions, not only of the Government, but of each individual inhabitant of the South.

CHAPTER XIV.

THE MISSISSIPPI CAMPAIGN.

ALTHOUGH foiled in the great aim of the Virginian campaign, and driven back after each successive attack on the capital of the Confederacy, the North firmly and persistently continued her endeavours to attain the accomplishment of her second and, after the capture of Richmond, the most desired object of the war, viz. the occupation of Vicksburg and the opening of the whole length of the Mississippi River. The general she had selected for this important enterprise possessed perseverance and resolution which could not be daunted by any obstacles, and which led him, as each successive attempt failed, to seek fresh means and to organise new plans for the continuance of the struggle.

After the failure of the Steele Bayou and Yazoo Pass expeditions, after the repulse of the Federal fleet from Port Hudson, and the evidence that the canal project across the isthmus opposite Vicksburg could not be carried out, General Grant determined on investing the town, and having turned the defences on the Mississippi and Yazoo Rivers, to cut off the defenders from all communication with the east. At a distance from the scene of these operations, but acting in conjunction with them, General Banks, advancing from New Orleans,

THE COUNTRY ROUND VICKSBURG.

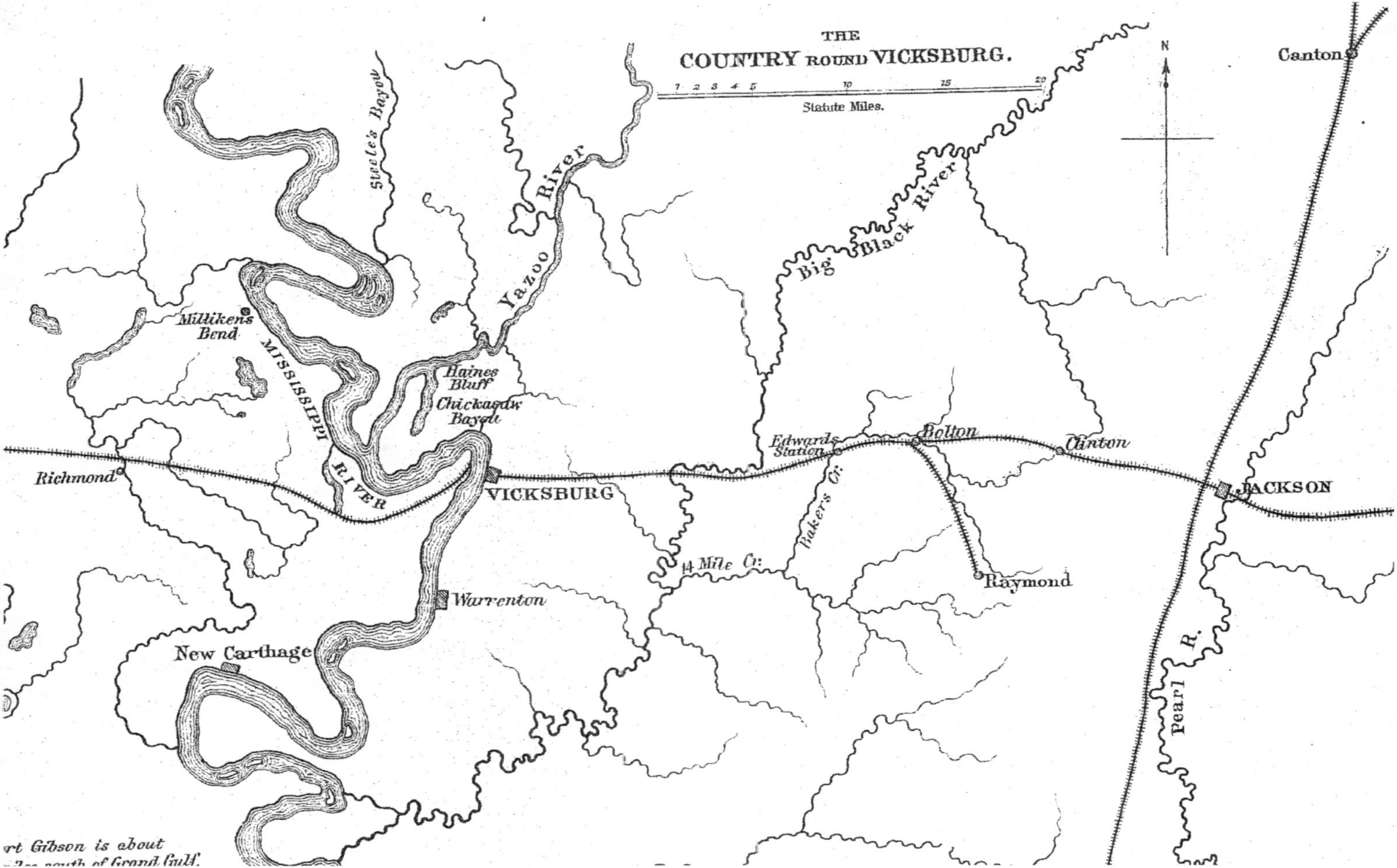

threatened Port Hudson from the land, and the fleet, although repulsed, yet not defeated, menaced it from the river.

The line of advance for the main army of Louisiana, under General Banks in person, had been through the rich and sugar-producing district of the Bayou Teche. Leaving New Orleans by the rail to Brashear City, the two brigades which composed the majority of the force, under Generals Emory and Weitzel, had rendezvoused in the neighbourhood of Berwick, a small town on the right bank of the Atchafalaya River; whilst a third brigade, under General Grover, had embarked on board transports on Grand Lake, and was prepared to turn any position which the enemy might take to bar the road up the Bayou Teche River to Opelousas. The Confederates, who formed a part of General Sibley's force, retreated up the Bayou Teche, skirmishing and delaying the march of the invaders. The planters forsook their houses, leaving their wealth on their plantations, and with their wives, families, and slaves made a hasty flight further into the heart of the country; the bridges were burnt, the course of the rivers impeded by obstructions, and every attempt made to hinder the advance of the troops and of the gunboats which accompanied them. The Confederates were not in sufficient force to offer much resistance: attacked in front by the two brigades marching from Berwick, and taken in flank by Grover's brigade, which had landed from its transports, they retreated towards Opelousas, destroying the steamers and other vessels which had hitherto navigated these inland waters.

On the 20th April the Federal force entered Opelousas, about 180 miles from New Orleans. By these operations General Banks had secured New Orleans and

Brashear City from the risk of a surprise during the absence of the main army, whilst at Opelousas he was within a short march of Port Hudson, and was prepared to cooperate in any attack made on that stronghold by a combined naval and military force from New Orleans.

Contemporary with these events, Admiral Farragut, with the Hartford, held command of the river between Port Hudson and Vicksburg, blockading the Red River, and bombarding any places at which batteries had been erected. To reinforce him, by running his gunboats past the works at Vicksburg, several attempts were made by Admiral Porter, attended with varying success. The ram Lancaster was sunk, and the Switzerland much injured, whilst engaged in this bold enterprise; but on the 16th April, an expedition on a far larger scale, and planned with greater care, succeeded in the attempt, and in conjunction with a land force which had been marched from Milliken's Bend to Carthage, was in readiness to execute General Grant's scheme of attacking Vicksburg from the south-east.

Well organised and boldly carried out was the enterprise of running the batteries. During the 16th April the preparations were completed, and eight gunboats, three transports, and various barges laden with supplies, lay moored to the shore near the mouth of the Yazoo River, ready to drop down the Mississippi when night had closed in. Eagerly was the result expected, and many an eye was anxiously directed towards Vicksburg, to endeavour to ascertain whether the garrison contemplating the attempt had added to their already powerful batteries. The night was clear and the stars bright, far too clear to accord with the wishes of the Federals, although, as the fleet left its moorings at 11 P.M., a light mist rising from the river partially concealed its movements.

Without light or noise the gunboats and transports glided down the stream, keeping near the Mississippi shore, and the spectators hushed their voices and drew in their breath as they watched their progress. For a few moments there was stillness; not a gun was heard; the bluffs on which Vicksburg stands loomed out dark against the sky, but all was quiet. Suddenly the report of a gun, broke the silence of the night, then from every battery in succession the artillery opened, from those above and near the town, to those as far down the river as Warrenton. The roar increased in fury, whilst from the summit of the hill, near the church, a bright light shot forth, which increasing in intensity, illuminated the whole breadth of the river, revealing with terrible distinctness each passing vessel. The firing became more rapid, but the light which so clearly showed the vessels to the Confederate artillerymen, enabled their crews to direct their guns against the batteries. Gradually the firing from the upper batteries ceased, whilst from the lower it increased in violence; the fleet had passed the town. Again a light shone forth, this time from the river, and the flames as they rose upwards revealed a vessel on fire. The beacon-light on the hill had now burnt out, the sound of firing gradually died away, and a message received from Admiral Porter on the following day, announced that the eight gunboats, and all the transports and barges excepting one, had passed the batteries with but little loss and few casualties. The enterprise had proved completely successful, more so than even the most sanguine had ventured to anticipate, and greater than should have been the case had proper precautions been taken by the defenders.* The beacon-light was fired a few minutes too late, and in dealing with so swift a current as that of the great river, minutes are of the utmost importance.

As at Port Hudson the Mississippi had favoured the defenders by delaying the upward progress of the gunboats, so at Vicksburg had it sided with the assailants in carrying their vessels swiftly past the batteries. The lesson might surely have been learnt from the passage of the forts at New Orleans that, unless where obstructions have been placed, steamers will run the gauntlet of almost any fire. Could not these lessons have been made available by the defenders of Vicksburg? If by carelessness, by want of foresight or energy, proper and requisite precautions had been neglected, bitterly must those who were responsible for the defence of Vicksburg have looked back on the past, when the succeeding events of the siege proclaimed the importance of preventing the passage of the Federal gunboats.

Encouraged by the success of his plan, General Grant ordered seven more transports to be got ready for a similar attempt. The boilers of these vessels were well protected with hay and cotton, and volunteer crews were raised from the army, there being no lack of men to offer themselves for this perilous adventure.† On the 22nd of April this second fleet, towing twelve

* See a well-written account of the passage of the gunboats taken from the *New York Tribune*, and published in vol. vi. *Rebellion Record*, page 546, Documents.

† General Grant, in his official report, thus notices this incident in the war:—'It is a striking feature, as far as my observation goes, of the present volunteer army of the United States, that there is nothing which men are called upon to do, mechanical or professional, that accomplished adepts cannot be found for the duty required in almost every regiment.'

barges loaded with forage and rations, succeeded—with the loss of only two steamers and six barges—in passing the batteries, and in joining Admiral Porter's gunboats at New Carthage, where two *corps d'armée*, under General Grant in person, had by great exertions, and after overcoming the difficulties of a march through a country intersected by marshes and streams, been brought by land from Milliken's Bend, a distance of thirty-five miles, carrying with them supplies of ordnance, stores, and provisions.

It now remained to reduce the batteries at Grand Gulf, which had been recently strengthened by General Pemberton's orders, and which defended the mouth of the Big Black River. To this task Admiral Porter addressed himself, and, on the 29th of April, the naval force commenced the action. As much of the Thirteenth Army Corps as could be conveyed in the transports having in the meantime been landed opposite Grand Gulf, prepared to storm the works after the guns had been silenced by the navy. With his accustomed energy Admiral Porter commenced the attack, General Grant witnessing the engagement from a tug in mid-stream. But the batteries had been erected on high bluffs, and proved too strong, and the guns too elevated to be silenced by the gunboats; therefore Grant, fearing to risk his men in an attempt at storming the works, determined to turn them by landing at a point lower down the river. To carry out this object he directed the army to march by its right bank, and to be prepared to cross opposite Bruinsburg; whilst the transports should, as soon as it became dark, run the fire of the batteries at Grand Gulf, and so take up positions in readiness to ferry the army across the river. These movements both by land and water were accomplished without loss, and with very little hinderance from the enemy.

On 30th of April the 13th corps landed on the left bank, and were immediately pushed forward towards Port Gibson, a small town near the mouth of the Big Black River.

We must now inquire what preparations had been made by the Confederate General to resist the threatened attack. The passage down the river of the gunboats and transports, the march of the army from Milliken's Bend, and the evident preparations for an advance against Vicksburg from the south-east, had roused General Pemberton—commanding the Confederate army of the Mississippi—to a sense of the danger of his position. He telegraphed the news of Grant's movements to General Johnston, the Commander-in-Chief of the Western armies, who was then at Tullahoma with Bragg, and, in answer, received orders to attack Grant at once. He asked for reinforcements, but was told that none could be spared from the army of Tennessee, which was only just able to hold its own against Rosecrans.

In the meantime General Bowen, commanding at Grand Gulf, crossed the Bayou Pierre, and attempted to oppose the march of the Federals to Port Gibson. At 1 A.M., on the 1st of May, the advanced guards of the two armies met, and at daybreak the action commenced. During the whole of Friday, the 2nd, amidst the ravines, swamps, cane-brakes, and jungles, the armies fought. As the several Federal divisions landed and received supplies of rations and ammunition, they were hurried to the front; and on the evening of the 2nd succeeded in driving back the Confederates and in occupying Port Gibson, General Bowen having recrossed the Bayou Pierre, after burning the bridges behind him, and abandoning his hospitals, and such of the wounded as could not be removed.

Such was the first of the engagements which heralded in Grant's successful campaign. The march from Milliken's Bend, the passage of the river, the rapidity of the advance, and the success of the action of Port Gibson, all bore witness to the good order and discipline which prevailed in the army, and to the improvement which campaigning and practical experience had worked, both in officers and men. Very different were the dispositions for the campaign of Vicksburg to those which preceded the first battle of Shiloh; and far more formidable was Grant's army of the Mississippi than his former army of Tennessee. The training of war began in 1863 to neutralise the superiority which the greater enthusiasm of the Southern troops, and the chivalry of the Southern gentlemen, had given to the Confederate armies at the commencement of the struggle, whilst the more numerous population and greater resources of the North enabled her to bring into the field larger armies and more abundant supplies, and at every point to threaten to overwhelm her antagonist by weight of numbers.

As has been seen in the Virginian campaign, the Federal cavalry of the East had begun to rival those of Stuart; and in the West, enterprises which may compare with the bold raids of Morgan and Forrest were undertaken by the cavalry colonels of the army of Tennessee. Colonel Grierson's famous march through Mississippi, from the borders of Tennessee, to Louisiana, may well challenge the admiration of all who appreciate enterprise, endurance, and perseverance. Leaving La Grange on the frontiers of Tennessee, on the 17th of April, Colonel Grierson, with three regiments of cavalry

—the 6th and 7th Illinois and 2nd Iowa—marched boldly into the enemy's country. Crossing the Tallahatchie River, he moved southwards, and struck the Macon and Corinth Railway; he tore up rails, cut the telegraph wires, and burnt stores, sending detachments in various directions, and carefully concealing his numbers and the direction of his march. He then turned towards the south-west, seized the bridge over the Pearl River, and burnt locomotives on the Jackson and New Orleans Railway. Moving southwards, along the line of railway, he crossed the Amite River, and after capturing a troop of Mississippi cavalry, entered Baton Rouge on the 2nd of May, amidst the acclamations of its garrison, who could scarcely believe that the weary and jaded troopers, who with their prisoners entered the town, were really Federal cavalry from Tennessee. In seventeen days the march had been accomplished. The distance, measured in a straight line, between the two places is about 350 miles; but, calculated by the length of each day's march, it must have been very much greater; and when it is considered that rivers were crossed, swamps and marshes with difficulty waded through, enterprises against detached towns undertaken, and skirmishes—which, although slight, tended to exhaust the strength of horse and rider—fought, the march of Colonel Grierson through the State of Mississippi will take rank among the boldest cavalry raids of the war.*

* The following is the route and daily distances of march of Colonel Grierson's cavalry as given in the *New York Times*:

April 17,	30	miles to	Ripley.
„ 18, } „ 19, }	60	„	New Albany, Pontotac.
„ 20,	40	„	Clear Spring.
„ 21,	45	„	Starkville.
„ 22,	57	„	10 miles south of Louisville.

Although unproductive of great results, this expedition tended to evince the weakness of the Confederate Government, which having taxed all its resources to fill the ranks of the main armies, could not afford men to guard the heart of the country owning its sway. That the knowledge acquired in this and other cavalry raids, exercised an important influence on the conduct of some of the subsequent campaigns, will be evident as the history of the war more fully developes itself.

To resume the narrative of Grant's operations:—Immediately after the engagement at Port Gibson, M'Pherson's corps was directed to throw a bridge over the Bayou Pierre, and to pursue the enemy to the Big Black River. These orders were promptly executed. Bowen retreated across the river and evacuated Grand Gulf, which was taken possession of by Grant on the 4th May. Stores and supplies were brought up to the mouth of the Big Black River, reconnaissances were made in the direction of Warrenton, and demonstrations directed by Sherman against Haines' Bluff, in order to deceive the enemy as to the real line of march. From information he had received, Grant abandoned his former scheme of detaching a *corps d'armée* to the

April 23, } ,, 24, }	80 miles to Newton.		
,, 25,	20	,,	Raleigh.
,, 26,	42	,,	Stone River Bridge.
,, 27,	37	,,	Gallanton.
,, 28,	30	,,	Union Church.
,, 29,	25	,,	Brookhaven.
,, 30,	28	,,	Summit.
May 1,	40	,,	Amite River.
,, 2,	12	,,	Baton Rouge.

Possibly the distances may be slightly exaggerated, but in the main they must be fairly correct.

assistance of Banks, in an attack on Port Hudson, and decided on marching at once on Jackson, the capital of Mississippi. He brought up Sherman's corps from Milliken's Bend, and, on the 7th May, advanced by two roads up the left bank of the Big Black River; M'Clernand's corps on the right, M'Pherson's on the left near the river, and Sherman in rear moving on both roads, the ferries over the Big Black River being jealously watched and guarded to prevent any attack from the garrison at Vicksburg. Diverging from the main column, M'Clernand marched on Raymond, a small town or village* eighteen miles from Jackson, and connected by a branch line with the Jackson and Vicksburg Rail. Here he was met by Gregg's and Walker's brigades, and an engagement ensued on the banks of a small stream which crosses the road in the vicinity of the place. After some severe fighting the Federals repulsed their opponents and entered the town; M'Pherson's and Sherman's corps at the same time, and after heavy skirmishing, forcing a passage across Fourteen Mile Creek. Immediately after the engagement at Raymond news reached Grant that Joe Johnston in person had arrived at Jackson, and had collected a force with which to relieve Vicksburg. He therefore directed M'Pherson and Sherman to move at once toward Jackson, as he was desirous of securing his rear from attack before attempting the investment of Vicksburg. But Joe Johnston was not in sufficient force to defend Jackson, the brigades of Gregg and Walker did not number much more than six thousand men, and although he was expecting a brigade from Port Hudson, yet it did not arrive in time to assist in the defence of the

* It is seldom that villages are found in America. Every place of more than two or three houses is a town or a city.

place. Johnston therefore ordered Gregg and Walker to fall back slowly, offering such resistance to the march of the Federal columns as to allow of time to destroy or remove the stores accumulated in Jackson. These officers carried out the orders satisfactorily, and retiring leisurely, and availing themselves of the woods and ravines, kept the Federals at bay until most of the public stores had been removed to Canton, to which point the Confederate army retreated.

What followed on the capture of Jackson must cast a slur on the Federal arms, and sullies this otherwise well conducted campaign. Sherman's corps was directed to occupy the town, and to burn the railway station, arsenals, workshops, &c., which might prove useful to the enemy, and of which the destruction was necessary, owing to Grant's intention of abandoning the place, and his fear lest it might become a base from which Joe Johnston should operate against him, whilst he was engaged in besieging Vicksburg. These orders were in accordance with the rules of war, but when an undisciplined soldiery, drunk with rum, and unrestrained by authority, burns, plunders, and sacks an unfortified and peaceful town, both the general who should restrain, and the troops who perform such acts, must incur the odium which will and ought to fall on them. Jackson was not a large town, among whose narrow streets men might hide and plunder without detection, but it was a small county town, of two main streets, and consisted of detached villas inhabited by wealthy planters, of a few shops, churches, and the state house and prison. The principal street was lined with trees, and the numerous gardens gave an appearance of beauty to the otherwise simply constructed buildings. The few inhabitants who remained offered no resistance to the Federal troops, and there is nothing which can justify the wanton destruction of the place. Private houses, the Roman Catholic Church, the hotel, the penitentiary, and a large cotton factory were burned, and the town of Jackson underwent the fate of its namesake, Jacksonville in Florida.*

In the meantime, from intercepted despatches, and from the reports of prisoners and deserters, Grant had made himself acquainted with the plans of his opponents, and learning that Pemberton was moving across the Big Black River, he directed M'Clernand's and M'Pherson's corps to march by the Jackson and Vicks-

* General Sherman's report thus alludes to the destruction of Jackson:—'In Jackson, the arsenal buildings, the Government foundry, the gun-carriage establishments, &c. were destroyed. The penitentiary was burned, I think by some convicts, who had been set free by the Confederate authorities; also a very valuable cotton factory. The factory was the property of Messrs. Green, who made strong appeals, based on the fact that it gave employment to very many females and poor families, and that although it had woven cloth for the enemy, its principal use was in weaving cloth for the people. But I decided that machinery of that kind could so easily be converted into hostile uses, that the United States could better afford to compensate Messrs. Green for their property, and feed the poor families thus thrown out of employment, than to spare the property. I therefore assured all such families, if want should force them, they might come to the river, where we would feed them until they could find employment or seek refuge in some more peaceful land. Other buildings were destroyed in Jackson by some mischievous soldiers (who could not be detected) which was not justified by the rules of war, including the Catholic Church and the Confederate hotel—the former resulting from accidental circumstances, the latter from malice. General Mónser occupied the town with his brigade and two companies of cavalry, and maintained as much order as he could among the mass of soldiers and camp followers that thronged the place during our short stay there; yet many acts of pillage occurred which I regret, arising from the effect of some bad rum concealed in the stores of the town.'

burg Rail, and by the road from Raymond to meet him; at the same time ordering Sherman to evacuate Jackson, and to take a similar direction. Grant was now between the two Confederate armies, and was superior in numbers not only to each, but to both united.

The want of direct and certain communication, and of a combined plan of operations, fully debated on and clearly understood, produced the usual bad effects on the strategy of the Confederate generals. Whilst Johnston had been engaged with Grant at Jackson, Pemberton had remained idle, not probably from any fault, but from a want of information; when, on the other hand, Johnston retreated, Pemberton crossed the Big Black River and offered battle.

He drew up his army, numbering from fifteen to eighteen thousand men, on the right bank of Baker's Creek, across the Jackson and Vicksburg Railway, his left resting on a line of well-wooded hills called Champion Hills. His front was covered with cavalry skirmishers (i. e. mounted men, armed with muskets and rifles), whilst by a skilful disposition of his artillery, he delayed the advance of the Federal divisions on the south side of the rail. Of Grant's army, three divisions were on the Vicksburg Rail, four on the road from Raymond, one still further to the left marching on the Big Black River, and two under Sherman in the vicinity of Jackson. After some skirmishing, Hovey's division commenced the action by an attack on the centre of Pemberton's line, held by Stevenson's division, whilst the two divisions in his rear took ground to their right, and threatened to turn the Confederate left. General Grant, who seems not to have expected that the enemy would have fought east of the Big Black River, seeing the strength of his position, and the probable serious nature of the engagement, sent orders for the three divisions advancing from Raymond to hasten their march, and to come into action as quickly as might be possible. Before their arrival Hovey's division had been repulsed with some loss, and having fired away all its ammunition, were in the act of replenishing their cartridge pouches, when Logan, commanding one the divisions on the right, brought word in person to Grant, that if an attack should be made against the enemy's front, he could act with advantage against his left flank. Grant ordered Hovey's division to advance again to the assault of the ridge of hills. The troops moved forward in three lines with great gallantry, and although the two first lines were thrown into some confusion by the fire which greeted them, yet the third pressed forward and drove back Stevenson's tired brigades. At that moment Bowen's Missourians on Stevenson's right charged, the ground lost was retaken, and again were the Federals repulsed and thrown into disorder. But the divisions from Raymond had in the meantime arrived on the field, the broken troops were rallied, and the line again advanced. Daunted by this renewed attack, and possibly suffering from the reaction attending their recent efforts, confronted also by fresh troops, the Confederates gave way to panic, and broke in confusion from the field. Barton, Lee, and other generals, after great exertion, restored some degree of order, but the army was defeated, and during the night retreated to the Big Black River. By the advance of the Federals, Loring's division, which had suffered comparatively slightly, was cut off from the main army, and compelled, with the loss of its artillery,* to effect a retreat in a different direction, with the ultimate

* Third Year of the War, Pollard.

object of joining Johnston. Pemberton retired with the larger portion of his army across the Big Black River; leaving, however, a considerable force to guard the bridge on the left or east bank.

On the following day, the 17th May, M'Clernand's corps was directed to advance along the Vicksburg rail, with M'Pherson in support, whilst Sherman, with the pontoon-train, was ordered to cross the river at Bridgeport. No opposition was encountered until the enemy reached the east bank of the Big Black River, where on flat and swampy ground some field-works had been thrown up, covered by marshes extending on either side of the railway towards the river. Behind these works, and sheltered by patches of wood, the Confederates had taken up their position. M'Clernand deployed Carr's division on the right, and Osterhaus's on the left, keeping Smith's division in support. After a considerable amount of firing, the Federal right advanced under partial cover until near the enemy's lines, when with a rush the leading brigade ran in, and having entered the entrenchments drove the defenders to the banks of the Big Black River, capturing eighteen pieces of artillery, and many prisoners (said to have numbered 1,500), who were unable to cross the river, owing to the bridge having been burnt. The Confederates had not evinced their usual courage; they had occupied works provided with a sufficient quantity of artillery, and manned by a considerable force, but either disheartened by their defeat at Baker's Creek, or wanting confidence in their generals, they had allowed themselves to be driven to the river in confusion, if not in discreditable flight.

On the following day, the Federal army crossed the Big Black River, Sherman by a pontoon-bridge at

Bridgeport, the two other corps near the scene of the action of the 17th. Sherman pushed forward, without losing time, towards Haines' Bluff, and Admiral Porter, who was anxiously awaiting the result of Grant's operations, hearing the firing, and descrying by the help of telescopes Sherman's advancing troops, sent his gunboats up the Yazoo River. The vessels and the troops arrived at Haines' Bluff almost simultaneously, and discovered that the works had been evacuated, the place abandoned, and the garrison withdrawn within the lines of Vicksburg. Guns and stores were found in the deserted works at Haines' Bluff, but what was of greater importance, communication was established between the army and the fleet, and the base of operations changed from Grand Gulf on the Mississippi to Haines' Bluff on the Yazoo.

Vicksburg was invested on the eastern side; Sherman holding the right of the lines, M'Pherson the centre, and M'Clernand the left. Thus General Johnston's orders, which, after receiving intelligence of the defeat at Baker's Creek, he had sent to Pemberton, directing him, unless he could hold the position of Haines' Bluff, to evacuate Vicksburg, and to form a junction with his own army at Canton, were impossible of execution. Pemberton, with sixty days' provisions, was besieged in Vicksburg; whilst Johnston, although using every endeavour to collect a force to march to his assistance, foresaw the difficulties attending the enterprise, and foreboded the surrender of the place.

As the Confederate army entered the lines at Vicksburg, after the defeat at Baker's Creek and Big Black River, the citizens saw that evil times awaited them. Their confidence in Pemberton was shaken, and looking back sorrowfully on all they had undergone during the past year, since on the 18th May, 1862, Farragut had fired his first shot into the town, they anticipated disaster, and lost hope in the ability of the army to hold the place. But the Confederate generals were not men to despond: Baldwin solicited and obtained the post of honour and danger on the left of the line, Smith and Forney held the centre, and Lee the right. The axe and spade were diligently used, and when Sherman moved forward to assault the works on the 19th May, he found the defenders well-prepared to receive him. At 2 P.M. the Federals advanced, Blair's division forcing its way, with courage and perseverance, through the standing and fallen timber which concealed the chasms and ravines on either side of the road leading to the enemy's works. The 13th Regulars advanced even as far as the slope of the entrenchments, and there its commander, Captain Washington, fell mortally wounded, 75 out of 250 men of the regiment being likewise put *hors de combat*. The colours of the regiment were planted on the works, and the men, sheltering themselves as best they were able, kept up a fire on the defenders. With equal fortitude these held their ground; the assailants could not cross the parapet, and when night afforded an opportunity of withdrawing his troops in safety, General Sherman ordered a retreat.

This success inspirited the garrison, and the comparative harmlessness of the fire from the gunboats tended rather to create confidence than to inspire terror. The citizens, women and children, many belonging to the families of the rich planters of the neighbourhood who had fled to Vicksburg for safety, prepared caves in the hill, where they took refuge during the almost incessant bombardment; and the spirits of the soldiers were kept up by news received from

Johnston's army, by means of messengers who found a way through the swamps and thickets of the Yazoo, bringing with them a supply of caps for the rifles, of which the troops were in great need.

During the 20th and 21st, the Federal army rested; food, especially bread, and ammunition, was served out to the men, and orders issued for a grand assault on the whole line of the enemy's works on the following day. Grant hoped that he might capture the place without the tedious operations of a regular siege, and without the necessity of reinforcements, which would be required should he decide on sitting down before Vicksburg in due form, at the same time that he secured himself from interference from Johnston's army in his rear.

Precisely at 10 A.M. on the 22nd May, the three *corps d'armée* moved forward to the attack; the artillery kept up an incessant fire on the Confederate works, and the skirmishers under shelter behind the trees and in the ravines, directed their shots at any head that showed itself above the parapet. All was quiet in the enemy's lines; not a man could be seen, until the storming-party, having issued from the shelter of the woods, attempted to ascend the ridge. Then the Confederate troops rose up and poured a deadly fire on the assailants; these, disdaining to retreat, replied, availing themselves of such cover as they could find; but their loss was very heavy. At one time M'Clernand reported that he had gained the outer line of the Confederate entrenchments, but it subsequently appeared that his corps had been repulsed equally with those of M'Pherson and Sherman; and although the assailants evinced determined bravery, they met with such stubborn resistance that their efforts were unavailing. With an acknowledged loss of 2,500 men, they retreated to their own lines, and all attempt at capturing Vicksburg by assault was given up. During the attack on the land side, Porter had engaged the river defences, bringing his gunboats as near the water-batteries as he could, and throwing shells into the town from the mortar-boats; but in the river forts, equally as in those on the land side, were the defendants prepared; they inflicted more injury than they sustained; several of Porter's vessels were struck below the water-line, and the fleet, after firing away almost all its ammunition, dropped down the river.

The 22nd May was indeed a terrible day for the citizens of Vicksburg. From all sides shot and shell poured into the town; the inhabitants crept into their caves, and awaited the event with awful anxiety, anticipating the horrors which accompany the entry of troops into a town carried by assault.

On the next day, and almost without intermission for six weeks, was the bombardment sustained. Shells from the mortars, shot and shell from the heavy Parrott guns, rifle-bullets from sharpshooters on the right bank of the river, crossed and recrossed each other, in and over the unfortunate town. The Roman Catholic Church presented a conspicuous mark for the shells, but notwithstanding, on Sundays, in this and other churches was Divine worship celebrated, sometimes resulting in injury to the members of the congregation. The casualties were, however, surprisingly few in number; and it is recorded by one who was present during the whole of the fearful bombardment, that the people grew so familiar with the mortar-shells, that they almost ceased to regard them with fear.*

* Diary of a Citizen, page 165. *Rebellion Record*, vol. vii.

In the month of June heavy rain fell, which threatened to drown the inhabitants out of the caves, their last shelter, and a scarcity in the supply of provisions seemed to point to famine as a probable augmentation of their sufferings. With fortitude worthy of the brave women of the South did the inhabitants bear their sufferings, and gallantly did the troops undergo the hardships, dangers, and fatigue of a prolonged defence. Pemberton, in allusion to a report circulated by his enemies that he intended to sell the town, published an order, that he would indeed sell it, but only at the price of his own life, and that of every man under his command. He strengthened his defences, at the same time that he encouraged the soldiers to renewed efforts and continued endurance, by promises of the speedy arrival of Johnston with a strong army to relieve the place, by attacking the enemy in his rear.

The defences of Vicksburg, on both the land and water sides, had been constructed with much engineering skill; the hills were crowned with field-works, connected together by entrenchments covered with abattis; and the ravines, coated with the jungle so frequent in the forests of the more Southern States, presented an almost impassable barrier to the steady advance of troops.

Against these works did General Grant, after the repulse of his attack on the 22nd of May, prepare to conduct a regular siege. He had shown talent of no ordinary degree both in the conception and execution of the campaign which had led to the investment of the town. He had been ably seconded by the navy, his subordinate commanders appear to have acted with zeal and unanimity, and the conduct of the troops in enduring hardship and facing danger deservedly increased the fame which had ever attached to the Western men. Grant had now established a depôt for supplies in a situation easily accessible and secure from attack. The resources of the Western States were open to him, and the nature of the country in which he was encamped was equally favourable to the besiegers in furnishing easily defensible positions against Johnston's army, as to the besieged in enabling them rapidly to throw up fresh works.

Through the months of May and June did this memorable siege continue, its incidents alternately raising the hopes or exciting the fears of the South; but the final result belongs to a later period; and other events which, although not directly connected with the operations of the main armies, yet incidentally affecting their movements, require a passing notice, in order that the several threads of the narrative of the Western War may not be lost.

The connection between the movements of the army in Louisiana and that of Mississippi has already been shown, and as these operations received a further development, they tended in a still greater degree to exercise on each other a more direct influence. By an attack on Port Hudson and by his investment of the place, Banks hindered reinforcements from reaching Johnston, and added to that general's difficulties in collecting an army, first to prevent, and afterwards to raise the siege of Vicksburg.

At a further distance from the seat of war in Mississippi, but greatly affecting its conduct and results, was the army under Rosecrans, which, although comparatively quiescent since the battle of Murfreesboro, yet gave such signs of vitality as prevented Bragg from detaching any regiments to act with Johnston, and induced that general to inform his Government that either Tennessee or Mississippi must be given up. He showed that should troops be drawn from Tennessee, Bragg would be forced to retreat and abandon the State; should no troops be sent, Vicksburg would in all probability fall; with Vicksburg, Port Hudson must also succumb, and the line of the Mississippi River be abandoned.

The third army which, it was hoped, might have had some power in delaying if it did not prevent the ultimate disaster, was the Confederate army of the Trans-Mississippi department, and to that we must now direct attention. Its desultory and scattered operations present but few features of interest, but inasmuch as they tended indirectly to influence the great events of the war, it becomes necessary to notice them in order to present a picture of the whole campaign of the West.

Early in the year 1863, General Marmaduke, who had attained some fame as an enterprising officer, entered South-Western Missouri, and made an attack on Springfield, where had been concentrated the stores and depôts of the Federal army of Arkansas. His force, composed principally of mounted riflemen, proved too weak to capture the place; and after some severe fighting, dignified by the names of the battles of Springfield and Hartsville, fell back on Arkansas. Nothing more was heard of him until the end of April, when news reached General M'Neil, that the Confederates were advancing in force into Eastern Missouri, and threatened Cape Girardeau, a small town on the Mississippi River, above Cairo. M'Neil hastened to reinforce the garrison, and succeeded in occupying the place before the arrival of Marmaduke. A demand to surrender was sent, but indignantly refused, and on reinforcements reaching the Federals, Marmaduke retired, carrying with him fourteen pieces of captured artillery and several prisoners. M'Neil followed, but did not press the retreating force, which, with little molestation, reached the Arkansas frontier.

If Cape Girardeau had fallen, the effect produced might have been of some importance, as a considerable amount of Government property had been collected there, which would have fallen into the hands of the Confederates, and their guns might have hindered the navigation of the Mississippi, and diverted the reinforcements and supplies destined for Grant's army, to other purposes; as it was, Marmaduke's advance into Missouri was a raid similar to the many which characterised Western warfare, and was productive of little real result.

More intimately connected with the garrison of Vicksburg, but equally unattended with benefit to the Confederate cause, were the operations of General Kirby Smith's forces in Louisiana. When General Johnston found that he was unable to raise a sufficient force to attack Grant's rear strongly entrenched on the Big Black River, he fixed his last hopes on the Trans-Mississippi army; but either through mismanagement or deficiency in numbers, the attempts to open communications with the garrison from the right bank of the Mississippi proved abortive. In the beginning of June, an attack was made on the Federal camp at Milliken's Bend, which at first promised to be successful, as the defenders were driven from their outer line of entrenchments to the river's bank; but here, aided by a gunboat, and supported by the fire of some newly-raised negro troops, the Iowa regiments rallied and repulsed the assailants.

Shortly after this action, the last attempt at assistance from the West was defeated by the repulse of the Confederates forming Kirby Smith's advanced brigades, from Richmond, a small town about nine miles from Milliken's Bend, important from the fact that good roads connect it with Milliken's Bend, New Carthage, and Vicksburg. From this place the Confederates were driven with little difficulty; Kirby Smith retired further into Louisiana, and all hope of help from the West was at an end. Shut in on all sides, the fall of Vicksburg seemed to be only a question of time, and that such was General Johnston's opinion is clear from the expression he used to the War department, when he wrote—'That without some great blunder of the enemy, the Confederates could not hold both Mississippi and Tennessee, and that he considered saving Vicksburg hopeless.'

Almost cotemporary with the investment of Vicksburg by Grant, was that of Port Hudson by Banks. General Gardner, who held the place for the Confederacy, as soon as he knew for certain of the arrival of Banks from the Atchafalaya, telegraphed to Johnston for reinforcements; but before he could receive the answer informing him that none could be sent, and that he was to abandon his entrenchments, and march to join the main army of the Mississippi, Port Hudson had been invested, and Gardner, cut off from communications with the commander-in-chief of the West, was left to his own resources.

Banks had brought with him the whole of the force with which he had conducted operations in the Bayou Teche district, and having crossed the Mississippi, had effected a junction with T. Sherman,* who had ascended

* Not to be confounded with General W. Sherman, of Grant's army.

the river in transports from New Orleans. On the 25th May the enemy was driven from the outer works, but it was not until the 27th, after Weitzel's division, which had covered the rear of the army during the march from Alexandria, had joined, that the real assault of the works was made. Five infantry divisions,* besides artillery and a small force of cavalry, composed the besieging army; in addition to the formidable fleet of gunboats which commanded the river, and kept up an almost incessant bombardment. A very powerful force of artillery had also been brought from New Orleans, and not only were the land faces of the town commanded by guns, but heavily armed batteries were likewise erected on the right bank of the river.

To this large army Gardner could only oppose a force of about 6,000 men, entrenched behind hastily constructed works, and furnished with artillery of far inferior calibre to that of the besiegers. He determined, notwithstanding the disparity in numbers and the faint hope of relief, to hold out; and his men, both in their endurance of hardships and in their courage in action, proved themselves worthy of the general who commanded them. Proud of their previous resistance to the Federal fleet, and desirous of emulating the conduct of the garrison at Vicksburg, both officers and soldiers fought with desperation, and repulsed each succeeding assault of the besieging army. Happily, the horrors of the siege were not augmented, as was the case at Vicksburg, by the presence of an unarmed population and of women and children; the sufferings fell entirely on

* General Banks's army comprised five divisions, commanded by Generals Weitzel, Emery, Grover, Augur, T. Sherman, and the artillery under General Arnold.

the garrison, who supported them with firm determination.

Scarcely a spot in the whole of the defences was safe from the shells, which were poured in almost without intermission by the gun and mortar boats. There were no properly constructed casemates, and the men could only take refuge, when the bombardment was especially heavy, in holes dug in the ground. So completely did the Federal fleet command the works, that when an assault took place on the land side, the vessels were forced to cease their fire, lest the shells passing over the Confederate lines should inflict damage on their own men.

On the 27th of May the first assault was made; both sides fought with courage, but the Federals were repulsed with considerable loss, especially among the black regiments, to whom had been allotted a prominent place in the attack, and who gained the applause of the commanding general more probably on account of the loss they had sustained than the courage they had displayed.* Various accounts were given of the conduct

* General Banks speaks of the conduct of these regiments as in many respects heroic; he says no troops could be more determined or more daring. A Confederate account of the action alludes to the circumstances of the attack in these terms:—

'On the left the attack was made by a brigade of negroes, comprising about three regiments, together with the same force of white Yankees, across a bridge which had been built over Sandy Creek on the night of the 25th. This force was thrown against the Thirty-ninth Mississippi regiment, commanded by Colonel Shelby. About five hundred negroes in front advanced at double-quick, within one hundred and fifty yards of the works, when the artillery on the river bluff, and two light pieces on Colonel Shelby's left, opened upon them, and at the same time they were received with volleys of musketry from five companies of the Thirty-ninth. The negroes fled every way in perfect confusion, without firing a gun, probably carry-

of these negro regiments; they appear to have behaved at first with some degree of dash, but becoming quickly

ing with them, in their panic flight, their sable comrades further in the rear, for the enemy themselves report that six hundred perished. If this be so, they must have been shot down by the Yankees in the rear, for the execution we did upon them did not amount to two hundred and fifty, and indeed volleys of musketry were heard in the direction of their flight. Among the slain were found the bodies of two negro captains, with commissions in their pockets.'

The *New Orleans Express*, in its account of the attack on Port Hudson, says:—

'While an occasional shot was being fired before the battle commenced in its more deadly fury, speculations were rife as to the manner in which the 2nd Louisiana (black troops) would act during the conflict. They had been placed in the rear, with white troops leading them. General Banks, however, in order to test their military capacity, ordered them to the front. The negroes at once rushed to the assigned point, and in the midst of the battle they proceeded to storm the rebel position opposite to them. They rushed in a body over the parapets and siege-guns, and reached the interior of the fort, in despite of the opposition of a large number of rebels. The presence of the black soldiers inside, not less than the probability of the pass they had made into the stronghold, seemed to create a spirit of fury in the enemy. They left their guns at all points, and rushed to the quarter where the negroes had prepared to make a vigorous struggle. The whites and the blacks, in a moment, had a hand-to-hand conflict unprecedented in its ferocity. The negroes in the conflict were soon disarmed, and in defending themselves they rapidly used the weapons of savage warfare. In every position in which the struggle placed them they fought with their teeth, biting their assailants in every available part of the body, kicking and scratching them. Soon, however, they had to succumb, the bayonet, the trigger, the revolver, and merciless hands at their throats, doing the work for them with fearful fatality. It may here be noted, as a key perhaps to other battles, that the presence of the black troops made the rebels in the fort almost as ferocious as the blacks. In the attack the enemy did not content himself with wounding the Africans; of eight hundred, six hundred were killed at once; when one was wounded, the assault was repeated till he died. Finding themselves thus overpowered, about two hundred of the negro troops rushed to the siege-guns, jumped headlong over the walls, and were saved.'

dismayed and panic-stricken by the terrible fire to which they were exposed, they seem to have completely succumbed, and sought shelter in flight.

After the failure of the assault on the 27th, General Banks commenced the siege in regular form; fresh batteries were erected, the parallels advanced, and a continuous fire kept up by the sharpshooters on the enemy's breast-works. By night and day the gun and mortar boats poured in shot and shell; and sickness, occasioned by exposure and bad rations, added to the hardships of the garrison. But Gardner held out, and to a summons to surrender, couched in courteous terms, and sent under flag of truce on the 13th of June, returned for answer that his duty required him to defend the post. General Banks then ordered an assault to take place on the following day (Sunday the 14th of June). The attack was to be made on the left of the Confederate line, whilst the Federal left engaged the enemy's attention by feints against his right. Shortly before daybreak the bombardment opened, and the storming parties assembled under General Paine, who was to lead the first column, composed of Emery's old division, and supported by Weitzel. Availing themselves of the shelter afforded by the broken ground, and by an ill-constructed parallel, the skirmishers which covered the front of the assaulting column approached the enemy's works. Following them was the fourth Massachusetts regiment carrying hand-grenades, and in rear of the 4th was the 53rd Massachusetts, of which each man carried a sack stuffed with cotton, with which to fill up the moat in front of the works. The main body of the infantry, headed by Colonel Currie's regiment—the 133rd New York—followed closely in rear. The leading regiments, although suffering from the heavy musketry fire, and disorganised by the obstructions of the ground, arrived within a few yards of the works, a few men even climbing over it; but the supporting column had not pressed forward with sufficient rapidity, the brave men who had entered the works were killed, and the others, having lost many of their best officers—including General Paine and Colonel Currie severely wounded—either straggled and retired, or lay down in the cotton furrows, or behind such shelter as they could find. Here for many hours did the survivors of the assaulting column lie, hardly sheltered from the storm of grape and bullets which passed close over them, and not venturing to move, lest a rifle bullet aimed with greater accuracy should strike them. General Paine, badly wounded, could not be removed; some brave men sacrificed their lives in endeavouring to help him, but it was not until night had closed in that he and many others could be conveyed back to their camp. It is said that, owing to General Banks's omission in sending a flag of truce to ask permission to bury his dead, many of the unfortunate wounded perished where they had fallen, in front of the Confederate works. Neither side could succour them, as they were exposed to the fire of both. The garrison had behaved with great courage; few in number, and weakened by fatigue and hardship, they had with difficulty repulsed the column of attack, which, had it pressed forward in sufficient numbers, must have overwhelmed them.

After the failure of the assault on the 14th of June, Banks resumed the siege operations, the trenches were steadily pushed forward, and the sharpshooters kept up an almost incessant fire on the lines of entrenchment. The provisions and ammunition of the garrison began to fail; the mules were killed for food, and it was evident that unless succour should arrive, a capitulation would be inevitable. Whilst affairs were in this state, news reached General Banks that Vicksburg had surrendered; a rumour to the same effect, passed from the advanced skirmishers, was communicated to General Gardner, who having by flag of truce ascertained its truth, and knowing that all hope of relief was at an end, determined that it was useless to prolong further resistance, and surrendered himself and the garrison as prisoners of war. On the 9th of July the Confederate troops were drawn up in line, and General Andrews, chief of the staff to General Banks, received the formal surrender of the place. The appearance of the officers and men, their calm and dauntless bearing, the firm confidence they had in the justice and strength of their cause, and above all the gallant resistance they had made, aroused the admiration and elicited the praise of their enemies. The bitterness engendered by war was soon forgotten, and shortly after the surrender the men of the two armies joined in friendly conversation, the Confederate officers receiving kindness and civility from their former enemies. The amount of loss sustained by the defenders during the siege fell far short of what might have been anticipated as the results of the incessant bombardment and of the two assaults; the casualties during the whole of the long siege did not reach eight hundred.

So fell Port Hudson on the 9th of July; her sister fortress had in the meanwhile suffered the same fate; and in order to close the narrative of the siege, we must return to Grant's army, which in the month of June we left besieging Vicksburg, itself threatened in its rear by the Confederate forces of Joe Johnston.

The strength of Grant's position, his uninterrupted communication with the North-west, together with his numerous forces and powerful artillery, enabled him to defy any attempt at an attack on his rear; and whilst he strengthened his position by works on the Big Black River, he carried on the siege with increased determination. Regular parallels and approaches were constructed, mines were sunk, and attempts made to blow up the enemy's works. His artillery played almost incessantly on the opposing batteries, keeping down their fire; and his riflemen, become expert by long practice, prevented a head from being shown above the parapets. A space of not more than twenty or thirty yards separated the sharpshooters; and the batteries on either side were within three hundred yards of each other. By both Federals and Confederates were many gallant deeds performed, and the obstinacy and endurance of the besieged were only equalled by the steady perseverance of the besiegers. Oftentimes hand-grenades would be thrown into the Confederate lines, which inflicted considerable loss, and mines would be sprung, which would bury in the *débris* many a brave officer and soldier.* As a specimen of the warfare, M'Pherson's attack on the fort which fronted his lines may be instanced. His sappers had worked nearly up to its ramparts, but a deep chasm in front of the work prevented further progress. Availing themselves of an opportunity offered by a heavy bombardment, two sappers crossed the ravine, and commenced an excavation in the cliff on which the fort was built. Covered by the rifles of the sharpshooters, the mine progressed, the powder was secreted, and all was prepared for the explosion.

* See the Diary of a Confederate soldier in vol. vii. *Rebellion Record*, p. 170, Documents.

On the day fixed, a heavier bombardment and more vigorous musketry fire was kept up along the whole line, to distract the enemy's attention from the point of attack, whilst a storming party was in readiness to rush in at the breach at the moment of explosion. In the midst of the heavy fire, a column of white smoke and a rumbling noise announced that the powder had done its work, and before the smoke had cleared away, the Federals were in the fort; not sooner, however, than their opponents, who rushed in at the opposite angle. On either side of the chasm created by the explosion did the fight continue; both sides entrenched themselves, hand-grenades were freely used, and shot and shell poured in from the batteries in rear, with the fearful risk of killing their own men. A new line of breastworks was raised inside the fort, and the Federals, although they had gained an important position, yet found that fresh obstacles awaited them.

During the month of June the siege was pressed with vigour; the Federals gradually but successively advanced their lines; and food and ammunition were beginning to fail the garrison. Then despairing of succour, and unwilling to sacrifice the lives of his men, General Pemberton, on the 3rd of July, sent a flag of truce with propositions of surrender. After a conference between the generals, and further propositions and counter propositions, the terms were agreed on; the garrison were parolled and allowed to return to their homes, not to serve again until properly exchanged; the town, stores, arms, and trophies became the prize of the conquerors; and the 4th of July received additional celebrity in the North, as the day which witnessed the capture of one of the most important strongholds of the Confederacy.

Great was the loss sustained by the South; not so much from the vital importance of the position, as from the fact that she had, to add to the strength of Vicksburg, drawn largely on her resources in men and material, weakening for that purpose other important lines of defence; that she had fought a succession of battles, on ground selected by herself, and, after a display of indomitable courage and resolution, had failed and been defeated. From the difficulty experienced by Johnston in raising an army in Mississippi, and from the numerically inferior forces which were everywhere opposed to the far more powerful armies of the North, evinced by a comparison of Banks's army with Gardner's, and Grant's with those of Johnston and Pemberton—shown also by the gradual retreat of Bragg towards the frontiers of Alabama and Georgia—it became evident that the fighting population of the South were much reduced, and that the difficulty every day became greater of meeting, at so many and widely separate points, the armies which were mustering against her, and which, augmented by recruits from Europe, were seemingly inexhaustible. The loss by the surrender of the garrison of Vicksburg of nearly five and twenty thousand men, and vast stores of small arms,* was one which the resources of the country, neither in men nor means, could endure without great strain; whilst the separation

* Pollard, in the *Third Year of the War*, estimates the numbers which surrendered at the capitulation of Vicksburg at twenty-three thousand men, with three major-generals and nine brigadiers, upwards of ninety pieces of artillery, and about forty thousand small-arms.

General Grant states, that during the campaign he had captured thirty-seven thousand prisoners, and among them fifteen general officers, and that arms and munitions of war for sixty thousand men had fallen into his hands.

from the Trans-Mississippi department, caused by the now unfettered movements of the Federal gunboats, tended to isolate the States west of the Great River from the main body of the Confederacy, and deprived the armies east of the Mississippi of the supplies they had drawn from Texas.

The 4th of July, which for two succeeding years had witnessed defeat and humiliation to the Northern arms, had now dawned on a victory which was the more appreciated as it had been so long delayed. At Vicksburg itself fireworks were let off, and the day celebrated with rejoicings; although nothing in the conduct of either officers or soldiers in the Federal army could be construed into a wish to insult a fallen but brave enemy.* In the South, the news was received with astonishment and some degree of irritation; which last was principally directed against General Pemberton, who, it was asserted, was responsible for the misfortune. To a certain degree he possibly may have been; but, before condemning him, the difficulties which attended his position should be remembered, and the ability with which he conducted the defence taken into consideration.

The passage of the gun-boats and transports was the first step towards misfortune; without them Grant would have found it difficult, if not impossible, to have carried his army across the Mississippi; or, if that had been effected, to have furnished it with supplies for a

* Extract from the Diary of a private soldier C. S. army:—'*July* 4. The enemy came into the town in small numbers about twelve o'clock. They put their fireworks into operation after dark, by way of celebrating the 4th, but were very civil, and treated us with a great deal of kindness.' *Rebellion Record*, vol. vii. p. 173, Documents.

campaign. The want of co-operation with Johnston was also productive of calamity, inasmuch as it allowed either general to be beaten in detail; but Johnston's late arrival at Jackson, the difficulty of communication with Pemberton, and, in respect of the latter, the indecision of his movements, resulting possibly from a sense of his own responsibility, and from the necessity at the same time of obeying the orders of his superior, may partially account for, if they do not wholly excuse, the strategy which preceded and led to the actions at Raymond and Jackson, and those of Champion Hills and Big Black River. General Johnston's orders arrived usually too late for execution, and seemed to admit of the exercise of private judgment on the part of Pemberton; who by endeavouring partially to carry them out, met with the usual fate of those who attempt half-measures, as he injured his own position without benefiting the cause by cooperating with his brother general. After the investment of Vicksburg, Pemberton seems to have done all in his power to defend the place; he resuscitated the morale of his army, injured by the battles of Champion Hills and Big Black River; and if the courage and determined conduct of a garrison may be taken as any proof of the ability of the commanding general, the events of the siege of Vicksburg afford sufficient refutation of any charge against Pemberton during its continuance. Of the propriety of surrendering when he did, without awaiting the extreme pressure of famine, or the result of a final assault, there may possibly be much difference of opinion, as it opens the question of how far an officer in command of a fortified town is bound to carry his defence, when all hope of succour seems to have disappeared, and when the unarmed population and the women and children would, by a prolonged resistance, be called on to endure sufferings of which only the direst necessity could justify the infliction. When Vicksburg surrendered, it was sufficiently evident that no help could be looked for from Johnston, and the failure of the operations of the Trans-Mississippi army annulled any hope of assistance from that quarter. For the garrison to have cut their way out through Grant's strong entrenchments would have been impossible, and to have retreated across the river in the presence of the fleet of gunboats seemed equally impracticable. Under such circumstances ought the general in command to be blamed, if he sought to save the lives of his soldiers and of the inhabitants by a timely surrender? It is not easy to decide so difficult a question; and happy is he who is spared the responsibility of choosing between lines of conduct of which the consequences are so momentous, and which are usually judged, not by fair criticism, but by their results.

The consideration of what followed on the capture of Vicksburg must be deferred until other events, which were as important in their consequences, and which occurred during the great siege, have received their due amount of attention. Of the armies of Tennessee brought more immediately into relation with those of Mississippi, only a passing notice will now be requisite, as the great events of that campaign occurred at a later period of the war; but of those of Virginia a careful perusal of the strategy becomes necessary, in order to understand the circumstances connected with the great battle fought only a few days previous to the surrender of Vicksburg.

CHAPTER XV.

ARMIES OF THE CUMBERLAND AND OHIO.

NOTWITHSTANDING the efforts made by the Federal Government to promote the efficiency of the army of the Mississippi, the army of the Cumberland under Rosecrans had not been neglected, but had been increased in numbers and improved in its organisation since the battle of Murfreesboro. A new army under General Burnside was likewise in process of formation at Cincinnati preparatory to a combined movement with that of Rosecrans on southern Tennessee. Against these forces General Bragg, weakened by detachments sent to the army of the Mississippi, felt himself unable to contend and at the same time to maintain his position on the Duck River; he therefore prepared to retreat to the line of the Tennessee River and to Chattanooga.

Irrespective of the operations of the grand armies, there were skirmishes in various parts of Kentucky and Tennessee, to which the names of battles were given, but which exercised little influence on the progress of the war. The Confederate Generals sent several expeditions into Eastern Kentucky with the object of enforcing the conscription or procuring horses, and their possession of the passes in the Cumberland mountains enabled them to make these raids with more or less impunity; but neither in their magnitude nor results can the operations in Kentucky in the spring of 1863 compare with those of Morgan and Kirby Smith during the preceding autumn, or still less with the great invasion of the State by Bragg. There were skirmishes at various places, and as the Federal cavalry penetrated into Georgia and Alabama, so did the Confederate horsemen ride through Kentucky, and even cross the Ohio into Indiana. Many a brave deed and many a dashing affair must be passed over in order to hasten on to the greater battles of the war; and if one event resulting in the execution of two gallant officers receives especial notice, it is more as illustrating the incidents of civil warfare, than as forming matter of peculiar importance.

At dusk on the 8th of June, two officers in the Federal uniform, with proper horse accoutrements, rode into the small town of Franklin, in Tennessee, and immediately reported themselves to the officer in command, showing their passes, and stating that they were the Inspector-General and Assistant Inspector-General appointed by General Rosecrans to visit the outposts. They gave their names and answered questions freely, stating that they were anxious to proceed to Nashville on that evening. Something in their manner excited the suspicions of the Federal Colonel, who telegraphed to Murfreesboro to inquire whether there were any inspectors of the names given in the army of the Cumberland. An answer in the negative was immediately received. The circumstance of the presence in Franklin of the two officers was then detailed, and a telegraphic order returned from Rosecrans's head-quarters to assemble a drum-head court-martial, and try them as spies. Finding that no hope remained of preserving their disguise, the officers confessed themselves to be Colonel Williams, formerly an officer of the regular army, and aide-de-camp to General Scott, latterly chief of artillery to General Bragg, and Lieutenant Dunlap, also of the Confederate States army. They protested against the charge brought against them, saying that they were not spies in the ordinary sense of the word. Notwithstanding their plea, a reiterated order was sent from Murfreesboro to hang them at once, for fear lest Forrest, who was known to be in the vicinity, should profit by any information they had gained; and although Colonel Williams, as a last appeal, asked for clemency on the ground of his father's services and death in the Mexican War, the execution was proceeded with, and on the morning of the 9th a telegram announcing the fact was sent to Murfreesboro. There can be no doubt that the laws of war sanctioned this severity, and the caution necessary in conducting operations against an enemy, speaking the same language and identical in manners and appearance, will excuse any harshness on the part of General Rosecrans; but at the same time few can read of the devotion of these two gallant officers, without admiring their courage and lamenting their fate.

Shortly after this melancholy event, Bragg retreated from his lines on the Duck River, and taking the road to Chattanooga, crossed the Tennessee River. His retreat was harassed by the Federal cavalry, and his army was weakened by numerous desertions, caused probably by the abandonment of Tennessee, and the return to their homes of men who considered their duties terminated when the defence of their State no longer claimed their services.* On the Tennessee River the

* Loyalty to the State rather than to the Commonwealth of States, which formed the groundwork on which those who advocated the constitutional right of secession based their arguments, proved more than once to be an element of weakness to the Confederacy.

Confederate army was concentrated, the forces under Generals Bragg and Buckner being opposed to those of Rosecrans and Burnside.

The last-named general, after his resignation of the command of the army of the Potomac, had distinguished himself in his new department of the Ohio more by arbitrary acts of military power, than by operations against the enemy. By the arrest of supposed Southern sympathisers, by the censorship he established over the press, and especially by the imprisonment and trial by court-martial of one of the most able of the members of Congress, he incurred the hatred of the Democratic party, and perhaps of many others who valued the conservation of their liberties more than the augmentation of the authority of a strong central power.

Mr. Vallandingham had for some time rendered himself conspicuous as the leader of a party, known by its enemies as Copperheads,* whose aim was to arrange an armistice, preparatory to a convention, at which the difficulties attending reunion should be arranged, and, if need be, full concessions granted to the Southern States. At a meeting held at New Jersey Mr. Vallandingham had spoken vehemently against the continuance of the war, at the same time protesting that he was equally opposed to disunion, and that he belonged to the party who wished to try the experiment of bringing back the South by conciliation and compromise. At Mount Vernon in Ohio, before an assemblage of about 20,000 people, he had used nearly the same language and arguments; but among his audience were two of Burnside's staff in civilians' clothes, who had been detailed by the General to take down his

* So called from a small and venomous serpent.

words. In consequence of the presumed treasonable import of the language, a detachment of troops was sent to Mr. Vallandingham's house, and, without authority from the civil power, entered it at night, and having arrested Mr. Vallandingham, brought him under escort to Cincinnati. The arrest was made in conformity with an order issued by General Burnside on the 13th April, 1863, announcing 'That all persons found within our lines who commit acts for the benefit of the enemies of our country, will be tried as spies and traitors, and, if convicted, will suffer death.' To which the following order was added:—'The habit of declaring sympathies for the enemy will not be allowed in this department. Persons committing such offences will be at once arrested, with a view to being tried, as above stated, or sent beyond our lines into the lines of their friends. It must be distinctly understood that treason, expressed or implied, will not be tolerated in this department.'

On the day following his arrest, Mr. Vallandingham applied, by the advice of counsel, to the Judge of the Circuit Court of the United States at Cincinnati, for a writ of *Habeas Corpus*. The application was argued at length and refused by the Judge, who said that the legality of the arrest depended upon the extent of the necessity for making it, and that that was to be determined by the military commander; he added—'Men should know and lay the truth to heart, that there is a course of conduct, not involving overt treason, and not therefore subject to punishment as such, which nevertheless implies moral guilt, and a gross offence against the country. Those who live under the protection and enjoy the blessings of our benignant Government, must learn that they cannot stab its vitals with impunity. If they cherish hatred and hostility to it and desire its subversion, let them withdraw from its jurisdiction, and seek the fellowship and protection of those with whom they are in sympathy. If they remain with us, while they are not of us, they must be subject to such a course of dealing as the great law of self-preservation prescribes and will enforce. And let them not complain if the stringent doctrine of military necessity should find them to be the legitimate subjects of its action. I have no fear that the recognition of this doctrine will lead to an arbitrary invasion of the personal security or personal liberty of the citizen. It is rare indeed that a charge for disloyalty should be made on insufficient grounds. But if there should be an occasional mistake, such an occurrence is not to be put in competition with the preservation of the nation; and, I confess, I am but little moved by the eloquent appeals of those who, while they indignantly denounce violation of personal liberty, look with no horror on a despotism as unmitigated as the world has ever witnessed.'

Such was the judgment and opinion of a judge of the Circuit Court of the United States, and it may be doubted whether a similar instance of a disregard of justice, and of pandering to the violence of party, can be found in any judgment delivered in any court of justice during the present century. The Judge commences by asserting that there is a course of conduct which implies moral guilt, and a gross offence against the country which does not involve direct treason. No doubt such may be the case; but the moral guilt cannot be recognised or punished by law unless it shows itself in unlawful acts. Therefore, Mr. Vallandingham's conduct would not come under the cognisance of a court of justice. But he proceeds to imply, that overruling all law is the stringent doctrine of military necessity, and that the actions of such military necessity are legitimate. It may be fairly asked, What is this new doctrine of military necessity? It cannot be martial law, for Ohio had not been placed under martial law, and therefore its courts of civil judicature were in full operation. Forming an opinion from the case of Mr. Vallandingham, it would seem that the law of military necessity is merely the order of a general officer commanding the troops in the neighbourhood; or, possibly, it may be explained in Judge Leavitt's own words, *as the great law of self-preservation*, which great law would justify equally the violence of a mob as the arbitrary conduct of a soldier.

And here let the distinction be clearly drawn between the action of the judge, appointed to his high position to uphold and administer the law of the land, and that of the executive Government. Unconstitutional was the act of Burnside, and, of course, equally unconstitutional was the approval of that act by President Lincoln. But in times of peril the rulers of nations have frequently been found to act arbitrarily, and have even been acquitted of blame whilst overstepping the bounds of the law. Dangerous as such a course must be, it may possibly be justified on the plea that virulent diseases require violent remedies; and such an excuse may be alleged for the President and his subordinate—General Burnside. But when a judge, to whom the case is referred, not only refuses to put in force the law, but justifies such refusal by false and contemptible reasoning, he weakens the cause of order, and throws discredit on the administration of justice in the land which has the misfortune to entrust to such hands its guarantees of liberty and social order.

Numerous remonstrances from the Democratic party

were addressed to President Lincoln subsequent to Mr. Vallandingham's trial by court-martial. To these addresses he returned full and lengthy answers, but failed either to convince the applicants, or probably anyone else, that the line of action he had adopted was defensible on other grounds than those resulting from the peculiar danger which menaced the country. There can be no question but that the arrest and trial by court-martial of Mr. Vallandingham were illegal, and can be defended only by such reasoning as would equally justify what are called in France *coup d'états*.

The trial followed soon after the arrest, the charge preferred against the prisoner being, 'That he had publicly expressed sympathy for those in arms against the Government of the United States, and declared disloyal sentiments and opinions, with the object and purpose of weakening the power of the Government in its efforts to suppress an unlawful rebellion.' He was found guilty of the charge, and sentenced 'to be placed in close confinement in some fortress of the United States, to be designated by the commanding officer of the department, there to be kept during the continuance of the war.' This sentence, specifying no certain duration of the imprisonment, was as illegal as the arrest and trial; and the modification of the sentence by the President, decreeing the punishment of banishment in place of that of imprisonment, was also on a par with the rest of the proceedings. The President, in a telegram sent to General Burnside, directed 'that Mr. Vallandingham should be sent without delay, under secure guard, to the head-quarters of General Rosecrans, to be put by him beyond the military lines; and, in the case of his return within such lines, that he should be arrested and kept in close custody for the term specified in his sentence.' In pursuance of this order, Mr. Vallandingham was transported beyond the Federal lines, and, after travelling through the Southern States, ran the blockade to Bermuda, and subsequently went to Canada, from whence, at a later period of the war, he returned to Ohio.

Such, briefly, were the incidents attending the arrest of Mr. Vallandingham. At the time it was thought by many that disturbances and insurrection might ensue, especially as Mr. Vallandingham was much respected in the Western States; but in this, as in other instances, the Americans showed what some would call the love of order, and which others would term civil cowardice,* and remained impassive under the provocation. With their minds fixed on one object—the restoration of the Union—they disregarded the sacrifices which attended the prosecution of their enterprise; and, as they willingly offered up life and property, so were they equally ready to give up their hitherto much-prized freedom for the object they so earnestly desired. It would seem, however, that the strong feelings and urgent remonstrances which Mr. Vallandingham's arrest, trial, and punishment called forth, taught the Government that it would be unwise to try too far the patience of the Western people. Fewer political arrests were subsequently made in the loyal states; and Burnside, not long after this occurrence, marched from Ohio into Kentucky to cooperate with Rosecrans.

* The author inclines more to the former than the latter opinion as to the motives which regulated the actions of the mass of the people.

CHAPTER XVI.

CAMPAIGN OF GETTYSBURG.

AGAIN, on the third succeeding summer, does the interest of the great struggle centre in Virginia; the names of villages, streams, and hills already familiar as the scenes of battles, of lesser engagements and frequent skirmishes, are again to become signalised, as the wave of war returns over the country, still suffering from its previous inundations.

Taking up the narrative of events from the time of the retreat of Hooker across the Rappahannock, we find that during the remainder of May the two armies had watched each other from either side of the river. Apparently all was quiet; and if, as May drew to a close, vague reports were in circulation of an important movement on the part of Lee, which the month of June was to develop, they were treated in the North as mere rumours to which little importance should be attached. Nevertheless, preparations for a great campaign were diligently made in the Confederate camp. Longstreet, with two veteran divisions, was recalled from North Carolina; the cavalry was concentrated and reviewed by General Lee in person, in the vicinity of Culpepper Court-house; and the army, reorganised and divided into three equal and distinct corps, awaited the orders for a march, of which perhaps no one excepting the President and the Commander-in-Chief knew the ultimate object.

To General Longstreet was the command of the first corps assigned, consisting of the divisions of M'Laws, Hood and Pickett; to General Ewell, who, according to General Jackson's wish, had succeeded to the command of his old corps, were the divisions of Early, Rodes, and Johnson allotted; and to General A. P. Hill was the third corps given, consisting of the divisions of Anderson, Pender and Heth.* Each of these three corps numbered about 25,000 men, making the total strength of the army 75,000, irrespective of Stuart's cavalry.

To supply so large a force, and at the same time not to neglect the armies of the West, taxed to their utmost extent the resources of the Confederate authorities. The daily rations of the men were sufficiently difficult to collect and to forward to their proper localities, but the large quantities of forage necessary for the horses, and the relays of horses required to sustain the wear and tear of war, were almost beyond their capabilities. For these reasons, a change in the scene of operations was rendered advisable. But irrespective of the actual necessities of the army, other causes tended to influence the President and General Lee in advocating an alteration in the strategy of the summer campaign. The continual defensive attitude maintained during the autumn, winter, and spring by the Army of Virginia, was not only trying to the resources of the country, but was also galling to the spirit of the people and the soldiery, flushed with the victories of Fredericksburg and Chancellorsville. They could perceive no termination to a struggle in

* See Pollard's *Third Year of the War*, and Captain Chesney's *Campaigns in Virginia*.

which the aggressors, continually recruited from a numerous population and from European immigrants, and ignorant of the horrors and sufferings of war, pushed forward army after army in order to weary out, if they could not conquer, the only force which stood between them and Richmond. But it was contended, should war visit the Northern territory, and should the farmers of Pennsylvania learn by practical experience the sufferings endured by those of Virginia, they would sooner listen to the arguments urged in favour of peace, and would bring their influence to strengthen that large party in the North which was unfavourable to the continuance of the struggle.

That an irruption into the Northern States might relieve the pressure on the Confederate armies of the West, may also have been an additional argument in favour of an offensive campaign, and possibly the desire of counterbalancing the continual retreat of the armies of Tennessee and Mississippi by an advance into Northern territory, and of offering a counterpoise to Grant's brilliant movements against Vicksburg, may have exerted its influence in determining the President to listen to the reasonings of those who advocated bolder measures than he in general approved of.

The design of the campaign having received the sanction of the head of the Government, it remained for General Lee to put it into execution. He could not attack the army entrenched in his front with any hope of success, strong as it was in numbers and supported by a powerful artillery; and to turn its flank, and to threaten its communications without exposing his own, was a task which required all the talents of a consummate general. Strict secresy as to the intended movement must be maintained, and to secure such secresy, few, if any, excepting the President, could be entrusted with the plan of operations. The march of a large army and the transportation of its supplies were to be conducted in presence of a superior force, provided with a numerous if not very efficient cavalry; and a semblance of strength was to be preserved, in order to deceive the Federal general at Falmouth, and to conceal the departure of the main body of the army from his front.

The reoccupation of the Shenandŏah Valley, the invasion of Pennsylvania, and the change in the theatre of the war from Virginia to the enemy's country, were the immediate objects of Lee's intended movements. Whatever might result from these operations could not be foreseen, and the ultimate, and perhaps as yet scarcely defined, designs of the campaign could only develop themselves as success, or the reverse, should influence the conduct of the war.

To gain the Shenandoah Valley, and to relieve the town of Winchester, which since the campaign of Antietam had suffered under the tyranny of General Milroy, was the first aim of the intended movement; but how to transfer the army from its present position on the heights above Fredericksburg to the Shenandoah Valley, without the intelligence of the movement reaching the enemy, was a difficulty which can scarcely be over-estimated. General Hooker, by means of the rail to Aquia Creek and the transports on the Potomac, could move his supplies with greater facility than could his opponents by the circuitous rail to Gordonsville, and so by roads into the valley, whilst the distance that the army would have to march from Falmouth, by either Warrenton or Manasses, was considerably shorter than the route which the Confederates would be forced to take by Gordonsville and Culpepper. It depended therefore on secresy and rapidity, whether Lee would be able to gain a march on Hooker, and so outmanœuvre him, at the same time that he guarded against the danger of exposing his rear or right flank to the attack of the whole Federal army, when the leading columns should have advanced beyond supporting distance. Such were General Lee's difficulties. On the other hand, he had the advantage of *prestige*, both as regarded his own capabilities and the qualities of his troops, and he was operating against a general who possessed neither the confidence of his men, nor the education or talent necessary for the command of a large army.* Lee knew also that he could act on the fears of President Lincoln and his Government for the safety of Washington, and possibly induce them to interfere with the conduct of the campaign, in order to provide for the greater security of the capital.

During the first week in June the movement commenced. Longstreet's and Ewell's corps were directed to march on Culpepper, their right flank guarded by detachments of Stuart's cavalry which watched the fords of the Rappahannock, whilst A. P. Hill's corps remained at and near Fredericksburg, to deceive the Federal general by an appearance of strength. But the movements of a large army cannot be kept completely secret, and reports of a reduction in the numbers of the enemy occupying the heights in his front reached General Hooker, and induced him to push forward a strong reconnaissance across the Rappahannock below the town of Fredericksburg. A division of the sixth corps was

* This remark is not intended to reflect on General Hooker's capabilities for an inferior command, but only for that of a large army.

detailed for this duty, and effected the passage of the river on the 6th of June; but encountering some resistance, and fearing to involve itself amidst the forests and thickets of the Wilderness, it did not advance far beyond the bank, and obtained little information of the strength or intentions of the enemy. With a similar object did General Pleasanton lead forward the main body of the Federal cavalry across the Rappahannock on the 9th of June, moving in such considerable force, and pushing onwards with such vigour, as to develop more clearly than the earlier reconnaissance, the direction of General Lee's march. The cavalry, divided into two columns, the right under General Buford, the left under General Gregg, and, supported by a small force of infantry, received orders to cross the Rappahannock at 3 A.M. on the 9th June, Buford by Beverley Ford, Gregg by Kelley's Ford, and to unite at Brandy Station, a few miles distant from Culpepper Court-house, for an attack on that place. Moving rapidly forward, the Federal cavalry crossed the river, and ascending the right bank, surprised the Confederate pickets, and fell unexpectedly on Jones's brigade, many of whose men were not mounted, nor were their carabines and pistols loaded. The regiments were formed up as quickly as possible, but were driven back, and Brandy Station, which had served for Stuart's head-quarters, was captured; there, according to the programme, Gregg united with Buford; but by this time supports of infantry had been pushed forward from Culpepper; and Pleasanton, fearing to be overwhelmed by numbers, retreated across the fords of the Rappahannock, followed by the Confederate cavalry.* Skirmishing, sometimes increasing

* General Lee, in his report of the campaign of Gettysburg, claims to have captured four hundred prisoners, three pieces of artillery, and several colours in this engagement.

to the dimensions of an engagement, had lasted for nearly ten hours; the firearm had been freely used, but although in several encounters between individuals the sabre may have been brought into play, it does not appear to have been the weapon with which the combatants were most familiar. Often in the tumult of the engagement, the troops became so intermingled that friend and foe could not be distinguished; and the little attention paid to uniform, together with the grey dust covering the blue coats of the Federals, and converting them into the colour of the Confederate cloth, added to the mistakes and confusion.

Even after this reconnaissance, which brought back intelligence of the presence of a large Confederate force at and near Culpepper, no suspicion of the magnitude of the movements in progress seems to have been entertained by General Hooker. An idea gained ground that a raid on a large scale was about to be made into Pennsylvania, but that the whole Confederate army was moving in that direction was not believed or even anticipated.

Expecting nothing of greater consequence than an irruption of cavalry, for which he considered himself prepared, Milroy, with about seven thousand men, remained in fancied security at his head-quarters at Winchester, merely sending out the usual patrols of cavalry to watch the roads—a duty which does not appear to have been performed efficiently. The people of the country, strongly Southern in their sympathies, and rendered still more so by Milroy's acts of oppression, furnished him with no warning of the blow, which, in the shape of the corps composed of Jackson's veterans, was impending over him.

Detached from the main army, and marching rapidly

from Culpepper to Front Royal and Winchester, was Ewell with his three divisions, whilst the two cavalry generals Jenkins and Imboden, who had long guarded the upper Shenandoah and Cacapon Valleys, were converging towards the same points. The Blue Ridge Mountains had been crossed, and the passage of the Shenandoah effected, before Milroy awoke to the danger which menaced him. Confident in Hooker's power to retain in his front Lee's main army, and relying on him for information of any strong detachment which might threaten the Lower Shenandoah, Milroy had neglected the proper precaution of watching the passes in the Blue Ridge, or the fords of the Shenandoah River.

After crossing the river, Ewell ordered Rodes to march on Beverley, and to seize the village and cut the communication between Winchester and the Potomac; whilst he himself, with Early and Johnson, moved onwards to Winchester. Instead of assaulting the place in front, Early's division moved round the south-western side of the town, and occupied a range of hills preparatory to attacking a small work which overlooked the main forts constructed outside the town.

On the 13th June, a prisoner was captured by one of Milroy's patrols; and from him the Federal general received the first intelligence of the nature and strength of the force which was now almost within gun-shot of his works, and which he had hitherto believed to be an advanced body of cavalry. Realising the danger of his position, but undecided as to the course of action he should pursue, Milroy withdrew into the two large forts outside the town, giving a preconcerted signal for the brigade stationed at Beverley to retire on Winchester and effect a junction with the main force.

On Sunday the 14th, Early placed his guns in position, and in the evening ordered the Louisiana brigade to advance to the assault of the work on the hill. With the dash which characterises these Southern troops, the men rushed forward, and with little loss carried the position, its defenders being driven across the valley which separated it from the main forts. Milroy was now hemmed in between Early's, Johnson's, and Rodes' divisions; and nothing remained for him but to hold out until succour should arrive, to surrender, or to endeavour to force his way through the enemy's lines to Harper's Ferry. The first course he considered to be impossible, owing to a lack of supplies; the second he was unwilling to adopt, possibly from proper motives, increased perhaps by the knowledge that, like Butler, he was an especial object of hatred to the Confederates; the third course he endeavoured to carry out; but, either from the absence of the qualities of a general, or from the want of discipline among the troops, which could not resist the demoralising influence of a retreat, or probably from both causes combined, the enterprise failed; and although Milroy secured his own safety, the majority of his troops, his artillery, and a vast accumulation of stores and ammunition, fell into the hands of the Confederates.

During the early morning of the 15th, at 2 A.M., the retreat commenced; Johnson's out-pickets were surprised, and with some difficulty that general held the Federals in check until reinforcements came up; but as Early entered the forts and despatched his artillery to follow up the fugitives, and as the brigades of Rodes' division came into action, the Federal column of retreat was broken and became dispersed; Milroy himself, with a few cavalry, was among the first to arrive at Harper's Ferry, and, shortly afterwards, other detachments which had held together joined him; but three thousand prisoners, thirty pieces of artillery, over one hundred waggons, and great quantities of stores, were captured in and near Winchester, and seven hundred men surrendered to General Rodes at Martinsburg.

Such were the successful results of General Lee's combinations. The first act of the drama had terminated, and although the whole plot was not thereby revealed, yet enough was discernible to cause considerable alarm and excitement in the Northern States; and to show General Hooker that he had been out-manœuvred, and that rapid marching could alone make up for lost time.

On the 14th of June, the army of the Potomac commenced its flank movement to cover Washington, and on the evening of the same day arrived at Fairfax Court-house, and the well-known battle-field of Bull Run. Hooker was thus on Ewell's flank, and threatened to interpose between him and the Commander-in-Chief. But this danger had neither been overlooked nor unprovided for by Lee; and whilst with seeming recklessness he pushed forward Ewell's corps into Maryland and Pennsylvania, he hastened to occupy the passes in the Blue Ridge Mountains, which alone afforded doors of entrance into the Shenandoah Valley. Stuart's cavalry, moving in advance, and on the right flank of the main army, covered its march, and occupying positions on the roads leading to the passes, presented a barrier to the Federal cavalry, which, under Pleasanton, was hurrying forward to seize Ashby's and Snicker's Gaps, in the Blue Ridge.

On the 17th of June there was a skirmish between the two cavalry forces in the vicinity of Aldie, a small village in the Bull Run Hills, from which the roads to Snicker's and Ashby's Gaps diverge; and, on the 21st, after Longstreet's corps had occupied the passes in the chain of the Blue Ridge, the action was renewed; Pleasanton having in the meantime brought up the greater portion of the Federal cavalry, with infantry and artillery in support. The engagement occurred near Middlesburg, and resulted in Stuart's repulse, who withdrew towards the infantry reserves which held the mountain ridges, and which presented far too formidable a front to permit of an attack, with any prospect of success, by Pleasanton's comparatively small force. General Lee had gained his object; he had seized the passes in the mountains which afforded the only means by which Hooker could fall upon his flank; he had established a communication between Ewell's and Longstreet's corps, and yet continued to keep open his communication with Richmond, by means of A. P. Hill's corps forming the rear of the army between Culpepper and Front Royal.*

Such was the position of the Confederate army during the end of the second and beginning of the third week of June, and it became sufficiently apparent, not only to the Government at Washington but to the people, from whom it had hitherto been considered desirable to keep the alarming news, that a formidable invasion of the Northern States had actually commenced. Ewell in person was in Maryland; the cavalry, under Jenkins and Imboden, were levying contributions on the farmers of Pennsylvania; and their numbers, the extent of their depredations, and their ultimate objects, were canvassed and greatly exaggerated,

* On the 22nd of June, General Lee's head-quarters were at Beverley, ten miles from Winchester.

as each man repeated to his neighbour the momentous intelligence, and as the busy reporters telegraphed the news to the several cities of the North. The uncertainty of the position of Lee's main army, and the secresy with which his plans were carried out, increased the alarm, and led to the circulation of the wildest rumours. Some asserted positively that Pittsburg and Ohio were the objects of his march; others that Harrisburg, and even Philadelphia, would fall into his hands; and others, again, pointed to Baltimore and Washington as the true points which were menaced by the invading army. President Lincoln issued a proclamation calling on the Governors of Ohio, Pennsylvania, New York, Maryland, and Western Virginia for 120,000 militia, for the express purpose of protecting the States; the Governors, in turn, issued their addresses, but found that large armies and trained soldiers could not be raised as quickly as proclamations could be issued. Pennsylvania asked for aid of New Jersey, and Massachusets offered to furnish its quota, to protect the more exposed states on the frontier.

But it was not on the hastily levied militia that the safety of the North depended; the army of the Potomac, although commanded by a man in whom neither soldiers nor people had great confidence, yet comprised in its ranks veterans of many battle-fields, led by officers trained in war, and possessed of far greater experience than the generals of the campaigns of the York Town Peninsula.

It was on this army and on the strongly fortified lines of Washington that the security of the North really rested, and it was palpably the true policy of the Government to strengthen by every means the regular forces, and to sacrifice all considerations other than those which related to their efficiency. To remove or to receive the resignation of General Hooker was obviously necessary; but whom to appoint in his place was a question which could not so easily be decided. To recall M'Clellan would gratify a large portion of the army, but it would also strengthen the hands of the political party diametrically opposed to the Government, and would be a confession that other motives than those which had regard to his military qualifications had led to his previous removal from the chief command. No other general had been brought prominently forward, and on Mr. Lincoln devolved the task of selecting, among the many good officers of the army of the Potomac, a man capable of contending at this crisis against the great general of the Confederacy. The selection was attended with much difficulty; whilst many had done their duties well, none had as yet conspicuously distinguished themselves; and when, apparently, the fate of the Federal cause depended on the man who at this crisis should lead the army, the responsibility which fell on Mr. Lincoln can scarcely be exaggerated.

On the 28th of June, General Hooker, at his own request, was relieved from the command of the army of the Potomac, and General Meade, whose antecedents although perhaps not especially brilliant, were yet those of an efficient division and corps commander, was appointed to succeed him. General Meade was no *sabreur* such as at the earlier period of the struggle the Americans delighted to picture to themselves, as the type of their generals; but a quiet middle-aged man of forty-eight years, formerly of the Topographical Engineers, and remarkable alike for his mild and gentlemanlike demeanour, as for his courage on the field of battle. He had served as an officer of the Regular army in the Mexican war, had embraced the Federal cause at the commencement of hostilities; and to the experience of the latter part of the York Town Peninsular Campaign, where he had been severely wounded, he had added that of South Mountain, Antietam, and the battles on the Rappahannock. His manner, his address to the troops on taking the command, and his former services alike recommended him to the soldiers, who had learnt to distinguish between brave words and determined action, and knew that for the commander of a large army a clear head and a sound education were of more consequence than brilliant exterior, or the outward show of military talent.* There was another circumstance connected with General Meade, which the enemies of the administration were not slow to notice, and to assign as one of the reasons which influenced Mr. Lincoln's choice. General Meade was not born in America,

* The following is General Meade's address to the Army of the Potomac on taking the command:—

'General Order, No. 66.

'By order of the President of the United States, I hereby assume command of the Army of the Potomac. As a soldier, in obeying this order,—an order totally unexpected and unsolicited,—I have no promises or pledges to make. The country looks to this army to relieve it from the devastation and disgrace of a hostile invasion. Whatever fatigues and sacrifices we may be called upon to undergo, let us have in view constantly the magnitude of the interests involved, and let each man determine to do his duty, leaving to an all-controlling Providence the decision of the contest. It is with just diffidence that I relieve in the command of this army an eminent and accomplished soldier, whose name must ever appear conspicuous in the history of its achievements; but I rely upon the hearty support of my companions-in-arms to assist me in the discharge of the duties of the important trust which has been confided to me.

'GEORGE G. MEADE,
'Major-General Commanding.'

consequently, by a provision of the Constitution, he was ineligible for the Presidency; and, therefore, could be no rival either to Mr. Lincoln, or others of his party at the next election. This may, and may not have influenced the selection; such was alleged at the time; but, assuredly, the appointment of General Meade was unexceptionable, and his subsequent acts fully justified the choice which Mr. Lincoln had made.

Previous to Hooker's resignation the main army of the Confederates had crossed the Potomac—Lee, with Longstreet's corps, at and near Williamsport, and A. P. Hill at Shepherdstown. With cheers, laughter, and the good humour engendered by confidence and hope, the ragged but well-disciplined troops of the Confederacy forded the Potomac, armed principally with rifles captured from the enemy, carrying knapsacks and accoutrements which still bore the names and numbers of Federal regiments, clad in brown home-spun cloth, well shod, and preserving strict discipline on the line of march—Lee's soldiers presented a spectacle which might astonish and perhaps instruct those who had been accustomed to the regular troops of Europe.* True to his character as a general, a gentleman, and a Christian, Lee had issued a strong order against plundering and retaliation, and the good behaviour of his troops in Pennsylvania contrasted strikingly with the conduct of the Federals, in several of the campaigns fought on Southern ground.

Yet the provocations of many of the officers and men had been great; they had left behind them desolated homes, and wives, and children, scarcely able to keep themselves from starvation, and they were now entering a rich and fruitful country, teeming with plenty,

* See Colonel Freemantle's most interesting account of the Gettysburg campaign, of which he was an eye-witness.

and inhabited by an unarmed but unfriendly population: notwithstanding these temptations and incentives to revenge, they refrained not only from outrage on the inhabitants, but even from the appropriation to their own use of what might be deemed necessaries. Such forbearance, when the strife of faction has been silenced by time, must ensure the respect and gratitude even of those who have been most opposed to the South, and in Europe must increase the admiration which the fighting qualities of the Confederate troops has excited among men of all parties and professions.*

* The following quotation, from a Northern account of the proceedings of Jenkins's cavalry in Pennsylvania, affords one among many proofs of the truth of the statements put forward with regard to the conduct of the Confederates in the enemy's country:—'By way of giving the devil his due, it must be said, that although there were over sixty acres of wheat, and eighty acres of corn and oats in the same field, he (General Jenkins) protected it most carefully, and picketed his horses so that it could not be injured. An equal care was taken of all other property about the place (Chambersburg), excepting half a dozen of our fattest Cottswell sheep, which were necessary, it seems, to furnish chops, &c., for his men. No fences were wantonly destroyed, poultry was not disturbed, nor did he compliment our blooded cattle so much as to test the quality of their steak and roasts. Some of his men cast a wistful eye upon the glistening trout in the spring; but they were protected by voluntary order, and save a few quarts of delicious strawberries, gathered with every care, after first asking permission, nothing in the gardens or about the grounds was taken.'

As we are on this subject, we cannot refrain from quoting some passages contained in a letter from a Confederate soldier to his wife, which is published in the *Rebellion Record*, and which was picked up on the battle-field of Gettysburg:—

'Camp, near Greenwood Pa., June 25, 1863.

'MY OWN DARLING WIFE,—I have written two letters to you since I left the trenches at Fredericksburg. I received a letter from you dated the 14th instant. You may be sure I devoured its contents with great eagerness, but oh! how I was pained to hear that you

After crossing the Potomac, the two columns under Longstreet and Hill were directed on Hagerstown, and from thence advancing into Pennsylvania, reached Chambersburg on the 27th June. It was there that Ewell had previously taken up his quarters, and had scoured the country for many miles with the object of collecting horses, forage, and provisions, paying for the

were so unwell! It makes me miserable to think of you as suffering bodily afflictions, with all the great troubles you now have to contend with, and I not there to help you.

'You can see by the date of this, that we are now in Pennsylvania. We crossed the line the day before yesterday, and are resting to-day near a little one-horse town on the road to Gettysburg, which we will reach to-morrow. We are paying back these people for some of the damage they have done us. We are getting up all the horses, &c., and feeding our army with their beef and flour, &c., but there are strict orders about the interruption of any private property by individual soldiers, though, with these orders, fowls, and pigs, and eatables don't stand much chance.

'I felt, when I first came here, that I would like to revenge myself upon these people for the devastation they have brought upon our own beautiful home; that home where we could have lived so happy, and that we loved so much, from which their Vandalism has driven you and my helpless little ones. But though I had such severe wrongs and grievances to redress, and such great cause for revenge, yet when I got among these people I could not find in my heart to molest them. They looked so dreadfully scared, and talked so humble, that I have invariably endeavoured to protect their property, and have prevented soldiers from taking chickens, even in the main road; yet there is a good deal of plundering going on, confined principally to the taking of provisions. No houses were searched and robbed, like our houses were done, by the Yankees. Pigs, chickens, geese, &c., are finding their way into our camp; it can't be prevented, and I can't think it ought to be. We must show them something of war. I have sent to-day to get a good horse; I have no scruples about that, as they have taken mine. We took a lot of negroes yesterday. I was offered my choice, but as I could not get them back home, I would not take them. In fact my humanity revolted at taking the poor devils away from their homes,' &c. &c.

same in Confederate money. As the main army entered Chambersburg, Ewell was ordered to send Early's division to the east side of South Mountain, as far as York, with the intention of threatening Harrisburg, the capital of Pennsylvania, on one side, and Baltimore on the other, and so keeping the Federal army of the Potomac from operating on Lee's communications. The remainder of Ewell's corps marched on Carlisle, and likewise threatened Harrisburg; at the same time that Imboden's cavalry, which had hitherto been employed in covering the left of the main army, and in burning bridges, and otherwise destroying the Baltimore and Ohio Railway, and Chesapeake and Ohio Canal, received orders to march by way of M'Connelsburg to join Longstreet and Hill at Chambersburg. The greater portion of Lee's army was thus concentrated in the Cumberland Valley, and the troops were living in plenty in the midst of one of the most fertile countries of the Union. Heavy requisitions were made on the towns, but all private plundering was forbidden, and the Generals in command of detachments carried out the orders of the Commander-in-Chief with equal strictness when away from head-quarters, as when in their vicinity. The population, mostly of German descent, looked on in sulky dislike and fear of the invaders, but showed little alacrity to add to the numbers of the militia, which, under General Couch, was assembling at Hagerstown, and which, having burned the bridge over the Susquehanna, had sought shelter behind that river, leaving the task of defending Southern Pennsylvania and Maryland to the army of the Potomac.

After General Lee's intentions had been fully developed, that army—its left flank covered by the cavalry—had crossed the Potomac at the fords between

Harper's Ferry and Washington, and had marched by the right bank of the Monocacy River on Frederick City (Maryland). The garrison of Harper's Ferry, which had withdrawn on the advance of Lee to the Maryland Heights, was called in, and the army concentrated in and around Frederick City. Here Meade assumed the command, and at once commenced the movement destined to culminate in the decisive battle of the campaign. Two plans of operation were open to him—either to march directly towards Harrisburg, and placing himself in a position to cover Washington and Baltimore, and in communication with the militia on the northern bank of the Susquehanna, to force Lee to draw in his scattered divisions, and either to fight or retreat; or, advancing from Frederick City by the roads formerly taken by M'Clellan, to endeavour to cut the enemy's communications with the Potomac, and oblige him to accept battle in a position where repulse would necessarily entail disaster. To this second plan there were objections. Lee's right flank was protected by the range of South Mountain, which furnished him with strong positions, where a comparatively small force could hold in check a much larger one, whilst, by a movement of the Federal army in the direction of South Mountain, the whole of the country between the Susquehanna and Baltimore would be open to the Confederates, who might possibly succeed in inducing the population of Eastern Maryland to embrace their cause, at the same time that they would cut off Washington from any communication with the North, excepting by sea. The first plan of operations was therefore adopted by General Meade, and orders were issued for the army of the Potomac to continue its march up the Monocacy to Gettysburg.

Receiving news of the presence of the Federal army at Frederick, but uncertain of its movements and of the intentions of the new General, Lee had ordered his own army to concentrate on the same place, as being central between York, Carlisle, and Chambersburg. Towards Gettysburg, therefore, the several divisions and corps marched, not however so rapidly as would have been the case had the Commander-in-Chief possessed accurate information respecting the enemy's movements;* but deprived as he was of the services of the cavalry under Stuart, he found it most difficult to obtain reliable intelligence, or to reconnoitre the country at any distance from the main army.

Stuart, who after the actions at Aldie and Middlesburg, had continued to watch the enemy, and to harass his rear during his march to the Potomac, had, by Hooker's march to Frederick, and by Lee's advance into Pennsylvania, been cut off from communication with the main army, which he only succeeded in rejoining by a bold and exceedingly hazardous march round the rear of the enemy, and between him and Washington. Great was the consternation he had occasioned; his troopers were known to have approached within twenty-five miles of the capital; and small detachments, sent for that especial purpose, broke up the Washington and Baltimore Rail, and thus for a few hours isolated the former city, not only from the army on which it depended for defence, but from communication with the North. Capturing stragglers and supply trains, Stuart marched round the Federal army, and—reaching Carlisle on the 2nd—rejoined Lee in the neighbourhood of Gettysburg.

On the 30th of June, and on the morning of the 1st

* See General Lee's report, contained in the *Rebellion Record*, vol. vii.

of July, the two most powerful armies of the North and of the South, and on which the subsequent fate of the war seemed to depend, were marching on the same point. To fill the ranks of the Confederate army every nerve had been strained: Richmond had been almost denuded of its defenders, and the country between it and Washington laid open to the incursions of even small bodies of roving cavalry. Not only was this known to the Southern President and to General Lee, but owing to an accidental circumstance the weakness of the defenders of the Confederacy became revealed to the Federal Government. Whilst reconnoitring the passes of South Mountain, Captain Dahlgren had captured an orderly carrying an important despatch from President Davis* to General Lee, in which the former stated his disapproval of the advance into Pennsylvania, throwing the responsibility of it entirely on Lee, and informing him that he could expect no reinforcements, as Richmond was almost stripped of troops; also that no assistance could be furnished by Beauregard from South Carolina, as his hands were full, and he could not spare a man. As an instance of the want of troops in and around Richmond, President Davis regretted to inform General Lee that his nephew, who was lying wounded in a house not far from Richmond, had been captured by a detachment of Federal cavalry. This important despatch fell into the hands of Captain Dahlgren, and was at once forwarded to the Federal Government. It sufficiently proved that if the maintenance of the Northern cause in a great measure depended on the success of Meade's army, and its power to repel the invaders, so was also the fate of the Confederacy in

* The despatch was written by General S. Cooper, Adjutant-General at Richmond.

Virginia thrown upon the event of the approaching battle, and that, could the army under Lee be defeated and crushed, no barrier would remain between the victorious troops and Richmond.

Unknown to the Generals commanding, the two armies on which such important events hinged were on June 30th within but a short distance of each other. At Fayetteville, a village between Chambersburg and Gettysburg, but on the western side of South Mountain, were the corps of Longstreet, and one division of A. P. Hill; on the other side of the ridge, at Cashtown, were the remaining two divisions of A. P. Hill, and marching from Carlisle and York was the corps of Ewell. Gettysburg, another small town where the roads from Chambersburg and York meet, had been fixed by Lee as the point of junction of the three corps. Of Meade's army, on the same day, the left, consisting of three corps d'armée under General Reynolds, was at Emmetsburg, a village on the direct road between Frederick City and Gettysburg, about ten miles from the latter town; and the right was at Manchester. The front of the left wing was covered by Buford's cavalry, which had already passed through Gettysburg and encountered the Confederate pickets on the Fayetteville Road, near the village of Cashtown.

On receiving intelligence of the vicinity of the enemy, General Meade ordered Reynolds to occupy Gettysburg, which he accordingly did, entering the place on the morning of the 1st July with the 1st corps, but finding Buford engaged on the Cashtown Road, he pushed forward through the town, and deployed his troops on either side of the road, ordering up the 11th corps under Howard in support. This corps, smarting under the reproaches heaped on it for its panic at

Chancellorsville, and under a brave and distinguished general, hurried forward on hearing of the anticipated engagement, and finding the Emmetsburg Road blocked with the train of the 1st corps, took advantage of a bye-lane, and entered Gettysburg by the road from Taneytown.

On the same day—the 1st of July—the two leading divisions of A. P. Hill's corps continued the advance towards Gettysburg, his third division crossed the South Mountain, and Longstreet's corps, following the same road, commenced the ascent of the western slopes. At 10 A.M. Heth's division (A. P. Hill's corps) became engaged with the advance of Reynolds' corps, and drove in the pickets. Reynolds in person rode forward to superintend the dispositions of his troops, but met his death almost immediately, pierced by a rifle bullet from the Confederate line of skirmishers. By his fall the command devolved on Doubleday, who brought into action his own, Robinson's and Wadsworth's divisions; but Heth's division had now been joined by Pender, who formed up on the right, and the Confederate line steadily advanced.

The battle raged with great fury; the Federals fought well—so well as to draw from the enemy a favourable comparison with their behaviour on other fields. The railway cutting was stubbornly held, and the open fields on either side became the scene of hard fighting. Eagerly was the 11th corps expected, and about 1 P.M., Howard, riding in advance of the troops, arrived on the field and took command; his men followed shortly afterwards, and passing through Gettysburg, formed up on the right of the 1st corps. But, at the same time, marching rapidly towards the direction from whence the sound of the firing was heard,

SKETCH OF THE COUNTRY ROUND

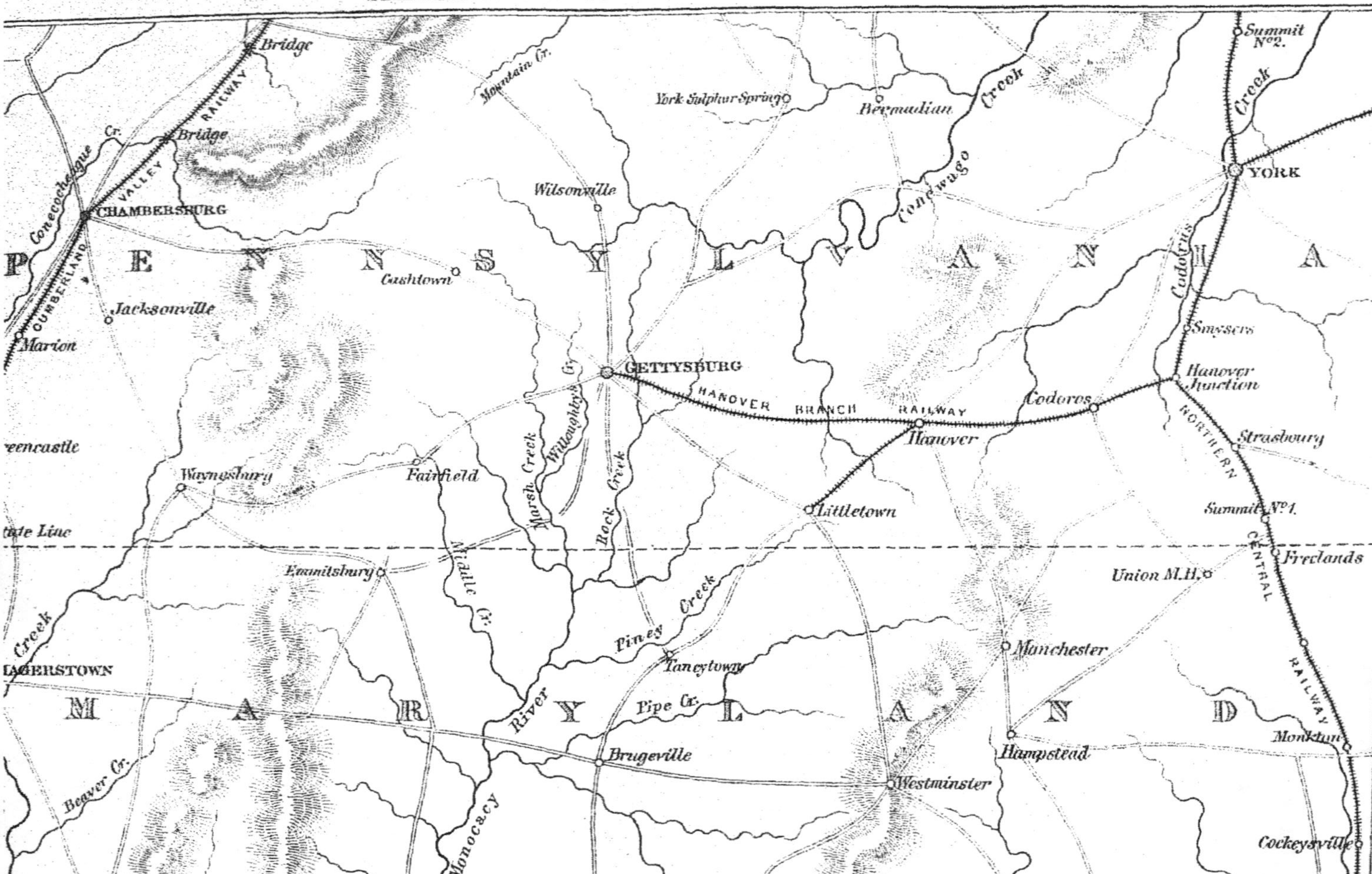

were the old antagonists of the 11th corps, who had driven them in such terrible confusion from the woods of Chancellorsville; the veterans of Jackson's former corps were approaching, and Rodes' and Early's divisions had already debouched from the York Road, and deploying in the woods on the ridge overlooking Gettysburg, had connected themselves with the left of Heth's division.

With them the 11th corps could not contend: rushing forward with a yell, these veterans drove back the Germans, who, however, fought far better than at Chancellorsville. The retreat of the 11th corps uncovered the right of the 1st corps, which had already shown signs of giving way. Both retired on Gettysburg, and the streets of the small town soon became thronged with fugitives: disorder ensued, the 11th corps lost its organisation, and poured through the town in rout and confusion, ascending the slopes of the hill towards a cemetery that covered its apex, whilst pressing hard on their rear came Early's division, followed by Heth's. On the crowded masses encumbering the streets of Gettysburg the converging fire of musketry and artillery told with terrible effect: many of the fugitives threw down their arms and surrendered, the remainder hurried up the hill towards the cemetery, where Howard, assisted by Hancock, who had been sent forward by General Meade to take command, re-formed the broken divisions.

Undismayed by the apparent strength of the new position, and commanding troops flushed with victory, Hill and Ewell prepared for a fresh attack, but, influenced partly by the lateness of the hour (about 5 P.M.), partly by the fear lest the woods on the summit of the ridge held by the Federals should conceal strong reinforcements, known to be in rear of the troops engaged, General Lee deemed it advisable to abstain from pressing his advantage until the arrival of the remainder of his army. Ewell, therefore, halted in the town of Gettysburg, and the action of the 1st of July terminated.

The loss in killed and wounded on the side of the Federals had been great, and in prisoners as many as 5,000 are stated by General Lee to have been captured on the field and in the town of Gettysburg. Had the 1st and 11th corps been followed up in their retreat, doubtless the disaster to the Federal army might have been far more serious than it actually was. The supporting columns were, up to 7 P.M., on the line of march on the Emmetsburg and Taneytown Roads, and it may be questioned whether they would have resisted the effect which would have been caused by the defeat and demoralisation of the two leading corps; but circumstanced as General Lee was, with his army not concentrated, and at a great distance from his base—uncertain also of the numbers of his opponents, and unable, by reason of the nature of the ground, to ascertain their exact position, which appeared to be one of great strength—it cannot be a matter of surprise that he refused to sanction an attack at a late hour in the evening, with troops already exhausted by their previous efforts, upon what might have been the whole Federal army.

During the action of the 1st of July, General Meade had remained at his head-quarters at Taneytown; but satisfied from the reports received from the field that the entire Confederate army was, or soon would be, in his front, he hastened up the 12th and a portion of the 3rd corps, under Slocum and Sickles, and directed the 2nd, 5th, and remainder of the 3rd to concentrate as rapidly as might be possible on the heights above

Gettysburg. Slocum and Sickles reached the scene of action soon after 7 P.M. on the 1st, Meade in person during the same night, and the remainder of the army by 7 A.M. on the 2nd of July, with the exception of the 6th corps (Sedgwick's), which, marching from Winchester, a distance of about thirty miles, arrived on the ground at 2 P.M.

Contemporary with the concentration of the Federal army, Lee ordered his corps commanders to close up their rear divisions. During the night of the 1st and early morning of the 2nd, the remainder of Hill's and Ewell's corps, and the divisions of Hood and M'Laws of Longstreet's corps were brought to the front,* and orders were sent to Stuart, news of whose arrival at Carlisle reached General Lee on the afternoon of the 2nd, to march on Gettysburg, and take position on the left of the army. Thus by mid-day on the 2nd July the two armies—on whose victory or defeat depended not only the result of the campaign, but possibly the fate of the cause which each represented—were drawn up opposite to each other, and within range of their respective artillery. Every soldier in both armies felt the importance of the coming battle. The Federals, fighting on their own soil, had the incentives of men contending for the defence of their homes; the Confederates exulting in the recollection of previous achievements, and looking forward to a new battle as to a fresh victory, were buoyed up by the hope that at length, after one supreme effort, they would be able to dictate peace on their own terms. But notwithstanding his success on the 1st, and his confidence in the troops he commanded,

* Pickett's division, which had been left to guard the rear, did not reach the field of Gettysburg until the morning of the 3rd.

Lee was anxious and doubtful as to the propriety of attacking the enemy in the strong position he had taken up. He knew the risk of defeat, separated as he was by many miles from his base of supplies; and he knew also that the troops in his front were well able to fight desperately behind the entrenchments, which they never failed to throw up, and which their own skill and perseverance, joined to the advantages of the country, would render most formidably strong. Yet retreat seemed to present even greater dangers than a battle. Without severe loss to his long waggon-trains he could scarcely hope to retire through the passes of South Mountain; and his doing so would open a communication between Meade's army and Couche's militia north of the Susquehanna. The country in the rear was unfavourable for collecting supplies, whilst a victory over the army in his front would open to him not only the fertile plains of Pennsylvania, but in all probability the gates of Baltimore, if not of Washington. The temper of his men justified almost any enterprise, however daring. Veterans of many battles, they were yet possessed of the enthusiasm of young troops, arising from confidence in their own prowess,* and not from

* The following are General Lee's reasons, as stated in his report, for fighting at Gettysburg:—'It had not been intended to fight a general battle at such a distance from our base, unless attacked by the enemy; but finding ourselves unexpectedly confronted by the Federal army, it became a matter of difficulty to withdraw through the mountains with our large trains. At the same time, the country was unfavourable for collecting supplies, whilst in the presence of the enemy's main body, as he was enabled to restrain our foraging parties by occupying the passes of the mountains with regular and local troops. A battle thus became, in a measure, unavoidable. Encouraged by the successful issue of the engagement of the first day and in view of the valuable results that would ensue from the

ignorance of the dangers and difficulties which awaited them; whilst the success of the first day's action had added to this confidence, and seemed to promise a repetition in Pennsylvania of the victories that had so often crowned their arms in Virginia.

It was a formidable position that General Lee had decided to attack. Sloping upwards from the town of Gettysburg, for about one mile and a-half, is a range of hills, partially under cultivation, partially rocky, and covered with woods; and along the western slopes, among the orchards and fences dividing the fields, the northern army was drawn up. The summit of the ridge was also occupied by the supports, and the lines extended from the slope of the hill—which rises above Rocky Creek, on which rested the right, and which was bent back in an easterly direction at nearly right angles with the front of the position—to the Round Top, a steep hill covered with timber, on the left, a distance of about five miles. Almost in the centre of the line, but nearer the right, and overlooking the town of Gettysburg, rose Cemetery Hill, which, elevated above the adjoining ridge, overtopped it on either side, and formed what may be considered as the key of the position. Below the ridge, and between it and a lower line of hills, an undulating valley, varying in width from one to two miles, richly cultivated—and at the time of the battle yellow with the ripening corn—separated the two armies; and on the eastern side of these lower hills, the Confederates were drawn up. Owing, however, to the

defeat of the army under General Meade, it was thought advisable to renew the attack.'

See also Lieut.-Colonel Fremantle's account of the battle of Gettysburg, and the letters from *The Times*' Southern Correspondent, both narratives written by eye-witnesses of the events described.

conformation of the land, and to the position taken up by the Federals, Lee had been forced—although with fewer numbers—to embrace within his lines a greater extent of country than that occupied by his opponent. His left, thrown forward in the direction of Rocky Creek, extended beyond the town of Gettysburg, whilst his right faced on the lower ridge, the high hill held by the Federal left.

It was not until 2 P.M. that the several corps composing the Confederate army had taken up the positions to which they had been assigned. On the right was Longstreet, with Hood's and M'Laws' divisions; next to him the divisions of Anderson, Pender, and Heth, under A. P. Hill, forming the centre of the army; and on Hill's left was Ewell's corps, of which Rodes' division was next to Heth, then Early's, occupying Gettysburg, and on the extreme left of the line beyond Rocky Creek, Johnson's division, which came on the ground after a long march on that same afternoon.

Of the Federal army, the extreme right, overlooking Rocky Creek, was held by Slocum, with the 12th corps. On his left was Newton, who had succeeded Reynolds in command of the 1st corps. Holding Cemetery Hill was Howard with the 11th corps; on his left was Hancock, commanding the 2nd corps; then Sickles, with the 3rd corps; and in support of the 3rd corps, and holding position on the extreme left of the line, was the 5th corps, under Sykes. Forming the reserve, between the Baltimore and Taneytown Roads, was Sedgwick, who had brought up the 6th corps from Winchester. Thus the Federal army was in position above Gettysburg, but as was the case with the Confederates, the difficulty of concentrating the troops had been great, and the rear-divisions of some of the corps did not reach the ground until the afternoon.

At 3 P.M., General Meade, who had placed his headquarters near Cemetery Hill, rode to the extreme left to inspect the ground, and to point out to General Sykes the position he wished his corps to occupy. Whilst visiting this portion of the line, he observed that General Sickles, either through misapprehension of orders, or under the impression that he could with advantage seize some rising ground in front of his allotted position, had moved his corps forward in advance of the rest of the army. Whilst discussing with him the propriety of retiring from his too exposed situation, the Confederate batteries opened fire, and the second day's battle of Gettysburg commenced. During the morning, among the corn-fields and orchards, frequent skirmishes had occurred, and the Confederates more than once had driven in the Federal pickets, apparently with the intention of drawing fire from the batteries, and so ascertaining their localities; but it was not until 4.45 P.M. that their own batteries ushered in the battle by a heavy fire along the whole line. Under cover of this fire, Longstreet advanced against the Federal left, and Ewell from Gettysburg and Rocky Creek moved forward Johnson's, Rodes', and Early's divisions against the right, his guns keeping up a continuous fire on the slopes of Cemetery Hill. Whilst the two corps on the flanks advanced to the attack, Anderson's division received orders to be prepared to support Longstreet, and Pender and Heth to act as a reserve to be employed as circumstances might require. In rear of this corps, on the slope of the hill, Lee had stationed himself: he had issued his orders, and confiding in the powers of his generals to carry them out, awaited the result of his dispositions, sending and receiving but one report* during the whole time the action continued.

* See Lieut.-Colonel Fremantle's account of the battle.

Under Longstreet in person, Hood's and M'Laws' divisions advanced; they encountered Sickles near the Emmitsburg Road, and outflanking him and driving back a portion of Hancock's corps which had been pushed forward to cover his false movement to the front, hurled back the 3rd corps with terrible loss on the heights in its rear. Sickles, badly wounded, was carried from the field. Birney succeeded him in command; and Humphries, an old and well-tried officer, resisted gallantly the enemy's victorious troops. Meade, seeing that against his left the real attack had been directed, brought up the 5th corps under Slocum, who, from the rocky heights of the Round Top, poured in a fearfully destructive fire on Hood's division. Hood himself was wounded; Robertson, who succeeded him, shared his fate; Barksdale was killed, and Semmes mortally wounded. Longstreet, hat in hand, and conspicuous on horseback, in person led forward the Georgians against the batteries; three brigades of Anderson's division advanced in support, and Wilcox and Wright almost gained the ridge; but reinforcements reached the Federals; the 6th and part of the 1st and 12th corps were brought up; and unsupported by the remainder of Anderson's division, Longstreet's men failed to gain the summit of the hill, or to drive back the enemy from the heights of the Round Top. Wright's brigade, almost surrounded, with difficulty rejoined the main body, which retiring from the attack, held the undulating ground near the Emmitsburg Road, previously occupied by General Sickles.

During these desperate efforts on the Confederate right, Ewell had moved forward to the assault of Cemetery Hill; Johnson's division forced its way across the broken ground near Rocky Creek, sustaining considerable loss from the fire poured down upon it from the higher ground; Early's division advanced to storm the ridge above Gettysburg, and Rodes on the right moved forward in support. But the attack was not simultaneous, nor does it appear to have been well-sustained or well-supported: Howard's, Newton's, and Hancock's men, posted behind entrenchments, kept up a destructive fire on the advancing troops, and although Hayes' and Hoke's brigades of Early's division distinguished themselves by their gallant capture of the first line of breastworks, yet not being supported, they were driven back, unable to resist the storm of bullets which from the higher ground carried destruction into their ranks. They retired, and considering the lateness of the hour and the increasing darkness, Rodes did not lead forward his division to a renewed assault; but even after night had closed in, a musketry fire from the vicinity of Rocky Creek proved that Johnson's men still continued the engagement, and retained their hold of the position they had seized on its right bank.

Both armies had suffered severely, and if the Federals had succeeded in beating back the assaults of their opponents from the higher ridges, they had only done so after great loss, especially among the troops of the 3rd and 5th corps. There were doubts at Meade's head-quarters, on the night of the 2nd, whether the army could sustain another attack, and orders had even been drawn up by the chief of the staff, in the event of a retreat being resolved on;* but the men had fought with great obstinacy and courage; and although for purposes of attack they were not equal to the more dashing troops of the Confederacy, they had yet evinced so stubborn a determination in holding their position

* See 'Campaign of Virginia and Maryland,' by Captain C. Chesney.

that their General considered himself justified in offering battle on the same ground on the following day. On the other hand, the Confederate army, proud of the advantage gained against the Federal left, and appreciating the courage which had won even temporary possession of the ridges of Cemetery Hill, attributing the failure in converting success into victory to the want of prompt support from the centre, and anticipating reinforcements from Pickett's division—known to be on the road from Chambersburg—looked forward to the morrow in the confident hope that the final victory, although postponed, was still within its grasp.

Casting a retrospective glance at the battle of the 2nd, it must be observable how much not only had the strength of the position but the conformation of the ground, assisted the Federals; to them it was easy to move reinforcements as circumstances required, and the short space intervening between the flanks of their army—occupying a convex position—contrasted with the distance between the right and left of the army moving against them in converging lines. Johnson's division, on the Confederate left, was removed beyond the possibility of assistance from the centre and right, whilst on the other hand, Slocum's corps—posted on the extreme Federal right—rapidly afforded reinforcements to the hardly pressed 3rd and 5th corps on the left. The late hour of the day at which the battle commenced was also favourable to the army acting on the defensive: the attack could not be continued after dark, and the period intervening between 5 P.M. and dusk was not sufficient to allow of the whole Confederate army being brought into action. This will partially, but not wholly, account for the comparative inactivity of a great portion of Hill's corps, and also for the tardiness of Rodes in supporting Early's attack. But the danger, in the presence of a superior force, of weakening the centre of the army to support its flanks, and of bringing into action the reserves, when a battle on the morrow may be anticipated, seems to have influenced either the General Commanding-in-Chief or his subordinates in holding back the troops which formed the centre of the army, and which were more especially under General Lee's supervision.*

Early on the following morning (the 3rd) Pickett's division of three brigades, numbering less than 5,000 men, joined Longstreet, and the batteries on the Confederate right were moved forward to the position gained on the 2nd. Encouraged by the partial success of the previous day, and strengthened by the arrival of the reinforcement, Lee determined to renew the attack; but from various causes, especially from the difficulty of bringing up reserve ammunition by the only road which led directly to the rear, the preparations were not completed until noon, when, under shelter of the woods, the several divisions lay down, awaiting the signal for the advance. Thus, as regarded the main body of the Confederate army, all was quiet during the forenoon of the 3rd; but on the extreme left, where Johnson occupied the broken ground on the right bank of Rocky Creek, the action had recommenced as soon as sufficient light enabled the artillerymen to sight their guns.

* Colonel Fremantle, in speaking of General Lee's position during the action, states that 'so soon as the firing began, General Lee joined Hill just below our tree, and that he remained there nearly all the time, looking through his field glass—sometimes talking to Hill and sometimes to Colonel Long, of his staff. But generally he sat alone on the stump of a tree.' It would thus appear that he was on the ridge of hill immediately in rear of Hill's corps.

Meade, fearful lest his right should be turned, ordered Geary's division of the 12th corps, detached on the previous day to support the left, to return to its former position, and to drive back the enemy to the further side of the stream. In this it was assisted by a brigade of the 6th corps, and succeeded after some hard fighting in regaining the ground lost during the battle of the 2nd.

Unable to assist the extreme left without weakening the centre and right, and exposing his line of retreat, and sparing of his ammunition, General Lee submitted to this repulse of Johnson's division, hoping to retrieve the comparatively slight disaster by a vigorous movement against the centre of the enemy's position. The delay which occurred in preparing for this grand attack, enabled the Federals still further to strengthen their lines, and also tended to restore the *morale* of the troops, somewhat rudely shaken by the repulse of the 3rd corps on the previous day. The men were able to see and appreciate the strength of their position; they could perceive the gradual concentration of the enemy in the woods on the opposite side of the valley, but they could also more clearly discern the preparations made to receive him, and standing on the higher range of hills could in some measure estimate the terrible slaughter which must await troops in their march across the valley, exposed to a converging fire of musketry and artillery.

At 12.30 P.M. the cannonade which was to inaugurate the attack commenced; upwards of one hundred guns of the batteries of Longstreet's and Hill's corps opened a simultaneous fire, whilst Ewell's artillery, from the neighbourhood of Gettysburg, played on the slopes of Cemetery Hill. The Federal batteries replied, and for the space of two hours a cannonade such as has seldom been witnessed continued across the narrow valley separating the two armies. Under cover of this fire, Pickett's division, composed entirely of Virginian troops, and accounted among the best in the army, proceeded to descend the slope of hills and to move across the open ground. The front was thickly covered with skirmishers; then followed Kemper's and Garrett's brigades, forming the first line, with Armistead in support. On the flanks were—Heth's division, commanded by Pettigrew, of Hill's corps, and Wilcox's brigade of M'Laws' corps, the former on the left, the latter on the right of the Virginians. Leading the attack was Pickett; whilst watching it, and only withheld by the urgent remonstrance of the Commander-in-Chief from commanding his men in person, was Longstreet, who remained at the edge of the woods to superintend the movement. Without discharging their rifles, and with the precision and regularity of a parade did the brigades descend the hill; firing over their heads, the Confederate artillery covered the movement, until Pickett's division had reached the Emmitsburg Road, when, fearful of playing on their own men, the guns ceased, leaving the assaulting force exposed to the uninterrupted fire of the enemy's batteries, and to the musketry of the troops of the 2nd corps, posted behind a stone wall. Armistead fell, mortally wounded; Garnett was killed; but Pickett pressed forward. Nothing could resist his impetuosity. The Federals were driven back; some guns were captured, and the ridge for the moment occupied. Longstreet's staff, on the opposite hill, congratulated their General on the success of the attack. But he, overlooking the field, saw that the less experienced troops of Pettigrew's division wavered under the heavy fire; for resolutely did the Federals hold their position; the men of the 2nd and 1st corps stood their ground manfully, and Howard's batteries from Cemetery Hill poured destruction into the flanks of the advancing brigades. Seeing the danger, and noticing that a strong force, composed of a division of the 2nd corps under Webb, was descending the hill and preparing to attack the left flank of Pettigrew's brigades, Longstreet sent an aide-de-camp to tell that General to throw back his left to meet the assault; but Major Latrobe's horse was killed, and he failed to reach Pettigrew in time to deliver the message. The troops wavered, and halted under the awful fire; its effects were consequently doubled, and Pettigrew's men fell back in confusion, exposing Pickett's division to attack both from front and flank. Overwhelmed, almost destitute of officers, and nearly surrounded, these magnificent troops gave way; slowly and steadily, as described by an eye-witness, did they yield ground, and under the heavy fire which the artillery poured into their broken ranks, did they retrace their steps across the fatal valley.*

Outwardly unmoved by the disaster, Longstreet made preparations to receive the anticipated advance of the Federals: he pushed forward a portion of a battery to command the approaches to the wood, rallied the stragglers, and attempted to reform the broken regi-

* Speaking of Pickett's division, Pollard, in the third volume of 'Southern History' thus notices its losses:—'On our side, Pickett's division had been engaged in the hottest work of the day, and the havoc in its ranks was appalling. Its losses on this day are famous, and should be commemorated in detail. Every brigadier of the division was killed or wounded. Out of twenty-four regimental officers, only two escaped unhurt. The Ninth Virginia went in two hundred and fifty strong and came out with only thirty-eight men.

ments. Lee in person superintended and assisted in the work. Riding alone among the throng, unruffled in temper, and kind in voice and manner, he comforted the wounded, encouraged the officers dispirited by the reverse and by the loss of so many friends, and as successive detachments were formed up in the woods, brought them forward and placed them in positions to resist the attack which all considered imminent. The personal influence of the Commander-in-Chief, and of other officers well known to the men, quickly remedied the disorder; quietly, and without noise or confusion, the regiments were rallied, and ordered to lie down in the woods to await the attack, which a prolonged cheer, heard about 6 P.M. from the Federal lines, was supposed to announce. But the cheer proved to be only the greeting awarded to General Meade, as he rode down the ranks of the 1st and 2nd corps; and the Federals, diminished in numbers, wearied by their efforts, and with ammunition almost exhausted, made no attempt to renew the battle.

With the repulse of the main column of attack, the crisis of the third and last of the battles of Gettysburg terminated. Portions of M'Laws' and Hood's divisions had been engaged on the right, but had effected nothing against the 5th corps, and in the evening, Hood's Texans drove back with great loss a body of Federal cavalry, having almost surrounded them in the woods and orchards. On the extreme left of the line Johnson had recrossed Rocky Creek, and had again threatened to occupy the ground on the right of Cemetery Hill. But these detached operations depended for their value on the success of the great attack against the centre: they were intended to distract attention, but failed to deceive General Meade as to the real point of danger. At the same time they weakened the strength of the Confederate line at the decisive point, and whilst Johnson was fruitlessly expending his force against the steep banks of Rocky Creek, Pickett, overwhelmed, was retiring, and no fresh troops were at hand either to support the attack at the critical moment, to renew it, or even to occupy the ground until the broken brigades could be re-formed. The defect in the tactics of the battle of the 3rd, as it had been in that of the 2nd, lay in the too great extension of the Confederate lines, the troops were not sufficiently concentrated, and, to quote General Longstreet's own words, 'the attack should have been made with 30,000 instead of 15,000 men.'* A large portion of Ewell's force was unemployed, and the operations on the flanks were but of little assistance to the troops engaged in the centre.

Probably General Meade showed wisdom in not risking the advantages he had gained, by an advance from his own strong position, to follow up the enemy in his retreat across the valley. Many of Hill's and Ewell's troops were still fresh, whilst crossing the valley the Federals would have been exposed to the full force of the enemy's artillery, and the previous history of the

* The following extract from Lieut.-Colonel Fremantle's account of the battle contains General Longstreet's criticism on the third day's battle:—'General Longstreet talked with me for a long time about the battle. He said the mistake they had made was in not concentrating the army more, and making the attack yesterday with 30,000 men instead of 15,000. The advance had been in three lines, and the troops of Hill's corps who had given way were young soldiers, who had never been under fire before. He thought the enemy would have attacked had the guns been withdrawn. Had they done so at that particular moment, immediately after the repulse, it would have been awkward; but in that case he had given orders for the advance of Hood's division and M'Laws' on the right.

Army of the Potomac scarcely sanctioned complete confidence in the capabilities of the troops for purposes of attack. The three days' battle, under the hot July sun, had severely tried the men, and the losses of the Federals had been equally serious with those of the enemy. The Northern army had been diminished by about 20,000 men,* including upwards of 7,000 prisoners, and the infantry had so exhausted the supplies of small arms ammunition that there remained scarcely sufficient for another day's battle.† These reasons were of sufficient weight to decide General Meade against following up his success on the 3rd, and prevented him from renewing the battle on the following day. The option of doing so rested with him, as General Lee—although compelled to make dispositions for a retreat—was yet prepared to fight an action to cover the march to Hagerstown of the long trains of waggons containing the plunder of Pennsylvania. In an enemy's country, and at so great a distance from his base of supplies, he could not hope to remain, as his ammunition was almost exhausted, and none had been captured from the enemy. He had, however, still sufficient for one day's battle, and he felt that he could confidently await attack in his present position. He therefore drew in his left, and concentrating his army to cover the Cashtown and Fairfield Roads, occupied himself on the 4th in burying the dead, and sending to the rear such of the wounded as could be removed. Stuart's cavalry, which had played little or no part in the last day's action, was detailed as an escort for the waggon-trains, and rendered efficient service in protecting them from the incursions

* See Meade's report. General Meade acknowledges to the total loss during the campaign of 23,186 killed, wounded, and missing.

† See Captain Chesney's *Campaigns in Virginia and Maryland.*

of Kilpatrick's and Buford's squadrons. Neither at Gettysburg, nor indeed at any of the great battles of the war, had the cavalry borne a conspicuous part, and although Kilpatrick had attempted a diversion against the Confederate right on the evening of the last day, he had accomplished but little, and had lost many men, including, among others, the brave officer who had led the charge—General Farnsworth.*

Heavy rain fell in the evening of the 4th, and continued during the night; the country roads, ill-fitted for the traffic of a large army, became almost impassable, and the waggon-trains made but slow progress. Late in the evening of the 4th, Ewell's corps retreated, those of Hill and Longstreet continuing to hold their position. During the same night and the early morning of the 5th they also retired, and the Federal pickets reported that the force in their front was in full retreat. Little attempt was made at pursuit; the Federal army was in no condition for rapid movements, and Sedgwick, with the 6th corps, which had suffered less than the others, was alone sent forward to follow the retiring columns. In the evening of the 6th, he came up with the enemy's rear-guard, posted in Fairfield Pass, and occupying so strong a position that he deemed it inadvisable to attack, and sent a report to that effect to General Meade. The Commander-in-Chief coincided in the opinion of his subordinate, and having detached a brigade of infantry and of cavalry to harass the rear of the retreating army, he directed his own march on Middletown, moving in a direction parallel with that

* Captain Chesney, in his admirable account of the campaign of Gettysburg, notices and adduces reasons for the absence of efficiency of the cavalry for important operations in both the Federal and Confederate armies.

pursued by General Lee.* At the same time he ordered General French, stationed at Fredericktown, to reoccupy Harper's Ferry and Turner's Gap in the South Mountain. But these orders had been forestalled by French, who had even sent cavalry as far as Falling Waters and Williamsport, and had burnt the pontoon bridge and captured the guard. An attempt was likewise made in the darkness of the stormy night of the 5th to cut in two Ewell's long waggon train by a detachment of Kilpatrick's cavalry, which had crossed the mountains and actually intercepted the line of retreat; but the confusion was so great, the road becoming blocked up, that but little real damage was inflicted: a few waggons were captured, and some burnt, but when daybreak appeared the small force of cavalry was glad to retire before they were overwhelmed by the troops forming the escort to the trains.†

On Wednesday, the 8th July, the Federal army was concentrated at Middletown, between the Catoctin and South Mountains, and on the 9th effected a passage over the latter range by Turner's and Crampton's Gaps. Kilpatrick and Buford had already crossed, and making their head-quarters at Boonsboro, had encountered in several skirmishes the cavalry of General Stuart. Even into the streets of Hagerstown and Williamsport had detached parties of Kilpatrick's men ridden; but as the main Confederate army approached they were forced to fall back on Boonsboro, where they awaited the slow advance of Meade's columns.

* See L. L. Crounce's account, entitled 'The Escape of General Lee,' page 345, vol. vii. *Rebellion Record*, Documents. Also General Meade's report.

† See the *Union Cavalry Service*. *Rebellion Record*, vol. vii. p. 183, Documents.

In the meantime, after an arduous march,* the Confederates reached Hagerstown on the night of the 6th and morning of the 7th; but the heavy storm which had commenced on the day following the battle of the 3rd, had caused a sudden rise in the waters of the Potomac, and had rendered the fords impassable; the bridges, both at Williamsport and Falling Waters four miles below, had been destroyed, and the vast train of waggons and the ambulances conveying the wounded were forced to halt at Williamsport until the river should subside or fresh bridges be constructed. The engineers performed their work well, and whilst the army took up a position covering Williamsport and Falling Waters, and threw up entrenchments and batteries, boats were built, and such parts of the pontoon bridge as had not been destroyed repaired and made serviceable. For a week the Confederate army held the lines, expecting an attack from the enemy, who had approached the position to within two miles. On the 9th Meade had established his head-quarters at Antietam Bridge, and on the 11th he had called a council of war to advise on the propriety of attacking the Confederate position. Of the seven corps commanders, two only favoured the project; but to these were added the chief engineer, General Warren, and the cavalry General, Pleasanton. However, influenced probably by reasons somewhat similar to those which caused M'Clellan a year previous, and on the same ground, to decline a second day's battle, General Meade resolved to await the reinforcements which, under Couch, were marching from the Susquehanna. A small number (4,000, under General W. F. Smith) had already joined,† but many more were

* See Lee's report. † General Meade's official report.

expected, and until their arrival it was decided that no forward movement should be attempted. It was also hoped by some of the senior officers that Lee, unable to cross the river, and straitened by want of provisions, might be forced to leave his lines, and to attack, and thus give the Federals the advantage of fighting on the defensive and behind the works which they had already begun to throw up. But the swollen waters of the Potomac commenced to subside, the pontoon bridges and boats were completed, and Lee decided on crossing into Virginia.

On the night of the 13th July, Ewell's corps forded the river above Williamsport, and Longstreet and Hill marched towards the bridge, but owing to the bad condition of the roads did not reach it until after daylight on the 14th,* when Kilpatrick's cavalry, which formed the videttes of the Federal army—and which had been ordered to prepare for an advance on that very day—discovered the movement. Without loss of time they followed the retreating enemy, and with considerable dash and enterprise they endeavoured to break the rear-guard which covered the approaches to the bridge. A squadron under Major Weber actually passed the earthworks, and attacked the rear-brigade, mortally wounding General Pettigrew, but Weber was killed, his men were driven back, and with the loss of two guns and a considerable number of prisoners, mostly stragglers, the Confederate rear-guard crossed the river and at 1 P.M. destroyed the bridge.

Thus was Lee again in Virginia; the invasion of Pennsylvania was terminated, and Meade, who by the final battle of Gettysburg had saved the North, had

* See Lee's official despatch.

yet left unfulfilled the task which his countrymen had allotted to him, of cutting off and destroying the Army of Virginia. With the greater portion of his waggon train, and with a long line of prisoners, Lee had accomplished his retreat; and two guns alone remained as trophies in the hands of the enemy.* On the 15th the army marched to Bunker's Hill, between Martinsburg and Winchester, where it remained for some days. No further pursuit was attempted, with the exception of a cavalry reconnaissance pushed forward from Loudon Heights under General Gregg, who had crossed the Potomac by a pontoon bridge at Harper's Ferry. A sharp engagement was the result, as Gregg encountered Fitzhugh Lee's cavalry between Shepherdstown and Martinsburg. The men for the most part fought dismounted, and during the morning little advantage was obtained by either side; but upon supports arriving from Martinsburg the Federals were repulsed, and at night retreated to the hills near Harper's Ferry.

At Bunker's Hill General Pettigrew died; General Pender also succumbed to his wounds; Barksdale, Garnett and Semmes had previously fallen; many of the leading generals of the Confederate army were wounded, and one, General Archer, captured. The

* General Lee, in a letter of July 21, 1863, denies the fact that any organised body of men was captured on the occasion of crossing the Potomac. He acknowledges to the loss of two guns which were left in the mud. General Meade on the other hand, in a letter dated August 9, 1863, referring to General Lee's statement, quotes General Kilpatrick's report, which states that the cavalry captured two guns, three battle flags, and upwards of 1,500 prisoners. General Meade, in his report of the operations of the campaign dated October 17, 1862, alludes to the occurrence in these terms:—'The cavalry in pursuit overtook the rear-guard at Falling Waters, capturing two guns and numerous prisoners.'

losses in men, in killed, wounded, and prisoners, had been very heavy, probably nearly if not quite equal to those of their opponents, and in their relative proportions as compared with the resources of the North, far exceeding them in magnitude. The numbers engaged on either side in the campaign of Gettysburg had been much more evenly balanced than in the previous campaigns of Gordonsville, Antietam, Fredericksburg, or Chancellorsville; and the result of the sanguinary battles fought in Pennsylvania proved that the Federal army of the Potomac had profited by the lessons of adversity, and under a general capable of leading it was equal to any task which might reasonably be required.

As the campaign which resulted in the capture of Vicksburg afforded evidence that the army of the West, under General Grant, had greatly improved in all soldierly qualities, and in these respects was very different to the army which had allowed itself to be surprised at Shiloh; so did the army of the Potomac under Meade at Gettysburg compare favourably with the force which had fought under Pope at Bull's Run, and under M'Clellan at Antietam. The teaching of war had worked great changes, affecting the officers even more than the men. The necessities of the country had opened the eyes of its rulers to the evils of political jobbery as regarded the administration of the army, and officers were now selected for high commands in respect to the qualities they had shown in the field. The regular officers, both those who had served in the old army and those who had more recently joined from West Point, upheld their position, and evinced the benefit of military training, and the advantages of professional education. The young men who at an earlier period of the war had been promoted to high commands had gained experience, their characters had become sobered, and after two years of training in the field, and in such rapidly recurring battle-fields as those two years had produced, they had acquired the gravity and *savoir faire* of older generals combined with the strength and enterprise of youth. The staff had learnt their duties, and in all the accessories of an army, that of the Potomac offered a pattern which many military nations might do well to study. The more brilliant talent, the more rapid movements, and the fiercer enterprise still remained with the South; but they were met by a stubbornness of will, by a determination which no disaster could daunt, and by an elasticity which seemed to render the Northern nation insensible to defeat. The natural features of the country, the somewhat similar tactics, and it may be said failings, of both armies, together with the use of arms of precision, had produced a peculiar mode of warfare. Battles were a succession of attempts to storm entrenchments, usually resulting in the repulse of the attacking force; the power and influence of artillery had become fearfully apparent, and the benefit of massing the batteries and of meeting with a concentrated fire advancing infantry was recognised fully by him who more than any other had evinced the qualities of a great general. Lee worked his batteries in battalions, and was averse to scattering his guns among the brigades and even the divisions of his army.

The cavalry on neither side preserved on the American continent the renown which that arm of the service has gained in European wars. In irregular warfare, the Confederate mounted men had proved of invaluable service, and as the scouts and purveyors of the army they had greatly distinguished themselves. In fact, the absence of Stuart previous to the battle of

Gettysburg was the principal cause of the ignorance of General Lee of his adversary's movements. But the Confederate cavalry effected nothing on a grand scale; they neither played a prominent part during any of the great battles, nor did they ever convert into utter rout the retreat of the enemy. Possibly this falling off from the traditions of European cavalry may have been partially owing to the natural obstacles which the country offered to the manœuvres of horsemen, and partially to the increased advantages which rifled cannon and rifled muskets have given to the artillery and infantry; but the imperfect drill and discipline of the men and horses must also have tended towards the inefficiency of the cavalry in masses; and assuredly the greater attention paid to these matters by the Federal officers already began to bear fruit in the campaigns of Virginia and Pennsylvania. It is said that Farnsworth's charge at Gettysburg was a gallant although unsuccessful attempt to break Hood's Texans; and it would appear that some of the engagements in the neighbourhood of Boonsboro are worthy to take rank among the achievements of cavalry in the former wars on the European continent.

There can be no doubt that the great improvements of fire-arms has and will work an important change in the tactics of armies, and well will it be for that nation who in time of peace prepares itself by study, and as far as possible by experiment, for the contingencies which may arise when its armies shall have to encounter and have to use the implements of modern warfare. The benefit of quickly throwing up entrenchments, and the necessity of rapid movements, covered by efficient skirmishers, employed more extensively than in the English army, seem to be some among other lessons taught by the American war. A well-organised method of supplying troops with ammunition in the field, and of replenishing its increased expenditure, is another difficulty which requires preparation to meet, and which does not seem to have been sufficiently considered by the Northern generals; nor do the hazardous operations of night attacks against positions to which the approaches were swept by artillery, appear to have been often attempted by the troops of either army; although with the better disciplined and more accurately drilled soldiers of Europe, men might possibly be saved by an occasional resort to such tactics.* These questions will doubtless suggest themselves to those who have considered the campaigns of America, as will also the importance of railways, and the possible contingency of a general laying down rails on an extensive scale for the special supply of his army. Railways and telegraphic wires have proved, and will prove, without doubt, of immense importance, and the latter have been far more extensively employed in the armies of America than in those of Europe; for not only for the transmission of messages between detachments, or between the general and the home government, has the telegraph been used, but for the more rapid communication between the head-quarters tent and those of the corps and divisional commanders, quickly extemporised lines of wires have in an American camp been frequently employed. These and other experiments have been tried on a great scale during the military operations in America, and although the earlier battles of the war may possibly afford but few lessons, yet the campaigns of the second year may

* The author offers these observations with some hesitation, as neither his position in the army nor experience would warrant him in putting forward opinions on such matters.

be studied with advantage both as regards their strategy and their tactics.

To return to the campaign. General Lee's army having crossed the Potomac, occupied a position almost identical with that which he had taken up nearly a year previous, after the battle of Antietam, whilst the Federal army prepared to effect the passage of the river at the same places as those selected by M'Clellan in his march to the Rappahannock. Crossing the Potomac at Berlin, Meade moved up the Loudon Valley, between the Bull Run and Blue Ridge Mountains, at the same time that Lee retired along the Shenandoah Valley. The former hoped to be able to cut off the retreat of the Confederates, or fall on their flank by seizing and occupying the Northern passes through the Blue Ridge, whilst General Lee, fully appreciating the importance of these gaps, sent detachments to guard them, until his army—in three columns—had crossed the Shenandoah, and had marched leisurely towards the Upper Valley and Chester Gap, through which it could pass into the valley of the Rapidan. With the object of seizing Manasses Gap, Meade pushed forward French, who had succeeded Sickles in command of the 3rd corps; and he, reaching a small village at the foot of the mountains on the 23rd July, ordered his chief of the staff to make a reconnaissance of the enemy's position. Having ascended the higher ridges, Colonel Hayden perceived a heavy column of the enemy in the act of crossing the Shenandoah River, and reported to that effect to General French, who supposing that it formed the centre corps of the army, and that the rear was still on the left bank of the Shenandoah, and being confirmed in this opinion by the information of spies, considered the opportunity favourable for making an attack on the enemy's flank, and cutting in two his line of march. On the 24th he advanced towards the mountains, driving back the enemy's pickets, who disputed obstinately every ridge. Hill after hill was gained, but only to show some fresh position occupied by the retiring troops, which were found to be a portion of Ewell's corps; and in the evening, when what seemed to be the last ridge closing the entrance to the valley alone remained to be stormed, orders came from the commander-in-chief to stay the attack, as information had been received that Longstreet's corps was returning, and that the whole Confederate army was closing up to offer battle for the defence of the pass. During the night of the 24th, other corps and divisions of the Federal army arrived and took up positions preparatory to the anticipated battle of the morrow. But when day dawned it was discovered that the enemy had withdrawn, and that the troops seen by Colonel Hayden had been the rear of the Confederate army, which was now well on its way to Chester Gap, and was out of reach of any attempt on the part of Meade to intercept its retreat. The Federal general had been out-manœuvred, and nothing remained but to march to the Rappahannock, following M'Clellan's footsteps of the previous year.

Thus closed the campaign of Gettysburg; and as the fall of Vicksburg and Port Hudson marked an important period in the war on the Mississippi, and as the retreat of Bragg to Chattanooga and the upper Tennessee River inaugurated operations in a new country for the defence and attack of the central States of the Confederacy, so did the termination of the Gettysburg campaign and the retreat of Lee to the Rappahannock conclude the second great invasion of the North, and again reduce the Confederate army to the necessity of acting on the defensive, in place, as it had been fondly hoped, of achieving peace by carrying the war into the enemy's country. It is alleged that overtures of peace had been made from Richmond on the receipt of the intelligence of the first day's battle, but the repulse of the Southern army on the final day had completely changed the aspect of affairs, and had rendered the North deaf to any terms which did not include the restoration of the Union.

Upwards of fourteen months had elapsed since M'Clellan's advance on the Chickahominy, and although numerous and great victories had added to the fame of the Confederate armies since Jackson had turned the tide of success in the Shenandoah Valley, and although the gallant defences of Vicksburg, Port Hudson, and Charleston, had atoned for the surrender of Fort Donelson, New Orleans, and Island No. 10, yet steadily but seemingly surely the Northern armies had advanced. Tennessee had been almost entirely, and Mississippi partially occupied, whilst Arkansas in place of Missouri had become the theatre of war in the Far West. The great generals of the Virginian army had without doubt waged war with success against far superior numbers, but the impossibility of reinforcing Lee, or even of retaining sufficient troops for the defence of the capital during the advance of the army into Pennsylvania, sufficiently demonstrated the straits to which the Confederate Government was reduced for men to supply the losses of war. To the Southern ports no vessels filled with emigrants brought fresh supplies of recruits, and the native population, far less numerous than that of the North, with the utmost difficulty furnished the sole resources of the armies. No help came from the great European powers, who although admiring the heroic qualities of the South, were yet content to maintain strict neutrality, and to allow Americans to settle their difficulties in their own way, and at their own time.

Almost every prophecy so rashly hazarded at the commencement of the struggle had been proved fallacious. On neither side had the republican form of government yielded to the despotic power of one man. In the South the negroes had proved quiet, and, apparently content with their lot, had shown no signs of a servile insurrection ; and in the Northern States the people had evinced a stubbornness of will and energy of purpose which those who had judged of them by the somewhat blustering tone of the Government and the press had not given them the credit of possessing. Neither in the Northern nor the Southern States had public calamities created serious* outbursts of mob violence, and although about the time of the success at Gettysburg, New York had shown symptoms of turbulence, and mobs had rioted in the streets of the greatest city of the Union, yet, on the whole, the tranquillity of the interior of both the Federal and Confederate States during times of great trial and suffering, is in a high degree creditable to the American people. As the good behaviour of the poorer classes contrasts with the turbulence shown by the mobs of some European cities, so does the absence of executions for political crimes testify to the humane principles which actuated both Mr. Lincoln and Mr. Davis ; and if some of the acts of the President of the Northern States may have been unconstitutional, and, as in the case of Mr. Vallandigham, extreme measures may have been taken to meet

* Not serious as compared with the revolutions in European cities during the years 1848, 1849, and at other periods.

a supposed necessity, yet no one can accuse Mr. Lincoln of harshness in the punishments he considered it necessary to inflict on political opponents.

There are warnings to be gathered and lessons to be learnt from the conduct of both parties in the great war; but in considering the important questions relating to the welfare and government of nations, it should never be forgotten that institutions which may work well in a new country are totally unsuited for the well-being of those who, inhabiting the thickly populated districts of Europe, have inherited through many centuries the advantages and disadvantages of a long civilisation.

END OF THE SECOND VOLUME.

CPSIA information can be obtained
at www.ICGtesting.com
Printed in the USA
LVHW111954050422
715401LV00006B/210

9 783752 588606